JENNIFER ROBERSON

DEEPWOOD

DAW BOOKS, INC.

DONALD A. WOLLHEIM, FOUNDER
375 Hudson Street, New York, NY 10014
ELIZABETH R. WOLLHEIM
SHEILA E. GILBERT
PUBLISHERS
http://www.dawbooks.com

First Paperback Printing, August 2008
1 2 3 4 5 6 7 8 9

For Drs. Beverly Scott (Phoenix) and
Jim Maciulla (Flagstaff),
veterinarians extraordinaire,
who have always gone those many extra miles
for my beloved Cardigan Welsh Corgis.

AUDRUN SLEPT. AND woke. Slept, and woke again throughout the night, and also the day. Mind and body refused to remain awake and aware of the world. When, for the barest flicker of a moment, she roused to consciousness, there was no strength in her limbs, no impulse to awake, to arise, to recall who she was, to remember where she was. To be cognizant of the world.

A world forever changed.

Alisanos.

Now Audrun's eyelids snapped open as she sucked in a strangled breath of recollection. Oh, yes, she remembered. She remembered all of it.

Vision, dazzled by a chiaroscuro of dark and light, of low-hanging, gnarled trees bearing broad, sharp-edged fronds glittering like crystal, struggled to find clarity. But vision was fractured.

She squinted, lifted a trembling hand to shield her eyes. The world was bright, and warm. Blindingly bright. Leaves rippled overhead. Fronds bent down on delicate, pendulous stems, as if to touch her. Beneath her body blades of grass stirred against her flesh, insinuating themselves within the weave of her clothing. She turned her head to escape the glare of double suns, one white, one yellow; the sky, through the trees, was a dusty sepia.

Davyn. The children.

Five children, now; the newborn infant had spilled from her body well before its time. And lived.

Sound broke from her mouth.

"Be still," someone said sharply.

Be still?

But no. Her body would not permit it. Her awareness, rousing now from exhaustion into tensile wakefulness, asserted memories. Audrun recalled the wind, the rain, the storm, the blackness rolling across the land, the absence of her family.

Alisanos. The deepwood. The nightmare.

And again the voice. "Be still."

She could not do that. Could not *be* that.

Alarm sent the blood rushing through her veins, filling her with memories, with awareness, with the terrible pain of loss. Her throat closed on a gasp, on a sob; on a strangled outcry of grief.

Be still, he had said.

But first she hitched herself up on one bruised elbow. To look. To see. To register what she saw. Yet to understand none of it.

The karavan guide . . . who was not Shoia after all,

but something else entirely. *Dioscuri,* he named him-self: the son of a god. An Alisani god.

His back was to her, bare save for the leather baldric hooked slantwise from left shoulder to right hip. And braids, so many copper-hued braids, twisted, tangled, and threaded one upon another into a complex cluster of ornamented plaits dangling down his spine. His posture was tangibly erect, with legs spread slightly, knees flexed, booted feet planted.

She could not see his face, but she could hear what he said. And understood none of it.

Rhuan stood his ground. Around him, with a stir-ring of vegetation, a trembling of leaves, came the sound of growling, of howling, of hissing, of noises she could not identify save for the tone, the threat. A suggestion of sinuous bodies. Of *beings.*

Human, none of them. This was Alisanos.

In a tone she had never heard, in a tongue not her own, he spoke to the bodies and beings. He was of Ali-sanos. He had said so. Confessed it, when she insisted on an answer. This was his world. These beings, these bodies, he knew.

He turned very slightly, still holding his place. She saw then that cradled within a leather sling con-structed from his tunic was the infant, clasped within his arms against his chest. The girl. Born four months before her time, yet inexplicably full-term.

Mother of Moons. The beings, the bodies, the demons and the devils, wanted her child.

"Be still," Rhuan said, in the midst of other words in a language she did not know.

This time she obeyed.

FERIZE WAS GONE. In Brodhi's last view of her, she had been in demon form, with wings, fangs, claws, tail, catlike eyes, and opalescent scales. She had flown into the sky, into the depths of the storm, riding tumbling currents. Now she was absent, no doubt overcome by the sheer elation of demon form, of her natural, wilding state. Brodhi wished he might share in that, but he was ground-bound, his form like men, human men. He was no demon to shift his shape, to taste the air with a sinuous forked tongue. And not for the first time he wished himself otherwise, capable of sprouting wings to ride the skies beneath the sun. Even if it were the puny single sun of the world belonging to humans, and not the double suns of Alisanos. No, he was no demon, but *dioscuri*. In time he would be a god.

In time. Too much time! Deserted by Ferize, whom the human tongue named wife, Brodhi was left behind. Forgotten. Trapped among the humans by vows he had taken before the primaries of Alisanos, most of whom would as soon see him fail his tests, to abjure his journey. If he did so, all was lost. He would no longer be the halfling son of a god with a future of immeasurable length, immeasurable power, but something else. Something less.

A neuter.

Even the thought made him flush with anger, with shame, with something very akin to desperation. His third eyelid dropped, a scrim of semi-opaque membrane that painted the world ruddy. To those who knew him, those of Alisanos, it was warning, as was the subtle darkening of his skin. But here in the human world, such things were not understood.

Brodhi fought for self-control. But it was a difficult battle, in the aftermath of a conversation with Darmuth, who was, as Ferize, a demon. Rhuan's demon. Darmuth had given him the news that Rhuan was back in Alisanos, having been overtaken when the deepwood, awakened, engulfed miles of new territory. Rhuan was in fact precisely where Brodhi wished to be. But that, Darmuth made clear, was denied him. If Brodhi voluntarily crossed from the human world to Alisanos, he would lose any chance of gaining the godhood he craved. Rhuan, who had been swallowed up entirely against his will, caught as humans had been, would not face the same reception.

The memory of Darmuth's words renewed bitterness and anger. If either were to be overcome, he needed release in physical activity. Brodhi turned on his heel and left a grove that had survived the storm, save for the youngest of trees, and strode toward what remained of the tent village. With every step he named the Names of the Thousand Gods, one of whom was his sire.

Chapter 1

*I*LONA STOOD BENEATH a clear blue sky empty of
the deadly storm. Her belted tunic and long split
skirts were soaked and mud-soiled, sticking uncom-
fortably to her body. Curly hair, loosed from a twisted
coil habitually anchored to her head with ornamented
hair sticks, hung to her waist in wet disarray, dripping
brown-tinged water. Though the sun was out again, no
longer obscured by banks of roiling black clouds, she
did not feel warm. She was too wet, too worn.

She and Jorda, the karavan-master who was her employer, had escaped the worst of the destruction
wreaked by Alisanos because they obeyed Rhuan's in-
sistent command that they go east. Both knew the karavan guide, both trusted his instincts. They asked no
questions; such things wasted time, and Rhuan said
there was little left for them. But before fleeing, she
and Jorda had done their best to send the karavaners
eastward as well, echoing Rhuan's instructions. She
did not know who survived and who did not. Only

that she had, and Jorda. She gave fervent thanks to the Mother of Moons for that survival.

Now there was something she needed to do, something to discover before she tended aches and exhaustion, the pain of a broken arm.

She was a diviner. Her gift, her art, was to read in others' hands glimpses of their futures, to interpret what she could of what was visible. In Jorda's hand she sought answers to many questions, to see, in the aftermath of the storm, what lay before him. She could not read her own hand, but knowing what lay in his, as her employer, might provide a peripheral knowledge.

Jorda, as soaked as she, stood before her, left hand extended. His riotous ruddy beard was drying in the newborn sunlight, though unless he undid the single gray-threaded braid at the back of his head, his hair would require more time. A lifetime of guiding caravans in all kinds of weather had carved deep seams into the flesh at the corners of his eyes, though much of his face was hidden by the beard. He was a broad, big, plainspoken man who had seen more than forty years, not given much to laughter because of his responsibilities as karavan-master, but was the most honorable man Ilona had ever met. The decision to apply for a position as karavan diviner, after years of working in various villages and hamlets as an itinerant hand-reader, was the best decision she had ever made. The travel could be wearing, but the security and companionship were not.

Now Ilona stared into Jorda's wide, calloused palm. She was aware of faint disorientation, of pain. Her left forearm, held lightly against her chest, had been broken in the fall from Jorda's stumbling draft horse, but she did her best to ignore it. Her right hand, from beneath, steadied his.

She saw the calluses, the scars, the thin lines common to all as creases in the palm. But nothing else. Nothing *more*. The hand was merely a hand, not a harbinger.

How can I see nothing? Stunned, Ilona looked into Jorda's face. Between the top of his exuberant ruddy beard and the lower lids of his eyes there was not much flesh. But he was pale; that much she could see. And in his green eyes, concern.

"Is it bad?" he asked in a deep voice made raspy by the shouting he had done to warn his karavaners of Alisanos' arrival. Something in her expression stirred him to repeat the question more urgently.

Ilona felt numb. "I see nothing." She stared again into Jorda's palm, mentally shoving away a burgeoning apprehension. "I see a hand. Just—a hand." *O Mother, tell me this isn't happening!*

Concern faded from Jorda's tone. In it now was a peculiar, conversational lightness, as if he spoke to a child. "Well, perhaps that is to be expected. Your arm is broken, Ilona. Who could concentrate enough to read a hand when pain is all they know?"

The sensible words held no meaning for her, and did not assuage her fears. Blankly, she said, "Not since I was twelve has a hand been closed to me." Not even Rhuan's, the time she caught a glimpse, despite him being of the Shoia, a race very different from her own.

And then she recalled that the last time she had attempted to read Audrun's hand, it had been closed to her. They had discussed whether the unborn child was blocking her art.

"You are wet, cold, exhausted, and in pain." Jorda disengaged his hand from hers. "Let it be for now. You may try again later, when you have rested and I have tended that arm."

"Jorda—"

"Let be, Ilona." That tone was a command. "We'll return to the grove, to your wagon—whatever may be left of it—to set and splint that arm, and to let you rest. I think it should come as no surprise that your art is in abeyance, considering what has happened." Jorda laid his big hands upon her shoulders, surprisingly gentle even in insistence, turned her around, and then touched her back lightly to urge her into motion.

Ilona permitted it, cradling her injured arm. Her mind was too full of thoughts and memories to protest, brimming with images seen in the midst of the terrible storm. Full, too, with a sick fear that tied her stomach into knots.

And then from ahead, from near the settlement, came the unexpected call of a woman. Ilona heard Jorda's brief grunt of discovery and relief; she lifted her head to look and saw a slight, wiry young woman clad in the boots and leather gaiters of a courier jogging toward them. Fair hair, cropped short, was drying in the sun, standing up in tufts. Brass ear-hoops glinted.

Behind the woman, moving ponderously, came a heavy, thick, dark-haired man with a leather patch tied over one eye. Ilona murmured thanks to the Mother of Moons: Bethid and Mikal. Alive.

Bethid's thin face was alight with joy. Laughing now in joyful relief she dropped to a walk and came up to them, reached out to embrace them. Ilona thrust her right hand up in a defensive gesture before Bethid wrapped arms around her.

"She's injured," Jorda said, then bent to embrace the young courier. "Thank the Mother!" He closed his eyes as he bear-hugged Bethid, grinning inanely. Ilona, murmuring her own gratitude, shared a measure of his joy, but was now so shaky she wasn't certain she could walk any farther.

Mikal joined them, clasping Jorda's arm firmly. Small Bethid, wrapped now in one big arm, was laughing. But the reunion was short-lived; Jorda untangled his arms and bent his attention to his diviner.

"Come," he said. "Ilona's hurt—that arm wants setting. We're going to her wagon."

Awareness attenuated. She heard Mikal and Bethid talking, expressing concern for her, sharing comments about surviving the storm. She felt distant, disoriented. The throbbing ache in her arm spread to engulf her body.

"Here," Jorda said, and swept her into his arms. "This will be faster."

Ilona wanted to protest, but held her tongue. She felt

odd. She could make no sense of the day, of her surroundings. Held against Jorda's broad chest, she gave over control of her body to him. She began to shiver uncontrollably.

"She needs to get out of those wet clothes," Bethid said as they walked. "I can tend to that, if you can find some dry ones."

"If we find anything at all, I will sing praises to the Mother," Jorda replied, "though I may deafen you all. What have you seen of the settlement?"

"Nothing yet," Mikal said. "But we were some distance out, and we headed in this direction when Bethid recognized you."

"Surely something survived," Bethid said. "*Everything* can't be gone."

Ilona, held against Jorda's big chest, wanted to disagree. But shock had set in, taking control of her body. Despite the distraction of her arm, she remained aware of her surroundings, of the sun upon her face. Aware, too, of the pain. Perhaps Jorda had the right of it; perhaps she was unable to read his hand because of that pain. She had never been injured before, save for bumps and bruises, or a few innocuous cuts.

"Later," she murmured, as her eyes drifted closed. *I'll try again later.*

Within moments as they walked, she heard Bethid's breathy gasp of shock. "Look! Oh, Mother, this is a graveyard, not a settlement!"

Ilona opened her eyes as Jorda carried her into what remained of the settlement. Indeed, little was left. The

remnants, burned in part by Hecari warriors on a decimation mission—killing one person in ten, regardless of
age and gender, where too many Sancorrans gathered—
had succumbed to the storm. Killing winds, crimson
lightning, skull-shattering thunder. And rain, hot rain,
striking hard, merciless, heedless of petitions or
prayers. The remaining tents had been blown down,
blown apart, carried away. The loose dust of foot-stirred
pathways was banished, leaving only hard-packed
earth that still ran with cooling rain. Every blade of
prairie grass was flattened into the mud made by standing water. And most of the grove, the wide-crowned,
comforting trees that had served to shelter karavans,
had been upended, shattered; raw, twisted roots torn
free of the earth now reached skyward as if in supplica-
tion; broken limbs and branches were stripped naked.

There were bodies. Humans who had not heeded the
warning of Alisanos' imminence, of the destruction and
danger that threatened all in the deepwood's path. For
forty years the boundaries of Alisanos had been known
and avoided. Danger was rarely considered in a gener-
ation unfamiliar with the peril. Though most of the tent
village's inhabitants tried to flee the storm as it swept
down upon them, some were too late. Some were
caught. Some, like the trees, had been battered to death.

"Bethid," said Mikal in a tone harsh with shock and
grief, "you tend Ilona once Jorda has her settled. He
and I will look for survivors."

Ilona, cradled in Jorda's arms, felt a rumble in his
deep chest. "Pray there are some."

She wanted to protest. She wanted to remind them that *they* were alive, the four of them; that Alisanos had tasted of them and let them go. But that was a selfish impulse and she chided herself for it.

"Oh, Mother," Bethid murmured. "Other than the oldest trees, most of the grove is blown down!"

"But the wagons remain," Jorda said. "Many of them—see? That one there, that's Ilona's. It may be lacking its canopy, but otherwise it looks whole." He shifted Ilona slightly in his arms. "Almost," he told her. Then, "Bethid, run ahead. Make certain her cot is clear of debris, and brew some willow bark tea. Mikal, look for wood suitable for a splint. Try the supply wagon—even tree branches would do."

Ilona wished to say they need not do so much for her, but her awareness had begun to fray at the edges. She was dreadfully tired. Her eyes insisted on closing.

Jorda raised his voice. "And Mikal, perhaps you can check your tent and see if there are any bottles of spirits left intact. She will need it when I set this arm."

Ilona, who drank ale or wine and did not care for spirits, tried to override the suggestion. But there was no strength in her voice, and Jorda simply ignored the attempt.

BENEATH THE DOUBLE suns of Alisanos demons gathered, and devils. And beasts and creatures. Some slithered, some walked, some dropped out of the trees. In brambles, in briars, shielded by dense vegetation, tangled groundcover, and thick, twisted tree trunks, they waited. Tails whipped. Eyes stared. Bodies trembled. Forked tongues tasted the air, lured by the scent of human flesh. In particular, the flesh of a newborn human.

Rhuan could feel them on his skin, all the avid eyes fixed upon him. Hair rose on his arms and legs, prickled at the nape of his neck. He stood very still before the assemblage. He saw the glint of an eye here, the twitch of an ear there; heard the subtle susurration of muscles flexing, of bodies tensing to leap. He had been long out of Alisanos, bound to his journey in the human world, but he had forgotten none of the deepwood's dangers, or its denizens.

He stood before them all, holding a human baby. That baby was, wondrously, made mute by sleep. Behind Rhuan, the farmsteader's wife had stopped moving. His attention no longer needed to be divided between baby and mother. Instead, he gave it all to the creatures, to the devils and demons, to the children of Alisanos.

If he were to survive, perhaps it was time he summoned the arrogance of his sire, donning Alario's certitude of power, the implacable aura and arrogance of sheer superiority. The primaries ruled their own in Alisanos, but even they could fall victim to the jaws of predators, to inhabitants who were power made tangible, inexplicably alive; to progeny born of the deepwood's bones and blood. No one, no *thing*, born of and in Alisanos, was immortal, save for the deepwood it-self. The battle to survive amid the deadly challenges of capricious Alisanos began again with each dawn, beneath the double suns, beneath the sepia sky.

He raised the ruddy membrane that turned his eyes red. He let the heated flush of blood rise beneath his skin, deepen its hue. He stood his ground in the very posture he had seen in his sire, when Alario engaged in a battle of wills with the creatures, the demons, the beasts, who would pull him down if given the chance. Half of Rhuan was human; yet at this moment, the other half was completely, and incontrovertibly, Alario's get.

He used the language most familiar to demons, devils, and beasts. He had been raised to know sev-eral forms, from his milk-tongue, to the careful enun-ciations of adolescence, to the burgeoning of self-awareness, to the finding of one's place amid all others as a young male. But he was *dioscuri,* and he knew additional tongues, additional inflections. Such things as marked him different.

Rhuan summoned what he had witnessed in his sire; summoned the words and tones and postures of an Alisani primary, who held dominion among his own. Who was of the first litter of get whelped by Ali-sanos, thousands of years before.

They knew what he was. They knew *who* he was: Alario's half-human son, the first *dioscuri* born to Alario in three hundred years.

He sought the eyes, captured them, held them with

his own. He felt the first faint stirring in his genitals; the initial tingle of pure, concentrated *maleness* rising from his skin. He entirely subjugated any part of him that questioned, that wondered, how he could do this thing; to do what he had never attempted before.

"I say no. *I* say no. I say *no*. You cannot; you shall not. This is not for you."

But all of them wanted. Very badly, they wanted. From a hundred mouths came the hissing, the chattering, the guttural clicking sounds of denial, of warning; that much they allowed him. Heads tipped sideways. Bodies wove from side to side. Jaws dropped open, displaying tongues and teeth.

"I say, *I* say: You shall not."

The child, cradled in a sling made out of his leather tunic, neither stirred nor made noise. She slept on, the infant; the girl-child they all of them hungered for. Sweetest flesh, human flesh, infant flesh. Such a rare delicacy had not appeared in Alisanos for forty years.

Rhuan felt his lips drawing back from his teeth in a rictus of challenge. *"She. Is. Mine."* Heat bathed his flesh, rising from his bones. He viewed the world from behind the ruddy membrane. Fingertips twitched, itched, as if he might grow talons. "You. Shall. Not. She is mine. I claim her. I name her my get. I shall raise her to be *dioscuri*, as I am, and to one day become a primary, as I shall. She is fated, this child. She is not for you. Not for *such* as you."

He held his tongue, his breath. He waited. He did not permit his gaze to waver, to flicker aside for even a brief moment. He maintained the posture of sheer superiority, that of an alpha male, a primary, a god, standing before them regardless of his shape. They could assault him. They could mutilate his flesh, shatter his bones. They could dismiss his posture, his attitude, the language in his mouth. It was a daily fight, this; a deeply ingrained acceptance of the need to dominate. To perservere. To be *more* than any of them.

Enemies, all of them, but in this they were united. They scented the child. They wanted the child. They could, one or all of them, take that child. And he, Alario's most recent *dioscuri,* would be taken down, torn apart, supped upon by those whom he, in this moment, dominated. Whom he had to dominate, were he to survive. Were any of them to survive, including infant and mother.

Fear did not shape him. Fear did not fill his eyes, his belly, nor the words, the tones, in his mouth. Fear could not exist.

"Go," Rhuan said. "Go now, each of you. You are not wanted here. You have no business here." And then, without turning, without breaking his gaze, he said to the woman, the mother, who waited in silence behind him, "Come here to your child, and draw one of my knives."

For a moment she did not move. And then Rhuan saw all the watching eyes shift focus, departing from him to make note of the woman. He heard her rise, heard her walk, heard the raggedness of her breathing. But she said nothing. She stepped up beside him. He could smell her fear. But she showed none of it.

"Draw a knife."

She took one of his throwing knives from his baldric, shorter-hilted, shorter-bladed, than the horn-handled weapon at his hip.

Rhuan, who held the infant, displayed the palm of one hand. "Cut me. Bleed me. Do not hesitate."

But the woman's pause was long, was fraught with doubts.

"Do it," he told her, "or all is lost. Cut me. Bleed me. Now."

He felt her cool fingers close around his wrist, steadying his hand. "Just—cut?"

"Just cut." He showed nothing at all as the blade nicked his palm. "Deeper, if you please. Bleed me."

She cut him. She bled him.

"And now," he said, "something more, something difficult, something you will cry out against as a mother, but you must do it. It is the only way."

She was frozen beside him.

"Do it," he repeated. "Now. Waste no time."

He felt her disavowal, her denial, her despair.

"I am fighting for her life," he said, "not for her death. I promise you this."

She cut into the tiny palm, brought blood to the surface of the new, pink flesh. The child awoke crying.

Rhuan closed his much larger hand over the tiny knife-cut palm. Felt against calloused flesh the softness of her palm, the perfection of her skin that now was scarred. His blood mingled with hers. Her cries increased in volume.

To the creatures, to the beasts, to the demons and the devils, in the tongue that made him their superior, he declared, "She is mine. I claim her as my get."

Audrun, beside him, trembled. Tears ran down her face. She could not understand his words, but she understood his tone.

"She is *mine*," he repeated, with purposeful emphasis. "Go you, each of you, *all* of you: away. This girl-child was born in Alisanos. She is *of* Alisanos. She is not for you."

He stood his ground, and waited. And inwardly, he rejoiced; one by one, the children of Alisanos deserted him, disappeared into the shadows.

The woman's voice was unsteady. "What have you done? What have you done to my child?"

In the language of the humans, he explained, "I have adopted her. She is now as much my daughter as she is yours."

Audrun recoiled. "*Davyn* is her father! Not you!"

"What little protection there is, she now has."

"She is mine," Audrun said. "Give her to me."

He might have protested. He did not. He handed the baby over, watched her settle into the arms of a visibly angry mother.

"I do what I must," he told her, "to keep my charges safe."

Chapter 2

*D*AVYN HAD WEPT himself dry. His eyes, swollen by tears, stung now in the glare of the sun. No more wind. No more rain. No more blackened sky. And around him, filling the horizon, stretched empty, barren miles of untenanted grasslands, beaten flat.

He had called his wife's name, and the names of his children, until his voice broke. Now, as he offered prayers aloud, he spoke in a hoarse rasp.

He had returned to the wagon, hoping against hope that somehow his family had made their way to it as well. Instead, he found it absent of wife and children, still canted sideways on its broken rear axle. The canopy had been torn free and carried away by the wind. Naked curving ribs jutted skyward. The Mother Rib now was empty of charms intended for protection, for luck. In the flattened grass near the wagon lay the bodies of two fawn-colored oxen, hides wind-beaten, eyes scoured from their sockets.

Mother of Moons, but how was he to find Audrun

and the children? The storm had scattered them all. Rhuan, the karavan guide, had taken the two youngest by horseback to what safety he could find; Ellica and Gillan, the eldest, had fled after him on foot. And Audrun . . . Audrun had disappeared in the midst of the storm, her hand torn from his.

Davyn turned in a circle. Where? *Where?*

The sun, so warm after the chill of the wind, beat down upon his body, beginning to dry his mud-stained, sodden clothing and dirt-crusted fair hair. Beneath caked mud the leather of his boots was still damp and pliable; he dared not take them off lest they dry too rigid to put on again.

Where?

"Mother," he rasped, "show me where they are."

Desperation crept up from his belly and lodged in his chest and throat. Gone. *Gone.* All of them. He was stiff-jointed with dread, with the immensity of his fear. He could see nothing, where he stood, beyond the horizon. Were he a bird, he could fly and see the land stretching below him.

Fly. He could not. But the wagon stood upright, canted though it was.

Davyn clutched at rain-soaked wood, pulled himself up into the back of the wagon. Inside, amid the tangle of storm-tossed possessions, were two narrow cots, a massive trunk, a chest of drawers he had fashioned for Audrun in their first year of marriage, and other belongings. He was a tall man, but no oilcloth canopy remained to hinder his height. Davyn climbed up onto the chest, balanced himself against the tilt of the wagon with a hand on one arching rib, blocked out the sun with his other hand, and stared across the land. He turned, searched. Turned and searched again.

Where?

Four children, lost. Audrun, gone. And no guide on horseback offering answers to his questions.

North. South. East. West.

A harsh, strangled sound broke from Davyn's throat. For a long, excrutiating moment he battled freshening tears, struggled to tamp down panic. And then he began to think.

There was food in the wagon. Waterskins. And now, in the brilliance of the day, he could see in all directions. He could orient himself. His sense of direction, overwhelmed in the storm, was restored again.

Bless you, Mother. Thank you.

Davyn began to gather the items that would be necessary for his journey.

BETHID SAW THAT Jorda was correct: Ilona's wagon was missing its colorful canopy, but the rest of it appeared to be intact, if in disarray. She jogged ahead, hastily dropped the folding wood steps, and pulled open the door. Bethid kicked aside various objects to clear a path for Jorda, and lifted a scattering of fallen possessions from the narrow cot. Part of her was aware that she paid no attention to neatness as she stuffed objects here and there away from the cot, but there was no time for such things.

"Willow bark tea," she muttered, kneeling down beside the cot. Beneath it was a many-drawered cabinet with brass pull knobs. Bethid began pulling them open one by one, inspecting the contents. She was no diviner and knew nothing of such objects as one might use, but herbs she was familiar with. The fourth small drawer contained a small drawstring muslin bag through which she smelled the astringency of the tea that, steeped, might offer surcease from pain. "I think Mikal's spirits will do better . . ." Bethid tucked the bag into her belt, then cast about for a kettle.

Jorda was at the steps. "Is there room?"

"A moment . . ." Bethid looked this way and that. "Ah—here." She rose quickly and made her way to the door, slipping out with the kettle in one hand and the muslin bag of tea plus flint and steel in the other. Ilona, she saw, was markedly pale but for a bluish bruise rising on her brow and left cheekbone, and unconscious. Bethid waved Jorda in and searched for a nearby fire cairn or ring. With trees upended all around her, branches stripped of leaves, she was even more aware of a funereal feeling. The world was upside down.

She had a task, and was grateful for it. Yet part of her was aware of a burgeoning anxiety, an apprehension that, once marked, twisted her belly upon itself. Two fellow couriers had also been in the settlement, sharing the common tent. She had seen neither Timmon nor Alorn in the midst of the storm as she, with Mikal, ran through the tents shouting for people to hasten eastward. There hadn't been time to look for specific individuals, only to cry over and over again that all should flee the settlement. Many had, but some had not. They remained behind now as corpses, clothes made muddy and sodden. Bethid prayed Timmon and Alorn had heard her shouted instructions and obeyed them. Later, she would search for their bodies, hoping not to find them.

Beneath a sky now naked of shielding tree canopies, where grass did not grow, beside a massive grandfather oak that had withstood the storm, Bethid knelt in the mud. With a handful of rocks she built a haphazard fire ring atop a broad, flat stone. But the deadfall of leaves dropped from trees, of small twigs and brittle leaves, had been torn from the ground by wind. "Tinder . . . tinder," Bethid muttered absently, glancing around. But anything stripped from the trees by winds would be too green, too damp to catch fire.

She rose and went to the wagon, climbing onto the bottom step. "I need kindling," she told Jorda, who was bent over Ilona. "Anything of wood, to burn. Everything on the ground is wet."

Jorda dwarfed the tall wagon, despite its size. Muttering, he cast about awkwardly, eventually scooping up something he found on the floorboards. "Here." He thrust the handful to Bethid. "Wood."

She stared at what she grasped. Her spine felt cold. "These are rune sticks."

"They'll burn. And here is dry cloth to help—we'll hope Ilona forgives the sacrifice."

"But these are *rune* sticks, Jorda."

"Beth, not now. You wanted kindling. There's kindling."

"But, Jorda—"

The karavan-master was clearly impatient and irritated. "*Burn* them, Beth! Ilona's a hand-reader—those are for show."

Bethid felt slow and stupid under his green-eyed gaze. "But *I* use a rune-reader."

That he understood; everyone in Sancorra province relied on diviners as something akin to extensions of the gods, to learn if their futures were good or bad, if they were worthy of a good afterlife when they crossed the river, and to confirm that plans were auspicious.

Jorda's irritation was dispersed behind an expressionless face. "You do this to aid a diviner, even if her art is not the one you rely on. In these circumstances, I think the gods will forgive you."

It felt wrong, utterly wrong, but Bethid, with effort, mentally shoved that feeling aside, dismissing it with the discipline of a trained courier. Yet even as she knelt and began to arrange the rune sticks within the small stone ring, a rebellious portion of her mind betrayed that discipline. "Mother of Moons, forgive me. I do this for one of your daughters."

A man's voice, heavy with irony and scorn, yanked her attention from the fire ring. "Your Mother of

Moons has nothing to do with this, Bethid. It's Alisanos you should concern yourself with."

"Brodhi!" Bethid stared at the copper-haired, many-
braided Shoia. He was wet as all of them were, but
cleaner, and moved with the efficient grace of a man
unaware of personal discomfort. In fact, he looked
angry. That was not an emotion she was used to seeing
in her fellow courier, who generally wore an implacable mask that hid all feelings except for a habitual and
annoying arrogance.

It struck her then with a tangible shock that though
she remained concerned for the safety of Timmon and
Alorn, she had not thought of Brodhi at all.

TORVIC PEELED BACK the blanket and oilcloth he had clutched around his body in the
midst of the storm. Beside him, Megritte was crying.
The rain had stopped, the wind, the lightning and
thunder; the world was calm again. Steam rose from
the ground, filling the forest and muting sound.

He and his sister had been put into a crevice between two huge tree-shielded boulders, cautioned by
Rhuan, the karavan guide, to remain where they were,
to not stir until the storm died. Well, the storm was
dead; Torvic saw no sense in continuing to hide.

He folded back additional layers of fabric, baring a
damp blond head and equally wet shoulders. "Meggie, stop crying."

She did not.

"Meggie, there's no storm anymore." Torvic shed the blanket and oilcloth and stood up, climbing down out of the crevice. Indeed, beneath the wide, drooping tree canopies there was no storm; but something was not quite right. The colors looked different. The sun was brighter. Squinting, Torvic looked up past the leaf canopy to the sky overhead.

The world they inhabited was not the same.

Torvic stood utterly still. He felt pressure in his chest, rising to fill his throat. He swallowed back a painful lump. He would not cry. Would *not*. He was a year older than four-year-old Megritte—that year made him better, braver. But he could not suppress the trembling that began in his body.

Megritte climbed down next to him. Her hair was a tangled thicket torn free of its braids. Her face was wet with tears. "Torvic—"

But he interrupted. "Meggie, we have to go." He didn't like his tone; it was thin and weak. He tried again. "We have to go. We have to find Da and Mam. We can't stay here."

That diverted her. "*He* went to find them. The guide. He said he'd find Ellica and Gillan, and then Mam and Da. He said we should stay here."

"I don't want to stay here, Meggie. The storm's over. We should go find Mam and Da."

Megritte opened her mouth to say something further, but the air was filled with a high-pitched, inhuman, ululating scream.

AUDRUN TOOK BACK her screaming infant from Rhuan. "How could you make me *cut* her? Mother of Moons, she's but a newborn!" She uncurled the baby's fist to inspect the damage done, spat into the tiny palm, then used the hem of her long-tailed tunic to wash the blood away.

He was cleaning the knife she had used. "It was necessary."

"And now you believe she's yours?" Automatically she cradled the baby in such a way as to calm her, rocking her slightly. "Hush, hush, little one—all is well." As the thin crying died out, Audrun unwadded the tunic from the baby's fist. She blinked. "It's not bleeding anymore. The cut is closed. There's just a small scar."

He nodded. "She's a child of Alisanos, as I am."

"She is *not*," Audrun declared with vigor. "She is no such thing. This is Davyn's child, not yours, and she's Sancorran-born. She has nothing to do with Alisanos!"

"We have commingled blood," he said with a calmness she found distinctly annoying. "Hers passed into me, mine passed into her." He displayed his right hand. "You see? I heal quickly, if the wound is not too severe. She will also, should she be injured. But neither of us is immortal. Not here. Alisanos rules here."

That startled her. "But you revived before, when the Hecari dart struck you. I saw it."

"In your world. Yes."

She shook her head, frowning. "But if you're not Shoia . . . there's no such thing as six deaths before the true death, then, is there?"

"For a true Shoia, there is. But I'm not Shoia. In your world I can't die." He paused. "Well, other then temporarily. Here," he shook his head. "Here, it's different. Alisanos is deadly even to *dioscuri.*"

Audrun felt an upsurge of desperation accompanied by an underlying nausea. Too much had happened, too much had changed, too much yet *would* change. Her husband and children were missing, save for the infant born too early in any world but this one, and she hadn't the faintest idea where any of them were or where she should begin searching. Or even if they lived. Mired in exhaustion and worry, she could not wholly comprehend what Rhuan was telling her, though she knew it was important that she should. "When—" She paused as her voice broke, cleared her throat, and tried again. "When will it begin? The changing?"

"It has begun," he told her gently.

"Oh, Mother." Audrun held the infant more tightly yet, closing her eyes against the sympathetic expression on the guide's face.

"But if it calms you to know, you will likely see nothing immediately. Alisanos seeks out the blood and bone, first. Lastly the flesh. It may take years, Audrun, for a complete change. By human reckoning."

She swallowed around a painful lump in her throat, fighting back tears of fear, of anger, of helplessness.

"And are they gone? Those creatures that wanted the baby?"

He grimaced. "For the moment. But I am neither my sire, nor a primary, for all my recent posturing, and they will remember that at some point. They will seek us again."

Anger, oh, yes, anger was in her heart. Anger and utter despair. The baby was safe again in her arms, a warm bundle wrapped in the remains of Rhuan's leather tunic, but the karavan guide—the *Alisani-born* karavan guide!—had laid claim to her daughter. Yes, he explained it was for the child's safety, and a part of her accepted that, but the balance of her mind and emotions rejected the idea outright. With Davyn absent, with Davyn *missing*, she could not bear to think of his daughter being claimed by another man. *O Mother, let him be safe. Let us find him, let him see his child!*

Even as she cradled the baby against her chest, Rhuan stepped in behind her, undid the knot in his tunic sleeves, adjusted the length of the sling, and retied it at the back of her neck.

She felt a mixture of gratitude, embarrassment, and annoyance because he performed the act of a husband. "You may take it back," she said. "Your tunic. I can carry her."

He shrugged bare shoulders. "It's easier with the sling."

Yes, it would be, but he was a stranger, and male. It stirred a question. She latched onto it, relieved to find a topic that did not emphasize their danger. "How do you know about such things?"

His smile was fleeting. "*Dioscuri* help in the creche."

The words meant nothing. "What is that?"

"Children are kept together from birth. They are raised by secondaries and neuters, not their parents. Part of a *dioscuri*'s duty, before puberty, is to assist in the creche."

She could not keep the skepticism from her tone. "And you said *dioscuri* are—children born to gods?"

Dimples flashed as he grinned. "Is it so difficult to believe I'm the son of a god?"

"Difficult?" The impulse was to laugh in desperate disbelief, but she curbed it even as she answered with pointed honesty. "More accurately impossible."

Unoffended, he nodded, irony twisting a corner of his mouth. "Yes, well, Brodhi has said the same. I will have to tell you about Alisanos and the lives of my people, but later. For now, we would do best to move on." He placed a warm hand on her shoulder and turned her. "I suspect we'll be followed anyway, but if we can make it to the Kiba, we should be safe."

Distracted, she allowed him to urge her into motion. "Where and what is that?"

His tone was odd. "Well, I know where it was the last time I was here. It may be elsewhere, now. But we'll go first to where it was when I departed Alisanos."

Audrun stopped dead, turning to face him. It took all of her strength to keep her voice level and noncon-

frontational, to banish panic. "You will forgive me, I
do hope, that I must ask you to be clearer. That I require more information, more *explanation*. I know only
that somehow we have come to be in Alisanos, that my
pregnancy was inexplicably escalated, and that I now
have a newborn to tend four months before the proper
time. I am not alone, you see. I have more than myself
to deal with. And also, there is my family to find, my
children, my husband." She drew in a breath that
shook; steadied it with effort. "I know you mean well,
but I must ask questions. I must *know* things. I require
answers."

The dimples were gone, as was the irony in his tone.
He looked away from her a moment, glancing into the
forest depths, then met her eyes again. "I will answer
you as best I may. Always. I will keep you and the
child as safe as I can. Always. But this is Alisanos. Very
often, what once had answers may now have none."

Abruptly, she was tired. Strength had run out in the
aftermath of childbirth, of fear, of terrible anxiety. Her
mind felt slow, sluggish, distant. Even the weight of a
newborn taxed her. She let the sling take more of the
baby's weight. "But you know this place. You said you
were born here."

"I do, and I was. But Alisanos is . . . capricious. At
present I don't know where the borders are, where the
heart of the wood—the Kiba—is. There are no maps of
Alisanos, not even here." He touched his head. "All
that you have heard about Alisanos, all of those things
that seem impossible and thus not to be believed, are

true. I will do my best for you. But I have been in your world for four human years. Here time is reckoned differently." His tone intensified. "Audrun, you must understand—Alisanos is chaos. Is maelstrom. There are no such things here as roads, tracks, or pathways. The wood is wild. Things change overnight . . . or even by the moment, as human time is reckoned."

"And this—Kiba?"

"My people are there, much of the time. We may find safety among them."

Her tone was sharp. " 'May'?"

"May," he repeated, with simple emphasis. "I can give you no certainties, Audrun. Not here."

She found the correct term. "But you're *dioscuri*."

"I have some advantages," he said carefully, "in some circumstances, against some of the inhabitants."

Some, some, some. Tears formed unexpectedly. To Audrun, *some* was simply not enough. Angrily, she dashed the tears away. She looked at her fingertips, where moisture glinted. And recalled the words of the karavan diviner: blood, grief, loss.

She looked up and found calm brown eyes watching her. "The son of a god," she began, "should know many things."

"He does," Rhuan said. "He just may not know the *right* things."

It made no sense. She opened her mouth to ask a question, but froze. In the near distance, slicing through the forest, came a high, shrill, ululating scream.

"The baby," Rhuan said, and before she could protest he had relieved her of sling and infant. "Go before me." He turned her, pushed her into motion, even as he slipped the sling over his shoulders. "Run, Audrun. *Run.*"

Chapter 3

BRODHI WAS BROUGHT up short when he came upon the battered collection of surviving karavan wagons amid a storm-sundered grove. He looked upon the young woman kneeling before a small fire ring beside a huge elderling oak. He knew Bethid better than any of the assortment of humans he had met as a courier, but that did not necessarily explain her values to him, her thought processes, the motivations for her behavior. Now, as she worked, her thin face was strained, freedom of movement somewhat impeded by wet, sticky clothing. That she didn't know he was present was obvious.

Though his eyes were now clear of the red membrane, and his flesh freed of the blood engorgement that deepened its hue, Brodhi could not stem the tide of anger rushing back as Bethid petitioned the Mother of Moons. Nor could he control the trace of bitter desperation threading his words, though she wouldn't recognize it. No one had heard that tone in his voice before, so none could interpret its meaning. "Your Mother of Moons has nothing to do with this, Bethid. It's Alisanos you should concern yourself with."

She looked up sharply, clearly startled. "Brodhi!"

She had built a sad little pyramid of carved wooden rune sticks within the modest rock ring atop a flat stone to keep it free of mud and puddled water. He recognized the instinct: as much a need to kindle flame against the memories of the terrible storm as anything else. Light. Heat. Warmth. But also a shield against fear, a method to restore familiarity with, and faith in, the world.

Anger stirred anew, tinged with a brittle chill. "Nothing you do will make it the same. It's gone, Beth."

She stared at him. "What's gone?"

"The world you knew."

It surprised him when she didn't protest, but merely nodded. "Yes. It won't—it *can't*—ever be the same. But we can rebuild." A sweeping gesture encompassed the remains of the grove, the wagons, the detritus of what had been a settlement. "There's enough here to make a beginning."

He took a step closer. Inside him, there was pain and a sense of futility. His eyes hazed red briefly; it took all his will to force the nictitating membrane back beneath his eyelids. "Do you even realize what has happened?" He flung out an arm. "Alisanos has *moved*, Bethid. It's now but a half a mile away in that direction, not days away. Can you risk that? Any of you?"

Her blue eyes, which had followed his arm, now flicked back to his face. "We have to."

Inexplicably, he wanted to cry. Too many emotions, too much frustration, filled his chest. His throat ached with the impulse, with the conflict in his soul. He was weak, he knew, to walk so close to the edge of a loss of self-control, particularly before a human. And that fanned his anger, refined it, aimed it at the woman who knelt before him. "You're fools. All of you. You put blind trust in gods you don't know, in rituals and prayers and petitions. You wear charms around your necks and hang them from tent poles and invoke the Mother's mercy." He spat aside. "You *waste your time*. And mine."

Bethid's expression was startled for a moment, then closed. She bent her attention to striking steel against flint in an attempt to light the shredded cloth and rune sticks. "This has nothing to do with you, Brodhi."

His lips drew back from his teeth. "So long as I am in this world, it has everything to do with me!"

She merely shook her head, not bothering to answer. She had raised a shield against him, was now dismissive of anything he said. And that further infuriated him.

"Do you think you can withstand Alisanos? You can't even light a fire!"

Bethid did not look at him, though her jaw was clenched.

The wild, burning rage threatened to burst out of him. Once again he needed physical release. Brodhi reached blindly to the elderling oak next to him and employed a sharp flick of his wrist to yank a tattered branch from the trunk. With quick, vicious economy, he broke the branch into pieces. One step forward placed him looming over Bethid and her fire ring. He bent and quickly laid out the lengths of broken branches atop the rune sticks.

Bethid's tone was crafted as if she spoke to a child. "That wood is green, Brodhi. And wet. It probably won't catch fire, and even if it does, it won't burn clean. It will only smoke."

He knew that *she* knew that he knew that. She was patronizing him. It set his teeth on edge.

"Leave it," he said sharply as she reached to remove the sticks. He leaned down abruptly, grasped her shoulder, and without gentleness shoved her from a kneeling position onto her buttocks in the mud. "I said, *leave it*." He drew his knife, cut into the heel of his left hand, and, as it bled, held it over the fire ring. Smoke curled up as droplets struck the branches and rune sticks, followed by a flicker of clean, pure flame. He glared at her. "If you want to petition the Mother or any number of other gods, you might as well petition me. After all, I'm not in Alisanos. I am very much *here*."

Bethid, still sitting sprawled with gaitered legs spread and elbows holding her torso up, stared at him in a mixture of shock, concern, and disbelief. "What is *wrong* with you, Brodhi?"

As the fire blazed up, Brodhi closed his bleeding hand. "What is wrong with me, you ask? I am *trapped*, that is what's wrong with me! They have put me here and refuse to listen to any arguments I may muster, even in the wake of Alisanos going active. Rhuan they allow home, but me they do not." He turned away awkwardly, took two long steps, then wheeled back to face her, repeating his words in a ferocious, bitter resentment. *"Rhuan they allow home, but me they do not."*

"Brodhi—"

He gestured sharply, overriding her. "There is your fire, Bethid. I spilled my blood for it—let it not go to waste."

She sat upright, wiping muddy hands against her leggings. "Wait, Brodhi."

But he listened no more to her. He turned on his heel and strode away, taking long, ungraceful steps, steps that carried him from the grove, from the fire, from a young woman who could not possibly comprehend what manner of complexities, ambitions, and needs ruled his life.

She was *human*. She was not of Alisanos, to know what he was.

ELLICA, TUMBLED INTO the black floodtide of Alisanos as it consumed the Sancorran grasslands, roused to consciousness incrementally. But when at last she blinked the world into focus again, she discovered she lay sprawled on her back beneath a brown-tinted sky, bathed by the heat of two disparate suns. It was difficult to think, as if her mind were bruised. Her body felt heavy, too heavy; various portions of it ached, or stung as if scratched. Her spine in particular burned, and now that she was nominally awake, she slipped a hand beneath her back to discover the cause of the pain. She felt thick, blade-edged grass. Exploring fingers found that the grass appeared to have *grown through her tunic and into her skin.*

Panicking, Ellica heaved herself upward, fell sideways, landed on hands and knees. The grass beneath her body had not been crushed or flattened by her weight, but grew in perfect, rigid verticality, edges glinting like shards of ice. The webbing between her spread fingers, where she braced herself, bled from multiple hair-thin slices.

"Mother—" She lunged to her feet, holding her splayed, bleeding hands out in front of her, nearly fell again as a root or vine wrapped itself around an ankle, and remained upright only by virtue of grabbing at the striated, knotted trunk of the tree closest to her. But as she clung there, gasping in shock, the lower branches drooped down, down, and lower yet; uncoiling, unfurling, reaching for her, touching her scalp, her tangled hair, her wet shoulders, even her breasts, with a languid caress she found terrifying in its intimacy.

Crying out, Ellica tore herself free of the branches, twisting away to break their grip. Three more stumbling steps brought her to a large knobbed boulder half buried in the ground; she leaped onto its crown as if it were a savior. No more blades of cutting grass, no more seemingly sentient tree branches imposing themselves upon her. She stood there atop the boulder panting noisily as she tried to catch her breath, bleeding hands fisted. Her body tingled unpleasantly in the aftermath of sheer panic; perspiration stung her armpits. The edges of her vision frayed.

"*O Mother . . .*" Ellica shut her eyes tightly, willing her breathing to steady, her body to cease its obstinate trembling. *MotherMotherMother . . .* She clenched her teeth so neither outcry nor sob would escape. A farmstead contained its own occasional dangers, and her parents had taught her as she grew up to think through her actions, to sort out the appropriate response in a given situation, even if she were frightened. It was that fear, they warned her, that was the true danger.

But nothing they had told her spoke of *Alisanos*.

She knew. Even without opening her eyes, she knew. The grass had proved it. The tree. She was not in the human world any longer. The deepwood had claimed her.

Her hands crept up to her face. She bent her head. Fingers pressed into her brow; the heels of her hands squeezed the bottoms of her cheeks, shutting out the deepwood, shutting away the truth.

But knowledge remained, frenzied and painful. Despite her best efforts, Ellica could not stem the fear. As she lifted her hands away, tears dampened her cheeks, tracking rivulets through the coating of dust. Vision blurred.

Alisanos. She was in Alisanos.

Nothingnothing*nothing* had prepared her for this.

Though, she recalled with a stab of abrupt recollection, the Shoia guide had warned them all about it. In great detail.

O Mother of Moons . . . "Da," she said on a rising tone of despair, "Oh, Da, you were *wrong*—"

ILONA WAS WEAK, trembling, felt sick to her stomach, and her left arm throbbed unremittingly. Somehow she had lost a period of time; she recalled being swept up into Jorda's arms and carried, yet nothing at all of actually being taken into her wagon and placed upon her cot. But she *was* in her wagon and on her cot, atop the colorful coverlet with a pillow beneath her head, she roused now to pain, and to a curious detached sensation she feared was a precursor to fever.

But it seemed too bright. The canopy, even with sidewalls raised, should provide shade against the sun. Ilona opened her eyes, frowning, and realized there was no canopy at all. Just the carved, painted support ribs jutting against the sky. The Mother Rib was wind-stripped of dangling charms.

Ah. The storm. How could she forget, even for a moment?

The wagon creaked and shifted. Jorda appeared at the top of her steps, filling the doorway. "Bethid's brewing willow bark tea," he explained, ducking in, "and Mikal's looking for spirits." Yes, she recalled something of that being said before. "There's no way around it, 'Lona. Setting your arm will hurt."

Well, that was undoubtedly true. Bones were not meant to be broken. There was a price to be paid when they were snapped, cracked, or shattered. "Your horse fell," she said woozily. "I remember." She did, if not clearly.

Jorda dipped his head, moving closer to the cot. "You broke your arm, I smacked my head." He briefly touched the large blue-black knot on his forehead. "But nothing we need fret about, either of us. That storm was wicked—we might have got off far worse." She agreed, but at the moment didn't feel well enough to say so. Her body felt on fire, and yet she was cold. A shiver wracked her from head to foot, jarring her arm. And Jorda saw it; a moment later he was settling a blanket over her. "You'll do," he said. "Bethid can stay with you tonight, see that you're all right."

Her vision blurred. Jorda was an immense, looming form with four eyes, two noses, and beard enough for three faces. She frowned, blinking. "Let me see your hand."

"Leave it be for now. Later."

"Jorda—"

" 'Lona, my hand will keep. So will whatever future lies in it. You need to rest."

But she reached out to him. "Please."

Sighing, Jorda squatted down beside the cot and extended his right arm. Ilona caught and held the back of his hand in her palm, fixing her eyes on the calluses, the lines, the scars of his work. She blinked again, repeatedly, to clear her vision. The hand remained a hand, giving up nothing of substance.

After a moment she released it, aware of rising apprehension. "Sibetha," she murmured distractedly, "have you deserted me?"

"No," Jorda replied forthrightly. "Your god simply realizes you're in no shape to practice your art. Let it go, Ilona. Let be."

But desperation rose up through the pain, the weariness. "I can't read it, Jorda! It's blocked. Very like when I attempted to read the hand of the farmsteader's wife." She saw he didn't grasp the implication, and tried again. "Jorda—I can't *see*."

The wagon creaked. "Jorda?" It was Bethid, climbing the steps. "I've got some tea brewed. Here." She handed over the tin mug.

Ilona felt Jorda ease his left hand beneath her skull. His palm was broad enough to cradle it easily, as if she were a child. He lifted her head slightly, then brought the mug to her mouth. "I'll hold it," he told her. "Get as much down as you can. Mikal will be here soon."

The tea was dreadfully bitter, lacking any sweetener that would lessen the bite. Ilona managed three sips, then turned her face away.

"Beth," Jorda said diffidently. "I told her you'd stay the night with her."

"Of course," the courier said. Then, more tensely,

"But I would like some time before that to look for Timmon and Alorn. They are friends, and fellow couriers. I haven't seen them since before the storm."

"Bethid?" This time it was Mikal, but he did not attempt to climb into the wagon. "Here, I found some spirits." Ilona, squinting against the sunlight, saw him hand Bethid the cork-stoppered bottle made of heavy blue glass. "And I've got the makings for a splint."

Jorda, accepting the bottle from Bethid, smiled grimly at Ilona. "Not putting it off, then. Drink up, girl, and then we'll be about repairing that arm."

She attempted to tell him that she had no need of spirits. But then the world slid sideways.

"Ilona?"

Jorda. And Bethid, saying something. But though her eyes remained open, Ilona could see little that made sense. Only the world turned sideways; awareness was bleeding away. She was cold to the bone, fading from consciousness, sliding from comprehension of where she was, and why; of *who* she was.

Ilona. Ilona. Hand-reader. Jorda's employee.

But sense spilled away, like sand from a shattered hourglass.

"KEEP GOING," RHUAN urged as he ran. Audrun was in front of him so nothing would pull her down from behind without warning. "Run until I tell you to stop."

The infant in his arms had awakened, jostled from sleep by the headlong run. With one arm he pressed both body and head against his chest, protecting the fragile neck. Without both arms outstretched, grasping at branches to keep himself upright and in motion, his balance was affected, but Rhuan did not doubt his ability to keep going, to keep moving, despite the hindrance of the child.

Audrun had yanked her skirts up initially, but dropped them when she realized her balance was almost nonexistent if she didn't use her arms. He caught glimpses of outstretched hands clawing vines and branches aside, shielding her face. Audrun pushed through impediments, working hard to remain upright even though she tripped and staggered. She fell twice, but each time pushed herself up again, regaining her feet and balance.

"Swing right—*there*, at the next tree . . ." One-handed, he caught the branch she released as it slashed toward his face. "Duck under that tunnel of drooping vegetation—see it? Straight ahead . . . duck under and crawl." He dropped to his knees behind her, bracing himself with one outstretched arm. Tall, sharp-edged grasses cut his flesh, vines and vegetation slapped at him as he fended them off haphazardly while shielding the baby.

On hands and knees, Audrun swung sideways to look back at him. Her eyes sought the child. Her face was a mask of grass cuts, sap from trees, welts from slashing branches. Strands of tawny hair stuck to blood and perspiration. He noticed that the front of her tunic was wet across her breasts. "The baby—" she gasped.

"Alive," he said. "Keep going. Keep crawling—we should be able to stand in a moment when it clears out . . . *there*. Just ahead. Go, Audrun. A crying baby is at least a living baby!" On two knees and one hand, he scrambled through behind her, lurching upright from the tunnel of vegetation under the last low tree branch.

Audrun stopped short in front of him as she came upon the bank of a rushing creek.

"Cross it. *Cross it*."

She splashed onward, working hard to hold her balance as the water-covered rocks rolled beneath her feet and the current caught at her skirts.

Audrun was across, hiking soaked skirts to climb up the knee-high bank. "Path?"

"None," he answered, leaping up behind her. "No paths . . . no tracks . . . Audrun, bear left. *Left*." She did, and he followed. "Ring . . ." he gasped, relief surging through his body. "Dreya ring . . ." She wouldn't know what that was. "Audrun, the silver-colored trees just ahead, see them? They form a ring—go through and stop inside. Stop in the center. You'll see." The massive pale trunks were close-grown, tangled branches indistinguishable from one another. He saw Audrun's clothing catch, slow her; saw her tear the fabric free. He ducked, felt a branch scrape his scalp, appropriating some hair, but he was through and into the dreya ring. "Here," he said, "halt. Audrun, stay here. Stay inside the ring."

She was bereft of breath, gasping for air in noisy whoops. His own ran ragged in his chest, burning his throat. He went to one knee, cradling the child in both arms. Still the infant cried, a thin, wailing, unceasing complaint. Speechless, he nodded acknowledgment as Audrun turned and reached out. No doubt allowing the child to nurse would quiet it, and ease the ache in Audrun's breasts.

With the infant held against her chest, she sat down hard. Still she gasped, sucking at air. He saw her fumble at the neckline of her tunic, watched her find a thorn-ripped hole. She tore it, tore at the smallclothes and binding beneath it, bared one breast. Within a moment the baby had latched on, cries silenced.

For a moment he watched, smiling, relieved beyond measure, until he became aware of a hard, fixed stare, the glare Audrun bestowed upon him over the head of the nursing infant.

Still short of breath, it took him a moment to sort out her expression. But he arrived at laggard realization, nodded understanding and waved an apology, then fell over onto his back as he continued to suck in air, staring fixedly overhead at the silvery canopy of interlocked branches. It was all the privacy he could give her, in the aftermath of their flight.

Chapter 4

GILLAN ROUSED TO crushing heat. A miasma of dampness, of clammy sulfur stench, bathed his body, filled his nose. He found himself on his back. He lifted a hand to cover his mouth and nose, and coughed. His lungs felt thick, laden with weight. Now that he had begun, he could not stop coughing.

He rolled onto his left side, levering himself up onto an elbow as his lungs continued to spasm violently. His world was filled with heat, humidity, steam, and clinging sulfur. His eyes, even closed, ran with tears. His skin itched. His chest ached. He began to bring up a sticky substance, and spat it out twice, thrice, until a steady, heavy coughing once again overtook him.

From close by, something exploded with a wet, phlegmy sound. A spattering of burning liquid rained onto Gillan, spotting his flesh. He cried out, lurched to his hands and knees, and tried to see through eyes awash with stinging tears. His skin was freckled with pain, with droplets that burned worse than the hot

rain that had swept over him in the grasslands of Sancorra. With the pain came a rolling wave of sulfur, a
thick stench that threatened to choke off his lungs entirely.

Desperate, Gillan thrust himself upward, into a
staggering, lurching run. He rubbed tears from his
eyes, caught a glimpse of steam cloaking the ground,
rising in plumes from blackened mounds. The ground
beneath his boots felt crusty, hot, frighteningly fragile.
It trembled as he ran, as he wiped at his eyes, waved
at steam, coughed unremittingly.

And then his right foot broke through the crust. His
leg plunged through into a liquid heat that swallowed
him to the knee. In agony, Gillan screamed.

In reply came a howling.

THERE WASN'T ENOUGH room for two men
as large as Jorda and Mikal in the hand-
reader's tall wagon. Mikal remained outside as Bethid,
answering Jorda's request, agreed to help him set
Ilona's arm. She could tell the karavan-master was
worried about his hand-reader. She was neither unconscious nor awake, but caught somewhere in between, as if fevered. And yet there was no heat in her
flesh. She was ashen beneath the smears of dust, dark
circles beneath her eyes.

"She'll choke if she drinks now," Jorda muttered,
setting aside the bottle of spirits Mikal had found

them. "Even though she's not truly conscious, we need to tend this now. If she wakes up all the way, I'll give her spirits then and hope she can sleep."

Bethid knelt next to him. "What shall I do?"

What gusted from Jorda's mouth was only half a laugh. "Odd as it sounds, I wish you to lie across her body. On the diagonal. Try to keep her legs and right shoulder pinned."

"*Lie* on her? Why not just hold her legs down?"

"Because that leaves her torso free to move. I need her kept still, Beth. Can you do this?"

Bethid's brows arched in speculation. "Well, I have ridden difficult horses. I suppose this is no different."

"Have any of them thrown you?"

"Not since I was a child," she replied tartly. "I'm a courier, remember?" She paused a moment, moderating her tone. "I have *fallen* off, but that's not the same."

Jorda grinned briefly, measuring the sticks Mikal had brought against the length of Ilona's forearm. "So it is. Well, then, keep aboard however you may. But it should be done quickly; the Mother willing, the bone hasn't broken the skin. If I can shift it back into alignment and bind it in place, she should heal well enough." He nodded at Bethid. "Go ahead."

Bethid crawled up over Ilona, then lowered herself across the hand-reader's body. Most of her weight was distributed from knees to right shoulder. Bethid laughed softly.

"What is it?" Jorda asked, tearing strips of cloth for bandages.

"Well, perhaps we shouldn't tell her precisely how this was accomplished. I'm not sure she would appreciate knowing I *enjoyed* it—or that you suggested it!"

His eyes flicked to hers, puzzled, then cleared as he recalled what was no secret among those who knew her: Bethid preferred women, not men. His teeth flashed briefly. "Better than Mikal or me, Beth. She'd smother." He wrapped his big left hand around Ilona's elbow, then closed the fingers of his right one over her wrist. "All right . . ." He pulled sharply, eliciting a cry of pain from Ilona. Bethid felt the lurch of the body beneath her, the reflexive attempt to escape. "There," Jorda said. "Stay there, Beth. Let me splint this arm, and then you can get off."

Bethid grinned, then sighed melodramatically as the body beneath her writhed. "I could but wish . . ."

"She's a woman for men, you do realize."

"That's why I said *wish*," Bethid retorted dryly. "She's with Rhuan, isn't she?"

"She says no . . ." With deft, practiced hands, Jorda cross-wrapped the splinted arm from wrist to elbow, tying off knots. "I thought so, too. But I don't interfere in the personal lives of my diviners. All right—climb off."

Bethid levered herself up and crawled backward, taking care not to plant a knee or elbow in flesh instead of cot bedding. "He's a fool if he's not interested."

Jorda was cradling and lifting Ilona's head again, holding the bottle of spirits to her lips. "Their business," he said briefly, "—and perhaps it's her not interested in him."

"*I* may not be interested in him, but from what I hear, they rather fall at his feet. One might think—"

"One might," Jorda said repressively, closing the topic. Then, "There, 'Lona, drink, if you please. It will do you good."

Bethid stood beside the cot, watching the diviner's ineffective attempts to escape Jorda's imprisoning palm and the trickle of spirits he poured into her mouth. As a courier, she spent more time on the road than in the settlements, but she had inhabited this one often enough to know those who came and went, those who visited Mikal's ale-tent when they were present in the tent village. Ilona usually appeared there with Jorda, or with Branca and Melior, and now and then alone, when they returned from a journey. She and Ilona usually exchanged casual smiles of greeting, but that was the extent of their relationship. Ilona was a hand-reader; Bethid consulted rune-readers.

She glanced uneasily out the wagon door. Well, she would if any rune-readers had survived the storm.

That prompted memory, and a frown. "Brodhi said something . . ."

"The Shoia?"

"He found me as I was making the tea. He said Alisanos had moved. He said it's only a half-mile from here." Now Jorda looked at her, green eyes startled. "I know," she said grimly. "If that's true, we may be in danger yet. What if it moves again?"

"Mother," Jorda muttered, glancing down at Ilona. Then he met Bethid's eyes once more. "I'll stay with her for now. Go ahead and look for your friends."

Bethid shot a glance at the hand-reader. The spirits had indeed brought sleep; her breathing was deep and slow. Bethid nodded and made her way out of the wagon. *Mother of Moons, let me find Timmon and Alorn.* She amended that immediately, fearing the Mother might take it literally. *Let me find them alive and well!*

HE WALKED ON. And on. Davyn had no sense of how far he had initially gone in the midst of the storm, directed by the Shoia guide, and his return to the wagon had been so fraught with worry and fear that he had not marked the distance. Now every step seemed to carry him farther and farther, with no result.

Beneath the warmth of the sun, his clothing had dried. Mud-stained and sand-crusted homespun tunic and trews were stiff, rubbing against his flesh as he moved. Leather boots remained damp, but mud still clung because the ground beneath his feet was soaked, puddled in places. Beaten prairie grass created a carpet of sorts to keep him from sinking in, but the going remained difficult. The top of his head was heated by the sun, while the wet, squishy footing kept his feet cold.

The day now was fine. The clear, cloudless sky was a brilliant blue, and the sun turned a bright, benevolent face to the world. But a look at the earth beneath told the tale: in addition to mud, puddles, and flattened grass, the prairie was pocked with lightning-dug divots like thousands of vermin holes, marked by the remains of explosions of earth, clods scattered in all directions. Some of the holes were as deep as Davyn's forearms were long. But the lightning had been amazingly precise, like a thin and tensile knife blade. And despite the overriding scent of mud and torn grass, Davyn smelled the astringency of power, the aftermath of extreme heat. The world, the air, the earth, had been selectively burned by capricious, malevolent lightning.

Hunger nagged. Davyn had no idea how long it had been since he had last eaten. The storm had blotted out all sense of time as well as of direction, stealing the sun from its path across the sky. He could not say if was the same the day, or another. But he refused to stop walking. From a drawstring bag attached to his belt, he took dried, salted meat. It was tough enough to threaten the seating of his teeth in his jaw, but it gave him something to do, something to mitigate the fear, the anxiety, that underscored every moment. His heart was filled with both.

He was alone upon the earth. The world felt larger, impossibly endless, less like a home than a challenge, akin to an enemy. The world had stolen his family, scattered those he loved. Davyn knew very well that no matter his efforts, it was possible he would find none of them. His children. His wife. Taken from him.

"No." He said it around the hard curl of dried meat

in his mouth. "The Mother of Moons is not so heartless."

But Alisanos . . . Alisanos was. And the guide had warned him: a *sentient* world, he'd said; a world that moved, that took, that changed the humans it swallowed. There was guilt in Davyn's soul, hag-riding him. But also an awareness that if Alisanos were truly so sentient, able to uproot itself and move at will, it was entirely possible nothing could have prevented the scattering, the loss, the winnowing of his family.

Except perhaps to have been in Atalanda province.

Davyn stopped dead. Around him spread the beaten grasslands, the lightning-scarred earth, the splattering of mud blasted up from the ground. Above him burned the sun. And within him, twisting like a knife, was the knowledge, the fear, that he was alone.

"Mother," he begged, tears threatening, "I beg you, let me find them. All of them." And he named them: the wife, and the children, each, so the Mother would know whom he sought.

THE INFANT, SATED, slept, cradled on her back in her mother's cross-legged lap. Having removed her muslin underskirt, Audrun set about making the child a few clouts she could wear against the anticipated end result of nursing. Already the girl had dampened Rhuan's donated leather tunic. Audrun untied it, shook it out one-handed, spread it across

the ground. She didn't dare look at the guide. Next she
tore her underskirt into several lengths of cloth that
would approximate clouts. Her muslin smallclothes
had taken as much of a beating as the homespun tunic
and skirts, full of holes, rents, tatters, and snags. But it
was better than carrying a naked baby in a man's ornamented leather tunic.

She had restored as much modesty as was possible
in the bodices of breast bindings, smallclothes, and
tunic. With Davyn she had birthed and raised four
children and was casual about such things as baring
breasts to nurse, but Davyn was her *husband;* and her
children, *her* children. Rhuan was a stranger. She knew
next to nothing about him. *Well, except that he can come
back to life after dying.* Not what one would expect to
know about another.

Oh, and that he was the son of a god.

Audrun ceased folding clouts. She looked across the
tree ring. Rhuan still lay on his back, sprawled in
loose-limbed abandon with copper-colored braids a
tangled tapestry against the ground. In fact, he appeared to be asleep. His belly, naked because the
baldric carrying his throwing knives had slipped up to
bare it, moved in even breaths against the low-slung,
belted waistband of leather leggings, every bit as ornamented as his tunic. God's son or no, he did not believe in subtlety. Or, she reflected, in modesty.

He was, Audrun supposed, as tired as she. Certainly
his flesh bore the same sorts of flight-engendered

wounds, though admittedly he had not given birth. But he had gone to great lengths to aid her family, finding them on the track in bad weather, transporting her two youngest, making suggestions to others, and coming back to her in the midst of the storm. He had done what he could to save her as Alisanos approached, and she had refused to let him. Now they were both trapped.

Or was he? Audrun frowned, studying his slack, tanned face with its clear-cut profile. He had said she couldn't leave. He had said, she thought, that *they* couldn't leave. But how could that be true? He was of Alisanos, a child of the deepwood, and the son of a god. Who—and what—could prevent him from going where he wished?

Had he said *they* were trapped merely for her benefit, so she didn't feel so alone?

If so, if he could indeed leave Alisanos, then he could do for her the greatest favor of all: he could look for her children, for her husband, to see if they were yet safe in Sancorra, or trapped as she was, as the littlest one was, in the dimness of the deepwood.

As if aware of her thoughts, he wakened. He did it all at once, body flexing into prepardness, eyes opening, fingers reaching to assure himself of the presence of throwing knives, of belt knife. He sat up, shook out his braids, and looked at her. Then he looked at the baby in her lap, and deep dimples blossomed. She had forgotten about those. "What will you call her?"

Audrun blinked. In the midst of chaos, she had not

thought that far. "Davyn and I decided if she were a girl, we'd name her Sarith."

Rhuan nodded. "Pretty name. As suits a pretty baby."

Not all men would find her so, at present. Audrun smiled down at her daughter—at *Sarith*—then glanced back at the guide. She waved a hand. "Where are we? And are we safe here?"

"For the moment." He rose up onto his knees, settling the wide leather baldric crosswise against his bare chest. "This is a dreya ring." He saw her puzzlement. "The trees. They're alive."

Audrun observed dryly, "Trees with sap and leaves usually are."

"But these are dreya trees." His gesture encompassed the close-grown, interlinked circle. The wood was a dull silvery color, the leaves nearly white. "Dreya live in them."

Audrun glanced up, and up. The canopy of each individual tree was woven together into a great, spreading, leafy vault. It was cool and shadowed in the ring.

"Not up there." Rhuan smiled, rising. He stepped to the nearest tree, gently touching the pale wood. "In here."

"In the *trunk*?" Audrun was astonished. "You're jesting with me!"

But he shook his head. "Not here. Not under these circumstances. No, dreya are beings. As I am."

"But—" She started to say *you are human*, because on the outside he was so like mortal men, then recalled he was something entirely else. "Beings who live in trees?"

"They *are* trees," he answered, "when in this form. They are born as all trees are born, from nuts that become seedlings, then grow into saplings, through adolescence, and eventually into adulthood. In maturity, the heart and soul of a dreya tree can also take another form. Very like yours, in fact; dreya are women."

Her response was reflexive. "No."

Rhuan's smile broadened into a grin. "Yes."

"I don't believe you."

He looked at the sleeping baby. "Tell me that again, who gave birth to a new being only yesterday."

Audrun frowned. "She isn't a being. She's human. Born of a man and a woman, a human man and woman, Mother be thanked, not from a *nut*." She then announced it, to make it so, to make it real, as her people did: "This is Sarith. She is Sarith. This is my daughter."

Gently, he said, "Sarith was born in Alisanos."

Unexpectedly, tears filled Audrun's eyes. She lifted the child, the human child, the infant named Sarith, and cradled her against her shoulder, one hand steadying the fuzzed head. "She may have been born here. That doesn't make her *of* here."

His smile had faded. "Doesn't it?"

"I will take her out of here," Audrun declared decisively. "I will find the way, and I will take her out of here, back into the world of humans. Back into *her* world."

"She is of both worlds, Audrun. Bred and born of humans, yes, but she drew first breath in the deep-wood. Your blood was spilled, the water of birth fed the soil. Alisanos is very aware of Sarith. Alisanos claims her as much as you do. And she—Sarith—she will know that. She will feel that. Even as I do."

She glared at him through tears of anger and desperation. "You have already claimed her, have you not? You 'adopted' her, you said. And now Alisanos, too, claims her? Well, what about me? This is *my* child. *My* daughter."

Audrun was startled to see sorrow in Rhuan's eyes. "I believe my mother, my human mother, said much the same about her son, when I was born. But, as you see—" his gesture indicated himself from head to toe "—I am what I am. Born in and of Alisanos."

She was moved to protest. She had to, to retain self-control. "But your father was from here," she said. "He's a *god*, you claim. Sarith's parents are human."

"One of them is," he agreed, "if your husband wasn't taken."

Astonishment banished growing tension. "You're saying *I* am not human? Now? Only a single day after Alisanos . . . uprooted itself?"

Rhuan's eyes were kind. "Not anymore."

Audrun lifted her hand into the air. She stared at it, turned it; saw the grime, the blood, the scrapes, the cuts. Familiar flesh, despite its wounds. She knew that flesh, knew the bluish veins running beneath her skin, the calluses on her palm. She was the same, exactly the same. The change, he had said, would take years. She was still herself.

He saw her denial, though she spoke no word. "Yes," he said. "Alisanos is aware of you, too. Decidedly aware."

Chapter 5

*I*LONA WANDERED IN dimness, in darkness, in shadows she could not reconcile with reality. Part dream, part fever, part vision—possibly of foretelling. She was a hand-reader, not a diviner of dreams, of bones, of ash, or tea leaves; of rune-sticks, of entrails. She was not a blood-scryer, nor any number of other divination sects and denominations. She took a hand into her own, sublimated her sense of self, and journeyed gently into the corners and layers of a soul, to the myriad potentials of future, the sense of self that belonged to another, occasionally unknowing. It was her gift to see, but also to knit together; to know, sometimes, how all the pieces of a person would merge into a future immediate or distant, and into reality. She had never doubted her gift, knowing it had come upon her for a reason, that she was destined by the Mother of Moons to be a diviner as other true diviners were.

Charlatans abounded, making up or copying rituals

to tell a nonexistent future for an ignorant paying customer, but she was not, and had never, been such a one.

What she saw was real. What she read was true. But sometimes even her art resulted in no sane answer, in no description that lent itself to good or bad as concerned a client, only to confusion. She was honest at those times, explaining when she could not see, could not read what she sensed within a hand, a heart, soul. Because for no diviner—except the charlatans—was anything plain, of such clarity and knowledge that a future might be sworn to. Sometimes it was suggestion, no more. Sometimes it was a hint, a wisp, like fading perfume, lost to the moment if not to memory, and indescribable.

She walked amid the shadows of self-doubt, of ignorance, of helplessness, of the terrifying inability to comprehend. No hand-reader could read her own palm; Ilona, as all did at the first blossoming of a gift, had tried. She had learned early on that dreams were no more to her than artifacts of what had gone before, of concerns about what was yet to come, the tedium, the minutiae, the mere unspooling of fragments, of scenes, of potentials that meant nothing. She was certain of the chasm that lay between dreams and divination. It was difficult to explain for any diviner, but all of them who were truly gifted knew. What was the unfolding of a many-petaled flower for one was mundanity for another.

But this, this was neither dream nor divination. This

was a tangled skein of instants, of incidences she could not grasp, not even for a moment; nothing she could take, could examine, could integrate. But neither could she banish those instants, the incidences, to mundanity. Something was afoot in her subconscious. *Something* was taking her somewhere, telling her fractured, fragmented tales. Some *thing* had ensnared her gift, her art, and was leading it astray. Was making that gift its own, a conduit for its intent.

She was, she believed, in the settlement, in the grove, in her wagon, in her cot. If so, she might find Lerin, the dream-reader, who could possibly make sense of what she saw, what she felt, what she *knew,* but could not comprehend. Lerin might, if Lerin had survived the storm.

Ilona stirred. Pain lanced through her left forearm, setting nerves afire. She said nothing, made no complaint because the words would not form, and in a moment the shadows came again, the dimness, the darkness. Portents and potentials, memories and vision. She was wandering, carried away from the self she knew, that she trusted. She was something less or something more; decidedly something *other*. Beneath the colorful blankets her body twisted, denying the comprehension that she was helpless, was an instrument of another's intent. She was Ilona. *Ilona.* Hand-reader. Sancorran. Jorda's diviner . . . *one* of Jorda's diviners.

But she was also lost. She knew it, and mourned.

BRODHI FOUND THE couriers' common tent collapsed, poles scattered, oilcloth tattered, but nonetheless present when so little else throughout the wind-wracked settlement was. Suspicion formed; weight of some kind had pinned down the oilcoth. He began to unwrap the tumbled fabric until he saw booted feet, outflung arms, mouths bloodied, and faces crusted with grime, dirt, blood, and sand. Alorn. Timmon. Fellow couriers, if not precisely companions. Brodhi had none of those, save for Ferize.

He peeled back the oilcoth until both forms were free of encumbrance. Brodhi did then what any human would do, but that an Alisani—not Shoia but *Alisani*—would also do: he checked the sprawled bodies for signs of life.

Neither man was dead. Neither man was conscious, but life yet quickened in them. Brodhi, squatting between the sprawled couriers, looked from one to the other. Eyes were closed, hair tangled, faces bruised and scraped, dusted with ash and soil. Well, he could leave them as they were, to come to themselves on their own, or he could take pains to make them more comfortable. For a moment Brodhi flirted with the attractive impulse to rise and walk away, putting them from his mind, but he remained upon his journey, was still to be tested, and he had, as always, absolutely no idea which occurences were tests, and which were mere coincidence.

In the wake of the storm, of Alisanos becoming active and uprooting itself in order to change locations, anything was possible but Brodhi believed it was far more likely that, in the wake of the deepwood's shifting, his actions and worth might be of more immediate interest, and thus were being considered by his people, by the primaries, who held the governance of his future in their hands. Ferize, in the guise of a young girl, had made it clear that he was to be seen as someone who cared for humans, to know their names, their habits, to *understand* them. He did not wish to. His interest, ambition, his *needs* lay elsewhere. But this journey, frustrating as it might be, was part and parcel of his rite of passage. He would not become what he wished to be if he did not complete the journey, did he not, in some way, become what the primaries demanded he become, were he to ascend. It was not for him to know what the journey entailed. Not until the culmination, the completion of his journey, was achieved, and his future settled.

Time, as the humans reckoned it, ran very differently in Alisanos. Here it was named as hours, days, weeks, months, years; there it was what it was, simple *continuation*. The suns of Alisanos, and its place upon the world, gave it day and night, daylight and darkness, but the rhythms of his body were not predicated on such things as dark or light, night or day, or even of time passing. Five years, the primaries had decreed; five human years. Brodhi was not entirely certain how those years were counted, other than being some conglomeration of hours, days, weeks, but he would know, he was told, when the time was up. When the journey was ended. Either because he had completed it, or because the primaries despaired that he ever would and ended it for him. He would be declared a neuter, unfit for godhood of any ilk; unfit, too, for the human world.

Unfair, he felt, that he, so patently prepared, so deserving to take his place among the primaries, to ascend to godhood, was nonetheless forced to undertake the journey. Such things belonged to Rhuan, his cousin, his kin-in-kind, who expressed a desire to become human himself. To *not* become a god. To *not* take a place among the primaries.

Brodhi could not blame Rhuan's human mother for that. His own mother had been human as well. Discussions among the primaries were ongoing as to whether it was the human element, the human blood, that had caused the seeds of Alario and Karadath to kindle into *dioscuri* in the wombs of two unrelated women when none had been born to either brother for hundreds of years by human reckoning, but as far as Brodhi knew no decision had been reached. And so the weakness he despised in Rhuan was present in himself: the blood, the bone, of humans. He was not just the legacy of primaries, who were wholly divine.

Sighing, Brodhi worked his hands beneath Alorn's shoulders and pulled him from the confining folds of oilcloth. He settled him a small distance away, beneath the brilliant sun, then retrieved Timmon as well. Side by side, they lay in silence, senseless.

"Are they alive?" Bethid's voice, much perturbed, as she arrived. She swooped down to kneel beside the two men. "Oh, Mother, tell me they're alive!"

"The Mother can't, or won't," Brodhi said dryly, "but I can. Yes, they're alive. Both of them. And not likely to die, from what I can tell."

She put her hand against Alorn's throat, waited, then nodded once. She moved then to Timmon's body and did the same.

"I don't lie," Brodhi observed. "Not even in the interest of tact."

Bethid, still kneeling beside Timmon, scowled up at Brodhi. "Pardon me for caring enough to want to find out for myself." Then her expression altered. "Did you pull them away?"

"Yes."

"Oh." Her mouth twisted. "And made sure they were alive."

"Yes."

"So perhaps you do care, and I do you a disservice." Bethid stood, knocking mud from the knees of her woven trews. "I'm going to find them water. Could you could fetch something to eat?"

"You do me no disservice." Brodhi glanced across the settlement. "I suspect fetching food means I must hunt." He gestured. "Little is left here of food storage and meals."

"Mikal found some spirits," Bethid pointed out. "You might go to the remains of his ale tent. Something edible may be left."

Brodhi shrugged. "But we will all need fresh meat soon enough. One might as well hunt."

She nodded, eyes narrowed, studying him thoughtfully. "One might. Or one may merely want nothing to do with tending injured humans."

He gifted her with a slight, dry smile. "One might not."

But she knew he was correct—fresh meat was a necessity—and waved him away. Brodhi found that dismissal more than a little irritating, but his choice was either to depart or to aid her with Alorn and Timmon, work that was, he felt, best left to her. Hunting would take him away from the remains of the settlement, putting distance between himself and human grief, human anger, human despair. Such things sat ill with him.

And then he remembered, startled by realization. "Our horses."

Bethid, walking away, stopped. Her eyes widened as she turned back. "Oh, Mother—how could we forget? How could *I* forget?"

This time he waved dismissal at her. "Fetch them water, Beth. I'll look to the horses."

They were couriers. Horses were necessary for their duties. But also helpful for hunting.

TO RHUAN'S RELIEF, Audrun stopped asking questions. She lost herself in tending the infant, wrapping muslin between and around her legs, criss-crossing it and tying it in place with a long piece of cloth. He left her to that tending, to a mother's joy—though he had, in the creche, changed many clouts himself—and set about giving thanks to the dreya, asking their support. This was their home, this ring; one did not remain within without permission, if one had manners at all. Unlike the human *hell*, where no good dwelled, not all of Alisanos was poisonous to humans, dangerous to others. Dreyas, unlike various demons, devils, and beasts, were not murderers, did not feed upon flesh. They took strength from the soil and suns. Born in and of Alisanos, they were nonetheless benevolent.

Rhuan, taking a step to the queen tree, grinned. *Rather like me.*

"What are you doing?"

Questions again.

He turned, standing at the foot of a tall, pale, wide-crowned, thick-trunked tree entangled on either side with the silvery branches of others. In the ring, dreya shared hearts and souls and blood; the latter humans called sap. "I intend to ask for protection tonight, so we may rest without concern for our lives."

Audrun blinked. "They can protect us? The trees?"

"The dreya, yes. A ring is sacrosanct."

She was astonished. "And demons respect that?"

"Well," he said, "not always. But mostly. Some-times." He shrugged, placing a hand against the trunk that was formed of thousands upon thousands of small, thin, silken scalelike plates of silver-hued bark. Each trunk bore a narrow cleft from ground to lowest branch. "Occasionally."

"That," Audrun mused absently, stroking her daughter's pale-fuzzed head, "is not particularly reassuring."

"They chose to admit us."

She looked up again, brows arching in startlement. "They could have kept us out?"

"Oh, most certainly. They allowed us to enter. In a way, they've granted us sanctuary . . . but I owe them gratitude, devotions, and my name. Your name." He smiled. "And Sarith's."

"It matters to them, our names?"

"Names define us, Audrun. Among other things." He turned then, turned away from her to face the tree. He placed both hands on the patterned trunk, and leaned in to rest his forehead against the wood as well. With eyes closed, he exhaled through his mouth and let the breath gust against the smooth trunk. In the tongue the dreya queen would know, he told her his name, the name of the woman, the name of the child; asked safety for the night; explained their need, and what brought them here. Then he offered her and her sisters all the respect of his soul, trained into him from infancy. He honored the ring, honored the dreya.

He might have used his sire's name, but he did not.

Alario had many sons, though only Rhuan remained of his *dioscuri*-born. The others were ascended, or neuters, or dead. And he, well, he would choose to be none of those things, but human. To live among the humans in the human world.

He wondered if his sire knew that. Alario might, if Darmuth had said anything after the Hearing. He was enjoined from such, but demons were not always dependable. And they could be tricked by beings who were gods.

Rhuan told the queen: *My mother was human, born into and reared by that world. Alisanos took her, as did a god—but her sap has quickened in me. The heat of Alisanos runs in my veins; I answer to the suns. But I answer also to the heartwood of my mother dwelling within me, the soul and the bone; and to the pull of the human world, the human people. This woman is one of them. She has young saplings in her world, growing straight and strong. She has a new-sprouted one here, stalked by that which, and by those who, would kill them both. When the suns rise tomorrow, it will be my task to protect the mother and daughter. Tonight, will you honor us with your protection?*

From without, from a distance, came a scream.

Audrun shot to her feet, clasping the baby. "That's Gillan!" she cried. "That's *Gillan!*"

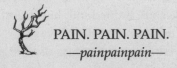

PAIN. PAIN. PAIN.
    —painpainpain—

He was stripped of self, of self-control, of all humanity save that which screamed in pain. He was name-
less, mindless, engulfed in agony. He could not speak,
could not pray, could not beg, could not petition the
gods, the Mother, for release. He could only scream.

His leg was afire.

To the bone, it burned.

Around him, heat turned stone to liquid. Heat bubbled up. Heat wreathed the world in steam. Beneath
him, his body was poised to fall, to follow his leg into
indescribable agony. If he fell, if he followed, would
the pain cease?

—*painpainpain*—

Gillan screamed again.

ELLICA, POISED STIFFLY upon the rock,
heard the screaming. It harrowed her to the
bone. It set the hairs on her flesh rising, her scalp
prickling. Not close, not close. Was it human? Demon?
Prey?

Was it something dying?

Some*one* dying?

INDECISION LOCKED AUDRUN'S joints,
held her transfixed in place. She could not
move. She could only clasp the child, only stare at the

man, only fasten every nerve upon the comprehension that her son was in pain. Her son was screaming. Her firstborn, the eldest of the siblings to the infant named Sarith, was not only in Alisanos, but in agony.

She knew his scream.

Ah, Mother . . . O, Mother of Moons . . . MotherMother-Mother . . .

She was torn, torn, torn. A baby here. A son there.

A baby, safe within a ring; Rhuan had told her so. And a son in pain.

"I have to," she gasped. "I must."

"Audrun—"

Her body insisted, and her heart, and her soul. "I have to go." She thrust the child into his arms. "Take her. Take her. Keep her safe."

"Audrun!"

"That's Gillan!" she cried. "That's my *son*."

"Audrun, no!"

She entrusted him with what was precious to her. She left the child, left the man, left the dreya ring. She ran.

Mother, she prayed, *O Sweet Mother, save my son.*

Chapter 6

WHEN DAVYN FIRST saw the smudge of trees along the horizon, his pulse quickened. He thought he recalled the guide shouting at them through the storm, saying something about a forest providing some shelter for them; was it here the Shoia had carried the smallest of the children, searching for safety? He had seen nothing of a forest as he'd stood upon the chest inside the wagon, but the land was not entirely flat.

Davyn broke into a jog. If the guide had gotten Torvic and Megritte to the forest, he may have done the same for Ellica and Gillan, and possibly even Audrun. Perhaps only *he* had been caught in the worst of the storm and the rest were safe.

Fear began to recede. Apprehension still rode him, but the idea that the others were safe became fixed in his mind. For some distance hope and the beginnings of relief carried him easily, but then his body began to flag. He dropped to a walk, stretching strides to cover

more ground, but before long that, too, seemed to require too much strength, more endurance than he had.
Davyn, panting, stopped, gulped water, caught his
breath, then forced himself into a jog once again. He
would go in spurts, as a man rode a horse cross-
country: walk, trot, gallop; walk, trot, gallop. It didn't
spend the horse unnecessarily, but steady changes of
pace covered ground.

Possibly, *possibly*, all were safe. Possibly they were
together somewhere in that forest, praying to the
Mother for *his* safety.

That made Davyn grin. All his worry for naught;
only *he* had been in danger while the others took shelter from the worst of the terrible storm. And he had
survived. He was uninjured. They would be together
again, a family again, and though the oxen were dead
and the wagon canopy destroyed, the wagon itself
was whole—or would be, when he changed the
cracked axle for the new one—and they could walk
back to the settlement. There they might be able to
find a team of mules or horses to borrow long enough
to pull the wagon back to the tent village. Audrun, Ellica, and the youngest could remain there with others
while he and Gillan took the team to the wagon, repaired it, and returned to the settlement. He thought
it likely that their journey to Atalanda would be delayed a good three or four weeks, but the baby wasn't
due for another four months. They had time. Plenty of
time.

In a much better frame of mind, Davyn jogged on-

ward toward the forest, the thick, massive canopy of
trees growing closer, clearer, larger along the horizon.

TORVIC HISSED AT Megrite, *"Be quiet."* And
when the fear in her eyes told him she might
very well cry out in reaction to the terrible scream, he
pressed both his hands over her mouth. "No, Meggie.
Be quiet." He glanced over his shoulder, saw rainwa-
ter dripping from leaves, drooping tree limbs. But
there was no sound—no sound at all. In the wake of
the high-pitched scream, everything had stilled. The
world seemed to have simply *stopped.*

Megritte reached up and tried to peel his fingers
from her mouth. He leaned very close, very close, and
whispered to her, "We need to hide. Go back in the
rocks, Meggie. Go back where we were."

She climbed unsteadily up into the crevice. There
was, once again, just enough room for him. Torvic
gathered in folds of fabric, pulling the blankets and
oilcloth up again, this time not as shelter but as shield.
Hunched next to him, Megritte pressed close. "We
have to find Mam and Da. You said."

Sound began again. Chirps and chitters, clicking. A
breeze ran through the trees, pushing leaves against
one another in a hissing susurration. The gloom intensified, as if the sun—the *suns*—were sliding below the
treetops.

"Torvic, we have to go. You *said.*"

"Not now." It came out trembling. Torvic pressed his lips together and tried again, whispering. "Not now, Meggie. Later."

The tears had stopped, but her voice sounded pinched. "What made that noise?"

"I don't know." The stone beneath his buttocks was chill. He scooted closer to his sister. "We'll wait a bit, Meggie. Then we'll go look for Mam and Da."

"Promise?"

"I promise."

TIMMON AND ALORN, conscious again, were wind-battered, filthy, scraped, and bruised, but otherwise whole. Bethid handed around the waterskin she'd found and told them to stay put; there was no reason they should do anything other than sit still and catch their breath. Both young men were pale and shaken, and dark-haired, brown-eyed Alorn nursed a long cut above one eyebrow while Timmon, lanky and long-limbed, with blue eyes and light brown hair, pressed a portion of his tunic against his swollen bottom lip to stem the bleeding. In the meantime, those tent dwellers who had fled the settlement began to return, straggling in. Bethid, seeing their shocked expressions, hearing despairing voices, was glad she had a task in looking after her fellow couriers. Others, those who had wisely followed instructions given out by her and Mikal as the storm swept down, now discovered that nothing in the world was left to them save their lives and the clothing on their bodies.

Too much, Bethid knew; simply too much for anyone to wholly grasp, to assimilate. But only days before a party of brutal Hecari warriors had arrived at the tent village, methodically killing one person in ten: men, women, children. They had also set fire to as many tents, culling dwelling places as well. In the days afterward, bodies were buried following various rites and rituals to see the dead safely across the river into a better afterworld, and burned tents were searched for what might have survived the decimation. On the heels of that had come Alisanos, swallowing acre after acre, mile after mile, its power made visible and tangible by the terrible storm.

Brodhi had said the deepwood was now but a half-mile away.

A chill pimpled her flesh. Bethid rubbed her upper arms vigorously. This was utter devastation, the tents left whole by the Hecari blown down, blown apart, tattered by and scattered on the wind. Oilcloth was gone, save portions that had been caught under something heavy, as had happened with the couriers' common tent, weighted by the senseless bodies of Alorn and Timmon.

She flicked a brief investigatory glance at both young men, judged them steady enough, then rose and began to peel back the puddled oilcloth that had swaddled them to see if anything remained. Sleeping pallets were gone, as were belongings. None of their rich blue courier cloaks remained, nor the silver badges of their office. She found two of the iron hooks that had hung from the Mother Rib of the tent, providing storage for cloaks and clothing, but little else. The ground beneath the remains of the tent was wet from the rain, scoured by the wind. Of the wooden pole framework, the scaffolding over which oilcoth had been lashed, only one pole remained in sight.

Bethid sighed, dropping the corner of heavy fabric. The common tent had stood on the edges of the settlement, and before it, stretching in all directions, was the detritus of lives altered forever. Here and there a woman knelt in the storm-purged place where a tent had stood, grasping children to her. Men walked through the lightning-scorched field of debris, searching out the footpaths, the landmarks, in hope of tracking belongings. Little was left to find.

Her mouth twisted grimly. *We meant to start a rebellion, to fight the Hecari . . . now we've something else to deal with.* She glanced sharply at her fellow couriers, still nursing their wounds. They had, with her, with Mikal, even Brodhi, discussed the possibility of a Sancorran revolt begun very quietly, very slowly, by careful, subtle couriers. Could they begin again? Could they continue to lay plans to take back Sancorra from the enemy?

But Alisanos had moved. Sancorra now had an enemy far less predictable than the Hecari.

"Mother of Moons," Bethid muttered, "there has to

be a way. There must be." But she knew that those who had survived both Hecari and the incursions of Alisanos would not now be willing to consider rebellion. She frowned, pondering. And then, abruptly, an idea unfolded before her. For a moment Bethid could not believe it herself, but with further consideration, layer by layer, thought by thought, a plan knitted itself together. "Stay here," she told her fellow couriers, gesturing with her hand. "No need to move; I'll see about more water, and food."

Bethid did not wait for any protests from Timmon and Alorn, though she wasn't certain any would come. She strode quickly across the settlement grounds, intent on finding Mikal. And Jorda—he was a natural leader, and could accomplish things she might not be able to, being small, slight, and a woman.

There was also Brodhi to find. The plan *required* Brodhi.

SHE RAN. SHE fell numerous times, tripped by tangled vines, exposed roots, thick ground cover, sharp-edged grass. Her legs and arms stung; her face burned. Blood was in her mouth. She spat, spat again, then rubbed haphazardly at her chin even as she ran. Once again she fell; once again she thrust her body upward, forced her body to keep moving, to ignore all physical insults. Cuts, scrapes, bruises . . . all these would heal. Gillan might not, were he injured.

And she feared he might be, recalling his scream. It rang in her memory, blotting out all other thought.

"Audrun!"

The guide. She clamped her teeth together. She could not spare an answer. Dared not; it would take time, and he would find her, would very likely insist she return to the dreya ring. She could not do so. Not with Gillan, her firstborn, in danger. Let the guide tend the infant while she tended her eldest.

"Audrun!"

Ah, Mother, but it was tempting to slow, to halt, to answer his summons. But the infant—no, she had a name: *Sarith*—was safe; Rhuan had said so, had promised it, upon entry into the ring. Gillan was not.

On and on. The deepwood continued to delay her, as if it were alive, mocking her, tricking her. No other scream had sounded. She depended on memory, on instinct, to find the direction. But overhead, above the thick canopy of wide tree crowns, *two* suns burned, not one. Could she rely on two alien suns in place of the single one she knew? Alisanos was ever changing, the guide had said; was it possible, was it *probable*, she would only accomplish getting herself lost?

Or were such doubts themselves products of the deepwood?

She opened her mouth and shouted. "Gillan!"

If he heard her . . . if he *heard* her, he could answer, and guide her.

"Gilllaaaaann!"

HE COULD NOT help but wonder if he still had a leg. He could not see through the layers of steam and smoke. But instinct and strength of will seasoned by sheer panic lent him the physical ability to quit the liquefied hole into which he had stepped, plunging foot to knee through crust. Without thinking, Gillan lurched upward and sideways all of a piece, aware of heated surface beneath grasping hands; aware also that he was blind amidst the choking, heavy layers of sulfur, could barely breathe, and could yet put himself into more danger. But the pain of his leg, so acute, provided a need, an overwhelming motivation so great as to make movement possible. Between one moment and the next he found himself lunging away, rolling aside, the hot crust beneath him somehow supporting his body, giving purchase to his clawing hands. Coughing, choking, eyes streaming with tears, he raised himself up on trembling arms. In a scrabbling, ungainly motion with his weight taken onto his right hip, he managed to move, to dig in with his fingers and thrust, to hook himself forward with elbows, to lift and drag his body, using the good right knee to both steady him and provide forward momentum.

He wept, he gasped, he coughed, but nonetheless he moved.

And moved.

And moved.

—*awayawayaway*— It drove him onward. —*away-away*— Still he dragged himself, thrust himself forward, pushed and pulled himself forward, with knee and hands. "Away—away—away—"

Oh, Mother—oh, *Mother*, but he hurt!

He crawled, he pulled, he thrust himself onward, dragged himself away. And when at last the sulfur fumes began to thin, when his eyes burned less, when he breathed clean air, he mumbled a prayer to the Mother of Moons. Of gratitude. Of amazement that he had survived; that he had somehow not lost all of himself in the burning liquid.

Gillan wept still. But now they were tears of pain, not of sulfur irritation; tears of disbelief, of confusion, of an awareness that he was hurt very badly. He dragged and hooked and hitched; he pushed himself onto cooler ground, onto reddish-black cinders, and farther, farther, until his hands touched grass. Until his body sensed shade. Until the trees drooped down, nearly touching the ground.

In the grass, half-blinded, head filled by the remains of sulfur fumes, the pain of his leg was so bad he vomited. He brought up everything he'd eaten until nothing was left but bile. That he brought up also, until his body was empty. He wiped a shaking forearm across his mouth, then, lizardlike, he turned half of his body aside while his legs remained in one place, distancing himself as best he could from the vomit. Sweat ran from his face. He felt hot, he felt cold. He began to tremble, to feel weak, to be aware of the world drifting away from him. He wanted to vomit again, to void his bowels and bladder. His entire body was in some form of revolt. And then at last came the blackness, the release; he slid faster and faster into the nothingness of extremity, deaf and blind to the world, thinking again and again the name, saying *Mother of Moons*, asking without speaking that she deliver him from the hell of his ruined leg, from the evils of Alisanos.

THE WOMAN LEFT trembling leaves and crushed vegetation in her wake as she ran from the dreya ring. Rhuan, poised at the edge, entwined boughs hanging around him, cursed her name in several different languages, even while understanding very well why she ran, why she ignored him.

It was dangerous. Much too dangerous for her to be alone in the deepwood. She risked more than her son's life; she risked her own.

He had carried the child while in flight before. But that had been to escape. This would be to track, to find, to grasp, to force a terrified mother back to such safety as the dreya offered. He could not afford the encumbrance of the baby. But he also could not afford to place that baby in danger by neglecting its welfare.

He turned and strode rapidly to the queen's tree. There he knelt and placed the swaddled, sleeping infant at the base of the huge, plated, tricolored trunk.

But he did not immediately place his palms against the tree. Instead, he drew a throwing knife from his baldric and cut into the ball of each fingertip. Bleeding, he replaced the knife. He touched the eleven blessing points: the middle of his forehead, the bridge of his nose between the eyebrows, each eyelid, the faint hollow between mouth and nose, the highest point of each cheekbone, his upper lip, lower lip, point of his chin, and lastly the notch that joined his collarbones. Then once again he pressed his palms and his brow against the tree. Once again he breathed against wood. Again, and at last, he appealed to the dreya queen. It was not his safety he asked for, neither was it that of the woman who tried to answer her eldest's need, but for the infant, the baby, the newborn named Sarith.

Come to her. Depart your tree. Tend her as is needed. Protect her. Let no one and nothing come into the ring to harm her. I entrust her to you; here, in the deepwood, she is as much mine as she is the woman's who bore her. We are both of Alisanos, this child and I . . . and also both human, to some degree. You understand that weakness. You comprehend the challenges facing us both, this child and me. Succor her. Shelter her. She is but a newly sprouted seedling bursting free of her shell. Let her grow to be a sapling. Keep her safe until her mother returns. Until I do. Rhuan drew a long breath. For the first time since childhood, he invoked his father's name. *I am Alario's get. I am dioscuri. I ask your protection for the human seedling.*

Chapter 7

*B*ETHID WENT DIRECTLY to the hand-reader's wagon in the denuded grove. There she found, as hoped, Jorda and Mikal. They stood outside, talking quietly near the folding steps. Large men both, weathered men, each responsible for his own business and thus accustomed to leading, yet markedly gentle in certain circumstances. That they were concerned about Ilona was clear as they spoke, brows furrowed over respective noses.

Her question was immediate, pushing aside other concerns. "How is she?"

Jorda rubbed a scarred hand over his head, absently smoothing hair the wind had torn from its single ruddy braid. "It's no kind of sleep I've ever seen."

Bethid pondered that a moment. "Well, she does have a broken arm. She may be getting a fever."

"I've seen fevers," Mikal put in. "I think we all have. This is like . . . it's like—"

"—her body's present, but she isn't," Jorda finished.

Bethid half-shrugged—couldn't they see it? "She's a diviner. They aren't like other people."

Jorda and Mikal exchanged glances, brows raised in consideration. Slowly, Jorda nodded. "It could be."

Mikal looked at him. "You know her best, of us."

"I do." The karavan-master pushed again at loosened hair. "But she's never been ill a single day, in all her time with me. Nor has she broken any bones."

"She's a *diviner*." Bethid believed it explained everything; or at least enough for the moment. "Look, I'll stay with her tonight, of course—but there's something we should discuss." Now she had their attention and continued crisply, counting points off in her mind. "The Hecari burned one tent in ten. The storm burned none. If we set everyone to searching in all directions, we may be able to find things carried away by the wind, things that are still useable. Oilcloth, poles, wagon canopies, bedding, clothing, food storage— even personal belongings. We have the wagons, too. Yes, things are damaged, and some can't ever be repaired, no doubt, but there should be enough material for us to rig makeshift shelters. We need also to set people looking for the livestock. The river provides water and fish aplenty, but we require more than that." Her expansive gesture indicated the settlement as a whole. "The karavaners planned to begin again somewhere out of Sancorra. They carry seed for crops. Grain. Herbs. Spices, flour, tubers, any number of other supplies. There is enough, if the Mother is generous, for us to rebuild the settlement. The rainy season is coming. We'll have a place to live for the time being, shelter and provender, and time to think. But we need to do this together. It must be communal, not family by family, person by person."

Mikal was frowning. "We call it a settlement, but it isn't. It's just a place people pass through. I think few of them will want to remain here, no matter how temporarily, after what's happened."

Bethid shook her head vigorously, ear-hoops swinging. "No, no, that's not true. *You* live here, Mikal. You aren't just passing through. And how many tents were here for more than a few months? How many karavaners stayed behind for whatever reason as their karavans left? Mikal, you have regular custom, people you see— you *saw*—every day in your ale tent. This is where karavan-masters, like Jorda—" She nodded in his direction, "—meet to gather their people. There's good water and grass, rich soil for crops, and safety in numbers. And in truth, many won't be *able* to go anywhere else. Not if they've lost everything but themselves." She scrubbed two-handedly at her short-cropped hair, now dry, splayed fingers shedding flakes of dirt and sand. "They'll need duties, these folk. Something to think about, something to *do*, and they'll require a few like you and Jorda to provide guidance and organization. Or things will only grow worse."

"Beth, you're talking about a *real* settlement," Mikal observed, scratching gently beneath his eye patch.

"Yes." She nodded. "Precisely. A place to put down roots." She briefly studied their expressions, gauged the interest in their eyes. "Alisanos has moved, do you see? Brodhi told me a portion of the deepwood is but a half-mile away, in that direction." She pointed. "Yes, we must send people out to recover what the storm took. But no one should go very far until we know how much danger we're in from Alisanos. We don't know where the borders are anymore."

Jorda understood her intent at once. "Someone should scout those borders."

"Exactly," Bethid agreed. "Alisanos didn't awaken for forty years, and everyone in nearly two generations knew where the deepwood was and how to avoid it—well, for the most part; some were lost, of course. Now, no one knows where it is. We need to map the borderland between the deepwood and safety. We need to *make* maps, and abide by them."

"Rhuan and Darmuth," Jorda declared immediately. "They'll be best at scouting and making maps. Rhuan says he is sensitive to the deepwood; he'll know how close we can or can't get. But for immediate concerns, we need only to find exactly where the deepwood begins and ends in the areas closest to the settlement. They need not map the entire perimeter. Others may do that later." He lifted heavy shoulders, lines deepening around his eyes. "For all we know, Alisanos reaches into multiple provinces."

Bethid nodded. "But if nothing else, Alisanos is a forest, which means it's visible. Just none of us knows how close we can go without being swallowed. In the meantime, we need shelter, meat, and crops." She looked searchingly at each man. "It may be that no supply karavans can come here anymore, if by some chance Alisanos *surrounds* us. There may be no way in, no way out. If that's true, we must find a way to survive on our own, on what may now be an island."

A tense silence ensued as the men grimly contemplated the possibility of being surrounded by the deepwood. Then Mikal raised a belaying hand. "Wait, Beth. For the moment, let's say we are not surrounded—though that is a harrowing thought! You're forgetting another danger. The Hecari. They came for a decimation once. They may do it again. Especially if this truly becomes a settlement. Yes, ordinarily there would be safety in numbers, as you said . . . but numbers is exactly what led the Hecari to cull one in ten here."

Bethid put a finger into the air. "I have an idea about that. The Hecari. If we're not, the Mother be kind, an island in the midst of the deepwood." When she offered nothing further, both men looked at her more sharply. "It concerns Brodhi," she explained, "and whether he'll agree."

Mikal scoffed. "If it requires aiding anyone, we cannot pin hopes on him."

"Only indirectly," Bethid replied. "Mostly it requires him to fulfill his vows as a courier, and that I believe he will do." She nodded at them both, heart lifting; it was a plan that could work. "We've an hour or more before sundown. Let me find Brodhi, talk to him, and then I'll return to see Ilona safely through the night."

"Wait," Jorda said as Bethid turned to depart. "Did you find your fellow couriers?"

She paused. "Yes, they're both well. Or will be, when the bumps and bruises heal." Then her thoughts skipped ahead. She looked thoughtfully at Mikal. "We have plenty to do for months, I daresay, in rebuilding, planting, mapping—but what we were discussing before the storm is still an issue, providing the deep-wood doesn't surround us. Perhaps you might mention to Jorda what we talked about, with regard to Sancorra and the Hecari. After all, a karavan-master is in his own way a courier, and I know we can trust him. I suspect we may *need* him."

STANDING STIFFLY ATOP the ridge of stone free of soil, of creeping vine and cutting grass, Ellica set trembling hands to her head, fingers spread across the crown of her skull. Was it human, the scream? Did it issue from a human mouth? It was not the shrill, piercing cry of a child. It was an older voice.

It might be prey. It might be human.

It *sounded* human.

A second scream carried through the forest. Indeed, human. Male. Someone in extremity, in agony. Someone possibly dying.

Was it Da? Could it be Da? Might it be Gillan?

Ellica breathed audibly through clenched teeth. Fingertips curled hard against her head. Every portion of her body shuddered, stiff as it was. As tears cut through the grime on her face, she pulled her hands slowly down the sides of her head, was tempted to dig fingernails into her cheeks and jaw. Anything to turn her attention from the screams, and the fear. Human. A *human* had screamed.

"Stop." It issued unexpectedly, breathily, from her mouth. "Stop this." Ellica drew in a very deep breath, exhaled sharply, then inhaled again. She tamed the trembling in her body in very small increments. *"Think."* Her parents had taught her that years before. She fastened upon it, slowly quashing the panic that made her want to cry, to wail, to give up everything in her queasy belly. She was not a child. She was not Torvic or Megritte. She was nearly a woman grown. Her parents would expect better of her. *She* expected better.

Think: *she was in Alisanos.* Demons dwelled here, demons and devils, all manner of beasts and creatures, so the tales told. She believed it now. She believed all she had heard. And she was alone, completely alone, wholly dependent on herself. There could be no rescue, not here. No discovery of her by father, mother, siblings. But she could not spend her days perched upon the crown of a boulder, starving to death, or, worse, waiting to be eaten. She must gather her wits and *do* something.

Upon the boulder's crown, no grass grew. No vines quivered. No branches reached for her. Ellica looked at each carefully: at grass, vines, trees. At the shadows of the forest. And, looking upward, squinting through the interstices of tangled tree canopies, at the double suns of Alisanos, one white, one yellow, against a sepia sky.

Ellica nodded. Once. Then stepped off the stone.

THE FOREST DREW closer, larger. Davyn, with a stitch in his side and breath ragged, slowed from a jog to a walk, pushing himself to keep going. He was wet again, but not from rain; sweat sheathed his flesh. It ran down his temples, stung his eyes, dripped from his jaw. He thought longingly of the waterskin, but had decided to save what was left. His family might need it. They might have spent many hours without water, and might be thirsty.

He wished he had the wagon. He wished he had a horse. Even an ox would do; he could place Torvic and Megritte atop the beast as they turned back toward the wagon. But he had none of those things, only himself, and now, so close to the forest, it became imperative to keep going just as he was, trotting and striding, never stopping.

Almost . . . almost. He nodded as he walked with long strides, waterskin slapping against his thigh.

His heart was full. The nightmare was nearly over. Renewed energy coursed through his body. He broke once again into a jog, wiping a forearm swiftly across his brow to clear the sweat away, so he could see clearly. Much of his hair, which had dried in the sun, was wet again, sticking to his skull. His chest hurt. His side ached. He kept jogging.

The guide had made certain his family was safe. Davyn remembered that, recalled the man riding out of the midst of storm to arrive at their wagon, to warn them, to see them to safety. Davyn remembered, too, that he had not wished the guide to accompany them. It had pricked at his pride, then, that the guide felt he, the husband, the father, could not protect his family. But in the midst of chaos, with the wagon canopy shredded and carried away, dust and dirt so thick no one could see a hand in front of his face, he had welcomed the guide with so profound a relief that he realized the soul inside him had feared that he, husband and father, was *not* enough. Yes, he had brought his family safely to the settlement, but doubts had risen, doubts and pride, as he measured himself against the Shoia guide. Memory recalled the man's efficient expertise with throwing knives, with the willingness and ability to kill Hecari the instant threat arose.

He coughed a laugh at that thought; one of the guide's throwing knives had ended up in Davyn's shoulder. But considering how swiftly the guide had reacted, how unerring his aim had been in sending blades into Hecari eyes and throats, the lone knife in his shoulder was a small price, Davyn felt. And by then the guide had a Hecari dart in his forearm, was dying of its poison. Still he had tended Davyn. Still he had thought of the children as death overtook him, to tell them not to fear. That he would revive.

And in that storm he had carried the youngest of them to safety, turning back for Gillan and Ellica, turning back for them all. With Alisanos on the move, the Shoia guide had put himself in harm's way to save a family of strangers.

I owe him much, Davyn thought. *More than I can repay.*

And then the thought left him, all thoughts left him. As he came upon the outer perimeter of the forest, he saw how the land changed. No grass existed beyond a certain point. It was charred, burned to ash. The area appeared to have *melted.* It was—nothingness. Blackened. Consumed. Beyond it stood the forest, but Davyn had never before seen its like. Twisted, odd-colored tree trunks, boughs knotted one upon the other, multi-hued leaves glossy as glass. The colors were wrong. *Everything* was wrong.

He fell out of his jog into an ungainly, broken transition. Then even walking was impossible. Panting, Davyn stumbled to a halt. For a moment he hung there on his feet, leaning toward the forest. But between his feet and the forest ran fissures in the earth, carved into the blackened, grassless surface.

The guide had taken his children into Alisanos.

A garbled cry fell from his mouth. He dropped heavily to his knees. "O Mother, O Mother of Moons, please, please . . . no . . ."

But Davyn knew the answer was incontrovertibly *yes.*

Chapter 8

*H*UNTING HAD BEEN successful. Brodhi, astride his chestnut gelding with the carcass of a small, field-dressed grasslands deer draped across the horse's withers, rode through the grove that had once hosted karavans gathering to depart, then those who had been wounded in the Hecari attack. It was empty now, branches stripped of leaves, boughs cracked and twisted, younger trees uprooted and thrown down in disarray. Empty, save for a handful of bodies. Two men and three women, clearly dead; three too weak, perhaps, to flee the settlement when the storm came down, while two had been burned by lightning. The latter were sprawled on the ground, faces muddied, hair and clothing charred.

Brodhi rode farther, leaving the bodies behind, then reined in beside a massive elderling oak. Most of its branches were stripped of leaves, but the grand old tree had withstood the rain and wind. Bare branches clove the sky. He heaved the deer over the left shoul-

der of his horse to drop it to the ground. Then he dismounted, took from the saddle the length of torn oilcloth he'd fashioned into a rope, tied the cloven front
hooves together, then flipped the end of the makeshift
rope over a heavy branch. Brodhi hauled the open carcass up until there was a foot of distance between the
ground and the deer's tail, then tied off the rope. The
delicate deer swung slightly; Brodhi stopped it with a
hand on one front leg as he unsheathed his long-
bladed knife.

Then, even with his back to her, he said, "What is it,
Bethid?"

He heard the gust of air exhaled in something akin
to a laugh. "I don't know how you do it."

"I listen," he said. "I know your walk. Your scent."

Her tone was dry as she approached. "How utterly
romantic." She stopped beside his horse, running an
experienced hand down the gleaming neck. "Did you
find the rest? Churri, and Timmon's and Alorn's
mounts?"

"I did."

"Are they well?"

Brodhi made a circular cut around the deer's neck,
then sliced downward to the cavity prepared by the
field-dressing. "My mount is fine, as you can see. The
other three have some welts, some scrapes, but all are
sound. They came when I whistled. I've hobbled them
so they can forage. The grass is wet, but the sun will
dry it soon."

"Poor Churri," she murmured. "I'm neglecting him.

I'll have to take him down to the river and let him soak."

He gripped the deer's hide at the cut on either side of the neck, then began to strip it downward, occasionally using his knife to slice with precision between skin and flesh. When Bethid made no further comment, he glanced over his shoulder at her. Her short-cropped fair hair, as usual, stood up in tousled spikes. Ear-hoops glinted. In the onset of the storm she had not had time to grab her scroll-case and other courier accoutrements; she wore a mud-caked, indigo-dyed homespun tunic belted at the waist, and baggy trews, gaitered in cross-gartered leather from knee to ankle over her boots. Her face bore the remnants of mud, dust, and grime, smeared by the applications of tunic sleeve and the back of her hand.

"What?" she asked, pale brows arching up beneath his steady gaze.

Brodhi hitched a shoulder in a slight, elegant shrug. "You came to *me*."

She frowned a little, eyeing the deer. A doe, young and small. "I don't think that's enough to feed the survivors."

"No," Brodhi agreed, pulling and cutting steadily, "but then none of us has any idea of how many survivors there are."

"We should take a head count," Bethid murmured absently, thoughts clearly active. "We need to gather everyone, find out who is injured. There are wagons in the grove across the settlement; we can gather there.

The trees will provide a little shelter, even if most of them lack leaves." She scratched at her neck, wincing as her fingernails found a welt. "So cursed much to do . . ."

"And you have decided this is your responsibility?"

She scowled at him. "This is everyone's responsibility. Even yours."

Brodhi indicated the half-skinned deer, making it obvious that he had contributed. "In the meantime, at your gathering divide the people into groups. Give them tasks. Some to assemble the dead. Some to bring water from the river. Some to fish. We'll need cookfires, if sufficient kindling can be found—"

"And will you bleed all over each pile of wood to set it afire? The wood's still damp, Brodhi."

His smile was slight. "Do we want people still in shock to witness such a thing? I think not. But then, you have a fire already, outside the hand-reader's wagon. It only requires one; others may be lighted from it."

Bethid nodded, gesturing the suggestion aside. "Yes, so it does. Well enough. But there's something more. Something you can do that might keep us safe. Something to buy us time to build again, so we've shelter when the rains come." She wiped the back of her right forearm across her forehead. "As a courier, it's your duty to advise the Hecari warlord of what's happened."

He stopped the skinning process to turn to her, to give her all his wary attention. "*A* courier's duty, yes."

"Yours," she said steadily. "Ride to Cardatha, Brodhi. Do that duty and tell the warlord what happened here. Tell him all about Alisanos, about all of its horrors—and how it moved. How it swallowed mile upon mile. How it destroyed settlements, took over roads, killed many, many people. Tell him this area is dangerous to all, even to Hecari warriors. That old roads no longer exist. That no man, coming near, can escape the deepwood. I can't go; he won't listen to a woman. Timmon and Alorn haven't your edge, your arrogance. Make the warlord *believe*, Brodhi. Make him understand that nothing remains . . . nothing worth his attention. You've scouted it, you see. You know what remains, and what lies now in Alisanos." She grimaced. "And for all we know, it may be exactly as I have described."

As he listened to her words, he realized precisely where she was heading. By the time she finished, he was nodding.

Her eyebrows quirked slightly. "I may be *only* a human, as you are constantly reminding me, but yes, I can think now and again."

He studied her a moment. This was the Bethid who'd come to the Guildhall in Cardatha years before, determined to take the trials to become a courier. She knew what she proposed was unlikely to be accepted. The courier service traditionally was made up of men. Other girls, he knew, had grown up wishing to become couriers. Other girls had even come to the Guildhall. But all had been sent away.

Bethid refused to leave. Bethid *insisted*. Eventually, Brodhi suggested to the Guildmasters that they permit the slight, small girl to undertake the trials. Horses, he told them, didn't care which gender rode them. And if she were to fail—he granted her that *if*—it gave the Guildmasters an example to present to any other young women who came sniffing about the Guildhall.

That Bethid, confident, determined, stubborn, willing to do whatever was asked of her to prove her worth—*and had*—stood before him now. And he knew very well that no amount of argument, no matter how persuasive his words, would sway her.

"Jorda told me that Rhuan is sensitive to Alisanos," she went on. "That he knows where its borders lie before they're visible, and when it's preparing to move. Is it a Shoia thing? Can you sense it also?"

He found that an amusing question, though she wouldn't understand why. Unless he told her what he was. "I have that land-sense, yes."

"Then you are ideal." She spread her hands. "A Shoia with land-sense, a courier who knows Sancorra better than any Hecari, who knows also where the deepwood lies. Who can *draw a map* for the warlord. Who can instruct that warlord, in precise, minute detail, as to how much of the province Alisanos has eaten."

"And so the warlord sends no culling parties when there is nothing to cull. Time is bought to recover. To begin your rebellion."

"But when he does send culling parties—because at

some point he will—perhaps we can lure his warriors *into Alisanos*. And out of Sancorra." She smiled. "A fitting fate for them, yes?"

"A few would be trapped," Brodhi agreed, "and thus could no longer trouble Sancorra. But not enough. Not nearly enough. The Hecari will learn, just as Sancorrans did, to avoid the deepwood."

Bethid nodded, stroking the gelding again. "But perhaps by that time we'll be better prepared to withstand them."

"Then you are proposing to rebuild here permanently. To encourage people to stay, and others to come."

Her blue eyes were bright, determined. "I am. Only this time it won't be just a place to pass through, to meet the karavans. It will be a staging area for the reclamation of Sancorra."

TORVIC ROUSED AT the sound of a human-sounding voice that was not his sister's. "You can come out now. It's safe, for the moment."

He jerked awake and felt Meggie do the same beside him. They were both squeezed into the back of the crevice as far as they could go, with blankets and oilcloth wadded around them. His eyes were sundazzled; waving branches and leaves caused the light to flash on and off, directly into his eyes. He squinted.

A woman knelt before them. She was poised on the

border between stone and soil, hands clasped loosely in her lap. She had brown hair braided back neatly and pinned against her head; in the blinding flicker of sunlight, he couldn't be sure of her eye color. Dark, he thought.

Meggie said, "Mam?"

That brought him to full wakefulness. "No, Meggie." And as she made to move he grabbed a handful of her tunic. "*Wait.*"

"Wise boy," the woman remarked, "here in the deepwood. No, I'm not your mam. Just one who would be your friend." She wore a tunic and skirt of rough, rust-colored homespun, a dark rope belt wrapped twice around her waist. Slowly she lifted her hands and displayed her palms to them. "I won't harm you."

Meggie's natural curiosity reasserted itself. "Are you a demon?"

The woman laughed again, teeth showing. Human teeth. "No. I'm like you. A human trapped in Alisanos." The laughter and smile died out as she lowered her hands. "I'm sorry. I know it's frightening. It's—very frightening." Brown eyes, Torvic saw now. Not a girl, or a young woman like Ellica. He thought she was perhaps the same age as Mam. "The deepwood took me three years ago. My husband and I were on the shortcut to Atalanda. We got—too close."

Meggie sat up straight. "*We're* going to Atalanda. Mam needs to have the baby there. The diviners said so."

The woman sighed. "I wish the diviners might have warned my husband and me."

"Where is he?" Torvic asked.

"My husband? Oh, he's dead. Something—took him." That struck them both into shocked silence. After a moment the woman managed a flickering smile. "It was in the first year. I've made my way alone since then." She rose, shaking out her skirts. "My name is Lirra. I have shelter. More room than a hole in a rock." She stilled, lifted her face into the air. She appeared to scent it, almost as if she were a dog. Relief brought a smile to her face again. "There. I smell the woodsmoke. It will lead us to my home. Remember, nothing in Alisanos remains the same. If you wish to find your way to a place more than once, you must do something to bring you back again. Tie rags on trees and bushes, burn stinkwood, something."

Now Torvic could smell it. "It does stink."

"I'm afraid so. But it grows aplenty here, and it's easy for me." Lirra looked up at the tree canopy overhead, shielding her eyes against the flickering light. "The suns are setting. It will be dark soon, and the nightbeasts will be out. Best we go now." She watched as Torvic and Meggie crawled from the crevice. Something akin to grief shone in her eyes. "You poor children. I know you're terrified and exhausted. Best to feed you something, then let you sleep. I'll tell you more in the morning. Here, I'll help roll up the blankets and oilcloth."

"Is it far?" Meggie asked as they worked. "Your home?"

"Sometimes," Lirra answered. And again, rising, "Best we go now."

AUDRUN FELL HEADLONG, right foot caught beneath a gnarled root. In midair, the world all in pieces, she twisted to land on hip and elbow, not facedown. The impact snapped her head on her neck, sending a fizzing thrum of pain from her skull through her shoulders. She rolled over onto her back, hands grasping her skull.

For a moment, she could only lie there dazed, thinking over and over again, *Let me not be hurt, let me not be hurt—* There was Gillan to find, an infant to tend. O Mother of Moons, *let me not be hurt*. It mattered. It mattered that she be whole. For her children, for all of them, each of them, when they were found. She must be whole.

Ah, but she hurt. Panic-bred strength was gone. She shook, now, as if she had a palsy.

And she lay within the deepwood, beneath double suns.

That drove her up, drove her to her knees, to her feet. But one step told the tale: she could put little weight on her right ankle. Off balance, she reached for support and found a gnarled branch. Flat, sharp-edged leaves cut into her palms. She bled. She burned.

Fury rose, coupled with helplessness. Screaming

with rage, Audrun struck out. She grabbed the limb, ignoring the slicing leaves, and twisted, *twisted*, trying to tear it from the trunk. But she had not the strength even for that. She ended up with a handful of stems, a few tattered leaves, stained with her blood.

"Audrun!"

Only instinct identified him as he came up on her, sidelock braids swinging. Still furious, Audrun faced him full on, trembling with rage, thrusting stems and leaves at him. "What good am I? What good am I to him?"

"Audrun—"

"I don't know where he is! I can't find him! I can't even make my way through a forest! *What good am I to him?*"

He stripped the leaves and stems from her rigid hands. He made no answer, merely drew up the long tail of her tunic and wadded it into her palms, rolling her fingers closed.

"O gods . . . O Mother . . ." She let go of the tunic and lifted her hands to her head, pressing bloodied palms against her temples. She was empty of all save failure. A terrible, harrowing failure. "I've lost my children . . ."

"There's no time," he said. "We must return to the dreya ring."

Gripping her head, she stared at him through a film of tears. Did he not understand? "I've lost my *children*!"

His face was calm. "Sarith remains."

That was too much. Audrun wept.

"Come," he said. "We must go now if we're to find the ring."

Her chest and throat ached, threatening to burst. "Don't you understand?"

"Come," he said again. "There is Sarith to tend."

She was too exhausted, too weak, to argue. And the guide was correct. Sarith needed her. Sarith she *could* tend. Gillan . . . Gillan was gone. Ellica and Torvic. Megritte and Davyn.

Gone.

Chapter 9

ABOVE THE PEAKS, against the sky, winged demons raged. Russet gold, both of them, terrifyingly beautiful, shedding scales as glints of gold. Talons struck, wings beat, forked tails whipped. Blood from slices, slashes, and gashes rained down, drop by drop, ruby in the unflinching light of double suns.

She stood below them, atop a peak, wind from their wings tangling hair, stirring clothing. Around her fell their blood, staining grass, staining cloth. It burned against her face.

Ilona roused abruptly as a large hand and forearm slid beneath her head, lifting it carefully from the pillow. A deep voice told her to drink as a cup was pressed gently against her lip. She did so; there seemed no other choice. Willow bark tea. She recognized its bitterness, its bite. She drank all of it. Then opened her eyes and saw a weathered, bearded face looming over her. Ruddy brows were knit together.

Ah. Jorda.

She felt odd. Distant. Detached. Her gaze traveled

upward, discovering in mild surprise that her wagon lacked a canopy. Oh, but that had been the storm. Though she couldn't recall when the storm had struck.

Above Jorda's head she saw the arch of glyph-carved roof ribs, and bare-branched trees. Was it winter? But amusement broke through, skittering across her mind: the grove, like her wagon, had been undressed.

"Are you with us?" Jorda asked, carefully slipping his arm from beneath her head.

She stood atop a peak as demons in the sky shed their blood in battle.

"Ilona?"

She said, "One of them will die."

Frowning, he leaned down to set the empty cup upon the floorboards. Overhead, perched upon a tree limb drooping over the naked wagon ribs, a mocking-bird sang tangled melodies.

"You're fevered," Jorda said. "You've broken your arm. It's set now, and splinted. Time will tell us if it's to grow straight."

Her arm was of neither consequence nor relevance. "One of them must die."

The karavan-master's lips flattened briefly. Then he sighed. "Sleep, Ilona. Rest. Bethid's to come and stay the night. You won't be alone."

The skies rained blood.

Ilona said clearly, "One of them *must* die."

THIS TIME, DAVYN did not weep. He spent no more of himself on tears, no more of his time in prayers. His family was taken from him as surely as the Hecari had burned the farmstead, swallowed by a forest he dared not enter. Yes, he wished to; what he wished most was to stride across the blackened earth and into the vanguard of trees that formed his horizon, filled his eyes. But now what rose up within him in place of grief, in place of frenzied impulse, was the cool and clear understanding that were he to enter Alisanos here and now, he could do very little to find or save his family; he might, in fact, do very much to lose them forever by losing himself.

The guide had been very clear that certain safety lay in the direction he took Torvic and Megritte on horseback. In the direction he sent all of them; to safety, he said. *Away*, he said.

And into Alisanos.

Davyn rose. He stood upon feet in mud-weighted boots and stared hard at the deepwood. Then he turned his back on it and began to walk swiftly, steadily, away toward the wagon. Food was there, water, clean clothing, supplies. There he could outfit himself for the journey that he knew would require time and determination and unrelenting endurance. The tent settlement lay days away by wagon; on foot, it lay farther, and longer yet. But it was there, and only there, that he was likely to find the guide; if not him, then the karavan-master, Jorda, who employed the guide. And who might be able to divulge where the guide was, since clearly he would not have taken himself into the deepwood. No sane man would.

But Rhuan, the Shoia, claimed to have land-sense, to know where Alisanos lay, to know when it intended to move. Likely he also knew *where* it intended to move. And he had come upon them in the midst of maelstrom, riding out of the storm, to direct them in a different direction than Davyn wished to go.

No sane man, no *human* man, would send a pregnant woman and four helpless children into the deepwood.

But the guide wasn't human. He himself had said so.

Questions would be asked. Answers would be demanded. Davyn intended to learn exactly who and what the Shoia was, because he would insist. As he would insist, too, that Rhuan, who knew the land, who sensed Alisanos, would take a husband and father into Alisanos safely and directly to his family, then guide them out again. Each and all of them.

Davyn repeatedly recited the names of those to whom he would speak, if not to the guide himself. Jorda. Ilona. And Darmuth, the other guide. Someone would know where the Shoia was. One of them, or all of them. Someone would know. And someone would tell him.

He would *insist*.

THE WOMAN, RHUAN saw, had injured her
ankle and could barely walk, though she tried.
Time grew short; it was vital they reach the dreya ring
as soon as possible. Ignoring her protests, he swept her
up into his arms and strode on steadily, ducking limbs
and vines.

He shielded Audrun as much as possible, and she
put up her left arm to fend off vegetation as well; her
right arm was hooked around his shoulders. Avoiding
the glittering edges of frondlike leaves that would slice
into their flesh, Rhuan stepped over the endless lattice
of roots broken free of soil, pushed through drifts of
leaf- and vine-mold, threaded his way through
groundcover and grasses. High overhead, tree
canopies merged, broke off, fell away from the suns.
He walked from shadow into light and back again,
over and over, lowering the red scrim of membrane
over his eyes against the worst of the blinding shafts
cutting through the canopy, retracting it again when
shadows defeated light. It painted the deepwood in
hues of rose and ruby, purpling the darkness.

When they came upon a stream, Rhuan halted.
Carefully he lowered Audrun until she stood in the
edge of the creek, water lapping above her ankles.
Rhuan gripped her hands so she wouldn't slip. "We'll
wait here a moment or two," he explained, "and cool
your ankle. It will help. But then we must go on."

Rage had left her, along with the feeling of helplessness. She was calm now, almost cold, and stood as he rec-ommended, balancing carefully. Tawny hair had come out of its braids entirely, snarled from shoulders to mid-back. Her face bore cuts, scrapes, and welts, was red-dened and swollen in places. Homespun tunic and skirts were in tatters—twigs, thorns, and leaves were caught in snags. Her forearms, too, were full of welts, criss-crossed from wrist to elbow. He knew beneath the skirts, bare legs were as damaged. But then he bore his own innu-merable blemishes, being bare-chested save for the baldric holding his throwing knives. He was grateful for his braids; they kept his hair from mimicking hers.

He tried to summon a smile, but failed. "I'm sorry," he said. "I know this is difficult for you. I wish I might improve matters."

Brown eyes were steady, as was her voice above the gurgle of the creek. "We should go on. I must reach my daughter. I know that you said the dreya would tend her, but they are *trees*. She needs a human. She needs her mother." Audrun lifted her chin and took in a deep breath, as if preparing for something. "And when I am there to tend her, I want you to leave us."

It startled him. "Leave you?"

"I ask you to look for my son."

He shook his head. "You and Sarith would be en-dangered."

Appeal in her eyes lessened the tension in her voice. "You said the ring was safe. You left my baby there, did you not? You can leave us both. Find my son, Rhuan. Please."

He desired very much to do as she wished, but could not. "Audrun . . ." He shook his head. "Forgive my bluntness, but he may already be dead."

She was vehement. "Then I need to know *that*." She pulled one hand from his and shoved hair away from her face. "Look, I mean no disrespect, but you aren't human. You've said so yourself. And that children, here, are raised in a creche, not by their parents. Possibly your folk don't feel the same way about children as humans do—*wait!* What are you doing?"

She was in his arms again, though stiff and awkward with surprise and dismay. Rhuan splashed his way across the creek and climbed out the other side. "My priority," he said, striding swiftly, "is to return you to Sarith in the dreya ring, then find us food. After that, we can discuss searching for your family. As to your implication that we don't feel the same way about children as humans do, well . . ." He sighed. "—unfortunately that may be so. Things *are* different here. But first we must survive, you and I, before we can search for anyone. We owe that much to Sarith."

The tone in her voice was raw. "Please don't tell me I must choose among my children!"

He didn't hesitate, though he knew it was cruel. "Audrun, it may come to that, yes."

"You can't ask a mother to do such a thing! No one can!"

"It wouldn't be me doing the asking," he said. "It will be Alisanos—and the deepwood won't *ask*."

"Rhuan—"

"We're here." He set her down and turned her, aiming her through two trees that formed a silver archway. "Tend Sarith." He pushed gently on her spine with his hand. "We can't have a fire in a dreya ring—too dangerous for the trees—but I saw fruit along the way. That will do for now. Remain here . . . it isn't safe for you to leave. I will return as soon as I may."

She had knelt, taken the baby into her arms, and now stood facing him. She was within the ring, he without; perhaps two feet apart, but it felt like two miles. "And if something happens to you?"

None of his habitual lightheartedness answered his summons. Only grimness. "Pray to your Mother that nothing does, else you and Sarith might not survive the night, let alone a ten-day."

Her brows shot up. "You said we were safe in this ring."

"You can't *live* in a dreya ring, Audrun. Seek respite for a night or two, yes; the dreya will keep out vermin and beasts, but they are not proof against everything that dwells in Alisanos."

The baby squirmed in her arms and began to cry thinly as Audrun tipped her head back to gaze a moment at the spreading canopy. She nodded blankly in his direction, thoughts on the infant, and turned away, fingers working to loosen tunic and smallclothes so the baby could nurse.

He did not believe, as she lifted the hungry child to her breast, that Audrun was aware the leaves of the dreya trees fluttered in response to Sarith's cries.

BETHID LED THE bay gelding down the beaten path from the settlement to the shallows of the river. Churri had been glad to see her when she found him, shoving his muzzle hard against her as she stroked his face. Now he moved with urgency, nearly clipping her heels as she walked ahead of him. Bethid paused long enough to remind him that he should walk on his own shoes, not hers, and he gave her space for a few moments, but soon closed on her again. She hadn't the heart to truly reprimand him, not under the circumstances, and simply stepped out more smartly.

She took him down along the river's edge and to a shallow pool, stripped off her gaiters, boots, and stockings and rolled up her pants legs, then led him into water that reached halfway to her knees. The halter rope was long, but she knew Churri wouldn't wander. Grazing along the river was good. Churri dipped his head and sucked in water, then let much of it dribble back out as he lifted his head and turned to Bethid, splashing her liberally. Smiling, she flipped the halter rope across his shoulders, then tied it loosely beneath his jaw so it wouldn't fall and hinder him, or tangle in his legs. As the bay grazed on the succulent grasses drooping into the water, she wetted a rough cloth she had unearthed in the settlement and began to tend the scrapes and swellings in his hide, and to cool down his legs. There were no true injuries, but the compress would soothe any inflammation possibly lurking in or beneath the skin.

As she worked, dipping, rinsing, and soaking the cloth again, Bethid could not help but reflect upon how profoundly her life had changed in just a matter of days. First, she witnessed a brutal Hecari decimation, then discussed province-wide rebellion with a select few; next, she aided Mikal in warning folk to flee the storm; last, she laid out specific proposals and plans to Brodhi, relying upon him to do as *she* suggested, which had never been his habit. The responsibilities she had set herself transcended the duties of a courier, and yet she could see no other way. She knew her ideas were sound. But she wasn't quite certain why she felt Bethid the courier could offer suggestions regarding the fate of Sancorra and of the folk remaining at the tent village. Yet it was a combination of certainty, conviction, and determination that drove her to speak, to act, when a matter of days before her only task had been to carry and deliver messages. Her world felt immensely larger, as if she saw more now, comprehended more, understood what could, and what should, be done. It was as if an entirely new future packed with brand new goals had suddenly unfolded, kindled by the Hecari decimation of the settlement, by the fury of a storm blowing out of Alisanos.

"Who am I to think I offer answers to an entire province?"

And yet she knew. *Knew* she was right to do as she did.

"I must be mad," she told the gelding. "Undoubtedly I am. But—*it feels right*, Churri. In my head and my heart and my soul."

Churri snorted, blowing dampness from his nose with a large clump of uprooted river grass clenched in his front teeth, muddied roots dangling. He shook his head hard, throwing mud off; much of it splattered Bethid. She grinned at him as she wiped the worst of it from her face with the wet cloth.

"Trust *you* to have an opinion." Churri chewed noisily, watching her with the classic, slow-blinking passivity of a horse thinking his own thoughts. Bethid tried to wipe away the clots of mud clinging to her tunic. "There's just no help for it," she explained, scrubbing. "We must find a way to defeat the Hecari, and relying on couriers is a good beginning. Brodhi's right that it will take years, but what else is there to do? Live like oxen beneath the Hecari yoke? Or become wolves, wolves hungry for freedom?"

She grimaced, giving up on the mud stains. Then a thought occured, and she leaned down and down, dipping her hair into the water. She scrubbed at her scalp with stiffened fingers, hoping to shed most of the grit and dirt deposited by the storm. When she stood upright again she slicked her hair back, squeezing out excess water.

"And Brodhi's right, too, when he says it's dangerous," she continued. "But something in me says Sancorra is worth that kind of service." Bethid rinsed out the cloth, watching absently as the horse yanked yet more grass out by the roots. "This is my home, Churri. This province. It's just . . . it's just something I feel that I *must* do." Bethid's mouth jerked briefly. "Well, if nothing else, the Hecari will never believe a woman is involved in a rebellion. That might be the only saving grace." She wrung out the cloth firmly, then tucked it into her belt and untied the halter rope. "Come, sweet boy. It's time for me to look after the hand-reader. I'll take you to good grass later this evening."

Churri protested briefly as she climbed back out of the shallows, but came willingly enough when she insisted. Bethid donned stockings, boots, and gaiters again, wondering how long it would be before she could go back on the road as a courier. Or if she ever could, depending on the whereabouts and the nature of Alisanos.

Chapter 10

*B*RODHI FASHIONED a cookfire and a spit near the elderling oak hosting the skinned deer, then lit the wood with his blood. He could very well have done as he'd instructed Bethid and brought a spill from the fire by the hand-reader's wagon, but this was quicker. And no humans were present to witness it. Those who had returned from the flight to escape the storm gathered now at the approximate center of where the cluster of tents had stood. From time to time, as he worked, he heard raised voices. Men, mostly, though occasionally women's voices punctuated the upended grove. The tones were tense, desperate, and occasionally shrill, rising and falling in response to varied emotions. Brodhi, shaking his head slightly, ran the spit through the carcass and fixed it over the fire. Thereupon he took a seat upon the ground, resting his back against the huge trunk, and waited, right arm draped casually over an upturned knee.

They came.

It was the aroma of roasting meat that penetrated the arguments, the appeals, the demands for answers. They arrived en masse, men, women, and children, drawn to the meat as flies to a body. Without rising, retaining his relaxed posture, he said quietly, "There are things to be done. Do them."

It silenced them all a moment, until one man demanded if Brodhi intended to eat all of the deer himself.

"There are other deer," he replied, waving a negligent hand. "Out there."

A woman said, "Some of us have children to feed!"

"Children may be depended upon to set snares," he replied, nodding, "and to catch fish, and to gather up scraps of food that survived the storm. Food is here. Water as well; you no doubt can find a bucket or two, if you look. Possibly a barrel, which can be rolled up the path."

A large male body pushed through the throng. A dark, one-eyed man, speaking gruffly. "What Brodhi means is that we may depend upon ourselves to see us through this. And he is correct. There is enough here to feed ourselves over the next day or two, if we spread out and look. And those of you who were in Jorda's karavan have foodstuffs in your wagons."

"And you *shall* share," Jorda declared, walking up to stand beside Mikal. "We'll have fresh meat tonight, thanks to the Shoia—" he nodded briefly in Brodhi's direction, "—but we'll need more. Tonight, those of

you with wagons may dole out blankets to those who
have none, and in the morning we all can sort out
what needs doing in what order. There are enough of
us that we can break up into groups. Some will fish,
some will fetch water—a wagon and team can bring
up a number of barrels—some make and set snares,
some search for oilcloth and lost goods. Those of you
from my karavan have tools and implements as well—
we can break ground for gardens, for fields. Get seed in
the ground. Dig up tubers. And any of you who have
horses and mules that are too injured to work, speak
up; we can butcher them and salt the meat, pack it
away. I say don't look at what we've lost, but at what
we *have*: enough to begin anew." His ruddy beard bris-
tled as he looked over the gathering. "For now, while
the meat cooks, I say we should gather up the dead and
clean their bodies, prepare them for the dawn rites.
When that is done, we'll have fresh venison and sweet
water. For tonight, thank the Mother, that is enough."

The karavaners were accustomed to Jorda's air of
command. Those who didn't know him answered his
tone as well. Brodhi, somewhat surprised to see that
the words were accepted without argument, watched
as the people counted out who should do what and
began to turn to tasks. A party of men went to get
shovels from wagons, while a handful of women vol-
unteered to clean the bodies. Within a matter of moments the gathering dispersed, discussing what would
come. Only Jorda remained behind.

"Where's Rhuan?" he asked.

Brodhi shrugged, drawing his knife. "Not among us, apparently."

"You're his kinsman, aren't you?"

"Alas, so I am. Not something I claim with any amount of pride. But I am not his keeper; Rhuan does as he will."

"He knew the storm was coming. That Alisanos was on the move. He would have saved himself."

"If he were not off attempting to gather up stray humans on a road very close—*much* too close—to Alisanos," Brodhi observed. "And what will a karavan-master do without a guide?"

"I have Darmuth."

"Do you?" Brodhi raised his brows. "Have you seen him?"

That told. He saw the realization in Jorda's green eyes, in the stiffening of his posture. "You know something, don't you?"

"I know many things, karavan-master. But the whereabouts of your guides is not one of them." Brodhi deftly flipped his knife one-handed, end over end. "Are you so sure Rhuan would risk himself for fragile human lives?"

"He would. He has."

"Ah. Well then, perhaps he is merely lost." He caught the knife by its point and stilled its rotation, looking steadily at the karavan-master. "Surely he is lost."

It was clear Jorda wished to ask him more. It was equally clear the man understood he would receive no replies that were not obscure. For a moment the green

eyes reflected a pure, unfettered dislike, a desire to re-
ciprocate, then cleared of emotion. Brodhi watched
him turn away, but before Jorda could leave, he rose.
"Care for some venison?"

Jorda swung back. "What I would care for," he said
tightly, "is someone to scout the borders of Alisanos
nearest this place. Preferably *before* men, women, and
children fall prey to it because they are ignorant of
where the deepwood begins, and where it ends. We—"

"No one knows where it ends." Brodhi leaned in to
test the meat with the knife's tip.

"Rhuan said he sensed it. That's why he instructed
us to go east."

Brodhi grinned. "You make a diviner of him, fore-
seeing things no one else can." He sliced off a piece of
meat and tested its taste.

"You're Shoia as well. Can you also sense such
things?"

"Not quite done," Brodhi commented lightly as he
swallowed a final bite. "Yes, I have the same kind of
land-sense. And yes, I could scout the borders . . . except I have been given a different task."

"What task?"

Brodhi resumed his position upon the ground, leaning against the elderling oak. "I'm to ride to Cardatha
to see the warlord. I am to inform him of what has
happened here in minute and lengthy detail, and explain how extremely likely it is that any Hecari patrols
coming to this area are in serious danger of being
swallowed by Alisanos."

Some of the anger left Jorda's expression. "Bethid's plan."

"So it is."

"Will it work?"

"It may," Brodhi flipped grease off his knife blade, "temporarily. But they will come eventually."

"We need to map this area," Jorda said. "We can't very well send people out to forage for food if they run the risk of stepping over some invisible border."

"It's visible," Brodhi said. "But it's quite true that the borders aren't stable just yet. Alisanos may have a few itches to scratch before it settles in for hibernation."

Jorda strode up to him, leaned down, loomed, and snatched the knife from his hand. "And would you happen to know in which direction those itches may lie? At least for tomorrow?"

Brodhi contemplated the hand now empty of knife. No wounds were visible. He looked up at the karavan-master towering over him. "Go north, or east. Not west. And probably not south, though I can't be certain of that. Land-sense has its limitations."

"Thank you," Jorda said evenly. Then he snapped the knife downward so it flew point-first at the earth and buried its blade to the hilt.

AS THE BABY sated herself, Audrun leaned her spine and skull against one of the smooth-trunked dreya trees and allowed her body respite.

Now that panic had subsided and her arguments were temporarily undone, exhaustion swamped her. She ached, inside and out. Cuts stung. Her face burned. The bitten lower lip no longer bled, but her tongue kept testing the tender, lumpy swelling on the inside of her mouth. She hadn't eaten in more hours than she could count—if Alisanos *had* hours—and hunger made her weak. Giving birth made her weak. Running and tripping and falling made her weak. Sitting alone in the deepwood with a newborn infant made her weak and worried and too muddled to think straight. She badly needed food, and sleep. But she needed answers just as badly.

She closed her eyes, losing herself in the physical release that came with nursing a healthy baby. "Mother of Moons, I beg you—" But that was as far as her petition got. She was abruptly aware of movement, of sound, of an undulation in her world that brought her to her feet, pressing Sarith against her breast. The *trees*—

The trees were moving. And it wasn't caused by the wind.

Audrun stood in the center of the ring, staring in shock. Branches lowered, interlaced, interlocked, formed a barrier. A tight net, a fence of silver boughs and limbs and leaves, encircled her. The sky was open to her now, the setting of the suns; no longer was she shielded against the blinding light. Audrun looked away, looked down, blinking dazzled eyes. Sarith, deprived of a nipple, began to cry.

Absently Audrun tugged up smallclothes and tunic to cover herself. On the other side of the barrier, from behind her back, she heard words she understood. Words in Sancorran. "Give it to me."

She spun. A man—*a man*—stood there, staring fixedly through breaks in limbs and leaves. Staring at the child.

She summoned her voice. "I will do no such thing."

"Give it to me."

With equal vehemence, Audrun said, *"I will not."*

The man came closer. She saw now that he wore loose dark leggings made of some kind of hide and a mis-shapen jacket hanging open crookedly so that his naked chest was visible from belly to throat. His flesh was very white, a stark contrast to the dark discoloration that climbed from the low waistband of his leggings. He looked human. He looked, and sounded, Sancorran.

"Who are you?" Audrun asked.

He made no answer, but came a step closer. She saw his chest more clearly, and its deep bruising.

No, not bruising. Not discoloration.

Scales.

"Give it to me."

Audrun didn't answer.

He came a step closer. She saw now that his hair, too, was black, hanging well past his shoulders. Amaz-ingly, it was combed. Astonishingly, it was clean. It fell in a shining curtain, parted only at his face. And in that white, white face burned piercing winter-gray eyes with slit, vertical pupils.

Definitely not a man.

"*No*," Audrun repeated, finding in that declaration and determination a modicum of strength.

He squatted suddenly, elbows hooked over knees. She saw his spine was also misshapen, deformed, as if he were hunchbacked. She had seen that in an elderly woman, once. But he was male, if not precisely a man.

Pale hands fluttered. His nails, long and curved, were black. Clawlike. The backs of his pale hands were also scaled. His head rotated sideways, back and forth. Then he sprang upward into the air, and Audrun saw that he was not hunchbacked at all. That in fact he was winged.

Winged.

Overhead, the tree canopy snapped together. Branch, stem, and leaf wove a shield against him.

ELLICA REMEMBERED SNEAKING in the midst of the night out of the house her father had built. She recalled how and where the floorboards creaked and squeaked, and how carefully and how slowly one stepped to avoid such things. Barefoot in childhood, she felt the roughness of the planed boards, felt the narrow gap between each, the depressions and slight lumps where pegs had been pounded in. Her da was a considerate man who wanted the best for his family. Occasionally the wood and best of intentions did not cooperate.

She crept now as she had then, step by step, alert to sentient grass that might attempt to impose itself again, growing up this time through the soles of her shoes. Step, step, step. As a child, the only risk had been that her da might hear, or her mam. Now, in the deepwood, Ellica knew worse than that awaited.

She paused. More than grass threatened; she saw briars, thorny vines, and tree limbs, all of them aquiver, as if waiting to attack. She felt the breath of the deepwood upon her: too warm, too wet, too intimate. Her body ran with sweat. It burned in her eyes.

Keep moving . . . keep moving . . .

She had no goal, no destination, except perhaps to find who'd screamed, if that were possible; if Alisanos allowed it. Human, she was sure. Perhaps not her da. Perhaps not her brother. But human. She was certain.

"Keep moving," she murmured.

Vines grew upward, vines grew downward. She avoided every stem, every thorn. She ducked beneath branches, slid around leaves, kept her skirts pulled tight. When the way she sought was too overgrown for her to manage, she went in another. But her memory was sound. She recalled from which direction the screaming had issued.

Perhaps not her da. Perhaps not her brother. In a way, she hoped not. And yet she hoped it might be, that it *could* be, so she would find someone she knew, someone she loved, someone who would buttress her spirits and provide the courage she knew she lacked.

Keep moving.

A vine whipped out of the trees. Like a rope, it snagged her throat, wrapped itself around her neck very tightly, setting thorns like fishing hooks. The human flesh beneath the thorns parted. In a gurgle, spraying blood, Ellica called for help. Called and called and called. Until no voice was left, only the knowledge that she was dying.

Adric, and the oak tree. Not far from the house her father had built, that she had slipped out of, avoiding squeaks and creaks. But Adric had gone to fight, and everyone she knew believed he was dead.

With hands locked into the vine at her throat, trying to yank it loose, Ellica recalled the last day she had seen Adric. The last time he had kissed her.

Maybe if I'm dead, too, I can find Adric . . .

Chapter 11

*L*IRRA LED THEM directly to her home, following the odor of stinkwood. Meggie complained about the smell off and on until Torvic hushed her, telling her it wasn't polite to insult a woman who intended to host them in her own home. But inside his head, he agreed with his sister: stinkwood *stunk*.

At last they broke through trees and vegetation and came upon a small cabin. It backed on more trees yet, but before the cabin lay a modest clearing. Torvic saw a neatly tended garden of vegetables, corn, and wheat; a small, crude well house with a winch and pulley system very like the one his da had built at their farmstead; and a bench beside the open door. The cabin itself was made of wood and mud, saplings cut down and laid in courses to form walls with plenty of clay chinking to fill the gaps. In the center of the clearing burned a small fire cairn, a thick plume of smoke rising steadily from it.

Lirra went directly to the cairn and proceeded to

throw dirt on the wood, eventually smothering the fire. "There," she said in satisfaction. "I only lay stinkwood fires outside, so the cabin won't smell so bad." She smoothed loosened strands of brown hair against her head, tucking them back into the knot of coiled braid at the back of her head. "Go in," she said, gesturing them toward the open door. "I have food and drink aplenty. My husband and I were swallowed whole with our wagon and livestock, so we were able to establish a good home and garden even in the midst of this evil place." She paused, eyes reflecting sudden grief. "Well, for a while."

Meggie followed orders and entered the cabin, but Torvic hesitated. "Can you help us find our mam and da? Can you show us the way out?"

Lirra shook her head. "I fear the answer to both is no. My husband and I spent days and days trying to make our way back into the human world, but it was impossible. There are no trails, you see, and Alisanos often rearranges itself during the night. That's why we learned to lay a stinkwood fire, as relying on strips of cloth would soon have had us naked." She followed Meggie into the cabin, dropping a hand on Torvic's shoulder as she guided him in. "You and your sister were taken together, as my husband and I were. But if there is distance between other members of your family, they would have been scattered like chaff. It would be exceedingly difficult to find them."

"You found *us*," Torvic declared as he stepped across the threshold.

"I did," Lirra agreed. "But that was great good fortune, and unexpected. I suspected that with Alisanos going active, many more humans would end up lost in the deepwood. I went out to see if I could find any." She smiled, mood lightening. "And there you were, tucked up in the rocks."

The cabin's roof was low, Torvic saw, too low for his da to be comfortable, but for Lirra it was all right, and for him and his sister. There was a bedstead tucked into one of the corners, a small table and two chairs in the center of the room, and a modest hearth and stone chimney, hosting a small fire. Rough-hewn shelving affixed to the walls allowed Lirra to display such things as a tea kettle, pewter plates, mugs, a handful of pots and pans, and other utensils. Along one wall rough, doorless cabinets had been mounted.

"I make do," she said, indicating the table. "Sit, won't you? I've bread baked fresh this morning, a little meat, and vegetables from my garden. I'll make you a fine stew. I apologize I haven't any milk—the cow died a few days back—but the water is sweet and pure."

Meggie contemplated the cabin. "Does the rain get in?"

"Oh, no." Lirra smiled, taking down a pot. "My husband was able to make the cabin snug and tight before he was taken. I have good shelter here, and the well and a garden, and I can set snares for some of the small creatures, so I eat well enough. But it does get lonely. I'm most glad to have your company." She worked quickly, Torvic saw, as he climbed into the chair across from Meggie, filling the pot with water from a pitcher and various foodstuffs and herbs from the cabinets. Once she'd hung the pot over the fire, she set out a tin plate hosting a generous chunk of pale yellow cheese. "I'm afraid with the cow dead I'll have no more cheese, so eat well of this, won't you? It should quiet your bellies until the stew is ready. And here is water." She set a mug down before each of them.

"Were you at the settlement?" Torvic asked.

Lirra looked puzzled. "What settlement?"

"The tent settlement," he answered. "Near the river. It's where we met up with the karavan."

"Where we were, no such settlements existed," Lirra told him. "We took the road beside the deepwood, bound for Atalanda—"

Torvic cut in. "That's where *we* were! Could we go back? Could we find the settlement?"

Lirra, stirring water, meat, vegetables, and herbs in the hanging pot, didn't answer at once. When she did, grief shone in her eyes. "There's no going back. Even if we found a way out of Alisanos, no one would aid us. We're different now, you see. The breath of Alisanos is upon us." She looked at them both. "It pains me to give you such news. But you need to know the truth. False hope hurts so much more."

"Did you *try* to leave?" Meggie asked.

"I told you: many times. We could find no way. After my husband was taken . . ." She hitched one shoulder. "I gave up trying."

"But if Alisanos has moved, maybe you can get out now," Torvic said. "Maybe you can *find* the way."

Lirra turned toward them, clenching her hands together against the front of her skirt. "You must understand. You must come to understand. Those of us trapped in Alisanos are different now. The breath is upon us. We can never go back. They won't have us, don't you see? They shun us. They kill us."

Meggie's blue eyes were huge. "*Who* kills you?"

"Humans," Lirra answered.

"That man." Torvic looked at his sister. "That man who came to the wagon, the one we thought was a demon."

Meggie fixed her eyes upon Lirra. "He had *claws*. Not hands."

"Yes," she said steadily, "that happens often. But I was fortunate." She unclasped and displayed her hands. "You see? No claws. No scales."

"Then you could go back," Torvic insisted. "You're like everyone else, not like that moonsick man."

"No," Lirra said, "I'm not." Tears shone in her eyes. "They would kill me. I can't go back. And now, neither can you."

Meggie, clutching cheese in one hand and a mug in the other, began to weep.

GILLAN ROUSED AT the sound of a voice speaking in a language he didn't recognize. It was full of sibilants. He lifted his head from the ground and attempted to look upward, but weakness was paramount. He let his cheek rest again upon the earth. The pain of his leg, the fear of what he might find—or *not* find—when he looked at it had drained him utterly. There was strength for nothing.

Someone squatted down beside him. Sibilants faded into words he understood. "You're the farmsteader boy. Ai, well, Rhuan did try to warn your sire. See what it brought you, that stubbornness? And now Rhuan is as much at risk as you are."

The voice sounded familiar. It nagged at him. Gillan lifted his head again and turned it even as it shook upon his neck, and saw beside him the karavan guide, the other guide, the one called Darmuth. The shock was such that it drew a blurted question. "You're here, too?"

"So I am, farmsteader boy. Though coming here was my choice; I wasn't trapped, as you were. As likely your entire family was. *And* Rhuan." He bent down low, folding himself upon the ground so that his face was no farther from Gillan's than the span of two spread hands. Pale gray eyes had elongated pupils. He flicked his tongue free of his mouth, and Gillan, in shock, saw that the tongue was forked. "You have interfered with the natural course of things, do you know that? Rhuan's journey has been ended prematurely, as has mine. *As has mine.* And now Rhuan is in danger, and so am I. All because a human was too pigheaded to heed the warnings from a *dioscuri*. A *dioscuri!*" He raised himself up again. Now Gillan could only see his lower body. "And you've hurt yourself, I see. Well, there's nothing to be done for it. You're a juvenile—you had no choice but to do as your sire instructed; I can't lay blame upon you for that. Here, let me look at your leg."

Hands were upon his homespun trews. Gillan tried to tell the guide no, not to do it, not to look, but the cloth parted. Darmuth peeled back the fabric. Gillan squeezed his eyes shut, clamping his teeth together. Air upon his leg set it afire.

"You'll likely limp," Darmuth said. "Muscle is burned as well as flesh. But the bone is whole. You'll walk."

His eyes snapped open. "I won't lose it?"

"Not unless I decide to eat it. Which is always possible." Darmuth leaned down again, all the way down, staring into Gillan's face. "You do understand, don't you? Or perhaps you don't." His lips drew back in a wide, wide smile, displaying the green gemstone set in a canine tooth. "I'm a demon, boy." His tongue slid out again, sinuous and forked. "I feast upon your kind."

No. No. No. It was the only word in Gillan's head. And the only one in his mouth, when he recovered his voice.

"No?" Darmuth grinned. "How about now?"

Gillan saw, to his horror, a scale pattern bleeding into Darmuth's face. The pupils now were slits. Even the shape of his face began to alter.

"No!" Gillan cried.

"Yes!" But the scale pattern faded as quickly as it

had come, and the eyes looked normal again. Human again. Darmuth straightened. "This is my home, farmsteader boy. Alisanos. The deepwood. I was born here. As for why I've been in the human world, play-acting the role of a human? Well, that's a tale to be told later."

Gillan had to ask the question. "Does Rhuan know what you are?"

That resulted in a gust of unfettered laughter. "Oh, I do think so. After all, he was born here, too. He knows exactly what I am."

It was shocking. "*Rhuan's* a demon?"

"Now, that's not what I said. Not everyone born here is a demon. Rhuan is—quite something else. Now, boy, I'm going to lift you up. I expect you'll pass out. If you're fortunate, you'll remain that way while I carry you to shelter."

Even the idea of movement was excruciating. But there was something to be said. "I have a name," he declared, "and it isn't 'boy,' or 'farmsteader boy.' It's Gillan."

Darmuth grinned. "I know that. Boy."

But before he could speak again, protest again, the demon put hands on him and began to lift. Gillan went screaming into darkness.

RHUAN ONCE AGAIN surrendered his leather tunic to a purpose other than the one for which it was made. He had tucked hard-rinded globes of blackfruit into it, along with a handful of pods containing sweet, rich, nutlike meat. He was hungry and knew Audrun was; of them all, only the baby was replete. He ducked through thick vegetation, following his instinctive sense of direction toward the dreya ring. Those born in Alisanos could generally find their way even without tracks and pathways, but there were never any guarantees that what they sought remained in the same place. Nonetheless, dreya rings were more deeply tied to the earth than other trees and landmarks, and were far less likely to uproot and move.

But when he reached the dreya ring, he saw that indeed the trees had moved. All of their branches stretched high overhead, forming an impenetrable roof against the sky through which little sunlight showed. Audrun, not screened by lower limbs, stood in the center of the ring holding the baby, staring upward.

"What is it?" he asked sharply.

Her head jerked toward him. "Rhuan, be careful! He flies!"

Rhuan sensed the shadow, heard the displacement of air, and threw the tunic full of fruit at the shape that came down upon him. He had the impression of dark, leathery wings and outspread human arms, but little else as he hurled himself to the ground and rolled. When he came up onto one knee, the other booted foot planted on the earth, he had a throwing knife in his hand. He snapped it, saw the winged creature jerk aside sharply, then had another in his hand.

One wing slapped down, an edge catching Rhuan across the eyes. He could not suppress the outcry of shock and pain even as he reached out with his left hand, trying to ward off the attacker. Claws closed upon the hand with the knife, sinking deeply into flesh. He felt other claws rake a thigh, reaching toward his abdomen.

He tried to duck away, tried to roll, tried to throw himself out of reach, but wings blinded him. He felt the clamminess of leathery membranes slapping around his body, felt claws again. On hands and knees, this time he grabbed for his long-bladed belt knife. He slashed blindly, heard a cry of pain and anger, and the creature opened his wings, climbing up and away, then plummeted down.

Rhuan rose to his feet, wiping briefly at a bloody forehead to clear his eyes. He saw what appeared uncannily like a human man crouching five paces away. Black hair tangled on his shoulders. One hand was pressed against his ribs. Rhuan saw blood, blood and patterned scales, and white, white skin. He saw too that the man—the creature—wore no shoes, and black, glistening claws extended from his feet, matching those of his hands. Pale eyes burned.

"He wants the baby," Audrun said.

"Well, he can't have her." Rhuan tossed back his braids, winced at a stab of pain, and tried to assume a posture of readiness. To the creature, he said, "Begone. You can't have this baby."

Blood spilled through clawed fingers, dripping

groundward. Wings, but loosely folded, snapped upward and spread. The creature leaped.

Rhuan threw himself aside again, ducking underneath the creature, but felt claws sink into his braids to cut the flesh of his skull. He stabbed, he slashed, smelled the creature's musk as it closed with him. Blinded again, upon one knee, he thrashed and fought, hoping to somehow hit something vital. The creature screamed and unlocked his claws, lunging upward raggedly. Blood rained down through the air, showering Rhuan. And then the creature was gone, rising up through the forest, lost to sight.

"Rhuan? Rhuan!"

He knelt, doubled over in pain. His abdomen hurt so badly he feared evisceration, was afraid to remove the hand splayed across his middle. His scalp bled unremittingly, painting his face crimson. His braids were soggy with blood. He drew in a long, trembling breath, then blew it out in a hissing stream between his lips.

"Rhuan?" Hands were on him, touching his shoulders hesitantly. "O Mother, oh, this is bad . . ."

He could not suppress the faint gust of laughter from his mouth. "So it is."

"Come into the ring. Can you come into the ring?"

He lifted his bowed head and saw, through the runnels of blood, the farmstead wife staring at him anxiously. Save for a lack of blood, he thought she looked no better than he.

"Come into the ring, Rhuan."

He made the effort. She closed her hands upon his

upper arm and tried to aid him, tried to urge him to his feet, but the best he could do was scoot on one hip, pushing himself with his free hand.

"Almost," she said, having given up attempting to physically help. "Not so much farther."

"The baby," he managed.

"Safe. She's safe. She's in the ring. Come, Rhuan." And then a brief, startled laugh issued from her mouth. "But I was forgetting! You'll heal. And even if not, you'll revive!"

He half crawled, half pushed himself across the invisible border between hostile forest and dreya ring. He left blood in his wake, running from his scalp, dripping from his braids, oozing out of claw scores. When at last he was in the ring, he found the queen tree. At its foot, cradled amid great silver-hued roots, he placed his spine against the patterned trunk. And finally, finally, he lifted his hand from his abdomen.

Relief made him weak. "Ah, no guts . . . not so bad as it might be . . ."

Audrun knelt beside him. "What can I do? I know you'll revive, should you die, but there must be something I can do for you now."

The membrane had dropped over his eyes so the world he saw, the woman he saw, hazed red. "Keep me alive."

"But—"

"*Do* keep me alive, if you would be so kind. In the human world I can't be killed, not permanently, but here . . ." He closed one bloodied hand around the woman's slender wrist. "*Here,* death is death. There is no revival. Not for any of us."

Her face blanched. Every cut, scrape, and bruise, and the dark circles beneath her eyes, stood out from her flesh. "But—your father's a *god*. You told me so!"

"In Alisanos," he said, "even gods die."

Chapter 12

*I*LONA AWOKE ABRUPTLY, with the sense that she'd been dreaming but no memory of the content. Her mind was clear; she recalled the violent storm, the fall from Jorda's draft horse, the realization that she was not in Alisanos. And there was pain. Her arm was broken; she remembered that well.

She looked upward, blinking, aware that there was no shielding oilcloth canopy stretched over the ribs of her wagon. She could not recall when that might have happened, though likely during the storm. Overhead she saw the spreading panoply of twilight as the first bright stars began to appear. She heard the rustlings of birds outside, the chirp and scraping of nightsingers. She smelled roasted meat as well.

Movement came from beside her. "Ah, you're awake." A woman leaned over her. The courier, Bethid. "I've brewed more willow bark tea; would you care for some? And Brodhi, of all people, came by with venison. Are you hungry?"

Ilona peered up at her. "What day is this?"

"The remains of the first day after the storm," Bethid replied. "You've lost no days and nights, only a handful of hours." She placed a hand on Ilona's brow. "I think you had a fever, but it seems to be gone now."

The courier's palm was calloused against Ilona's forehead. But it was still a palm, and her gift was not blocked by such things as calluses and scars. Ilona caught Bethid's wrist in her right hand. "May I read it? Will you allow it?"

The courier's expression was a mixture of reluctance and a wish to please her patient. "I go to a rune-reader."

"And you may again," Ilona said. "I wish only to read your hand this once—it won't taint you. A rune-reader won't turn you away."

Bethid looked abashed. "I'm sorry. I should know better." She knelt down beside the cot, a quick smile flashing. "Go ahead, then. I can bear it."

"This is not for you," Ilona told her, "but for me. I have not been able to read a hand since the storm."

"If you see anything bad, don't tell me. I'd rather be surprised."

Ilona pushed herself slightly upright with her right elbow to lean against the pillow and cushions someone had placed beneath head and shoulders, wincing against the pain in her left forearm. "This will be awkward, but I must try." She resettled her splinted arm, willed the pain to pass, then nodded at Bethid. The courier offered her hand. Ilona placed her own over it, but did not touch flesh to flesh. Her palm hovered over Bethid's.

Nothingness.

"No," Ilona said. "Oh, no . . ."

The courier withdrew her hand abruptly. "I said I don't want to know if there's anything bad in it!"

"No, it's not you. It's not bad. It's me. I see nothing. *Nothing.*" Ilona held her own hand up before her eyes, staring blankly at the palm she knew so well, but could not read. "Mother of Moons, what has become of my gift?"

"What do you mean? Is it—gone?"

Ilona looked at the concerned face. "I see nothing." Tears unexpectedly stung her eyes. "A hand is just a hand!"

"Perhaps it's the broken arm," Bethid said, seeking to reassure. "Jorda said that as long as he's known you, you've never been sick or injured."

Ilona considered that. "I've always been healthy. I've broken no bones before now. I've never been ill." She examined her palm again. "Could it be so? Could a broken bone block my gift?"

Bethid shrugged. "Why not? Pain and fever, and time needed to heal. Perhaps your ability is secondary to—to physical interference. It takes strength to heal, you know. Perhaps once the bone is whole, your gift will return."

Ilona dropped her right hand across the coverlet. Her eyes sought Bethid's. "Do you know Lerin, the dream-reader?"

The courier shook her head. "I haven't been here often enough to learn all the diviners. And, as I said, I see a rune-reader."

"Would you do a thing for me, and ask for her? See if you can find her, and tell her I'd like a consultation?"

"I will," Bethid agreed. "But first, let me fetch you a mug of tea, and the meat Brodhi brought. You can eat while I'm gone. But if you should fall asleep, do you want me to awaken you if I find the dream-reader?"

"Yes," Ilona declared. "Please." The courier nodded and ducked out, descending the folding steps. Ilona once again fixed her eyes upon the night sky. "Please. Let my gift not be gone."

She knew of no true diviner who had lost the ability to see the fortunes and futures of others. Not even a suggestion of it had ever been mentioned among diviners she knew. But the world was no longer the same. Who could swear that the coming of Alisanos had not affected them all?

Fear welled up, swamping her. What was she, without her gift? *Who* was she, without her gift? What under the sun and moon would she do with her life?

"Mother," she whispered, rubbing tears away, "let my gift not be gone."

AUDRUN FELT SICK to her stomach from a jumble of fear and shock. Holding her newborn daughter, she knelt beside a man she had believed invulnerable to serious injury, able to overcome death to live again. She had *seen* it, once. Impossible as it was, she had witnessed the guide's revival from death caused by a poisoned Hecari dart. But now he had told her death, a permanent death, was indeed possible for him in Alisanos, despite who and what he was. And he was badly hurt.

What can I do? What should I do?

Blood from the wounds in his scalp covered his face. His chest, naked beneath the baldric of throwing knives, was scored by dozens of claw marks. Blood seeped through rents in his leather leggings. But the worst were the deep, deep gashes on his abdomen.

Mother of Moons, what can I do? Guilt also rode her that she worried for herself and the child should he die. But she could not set that aside, even in the face of his injuries.

And then it came to her that despite what he was, a son of Alisanos, he was also a man. Not human, but a man, and a man who walked the thin blade of a knife's edge between death and life. What would she do if this were Davyn, slumped against the tree? Why, care for him! Give him her time, and what skill she had at healing. A wife and mother learned such things.

She cast a glance around the dreya ring. Branches and limbs had returned to the positions expected of trees. No shield blocked the sky and its two suns, no fence kept out such things as winged demons. Winged demons who spoke *Sancorran*. Who may have even been human once, fully as she was, but lost to the deepwood. Lost to the world. No longer a man, no longer a human.

Is that what will become of me?

Rhuan stirred. His breathing was arrested on a small grunt of pain, and then his eyes opened. Kind eyes, she had always felt. But now red, not brown. Now wholly alien.

He was no more human than the winged demon was.

"Mark your way," he said, barely aloud. "Always mark your way."

No more. No additional words. Lids dropped over his eyes. He was, she believed, unconscious.

At home, tending Davyn, she would ask for water. There was no one here, no children present, she could set to that task. So it was left to her. Were she at home, tending Davyn all alone, she would fetch the water herself. She would clean and bandage his wounds, offer water to drink and broth to eat. She would change the dressings as often as seemed necessary, try to keep a fever from setting in, let him know she was near, that he was not alone. That he should and would survive, because he was strong, and because she needed him. That the children needed him.

In her arms was cradled an infant. Around her, in a ring, gathered trees of the dreya, whom Rhuan had asked for help. And help they had offered. She was alive, and held a baby safely in her arms, *because* of the dreya.

Audrun nodded. Then she looked for and found a

tree in the ring that offered a form of protection within a tangle of roots upon the surface of the earth, and carefully set the baby into it. Sated, Sarith slept. Audrun drew in a deep breath, then rose. In the center of the dreya ring, she beseeched assistance. For the baby. For the man. For herself. Then she began to tear strips of fabric from her long tunic. She would, as instructed, mark her way, allowing her to return to tend the man and the infant.

A frisson of fear ran down her spine. This nightmare was not made of any images, fractured or whole, she had seen in her sleep. In no moments of the night, mired in darkness, had she envisioned herself trapped in Alisanos. Nor trapped with an infant wholly dependent upon her.

But the hand-reader, the woman named Ilona, had seen in Andrun's hand tears and blood and grief. And all had come to her in plenty. Her family, save for the child, was stripped from her. The knowledge of Alisanos that Rhuan, born to the deepwood, held was lost to unconsciousness. And the baby, tiny Sarith, knew nothing at all of anything, save of the woman who offered milk and warmth, a soothing voice and the beating of her heart.

Still standing in the center of the ring, Audrun looked at her sleeping baby. Looked at the man whose father was a god. And knew that the safety of both, as well as her own, depended solely on her.

But when had the safety of her children not depended on her since she'd borne her first?

She knelt beside Rhuan and took the long-bladed knife from his sheath. With precision she cut two long strips of fabric from the hem of her skirt. Her ankle pained her and would make walking difficult, but she had no choice. She dared not remove the boot to wrap her ankle because she might not be able to get it on again. So instead she carefully and tightly wrapped the strips around her boot, cross-gartering the leather, until her leg was encased from sole to midcalf.

She rose, testing her ankle. The compressed leather cut into her leg and would probably chafe, but she could bear that. With the weapon in her right hand and her left full of cloth strips intended to mark the way, Audrun limped out of the ring.

DAVYN REACHED THE wagon as the sun slid below the horizon. Twilight would soon bleed to darkness, and the slender crescent of Maiden Moon would rise in the sky. One day? Could all have happened in a single day? Or had the storm stolen more time than that from them, with none of them the wiser?

So much, *too* much, had occured. And now he was left alone with two dead oxen and the wagon canted sideways on its broken axle, with trunks, barrels, and chests set out upon the road. The arrangement, made so he and Gillan could lever up the wagon and replace the damaged axle, reminded him oddly of a hen with chicks.

He was exhausted, thirsty, hungry, badly in need of
rest. And yet something inside prevented him from
surrendering to the fatigue, from giving in to the need
for food and drink. He felt cold inside, icy, unlike himself. Anger was an emotion he knew, though one he
rarely gave in to. But this feeling wasn't anger. It was
a combination of several emotions, foremost among
them the acceptance that all this was the fault of the
karavan guide Rhuan, who had lost him his family.
That awareness fed him, that acceptance strengthened
him. He had a task to do, a journey to undertake. Panic
and fear would not do any more than unchecked
anger would. So he controlled it. Channeled it. Set his
heart upon it. A goal, a task, a journey, followed by a
rescue.

Davyn untied the waterskin from his belt and filled
it at the barrel. Then he sought and found food and
supplies in the wagon, and also Audrun's kettle and a
packet of tea. He built himself a small cairn, arranged
the tinder and kindling they always carried, fished
coals from the firepot and set them within the cairn.
With careful attention he encouraged a fire to blossom,
then set about making tea. It was a task Audrun always did as the children performed their predinner
chores; familiar motions brought him something akin
to comfort, small though it was.

At last he sat upon a blanket, poured himself tea, set
a dented tin plate atop crossed legs, and scooped cooling beans into his mouth with a crust of hard bread.
Tea washed it down. He banked the fire for the night,

climbed up into the wagon, and dug out bedding. Then he lay down upon floorboards beneath the open sky, under the Maiden Moon, and planned in his head what he needed to do come morning, what readiness was required before he set out upon the track that would lead him, eventually, to the settlement.

Davyn pulled the string of charms from beneath his tunic, closed his hand upon them, and fixed his eyes on the Maiden's crescent. *Keep them safe, Mother. Keep all of them safe. And let them not grieve for me, because I'm coming for them. I'm coming for them all.*

Chapter 13

*P*AIN, RHUAN DECIDED, did not simply hurt. Pain also exhausted a person, sapped his soul, thinned his spirit. Worse, pain was *tedious*.

All of his instincts told him to do more than slump against the queen tree, but his body did not respond. He remained where he was, spine against trunk, his legs sprawled loosely in front of him. His right hand, again, shielded his abdomen, where the worst of the gashes were. With his left, he explored his face, feeling for claw grooves. There were none, only the crusting of dried blood. Further exploration told him his scalp beneath his braids was lacerated in several places; no wonder he had bled so badly.

From nearby he heard a faint sound, the brief, fussy bleat of a young animal. He rolled his head to look, winced at the stabbing protest of his skull, and saw that at the base of the tree next to his, Audrun had left the baby. Sarith, swaddled in muslin but stirring, fussing more vigorously, very likely needed her clout changed. But he understood he was in no shape to do any such thing.

She had gone for water, he knew, the farmsteader's wife. It was what he himself would have done were their roles reversed. And though he had instructed her to mark her route, he had no certainty that Audrun could find her way back. Marked trail or no, Alisanos rarely cooperated. But it was his only chance, and certainly hers as well.

With nothing to do but think as he waited, trying to ignore the pain, Rhuan considered his circumstances. He was injured, and abdominal wounds were serious. He was in no position to tend his own welfare, let alone Audrun's and the baby's. Audrun would no doubt do what she could, but caring for both a wounded man and a newborn would be difficult even if they were *not* in the deepwood; in Alisanos, it was perilous. Her chances of survival and Sarith's, should he die, were nil. And he knew it was quite possible he might die.

Not a thought that pleased him, but it was the truth. He neither denied nor shirked the acknowledgment under the circumstances. He needed to think about the woman and the baby.

Darmuth would be of tremendous assistance were he present, but Darmuth was—missing. Or, perhaps more accurately, absent. Rhuan had no knowledge of whether the demon was somewhere in Alisanos, or among the humans not taken by the deepwood, had the settlement escaped. He was aware that Brodhi and

Ferize could communicate across distances, but they were bonded in a very different way. Humans called it *marriage* at its most simplistic level; here in Alisanos, when one was *dioscuri*, the bond was more complex.

Brodhi.

Where *was* Brodhi? In Alisanos? Still in the human world? He'd been at the settlement the last Rhuan had seen of him, but it was entirely possible that Alisanos had swallowed the tent village and everyone in it as well as Audrun and her family. If so, then possibly Brodhi might help him, though he doubted his kinsman's mood would incline him in that manner. And if Brodhi was in the deepwood as well, they shared a very similar and serious situation: journeys aborted, goals dispersed, futures unsecured. It wouldn't matter to the primaries that he and Brodhi had not voluntarily entered Alisanos. It would matter only that they had not completed the journeys set before them. They were, after all, *dioscuri,* and thus far more was expected of them. For instance, in the human world they could not die. An individual who could not be killed in that world should be able to overcome anything.

Claiming themselves Shoia was merely convenience; legitimate Shoia could indeed die six times, reviving until the seventh death, the true death. Assuming that racial identity afforded *dioscuri* the ability to revive should they "die," relying upon the legends of the Shoia to explain such things to startled humans. In general, *dioscuri* expected not to be killed even once in a human world far less dangerous than

Alisanos, let alone seven times; in fact, with the sixth death they were to disappear entirely to save themselves from inconvenient questions. They were not, upon their journeys, to confess to humans what they were, or that such beings as *dioscuri* existed. Central to the journey was living, as much as was possible, among the humans *as* humans, save for the necessity of cloaking resurrection in the fiction of Shoia blood, and admitting to the occasional art that humans viewed as magic.

But both of them were *dioscuri,* he and Brodhi, not Shoia. Not human. *Dioscuri* were expected to transcend difficulties that would challenge humans. It was part of the journey. Entering Alisanos before one's journey was completed was far more than a *difficulty.* Here, any death was permanent. And if called to judgment before time, the primaries would have no choice but to name failed *dioscuri* unworthy of ascension. He and Brodhi would be declared neuters. He and Brodhi would then be *physically* neutered.

Rhuan couldn't help it; the mere thought made his groin and thigh muscles clench. He shifted against the tree, then wished he hadn't.

If I could get out of Alisanos, return to the human world without the primaries discovering I'm here . . .

If he could. But in the meantime, there was a woman to care for, and her infant. Alisanos might well allow *him* to find a way out, should he survive, though it wouldn't be easy, but Audrun and Sarith were truly trapped. The baby, the first human child born in Alisanos in centuries, as humans reckoned time, would never be allowed to leave. And Audrun, given the opportunity to escape before the changes overcame her, would never leave her child. She had lost four already.

Shifting against the tree had broken open clotting wounds, kindling renewed, shocking pain. Blood trickled again from his bare abdomen. He pressed his palm against the gashes, trying to forestall additional blood loss, trying to control the pain, then realized, belatedly, that blood was possibly the answer to his present difficulty.

Rhuan lifted his trembling hand. Blood stained his fingers. Smiling grimly, he dabbed it onto closed eyelids, and summoned the blood-bond linking him to the one who was, in human words, his cousin; in the tongue of their people, kin-in-kind.

"You'll hate this, I know." Dimples appeared as his smile stretched to a grin. "And I don't care."

THE HAND-READER SLEPT. Bethid sat in the wagon's open doorway with booted feet propped on a lower step, sipping herb tea. She had dug up a pierced-tin lantern from Ilona's things and lighted it, then hung it from the nail over the arched doorway so that it shed illumination upon the steps and a small area beyond. She'd considered setting out several of the sherpherd's crooks and other lanterns as well, but decided that she should wait for Ilona's permission, especially as no one yet knew how much lamp oil had survived the storm.

Other wagons and people had settled in for the evening nearby. This sprawling grove, on the far side of the former tent village, was not ordinarily used for karavans, but the smaller, younger grove had suffered too much storm damage, and also hosted those injured in the Hecari culling. Upon his return, Jorda had brought his karavan to the older, stronger grove boasting massive trees, most of which had withstood the storm's fury. Earlier his folk had sorted through their wagons for things that could be given to the settlement residents who'd lost everything. Now the sun was down, twilight had passed into night, and the grove, providing some shelter, hosted multiple small fires. Karavaners had retreated into their wagons; those of the tent village gathered in family groups at the bases of trees, seeking a form of security. Bethid noted that the karavan-master was moving from wagon to wagon, quietly checking on his folk. Eventually, he came to her as well.

"She's sleeping," Bethid reported as Jorda walked into the lantern light. "And her fever appears to have broken. She took more tea and ate a portion of Brodhi's venison."

He nodded, relief limning his features. Illumination from the lantern glinted off silver threads in his ruddy hair and beard. He sighed, then squatted in the pool of light at the bottom of the steps. "I have a favor to ask of you."

She nodded, swallowing tea. "Ask."

He hesitated. "I would go myself, but Mikal feels I should stay to deal with the karavaners. The tentfolk are his responsibility. And I agree."

Bethid waggled fingers in a gesture to encourage an actual question. "Yes?"

"As a courier, you know the roads. So, I've come to see if you would ride out toward the Atalanda short-cut. Rhuan went to aid a family of farmsteaders before the storm broke. They may need help. And I need Rhuan."

Her brows arched. "What about your other guide? I'm willing to go, of course, but he and Rhuan are partners."

Jorda's expression was grim. "Darmuth's missing."

That was startling. "Did he go after Rhuan?"

"I have no idea where he is. He's a trustworthy man; I fear he may have been taken by Alisanos, or lost to the storm."

She understood the implication immediately. "Which means you need Rhuan more than ever."

"Brodhi has drawn us a very rough map of where he believes the Alisanos borders lie in the *immediate* area. It will do for the moment—it's far better than what we have otherwise—but he agrees it would be best if we scout the borders thoroughly before allowing anyone to venture farther. And we need to venture, Beth; there are things to search for, water to haul up from the river— what if part of *it* is in the deepwood, now? There are new fields to be plowed, hunting to be done, and so forth. It's imperative we have an accurate map. If we know how and where the borders lie, we can put up warning cairns, make sure everyone knows where they shouldn't go. Brodhi says his understanding is that most of the deepwood is forested and thus visible, but not all of it, and that the borders may creep one way or the other overnight. And even were it decided everyone should go elsewhere, it's simply too dangerous to travel without maps. We could all end up in Alisanos."

She grimaced. "And Brodhi's going to Cardatha, thanks to me."

"No, it's a good plan, Beth. And Rhuan has land-sense, too. It would be far safer for him and Darmuth to scout the borders than to risk folk who may blunder into the deepwood purely by accident."

"Then I'll leave in the morning."

"Bethid—it will be dangerous. For all we know, the road itself now lies in Alisanos."

"But it's visible, Brodhi said. If I see a forest where one wasn't before, I'll definitely know to avoid it!" She sipped her cooling tea. "I'll go, and I promise I won't take unnecessary risks."

"Brodhi said *most* of it is visible," Jorda clarified. Then he rose, shaking his head. "No, no, it's too dangerous." His abrupt gesture dismissed the idea. "We can hope Rhuan returns in a few days. That would be best."

"Yes," she agreed, "but what about in the meantime? And if Rhuan *is* lost to us, which is certainly possible—he's Shoia, not immortal—then we'll have to

scout the borders ourselves at some point, anyway.
And do it sooner than Brodhi can return from Cardatha." She shrugged. "How would we feel if *children*
wandered too close to a border none of us could see?
Better to risk one person, I think, than several, be they
children or adults. I do know the roads and routes,
Jorda, and where the shortcuts lie."

"Bethid—"

She cut him off. "I will do this. But if it would ease
you, I'll make a heartfelt vow to the Mother not to
take unnecessary risks." She grinned at him, patting
the string of charms around her neck. "After all, I'm
not Rhuan. I can't die six times and revive. I'll be most
careful."

Jorda passed a wide hand over his hair. "I don't
know . . . when I thought it through, I believed in the
plan. But now, speaking of it with you, I'm not so certain." He stared over her head into the wagon, brightening. "But if Ilona could read your hand, she might
be able to provide an indication of the danger." He
nodded, clearly relieved. "That might be best."

"Except," Bethid said soberly, "she already tried it.
She failed."

Jorda was stunned. "She *still* can't read a hand?"

"I told her it may be that she's injured." Bethid
poured out the dregs of cold tea beside the steps, then
shook the mug to rid it of residual moisture and set it
on the floorboards. "And it may. She says she's never
been ill nor injured. I don't know how a diviner's gift
works, but it seems logical to me that illness or injury

might interfere." That prompted a memory. "She had me look for the dream-reader earlier. Lerin. I couldn't find her."

Jorda blew out a noisy breath. "Mikal did. She's dead."

"Oh." That surprise pinched. "Well, surely there are other diviners here. *All* of them can't be dead. You have two diviners in addition to Ilona, don't you, for your karavans?"

His expression was grim. "Some diviners were culled by the Hecari. Then we told everyone to go east when the storm came down, but not all of those folk have returned. We can't be certain they didn't end up in Alisanos. Others . . . well, more bodies have been found. Lightning-struck, or crushed by falling trees. One man broke his neck, probably from falling off a frightened horse." Jorda briefly touched the knot on his forehead, gained in his own fall. His voice was bleak. "Branca and Melior are also among the missing. To my knowledge, after a head count, Ilona is the only surviving diviner here."

"Mother," Bethid murmured in shock. "*No* diviners left?"

"One," Jorda said grimly, "if her gift survives."

A chill ran down Bethid's spine. For a moment she scratched absently but vigorously at short hair, weighing consequences. "Jorda, without any diviners, we're all of us in danger. If anyone dies, and there are no diviners, there can be no rites. Without those rites, the dead can't cross the river. They'll be denied an afterlife. And we have bodies waiting already." She felt sick to her stomach. "Oh Jorda, we can't remain here if there are no diviners! We'll have to leave, all of us, no matter the threat of Alisanos. The deepwood's not a certainty. Without a diviner, damnation is."

Green eyes were dark in low light. His voice was tight. "Then when you make your vow to the Mother not to take unnecessary risks, ask her to rekindle Ilona's gift. If she is truly the only diviner, the fates of all of us, dead *and* alive, depend on her."

Chapter 14

*I*LONA DREAMED OF A MAN. *He was distant, and details could not be seen clearly, but she knew he was Rhuan. He came striding straight toward her, as if he knew she was waiting for him, and as he drew closer she realized he was not Rhuan after all. This man was taller, broader, older. But his skin was the same hue, his eyes the same warm cider brown, and he wore his pale coppery hair in orna-mented and complex braid patterns. His features were markedly similar to Rhuan's. But when he smiled, as he did in her dream, no dimples appeared. And she realized, as he smiled, that a flame burned within the man, hot and high. He wore power the way others wore clothing.*

Closer yet he came.

His apparel was as striking as he was. He wore a tight-fitting long-sleeved tunic and snug leggings made of a hide that was only a shade darker than his skin and hair, so that from head to toe he was a glossy pale russet, the color of au-tumn leaves. The clothing had a sheen to it, as if it were washed in gold, and wet. And then she realized, as the dream became clearer yet, as he walked closer still, that he wore the hide of a beast who was—that had been—scaled. She saw the interlocking patterns now, the delicate juxtaposition of scale overlapping scale. In the light of two suns, beneath a sepia sky, he glowed. But the hide was not ornamented, not as Rhuan's was, with shells and beads and fringe. The hide, in its clean, simple elegance, in the richness of its color and exquisite patterning, needed no adornment.

He stopped before her, close enough that she might touch him, that he might touch her. He did not. He smiled into her eyes, then lifted his arms over his head, palms turned up, as if to say "Behold."

She looked up, as he meant her to.

Above him, in the sky, beneath the double suns, winged beasts rose. That they did so to mate, she thought at first; but no.

To fight.

Still he smiled at her. "This is for you."

JUST BEFORE DAWN, Brodhi was wrenched out of sleep. Images impinged on his consciousness, flooding his mind. He sat bolt upright, staring into thinning darkness, and saw Alisanos. Was *in* Alisanos.

No. No. His body remained in the human world; only his eyes were in the deepwood.

Immediately he knew the instigator. Furious, frustrated, Brodhi clamped both hands over his face. *"Curse* you, Rhuan!"

His awareness of the human world attenuated, then snapped. With eyes closed, hands pressed against his eyelids, he nonetheless saw the pale trunks of the dreya ring, the leafy silver canopy spreading high against the sky, the light of two suns glittering among stems and branches. He saw the dappled depths, the shadows, felt a familiarity that reached out to him to yank demandingly at his spirit. He ached with yearning. For too long, much too long, he had been away. Brodhi longed to go home.

Then the view altered. He saw a booted foot—no, *two* booted feet—leather-clad legs, punctures in the leggings, and blood.

And blood.

The image shifted. Slid sideways. He had a cramped view of bare abdomen, and deep, ragged gashes.

Rhuan was not only in Alisanos, but *hurt* in Alisanos. And clearly was asking for help.

Brodhi already felt the first warning throb of the headache to come. Forced sendings always resulted in such. A moment later his skull felt like someone was pounding a tent peg into it. He leaned forward, clutching his head, and hissed through clenched teeth. "I know . . ." He swore viciously. "I see, Rhuan . . . yes, you're hurt; I see that. I see where you are. *Stop.*"

Rhuan didn't. A sending didn't work that way. They could not communicate beyond sharing, in silence, what Rhuan's eyes saw. Ordinarily a sending was indicated by a feathering of inquiry, a request for contact. But when forced upon a man, its repercussions were violent.

Brodhi thrust himself to his feet, blinded by pain, blinded by darkness, and stumbled forward. He reeled sideways a step, then staggered into the cookfire, knocking down the spit and the remains of the deer carcass. He swore, felt heat beneath his boot soles, and leaped forward to escape the coals. Tripping, he ended up on one knee, one hand thrust against the ground to hold himself upright. The other hand clutched at his brow.

Dreya ring.

Torn and bloodied leggings.

Torn and bloodied flesh.

He toppled to one hip, then down onto his side. He could not prevent his body's desperate bid for an interior escape as it curled upon itself. Childlike, he rocked back and forth, trying to stem the pain, or at least to assimilate it.

Rhuan's sending ended. Alisanos was gone. Brodhi saw night again, the crescent of Maiden Moon, the first faint thinning presaging dawn. Some distance away, tied to a tree, his horse snorted at him warily. A flood of invective fell from Brodhi's mouth, and all of it had to do with his kin-in-kind, the fool who'd forced a sending upon him.

When next he saw Rhuan, *if* he saw Rhuan, he'd murder him.

That is, if Rhuan didn't die of his wounds first.

Brodhi rolled onto his back. Ground chill seeped up

through his clothing, sheathing his flesh. He stared up into the sky, willing the pain to diminish, knowing it would require more time than he had before departing on his journey to Cardatha. He used the moon as proxy for his kinsman. "I'm *here*, not there, for all I wish our roles were reversed. And if you truly think I would go into Alisanos before my time and risk my ascension, then you don't deserve to live because you're too stupid!" Now, he was sweating. He felt sick to his stomach. "If you need help so badly, contact the primaries. Contact Alario. You know the way. You have the means. You don't want to ascend anyway—what would it matter?"

But it would. He seriously doubted Rhuan wished to be a neuter any more than he did. Which is why Rhuan had undertaken the sending. It truly was a cry for help.

"No," Brodhi declared. "It was your choice to put yourself so close to the deepwood as it went active. As the humans would say, you reap what you sow. I remain here."

Rhuan could not hear him, of course. But Brodhi's decision would be known when he failed to appear in Alisanos, in the dreya ring, and Rhuan would realize his fate was his own to make.

No, Rhuan would contact no one else for aid. Better to die intact than to live a neuter.

Sweat was drying on Brodhi's face. He lay sprawled and very still, afraid to move lest it make the headache worse. There beneath the Maiden he resolved yet

again, more determinedly than ever, to become what
he so badly wanted—needed—to become. Alario
would lose a son, but his brother Karadath would
have *his* son, his *dioscuri*, who would rise as the sire
had risen.

Ascension.

THE SENDING WAS done. Rhuan could well
imagine Brodhi's reaction. He did hold some
faint hope that Brodhi might shock him and actually
answer the plea for assistance, but doubt was foremost. Were Brodhi in the human world, he would not
enter Alisanos and risk ending his journey prematurely. He *might* answer the sending if he were in the
deepwood. But Rhuan doubted it. There had been distance in the sending, weakness in the blood-bond that
allowed the one-way communication.

He squinted up through the dreya ring's canopy,
noting the double suns had begun their descent. He
did not know if two days had passed in the human
world; it could possibly even be a week. What he did
know was that he would welcome darkness and the
chance to sleep, except that he feared sleep wasn't possible on two counts: first, he hurt too much; second, he
might die. The latter possibility sent adrenaline flooding through him as all his muscles clenched, which in
turn set his abdomen afire. No, sleep would not be
possible on any count.

The baby, still wet, still neglected at the foot of the nearest tree, protested with swaddled struggles and increasingly unhappy crying. Rhuan apologized to Sarith because he truly felt bad, but moving to tend her would worsen his situation. Audrun would be back soon. In the meantime, it would not harm the baby to be damp, any more than it would harm his ears to hear her cries.

He swore a series of increasingly obscene curses through clamped teeth, trying to concentrate on conjured images of quietude and rest. That, too, was impossible. Then he switched to telling over the Names of the Thousand Gods, hoping the devotion and respect he offered might be rewarded; knowing, however, that it was most unlikely, as the primaries would know why he was doing so. False devotion, devotion under duress, was viewed as a time waster. But it nonetheless gave him something to do. Something to distract himself.

Then fire flared.

Rhuan could not help himself. He thrust himself up from the ground, turned swiftly and knelt, hunched, bracing himself against the ground with one hand. The other went to his belt, only to discover his knife sheath was empty.

Audrun. Of course. And she had been right to take it. Conscious, he would have told her to do so.

He still had throwing knives. But now, as he saw clearly despite the pain in his midriff, he made no move to draw them.

Just outside the ring, the winged demon stood. Pale eyes showed vertical slits for pupils. Black hair was again neat and shining, hanging past his shoulders. The black hide jacket hung askew and slightly open from his shoulders, baring the scale pattern creeping upward across his flesh from the waistband of dark leggings. Wings were folded against his back. In one hand, he held a lighted torch.

The dreya ring, threatened, yanked branches as far from the torch as possible. Rhuan felt the fear, the thrumming of tension within the ring. Dreya trees were immune to blight, to insect damage and fungus, but lightning and fire could be devastating.

The demon smiled. *"Give it to me."*

Rhuan said, "No."

In one stride, the demon stood beside the queen tree. Pale eyes were locked on Rhuan's, which hazed red. An undulation went through the ring again as trees leaned away. In a matter of moments, feeder roots would begin to break free of the earth. In a matter of moments, any protection the dreya offered would end. Not because they surrendered, not because they gave up the child, but because they could not save themselves *and* the child.

"This infant," Rhuan said tightly, "has both a mother and a father."

The demon displayed fangs. "I. Don't. Care."

"You were human once. Sancorran, yes? This child is also Sancorran. Sancorran and Alisani."

The demon leaned forward, raising the torch higher yet. *"As am I."*

"This child has the protection of the dreya. This child has *my* protection."

The demon laughed. "The latter is worthless. The former? Well, that shall end. See you?" And he thrust the torch up into the gleaming branches of the queen tree.

Dreya screamed as fire took hold. Rhuan immediately lurched toward the baby, reaching for the small, squirming bundle before the demon could do the same. But his hands and clawed hands closed upon swaddling at the same time. Muslin tore, tiny limbs fell free. Rhuan caught an arm. The demon caught a leg.

Flame ran up through pale branches into the high canopy. Trunks twisted and writhed. Within moments the crown of the ring was afire. Roots pulled free of the earth. Women, pale and silver, wrenched themselves out of trunk clefts. Rhuan had an impression of terrified eyes, of clothing of mist and starlight, of blazing hair. Sarith, caught in opposing hands, opposing convictions, screamed even as the dreya did.

Without their trees, all would die.

"I'm sorry!" Rhuan cried to the dreya, redoubling his efforts to claim the infant. But then a leathery wing slapped into his temple. He was flung aside, slammed into one of the now empty trunks. Within the ring, dreya burned. Above, the silver canopy became a conflagration.

Rhuan lost the child.

"*Mine,*" the demon crowed.

Crumpled at the base of a burning tree, despite the flames, Rhuan fell into darkness.

 AUDRUN HEARD THE screaming. Smelled the smoke and fire.

Women screaming. Close by.

Instinct nonetheless made her kneel, made her carefully set aside the melon-bowl of water. Then she ran.

O Mother, O Mother, no . . .

She ran, and came almost immediately upon a firestorm. Stunned, she found the ring ablaze. Saw woman-shaped pyres. Saw a roof of flame. Rhuan, unconscious. And a demon taking flight, cradling a baby.

No. No. No.

Yes. Oh, yes.

Burning brands and branches fell into the ring. Dead dreya, still ablaze, collapsed into smoking heaps at the bases of their trees. Rhuan, too, was threatened, blind and deaf to all. Fire fell from the sky.

The baby.

Gone.

"Mother of Moons!" Audrun cried.

But this was Alisanos.

The baby was gone. The trees were afire. The dreya were dead. Rhuan wasn't.

Rhuan.

Audrun ran. She caught up a wrist, clamped her hands closed, and pulled. His body gave barely at all, slumping sideways. Audrun yanked. She set her booted feet, drew a huge breath, and yanked again and again. A sustained pull she could not manage; he was too heavy. But panic gave her strength and a desperate determination. Grunting, gasping, gripping his bare wrist, she pulled again, yanked again, tugged at him. From above sparks flew. All around her lay the remains of dreya, of women she'd never met but who had protected her child as best they could. Dead now, their trees ablaze, the child stolen.

Audrun cried out in extremity, expending all the strength she had left. She had moved him possibly six feet. Too close, too dangerous; the trees, she feared, would burn through and fall upon them.

"Rhuan! *Rhuan!*"

He lay sprawled on his back, one arm outstretched.

She leaned down over him, placed a boot on either side of his torso, and wrapped both fists into his tangled braids. "Wake up! Wake up! I can't move you!" By the braids, she shook his skull. *"Wake up!"* Behind her a branch fell in a whoosh of heated air. Desperate, Audrun placed one hand against the wounds in his abdomen. Gritting her teeth, she plunged two fingers into a gash. "Wake *up,* curse you! Do you want all of us to die? The demon has my baby and we're about to burn!"

The invasion of her fingers brought him abruptly from unconsciousness, crying out in pain. Eyelids flickered.

Audrun smashed the flat of her hand across his face, bloodying his nose.

"Now," she shouted as she saw glazed brown eyes upon her. "Now, curse you, *move! Move! Move!"*

Rhuan rolled as if to rise. Audrun hopped out of his way. On hands and knees, bloodied braids dangling, he made every attempt to crawl.

"Yes!" she cried. "Go!" She caught an upper arm in both her hands, setting nails into flesh as she urged him onward. "I can't drag you! I can't! Ah, Mother, lend him strength!"

He wobbled. He crawled.

"Yes!" Audrun shouted.

Rhuan was out of the ring. Behind him, tumbling down in gouts of flame, more branches fell. Audrun put up a hand up to shield her face against the upsurge of heat. Then, seeing him wavering, failing, she reached again and closed both hands around a wrist. In fear, in panic, in utter desperation, she yanked as hard as she could.

His body followed so fast she sat down hard. And she knew, meeting his eyes, acknowledging the failure of her own body as well as his, that they were both of them done. No more. No more. He was too badly hurt, and she had birthed a baby earlier that day. Audrun sat with legs spread, knees bent, leaning against arms braced behind her back, and sucked in air again, again, again. She had no strength for tears, nothing at all for words. All she could do was try to fill her lungs.

Rhuan levered himself onto hands and knees. She saw how his arms shook. He twisted his head and looked over a shoulder at the ring. Then he looked at her. "It won't . . ." he said, "can't . . ."

She barely managed, "What?"

". . . started amidst a dreya ring . . . there it stays . . ."

"The fire?" Still she sucked in whoops of air. "Won't spread?"

"*No . . .*" Rhuan said, and fell facedown.

AS THE SUN slid below the horizon, Davyn stepped off the nearly invisible shortcut. The ruts were broken by clusters of stone, some half buried, others on top, plus webby grass and groundcover, and he saw now why the axle had split. It was a punishing track, the condition indicating that no one traveled it to reach Atalanda, that all went around the long way, the way the guide had recommended. But none of them had been told by fourteen—no, *fifteen*—diviners that a child must be born in Atalanda; they knew nothing of the demands of time. Davyn believed he had made the right decision regardless of the outcome; what else could he have done? Set them upon the long route, so that there was doubt they'd reach Audrun's kinfolk before the baby came? The shortcut saved them weeks of travel. That the family now was scattered amid Alisanos changed nothing of Davyn's decision. The loss was not his fault. The loss was Rhuan's fault.

He had walked for hours. Now twilight came upon

him; it was time to stop for the night. He moved away from the track toward a tree that lay on its side, upturned roots displaying fresh, damp dirt. Yet another victim of the storm. Davyn found a place to spread a sleeping mat so that he could lean against the trunk and settled in. He wasted no time laying a fire. Tonight he would dine on dried, salted meat and water. And when the sun was gone and Maiden Moon rose in the heavens, he once again began the litany of prayers, the demands for aid. Alisanos was wholly unnatural, not a random act of nature. It was alien. It was maleficent. More than anything else in the world, it deserved the Mother's wrath.

And a measure of Davyn's. But most of that he reserved for Rhuan.

Chapter 15

BETHID AWOKE AT dawn. For a moment she felt competely disoriented, squinting up from a supine position at morning sunlight through naked trees, until she made note of the glyph-carved wagon ribs and the narrowness of of her place upon the floorboards. She was hemmed in by a large trunk on one side and the cot-cabinet on the other, lying on cushions with a thin blanket over her body. This was not the couriers' common tent.

Ah. Yes. Ilona's wagon. She had spent the night with the hand-reader, aware of when Ilona was awake and when she slept, while she, a mere courier, turned over plans for rebellion in her head.

Bethid sat upright, pushing aside the blanket. She rubbed absently at her hair, felt for brass ear-hoops, yawned, then looked at the hand-reader. Ilona's cot was atop the many-drawered cabinet, and she was a rumpled mound. Long, loose hair was a tangle of dark ringlets, untamed by the hair sticks Ilona usually wore to anchor a twisted, heavy coil of hair against her skull. Bethid assumed Ilona's hair and scalp bore a weight of dust and grit just as her own had before its haphazard washing. She thought longingly for a moment of descending to the river to bathe, but reflected too much required her attention before she could afford the luxury of a bath. She stretched again, then climbed off her pallet on the floorboards. Ilona was still asleep; that gave Bethid time to fix a new pot of tea. She also needed to talk to Jorda or Mikal about who could tend Ilona while she was gone.

That thought made her smile as she climbed down the wagon steps. It was amazing to her how various people had stepped forward to take leadership roles. Jorda had always been master of his karavan while Mikal's responsibilities had been solely to his ale tent and customers. Now he, as Jorda, worked to guide the karavan- and tent-folk into a sustainable future, regardless of where Alisanos lay. Undoubtedly at some point they would reestablish a Watch, now that Kendic was dead in the Hecari culling. Bethid was well aware that not every individual survivor in the settlement would necessarily work toward the common good; in all settlements, villages, and cities, people stole from others, injured or murdered others, looked solely for their personal gain regardless of potential repercussions for others and the community. Perhaps for a while those bent on thievery would lie low, simply because no one knew if anyone retained anything of worth following the settlement's destruction, but at some point stealing, drunkenness, fighting, raping, and death would occur. They always did. Meanwhile, *she* was making suggestions to Mikal and Jorda, and also to Brodhi, when such had never before occured to her.

Bethid knelt beside the modest cookfire, scraping aside ash with a stick to uncover dully glowing coals. Her thoughts ran on: Jorda and Mikal would assign Watch tasks to those they believed most reliable, while she spoke further of rebellion with Timmon and Alorn. Courier duties would not resume before Brodhi's return from Cardatha, so there was time to discuss those plans. In the meantime, their responsibility lay in assisting the survivors and preparing for potential visitations from Hecari. She wasn't certain enough people remained to trigger a formal culling, but it would be best to make it appear as though the settlement was but a shadow of its true self. They needed to plan a defense against the Hecari, even if it meant stationing people at various points to pass the word of a party's approach. Surprise had been a very effective strategy when the culling party had arrived. Now it was the task of the survivors to make sure surprise no longer played a role. Preparedness was required, along with a plan everyone knew.

And there it was again: she was thinking about the welfare of the settlement and its folk. Bethid shook her head, smiling wryly.

Two mugs sat beside the fire ring. The ground now was dry, or at least the surface was, so that Bethid could sit without having her trews soaked through. She

noted that the grass beaten flat in the storm was spring-
ing upright again. The smaller karavan grove nearest
the road hosted little grass because of constant wagon,
hoof, and foot traffic, but this grove, older and larger,
had not suffered months of such activity. Here the grass
grew thickly, though the various karavan draft animals
picketed throughout the grove would soon graze it
down. In the meantime, the grass provided an emerald
carpet that brought a sense of peace to Bethid.

She was in mid-stretch, yawning prodigiously,
when the hand-reader appeared in the doorway of her
wagon. She wore the storm-tattered clothing she'd
slept in, and tangled dark hair fell to her waist. She
supported her splinted left forearm with her right
hand, pressing it against her chest. Color stood high in
her face, and the pupils of hazel eyes were huge.

"Ilona, wait—" Bethid thrust herself to her feet as
the hand-reader climbed shakily down the steps. "Stay
in bed; I'm brewing tea."

But Ilona, now standing on the ground, stared at
Bethid blankly.

"Come." Bethid gestured. "Let's get you back in bed,
and I'll bring tea. Then I'll see about something to eat."

Ilona resisted, and Bethid was afraid to put hands
on her lest she jar the broken arm. The hand-reader
just stood at the bottom of her steps, gazing around the
grove. Eventually her eyes tracked upward through
the bare-branched trees. A confused frown drew her
brows together. "Where am I?"

O Mother. Bethid made her voice cheerful. "Come,

Ilona. Let's have you back in bed." Carefully, she touched one shoulder. "I suspect the fever's upon you again. Rest is what you need."

Ilona's eyes stared through her. "I'm being called."

Bethid was startled. "You're what?"

"They're calling me."

"Who's calling you?"

Ilona's expression was perplexed. "I don't know."

Bethid gently touched the hand-reader's brow. "As I thought—you're on fire. Come, Ilona. Back to bed with you."

"I'm to go to them."

"Well, you can't. We need you here." Bethid placed a hand on Ilona's back and urged her to turn toward the wagon. "We need you badly, Ilona . . . you're apparently the only diviner the storm left us."

Hazel eyes sharpened. "Let me read your hand."

And if she failed again? Bethid didn't wish to risk it. Not now, while the fever was on her. "Later. Right now you need to go back to bed, and I'll bring tea." Bethid pressed a littler harder, aiming Ilona toward the bottom step. "Up you go." Ilona obliged this time, climbing into the wagon. Bethid followed to make certain she put herself back to bed, and was relieved when she did so. "Rest," she said. "I'll see to tea and food. Let others tend you, Ilona. No need to do any tasks for a few days." A thought crossed Bethid's mind. "Do you need the nightcrock?"

Ilona, lying against piled cushions, shook her head. She seemed dazed. Distant.

"Very well. Rest here. I'll return in a moment."

When Bethid climbed down the steps, she found a woman standing near the fire. She wore fine-woven but stained russet skirts and a honey-colored tunic belted with a wide gold-studded leather belt that wrapped a narrow waist. Her tunic was slit to the tops of her breasts, edged with russet-colored embroidery. Propriety demanded a cover of some sort, and she wore a moss-hued light shawl around her shoulders, but the weave was openwork, and its sheerness provided little coverage.

Bethid, attuned to women she found attractive, saw the piquant features, the large brown eyes beneath heavy lids, and a mass of tangled honey-colored hair tied at the back of an elegant neck. Beauty coupled with fine but suggestive clothing told her precisely what the woman was. Resentment rose, resentment and a small anger, that a woman would demean herself by lying with men for coin. *Better she should lie with me*— But Bethid cut that thought off at once. Briskly, she said, "She's injured and fevered, and can't read any hands."

"That's not why I'm here." The woman had a low, husky voice. "Nor am I here for what you're thinking."

"Unless you're a diviner, which you're not, you have no idea what I'm thinking."

The woman tilted her head slightly, as if listening beneath the words. A very small smile touched her lips. "You're thinking a whore has no business bothering you. Yes, I am a whore—indeed, a Sister of the

Road—but I've come for something else. To offer my help."

"How can you help?" Bethid's mouth hooked wryly. "Yes, I prefer women, but I don't pay for it."

"The hand-reader is ill," the Sister said, ignoring Bethid's comment. "I came to tend her, if you'll allow it. You're a courier; you may have other duties."

So she did, though they had, at the moment, nothing to do with carrying messages. "Why?"

"Why am I here?" The woman lifted one shoulder in a small, elegant shrug. "The hand-reader and the karavan-master took pains to urge all of us to go east, to escape the storm. And so we did, and so we survived, my Sisters and I. The least we can do is to help her now, when she needs it." She turned slightly, gesturing. "Our wagon is just there. My Sisters and I can take turns tending the hand-reader. She won't be alone. And then you can do whatever requires doing, in *your* line of work."

Bethid sighed internally. It was a boon the woman offered, and there was no room in the post-storm world for bias. She, Bethid, had chosen a different road, but her life was no more conventional than that experienced by Sisters of the Road. "Then I thank you for it," she said. "There is tea ready."

The woman nodded. "My name," she said, "is Naiya. That is a true name, the name I was given at birth, not something men whisper to me in bed. It will stand surety for my intentions."

Bethid impulsively reached out a hand. Naiya

clasped it, palm to palm. "My thanks," Bethid said, "and now I must go. Churri and I have a long ride ahead of us."

Naiya nodded. "May the Mother keep you safe."

So even whores prayed to the Mother of Moons. Bethid smiled briefly, then turned away. Churri was picketed nearby; it was time to pack food and bedding, saddle up, and ride him down to the river for watering. Then they could go hunting for the missing Shoia.

GILLAN ROUSED TO excruciating pain in his left leg. He discovered someone had silenced him with a tight gag over his mouth, had stilled his arms by binding his wrists, and that he lay on a pallet that crackled as he moved, poking into his back. Leaves, he realized, and branches. But the pain in his leg was so bad that such thoughts only flitted briefly through his head. Tears rolled down his cheeks as he writhed, trying to cry out through the gag but managing only a keening moan. He blinked tears away, trying to clear his vision, and saw Darmuth bending over his leg. The man's—no, *demon's*—hands were massaging some kind of ointment or grease into his leg.

"Among us again?" Darmuth asked. "Well, I believe that won't last. Best to sleep, or swoon." He smiled. "You're gagged, yes, and tied. Quite often silence is necessary in Alisanos, if one is to survive. If you cry out in pain, or interfere with your hands, you will bring trouble down upon us." He paused. "Well, trouble down upon *you*."

Gillan levered himself up awkwardly with tied hands, balancing on one elbow. The flesh below his knee was raw as skinned meat, and weeping. It looked wasted, lacking the firm roundness of muscle and skin. This time his moan through the gag was not of pain so much as it was of grief and disbelief.

"You'll keep it," Darmuth said. "The bone is whole, as I told you. When this is healed, we can pad and brace the leg from knee to ankle for support. You'll walk." His fingers moved all the while he spoke. "But it's very unlikely you'll ever run again. Accept it."

Accept that he was a cripple? When the few cripples he'd seen in villages and hamlets were derided for their state, teased ruthlessly by children and mostly ignored by adults? Accept that?

Ah, but he was no longer in the world where villages and hamlets existed, where humans lived. He was in Alisanos, and a demon tended him.

Gillan fell back onto the leafy pallet, pressing the heels of his bound hands against his eyes. He wished not to cry, to moan, to writhe and twist in response to the pain, but he was helpless. His body acted of its own accord. Pain was paramount.

"You should be grateful," the demon said, "that I don't treat this leg as meat. It's quite tantalizing, you do realize, here in my hands, begging to be eaten. It makes my mouth water." Gillan removed his hands and his eyes popped open, staring; the gray eyes looking back at him appeared human despite the words. "But Rhuan would find that very upsetting, and no doubt you would as well."

Gillan nodded vigorously, making a sound of vehement agreement through the gag.

"And I do have my own journey, after all. So, I will tend this limb instead of dining upon it, and one day you will rise and walk. Perhaps at that point you will understand that all in Alisanos are not the same. Not even demons." Now the black pupils slitted. "Do you understand? You live here, now, in the deepwood. If you are to survive, you'll have to learn that which threatens, and that which doesn't. It's not a matter of black and white. This is your home. You'll spend the rest of your life here. There is no escape—well, only rarely. And then the humans kill you anyway, or send you from their home places. Because you won't be as they are anymore. You won't be human. Possibly—Alisanos does take some this way—you'll even end up a demon." He grinned, displaying his fanged canines, one of which bore a glinting green gem. "Just like me."

Gillan rolled his head aside, refusing to look at the man he'd trusted as a karavan guide. Darmuth was a demon. For all he tended Gillan's leg, he remained a demon, a creature of Alisanos. Gillan stared hard into shadows, willing himself not to cry, trying to let sense overtake pain. But his leg was afire beneath Darmuth's hands, and all he could do was whimper like a child.

Would he become a demon? Or something else? Something worse.

If worse existed in Alisanos.

He shut his eyes. Clenched his teeth. And resolved to remain human no matter what it took.

THE ROAD, BRODHI discovered, ended abruptly. It stretched out in front of him, beckoning him onward, but was encroached upon by a forest that hadn't existed when he rode from Cardatha to the tent settlement to speak of the Sancorran lord's execution. But he did not question it. He did not gasp aloud in disbelief. He knew exactly what it was, and why the road disappeared.

So if he continued on the road, he too would disappear into the deepwood. Thus it was incumbent upon him, if he wished to remain on his journey toward ascension, to avoid Alisanos and find another route to the Cardatha road. Accordingly, Brodhi swung his horse left. He would skirt the deepwood, avoiding the boundary that beckoned, that would lead him into the interior. Born of the deepwood, his land-sense was undeniable. He knew, he *felt*, exactly where Alisanos began and the human world ended.

Then he reined in his horse. He thought back, memory giving him a clear vision of how far he had ridden and the landmarks he had passed. Brodhi dug into his scroll case and took a tattered roll of parchment from it. He had delivered its message sometime before, orally, and the scroll had never left his possession. He next dug out lead, spread the soiled sheet across his thigh, and began to sketch. Maps were born thusly, and understanding. Taken back to the settlement, it would provide answers. So Brodhi was careful in his illustration, making certain to draw exactly what he had seen. Accuracy was paramount. Meanwhile, his horse dropped his head and began to graze on moisture-laden grass. From high overhead, the sun blazed. The skies were clear. It was difficult to recall that they had been occluded by black, heavy clouds giving birth to red lightning and shattering thunder only yesterday. The world was dry again. Birds sang, beetles rattled, buzzed, and chirped, small game sought safety in vegetation. Here upon the road, all were safe. A matter of paces away, no one, nothing, was.

Brodhi continued to sketch carefully but the task was interrupted as a large shadow passed overhead. His instincts warned him it could well be something out of the deepwood; during and after a shift in locale, Alisanos often disgorged creatures.

He glanced up as the shadow passed again. A soft, glinting shower of opalescent scales drifted down, and the winged creature came closer. Just as it arrived on the road directly in front of Brodhi, the creature convulsed, then took on human form. By the time it landed, by the time he had his horse under control again, Brodhi was smiling. And when the creature dissolved into a recognizably human form, sans wings, tail, and scales, it became a woman. A woman with wild red hair, green eyes, and freckle-dusted face, with features that were uncannily beautiful. She wore an indigo tunic and skirt, a silver-bossed belt, and slippers. Bright eyes laughed up at him.

Brodhi returned his attention to his map. "Back, are you?"

"To stay," she said. "Well, for a while." She strode gracefully forward, placing hands around the horse's muzzle. "Be still," she murmured to the bay gelding made nervous by her arrival. "All is well. I haven't come to eat you." Then her attention returned to Brodhi. "Where are you going?"

"Cardatha," he said absently, still sketching. "Where the warlord is."

The woman moved from the horse's muzzle to Brodhi's right leg. Slim, pale hands with perfectly human nails stroked his thigh below the parchment. "Come down," she said. "Come down off this horse."

Brodhi smiled inwardly. "I'm busy, Ferize."

"Busy doing what? Drawing pictures?"

"Exactly. Pictures that may mean the difference between death and life, between sanity and madness."

Standing beside the horse, she was not tall enough to see the surface of the parchment. "For humans?"

"For foolish humans, yes."

"Ah. And then what will you do, when this task is finished?"

"Go to Cardatha, as I said."

"Drawing pictures all the way?"

"Well, yes. So that when I return, I can offer the

knowledge to the humans who survived Alisanos going active."

"Tedious." Ferize closed fingers upon a tattered corner of the parchment. "Tedious in the extreme." She tugged slightly. "I think you need distracting."

"I find you immensely distracting," Brodhi agreed, "but this must be done while the memory is fresh. I came from here . . . to here." He tilted the parchment up to display it. "See? From here to here." Fingers traced the way. "Only to discover that the old road now lies in Alisanos, and so I must find another route to Cardatha. There, I will buy better parchment, perhaps vellum, and transfer the map to it."

"A mapmaker." Small white teeth showed between her lips. "Such a demotion for a *dioscuri*."

Brodhi continued drawing. "If I, as *dioscuri*, choose to do this, the task is elevated." He flicked a glance at her. "And if you spoil this, I will be most wroth with you."

Ferize laughed at him. "Wroth, is it? Because I spoiled something you intended for humans?"

Her fingers now lay across the parchment, obscuring his work. Brodhi gathered up the fingers in his own and lifted her hand away. "Not now, Ferize."

" 'Not now,' " she mimicked, adopting a pettish tone. "I have been away, undoubtedly leaving him bereft, and he says 'not now' when I return."

"Not now," he repeated. He slipped his foot free of the stirrup. "But if you wish to ride double with me when I set out again, you may as well come up now."

Ferize disdained the offered stirrup. In a swirl of full skirts, she leaped from the ground to land lightly atop the horse's rump. Then she snuggled herself close to his body, wrapping arms around his torso. One hand drifted down. "I could make you forget all about drawing pictures for humans."

"I'm sure you could. But that would not be the responsible thing to do when lives are at stake."

"Human lives."

"Human lives." He finished sketching a final tree, then carefully rolled closed the parchment. It and his lead were returned to the scroll case hanging from his saddle. "I think we need not allow additional humans to end up where they most want *not* to be when Alisanos has already fed so well."

Chapter 16

IN ALISANOS THERE was no moon, neither Maiden, Mother, nor Grandmother, only the Orphan Sky. But this Orphan Sky, here in the deepwood, promised no reappearance of the moon in any guise. Two suns, nothing more, and when they slid below the treetops and then beneath the horizon, giving way to the dark, only stars shed light, unless one had a torch.

Audrun did not. She sat in the clearing as the suns went down, beside the burned dreya ring, with a man's head in her lap. She had vastly underestimated how much time would be required to undo all the braids, to allow her opportunity to spread hair loose and tend scalp wounds. Rhuan had not roused at her touch. She had washed his other wounds time and again, wishing she had spirits. His breathing was regular, without hesitation, but that was not necessarily good, she knew. She had heard of injured folk who went to sleep, and remained that way. Their bodies withered, curling up on themselves, until at last they breathed no more.

So many braids, so much hair. It wanted, needed, washing. Audrun had no idea how often Rhuan undid the braids, or how often he washed his hair. She knew only that this was necessary, this unplaiting, to gain access to his scalp. Other wounds she had cleaned. Only these remained.

With the light gone, she halted her self-assigned task. Come morning she could begin again and unplait the balance of the braids. For now, so exhausted she trembled unremittingly, she needed rest badly. Her breasts ached, and the bodice of her tunic was damp with leaking milk. Though she had eaten the meat from the black-rinded melon she had opened to make a water bowl, she was hungry. She believed it very likely that she would topple over into unconsciousness if she didn't allow herself to sleep.

Earlier, she had found Rhuan's leather tunic. Now she folded it and slid it beneath his head as she backed away on hands and knees. They lacked mat, blankets, anything that might be used as bedding. The spare clouts Audrun had cut for the baby had been made over into bandages. She was tired enough, she believed, that it wouldn't matter that she lay on soil, grass, and deadfall. She had no idea how it might affect Rhuan. The only warmth was what their bodies carried. Audrun lay down carefully on her side, resting her body against his.

Night sounds in Alisanos were far different from those in the human world. Were there beasts in the underbrush? Creatures come to eat them? If so, nothing would hinder the predators. Nothing at all. Here, she and Rhuan were prey.

Her mind was as exhausted as her body. Slowly, she surrendered herself. And as she did so, she saw again in her mind the terrible image of the winged demon rising to the sky with Sarith in his arms.

Sarith. Megritte. Torvic. Ellica and Gillan. Her children, gone. The fruits of her womb were trapped in Alisanos, even as she was.

Now, in the dark, with nothing to do but sleep, Audrun, very quietly, allowed herself to weep.

IN LIRRA'S CABIN, Meggie cried herself to sleep when the double suns set—if night were called night here—bringing darkness to Lirra's cabin. Torvic had decided he must be strong for his sister, and did no such thing, himself. When he and his sister performed chores for Lirra, usually in the garden, or feeding chickens, he told Meggie that crying did no good. Crying wouldn't bring Mam and Da back, or Gillan and Ellica. Only the Mother of Moons knew where their kinfolk were, and perhaps one day the Mother would see to it they were reunited. Meggie always agreed to stop crying so much, but each night, not long after Lirra had tucked them into their pallets on the cabin floor, the tears came again.

Torvic kept track of the days by carving notches into a stick. But he knew time ran differently in Alisanos, because the days seemed to last longer than in the human world. He could only keep track of what he and Meggie experienced, not of what might be true in the human world. When they returned to their world, how much time would have passed? Weeks? Months? He dared not consider years. But the rhythms of his body were adapting to Alisanos. He could feel it.

And found it terrifying.

Torvic didn't tell Meggie. He didn't even dare hint to her that he felt different in the deepwood; it would worsen matters. And as she said nothing at all to him of feeling different, he believed she didn't experience Alisanos the way he did. Rather than plant ideas in her head, Torvic held his silence on the matter. And hid the calendar stick as well, returning the knife to Lirra's small collection after each notch was cut. He didn't know if Lirra was aware of what he did. He didn't know if she would care if she were. But he could speak to her of his feelings no more than to Meggie. It was a personal thing.

But he did tell Mam and Da. Each dawn, before Meggie awoke. Before Lirra awoke. In his mind, he told them everything.

BETHID MADE GOOD time, covering ground effortlessly atop smooth-gaited Churri. As on all assignments, she rested and watered Churri several times throughout the day, ate and drank in the saddle, stopped for the night as the sun went down, and was on the road again just before dawn. But this time she felt a sense of urgency far more demanding than usual. This time it wasn't a message she bore on her shoulders, but quite probably the welfare of karavaners and tent-folk. With Brodhi on the road to Cardatha, it was imperative she find Rhuan as soon as possible.

Thus, when she turned off the main road onto the shortcut to Atalanda and saw a man in the distance walking in her direction, relief came with a rush. The absence of a mount explained Rhuan's tardiness. She shouted, waved, and asked Churri to increase his pace so she might reach Rhuan more quickly. And yet as she drew nearer, her relief plummeted. The man wore no braids; in fact, he was blond. Nor was he shaped as Rhuan was. Within a matter of moments she recognized him: one of the farmsteaders Rhuan had gone to aid. The husband, in fact.

Hiding disappointment, Bethid reined in as she reached him. "What's happened?"

The man halted. He was red-faced and wet with sweat, hair sticking to his head. His voice was hoarse, as if he had not drunk in too long. But Bethid saw he had plump waterskins looped across his shoulders. "My family," he said, "has been taken from me."

"Alisanos," she breathed. "O Mother—I am so sorry! All of them?"

He scrubbed a forearm across his brow. "All but me."

"Did Rhuan find you?"

"Rhuan?" Color drained from the man's face. He was white now, blue eyes frigid. Anger was palpable, as was bitterness. "Oh, indeed, he found us. And delivered my family into Alisanos."

"*Rhuan* did?"

"The guide," he said. "The Shoia." He spat aside and made a gesture Bethid recognized as a curse.

She struggled to find words, to control her shock. "He wouldn't! Why would you think so? Why in the Mother's name—"

"*Because he did so!*" the man roared. "He put my youngest two up on his horse, sent my older two north, and instructed my wife and I to go as well. He was explicit—"

"He told the settlement folk to go, also," Bethid cut in, "before the storm got too bad. He meant us to escape, and likely wished the same for your family."

"He meant no such thing! He delivered my family to Alisanos. He probably intended the same for you, even if it didn't come to be."

Churri sidled, upset by the emotions. Bethid reined

him in, absently patted a shoulder. "Why? Why would he do such a thing?"

The farmsteader's tone was venemous. "Maybe he's not a Shoia. Maybe he's a demon out of Alisanos. Or maybe the Shoia *are* demons, and come from Alisanos. All I can tell you is that he sent us all north. He carried my youngest north. I looked, you see, when the storm was over. I searched. All I found was Alisanos! No wife, no children. Only the deepwood!"

She was sympathetic to his grief and anger, but couldn't believe what he said was accurate. "I can't imagine that Rhuan—" she began, and was sharply cut off by the farmsteader.

"Do you know him so well, then? Does he confide in you? Do you know his thoughts, his intentions?"

She did not. "I know Brodhi better, of course, but—"

"Swear to me," the farmsteader said. "*Swear* to me on the name of the Mother that the guide is incapable of doing such a thing."

On the name of the Mother? Bethid couldn't do that. She knew who Rhuan was, but not the heart of the man. "I can't," she said quietly.

"You see?" His smile was humorless, little more than a grimace. "I tell you, they are gone. All of them. Where they went is now part of the deepwood. Where he *sent* them."

She wanted to disagree. She wanted to convince him his belief was incorrect. But she had no evidence, and no words that might ease his anger.

"I'm assuming," the man said, "he's returned to the settlement. The Shoia."

Bethid shook her head. "No one has seen him since he set out after your family."

The farmsteader swore, spat again. "I want him," he said. "I want him so I can find out what's become of my family. So he can guide *me,* not a karavan, into Alisanos." He glared up at her. "Is the karavan-master at the settlement?"

"He is."

"Then he is most likely to know where his guide might be."

"I don't think Jorda knows," she told him. "The storm broke not long after Rhuan left. As I said, no one's seen him since."

"Convenient," the man muttered. "I have not seen him on the shortcut. Perhaps he's in hiding."

Bethid badly wanted to diffuse the situation. Accordingly she dismounted. "Here. Climb aboard. You're too heavy to ride double behind me; take the saddle, and I'll ride behind you. Best we get you to the settlement."

"I want," he said, "to find my family. I need the Shoia to do that."

"And the most likely place you'll find him, eventually, *is* the settlement." She indicated the saddle again. "We'll ask when he returns."

"If he doesn't?"

Bethid sighed. "Then there are two possibilities. He's either dead—"

"Or in Alisanos, where he sent my family."

After a moment, reluctantly, Bethid nodded. She did not believe, could not believe Rhuan would do such a thing, but she recognized that the farmsteader would not be convinced otherwise. Not yet. "Let's go," she said. "If what you say is true . . . well, Jorda needs to know."

"*Everyone* needs to know."

It was difficult to agree, but she did. "Yes."

Satisfied with that, the farmsteader mounted Churri. Then he shook the stirrup free of his foot and reached out an arm. Bethid set her left foot into the stirrup, caught his hand, and swung up onto the horse's broad rump.

He was wrong, the farmsteader. He had to be wrong. Bethid retained a very clear memory of Rhuan coming into Mikal's tent, urging them to go east, urging them to tell everyone in the settlement that safety lay in going east, that doing so might deliver them from Alisanos. It made absolutely no sense for Rhuan to send anyone *into* danger. Not on purpose.

And then another memory came. Rhuan had freely admitted, there in Mikal's tent, that he couldn't tell them *how* he knew they should go east. He simply knew, he said, and asked them to trust him. And they had, she and Mikal, when Jorda and Ilona expressed their faith in Rhuan. Those two knew him best. Those two believed. Jorda's and Ilona's trust in Rhuan had been enough for her, enough for Mikal.

Bethid had gone east, as Rhuan instructed. And she had survived. So had others.

This man's family had gone north, also directed by Rhuan. North was not east; she wondered why the change in direction. Especially now that all in the family but the farmsteader were lost to Alisanos. And Rhuan himself was nowhere to be found.

He's wrong. He must be. Rhuan wouldn't do such a thing. Not intentionally. Indeed, it was more likely, Bethid felt, that he might well be trapped in Alisanos himself, as helpless as the farmsteader's family.

But Bethid kept that thought to herself. The man in the saddle was understandably upset, desperate to find his family, and as desperately afraid he could not. Rather than give in to grief and despair, he conjured something in which he could believe, something that supported an irrefutable certainty that Rhuan was to blame for his family's fate because, she knew, it provided a goal. Something to which he could anchor himself. Something that allowed him to be a man, not a soul paralyzed by a terrible loss.

Perhaps once he spoke to Jorda, his conviction could be altered. But it would take two or three days to reach the settlement. She would not ask Churri to resume the pace she had required while on the way to the shortcut. The farmsteader was a big man, and now the horse carried two. But even walking, Churri would get them to the settlement more quickly.

So many things, *too* many things, to think about. To stave off confusion, to dismiss the image the farm-

steader had planted in her mind of a family sent intentionally into Alisanos, Bethid sought and found her
own certainty: *When Rhuan arrives at the settlement, he'll
explain everything.*

BEHIND A MASS OF underbrush and shrub-
bery near the river's edge, Ilona took the red
signal cloth from beneath the rock that weighted it and
hung it where it could be easily seen by anyone approaching from the settlement. Then she stripped out
of her soiled clothing. It was awkwardly done because
of her splinted forearm, but eventually she managed
it. Tunic, skirt, belt, and smallclothes; she would remove her felted slippers at the grassy verge just before
she stepped into the water. Then, odd as she knew it
was, she tied one end of the rope near the roots of the
largest bush and knotted the other end around her
waist. She acknowledged her weakness, seeing no
shame in it, and realized that though the river's current, here, might not be so strong, she wished to take
no chances. Jorda, Mikal, and probably the Sister
would admonish her if they learned what she did; the
achoring rope provided her with a small defense
against them.

She played out the rope as she walked carefully
down the riverbank, placed the towel and slippers
near the edge, then, gripping the ball of soap in her left
hand despite the splint, used the right to let herself

down. The entire process felt strange, almost comical, but eventually she stepped down into the water, balanced on stones beneath her feet, shivered from the chill, then worked her way carefully down into the pool carved out of the riverbank. The cool water would do well by her broken arm as well, she felt, and if there were any slight residue of fever, that, too, would be banished. Ilona slowly sank into the hip-high pool, hooking the splinted arm across the top of her head, though she imagined no harm would come to it if she got it wet. But she wouldn't do it intentionally; that would give Jorda yet another thing to chastise her for.

Ah. Bliss. After a long moment she raised the splinted arm into the air and tilted her head back, back, until her skull touched the water, soaking her hair. A somewhat deeper dip wetted the rest of her hair and her head, lapping at her face. Ilona released a sigh of relief; then, rising, clutching the soap ball in her right hand, began to scrub hair and skin.

She would be clean again. *Clean.* Ilona revelled in the water, shedding worries along with dirt. Such luxury!

It was as she lathered her hair, staring absently into the distance, that Ilona noticed the trees. New trees. Strange trees, all twisted upon themselves. They were unlike anything she had seen. The forest, perhaps a half-mile away, stood where no forest existed before. She was certain of it.

"Mother," she murmured, chilling again. "Alisanos?"

It must be so. No other forest could simply *arrive* where none had been before.

Mother of Moons, the deepwood. Much too close.

Then, unexpectedly, apprehension faded beneath awed curiosity. Alisanos, visible. Alisanos, here.

And Rhuan, there?

With that thought, Ilona made short work of rinsing soap from hair and body, of climbing out of the pool, of ringing out soaked hair, of removing the rope, drying herself, and donning fresh clothing and slippers. She had not yet washed the garments she'd worn in the storm and for several days after, but that could wait. This might not.

Rhuan might not.

Cradling her splinted arm, with loose, wet hair hanging to her waist, Ilona began to walk. Away from the settlement. Toward Alisanos.

Chapter 17

*A*S ALL CITIES DID, Cardatha began as a small hamlet. In time, more folk arrived to stay, then more and more, all eventually putting up permanent dwellings and businesses. The province lord took up residence, building a large, impressive stone palace. For purposes of defense a wall around the city was also constructed, with a single large barbican gate manned by a contingent of the lord's guard, permitting entry and exit. Originally all residents had lived within the wall, safe behind the defenses, but over time, later arrivals lacking the resources to rent or buy in the city instead assembled flimsy, impermanent market stalls, lean-tos, and shacks outside the wall. Cardatha, sited on a modest hill, sprawled downward, then outward, as if its skirt hem had been tattered.

Certainly the hem had burned.

Upon arrival at Cardatha, the Hecari, who, led by their brutal warlord, had overrun the province, killed every person living outside the wall, regardless of age and gender, and put to the torch the fragile dwellings and stalls. And though the heavy barbican gate, closed and barred against the warriors, initially promised safety to the citizens inside, the Hecari had proven too experienced at conducting a siege. In time, Cardatha— absent its lord, who fought elsewhere in the province because he believed Cardatha would stand—had fallen. And as the warlord and his warriors took possession, one tenth of the residents inside the wall were killed in a first decimation. Months later, another tenth died beneath Hecari warclubs. Shortly afterward, all in the city acknowledged the Hecari leader their lord, even as Sancorra of Sancorra, as he was called, had previously been their lord. Commerce continued. So did lives. No Sancorran suggested revolt. Not one soul made any kind of stand against the Hecari.

The city surrendered its identity. Cardatha retained its name, its dwellings, its businesses inside the wall, but all under the control of the warlord. The bodies of those killed outside the wall had been given rites and buried, but charred wood and collapsed huts, stalls, and shacks still lay in scattered piles against the encircling wall as a reminder to strangers and residents alike. Rain, wind, and time slowly broke down what had once been whole.

Disdaining stone dwellings, including the absent Sancorran lord's luxurious palace, the Hecari had put up large, round, conical-roofed hide tents called *gher* throughout the city, filling the open areas. Cardatha became an amalgam of pale gray stone and fawn-colored hide, all flying the gold-freighted crimson banners of the warlord. The high city wall now provided *the Hecari* with a defense, though in the face of their warlord's cleverness and the loyalty and brutality of his men, and with the former lord now in hiding, no one expected Sancorrans from elsewhere in the province to make an attempt to recapture the city. Cardatha was no longer home to Sancorra's lord, but the principal seat from which the Hecari warlord ruled. All matters of business were brought before him. All taxes and tribute from it and other provinces, accrued to him. His power was absolute. And to remind the residents of this fact every single day, the warlord had his own palace constructed, a huge round *gher* put up in the only available space large enough to host the Hecari palace: Market Square.

As Brodhi and Ferize approached the massive barbican tower and gate, Ferize took her leave, saying she had business of her own. It might or might not be true; for all he knew, she planned to surprise him again at some point in the city. So he rode on alone, and as expected his blue courier's cloak and silver badge gave him immediate entrance before others in long lines waiting to be questioned by the gate guards. Hecari gate guards, not Sancorran; the lord's guards had been executed. Cardatha was now a Hecari stronghold, but those from all provinces overtaken by the warlord had business in the city nonetheless.

Ordinarily, Brodhi would have ridden directly to the couriers' Guildhall to make his report, take some rest, and to accept new assignments, were any in the offing. But things had changed since the arrival of the Hecari; instead, he headed first to Market Square, to the warlord's lattice-and-hide palace. As always, the narrow dirt lanes were crowded, some nearly impassible because the market vendors, deprived of their traditional place in the city, had set up stalls along the lanes that radiated from the square like spokes on a wheel. With the populace strolling those lanes, pausing at various stalls to argue over the prices and quality of various items, and a plethora of loose dogs, cats, and poultry, it was nearly impossible for Brodhi to make his way through. Though Cardathans gave way at once to mounted Hecari, a stranger on horseback who was clearly not Hecari occasioned no such reaction.

Eventually he broke out of the crowded lane and entered the cobbled square, faced on four sides by an assemblage of various guildhalls. The warlord's palace was a huge affair. A broad wooden platform was raised several stair-steps off the ground, and a free-standing hide *gher*, large as six stone dwellings, rose from it. It was round and tall, with a flat-topped, conical peaked roof, incorporating criss-crossed lattices of saplings to form sidewalls over which the hides were laced into position. It also boasted an intricately carved frame for the single door. The exterior hides, stitched together with sinew and leather, were assembled skin-side out, forming rectangular, square, and triangular sections that alternated in color and texture from dark to light, spotted to plain. From the flat roof-ring a crimson banner flew; at each platform corner an iron crook taller than a man also displayed the red banner. As always, thirty Hecari warriors encircled the palace as guards, their hair shorn save for a scalp lock, eyebrows shaved, lower faces painted indigo. Ear-lobes, stretched long and wide, bore heavy golden spools. Four warriors upon the platform stood guard at the *gher*'s door, a heavy slab of joined wooden planks carved into curvilinear and interlinked patterns of immense precision.

Most Hecari warriors knew Brodhi because of his coming and going, reports given to the warlord, messages received from him. Those who didn't know him personally recognized his cloak and badge. He dismounted and a warrior came forward to hold his horse as he retrieved the scroll case from his saddle. Brodhi mounted the triple steps and stood silently upon the platform, the cloak pinned to his right shoulder and looped behind his back through his left arm. He waited.

As expected, one of the door guards eventually asked his business in weak Sancorran. Brodhi, speaking clear if not fluent Hecari, offered an abreviated version; details were due the warlord, not his guards. The warrior went into the huge *gher* and a moment later came back out and indicated Brodhi should follow him.

Brodhi took care not to step upon the golden threshold, which was offensive to the Hecari. He took care not to look at those gathered within the round palace;

from him, it was also an offense. He took care to watch
only his own feet, and to monitor his position in refer-
ence to the guard's. But he knew the palace well from
previous visits. And also he knew the warlord.

Within, the criss-crossed sapling lattices tied with
straps of red-dyed leather formed curving walls as tall
as a man. Above the walls, red painted wooden rafters,
carved in a spiral pattern and wound about with strips
of stamped gold, rose to a flat-topped peak where they
were fastened to the roof-ring. From the rafters hung
banner after banner, all of different colors, shapes, and
sizes, figured, painted, and plain. Also suspended
from the rafters were iron candle racks with fat ocher
candles set into iron cups. Gilt-edged prayer flags and
beaded gold wire wrapped around stone animal
fetishes dangled over Brodhi's head. Vivid tribal tapestries in an amazing array of colors divided the *gher*
into rooms, but half of the palace was reserved for the
warlord's private reception chamber. At that tapestry,
Brodhi halted as he was gestured to do. The guard
slipped in; a moment later he pulled the tapestry aside
and motioned for Brodhi to enter. Brodhi did so, keeping his head down. He also displayed the palms of his
hands, and knew not to withdraw them until bade to
do so, no matter how long it took.

This time, the warlord granted him the right to seat
himself immediately. Brodhi bowed slightly and did
so, placing his hands palm down on his thighs. The
platform within the walls was richly carpeted, and colorful cushions were scattered here and there for

guests. Brodhi knew to take the one placed in front of the warlord's low marble dais, also draped in vibrant tribal rugs. Light was admitted through the open roof-ring; it glowed as well from the hanging candle racks.

The Hecari warlord sat in a heavy wooden chair bound with strips of stamped gold, flanked by six guards, three on each side. The chair legs were quite short so that the cushioned seat was low, but the carved and painted back was very tall, curving forward over the warlord's head at its zenith like a wave in the ocean. Gold affixed to the wood gleamed in the light; gemstones glinted. The man in the seat, dark-skinned and black-eyed, wore amber-dyed silk trews and tunic, beaded slippers, and a fawn-hued tabard heavily embroidered with golden thread. His scalp lock was threaded with a few strands of gray hair, braided, and brought forward over his left shoulder. Decorative gold clasps ran the length of the braid from skull to just past his shoulder, and his ear-spools were gold set with emeralds. In the tradition of his people his head was shaved save for the scalp lock, as were his brows. But while the warriors merely painted their faces, the warlord was indelibly tattooed in indigo ink so that no amount of sweat, blood, or rain could make the paint run or smear, and the enemy, in battle, would always know him.

Brodhi, who reckoned the man around forty, kept his head bowed and his eyes lowered, fixed on the carpet directly in front of his cushion. It was not his place to open a conversation with the warlord, only to be prepared to answer any question, to follow any command. If he did not do so willingly, the guards would guarantee it.

This time it was command. "Tell us," the warlord said in accented but passable Sancorran, "about this—*Alisanos*."

Brodhi did.

OVER SEVERAL ALISANI days, as she reckoned them, Audrun made numerous trips to the stream to fetch water, following the fabric strips she'd tied onto bushes and branches. With the other half of the melon scraped out, she actually managed to fill and carry both, one carefully stacked on top of the other, then cradled in her arms. She still wore Rhuan's knife tucked into the drawstring waistband of her skirt and acknowledged that in order to use it she would have to drop the melons, but until that time came—*if* it came—she felt more secure armed. Her ankle yet pained her, but she kept it wrapped tightly for support, and her limp grew less troublesome.

Rhuan remained unconscious. Audrun began to suspect the demon's talons had contained some form of poison, though he showed none of the expected signs. Other than bruises, there were no discolored streaks radiating from his wounds; if he had a fever at all, it was low; and he never appeared to feel cold. In the dark, Audrun did. And she discovered that if she lay close to Rhuan, resting her body from back to ankles against his, the nighttime chill faded somewhat. Wryly, she reflected that he was rather like the heated, cloth-wrapped bricks she and Davyn put into their beds during winter to provide warmth.

His braids were at last undone. With water at hand, Audrun had spread the crimped hair, found and examined the scalp wounds, soaked them with wet muslin. All were shallow, causing no problem beyond pain and bruised flesh. The biggest concern continued to be the wounds in his abdomen, but Audrun felt those were improving as well, bit by bit. There was no smell of rot, and the edges were clean.

Food was scarce. The other two melons Rhuan had brought back provided sustenance for a while, if only enough to take the edge off her hunger, but didn't last. So Audrun took a hollowed half with her for comparison and went into the trees along the cloth-marked pathway, hoping to find where they had come from. She knew from harvesting pumpkin and gourds that the melons would grow on the ground, linked by woody stems, so she spent her time searching through thick grasses, brush, groundcover, and leaf mold. But the world was shadowed, the forest dense, and it was difficult to see much other than choking brush and vegetation. In the end, she tripped over a root and fell, nearly crushing her nose against a black-rinded melon obscured by undergrowth. Fortunately it matched in all ways the half she'd brought with her, and she harvested as many as she could carry, a clustered weight in a skirt held up to form a makeshift basket. When she returned, she made a small cairn out of them, piled within reach, keeping one aside to open at once.

She was seated next to Rhuan, hammering his knife into the hard rind, when he stirred and made a sound.

Audrun stopped bashing the knife with a rock. She let the melon and the crude hammer fall, but held onto the knife. She moved closer to him, kneeling at his side. "Rhuan?"

Lids fluttered. He inhaled a hissing breath. One hand moved to touch the bandages at his abdomen. After a moment he opened his eyes, frowning faintly.

Audrun smiled, relieved. "I have melon," she announced. "Will you take some? I've been giving you a mush made with water, but if you intend to stay conscious now, you can feed yourself."

His expression was perplexed as he peered up at her. Red flickered in his eyes, then retracted.

Audrun, who had witnessed the confusion in a wounded man when he first came to, decided to assist his memory. "I don't know how many days we've been here," she said, "not in Alisanos time, but I've seen three passes of the suns below the horizon. Three nightfalls. You've slept since then, or something akin to it." She smiled crookedly. "I did manage to get the mush down you and a little water, but you weren't particularly helpful. So if you're hungry, blame yourself." She paused. "Do you remember the fire? The demon?"

His voice was weak. "The dreya are dead."

"Yes, and their ring." She saw his gaze slip by her, saw it light upon charred trees. Saw the horror and grief enter his eyes. "I'm sorry," she said. "There was nothing to be done. You were badly injured, and the fire moved so fast—"

"Dreya trees are hollow," he rasped. "They conduct heat and flames as a chimney does. Once afire, no dreya tree, or dreya ring, can be doused." He shifted a little, winced, investigated with care the sore areas in his abdomen. Then looked into her face, acknowledged what she had not mentioned. "He took the baby from me."

She nodded. She could not speak of it. Not so soon.

Rhuan indicated his bandaged abdomen. "Is this all?"

"Some gashes in your thighs, and slices in your scalp. I cleaned all as best I could with water. I'm sure there are medicinal herbs and plants, even here, but I know none of them and dared not risk it. Perhaps you can tell me what to look for, now that you're awake."

Rhuan's right hand drifted from his abdomen to his scalp. Fingers searched a moment, finding damage, and then stopped. His eyes opened wide in shock. He could not even speak. He stared up at her fixedly, but his thoughts appeared to be somewhere else.

"I took out your braids," she told him. "It was necessary so I could get to the wounds. To wash them." She smiled. "I believe your hair will be longer than mine, once the crimping is out."

"No," he said. "Oh, no . . . no."

"It was necessary," Audrun repeated. "You can braid it again. And I kept all the ornamentation safe."

Rhuan shakily combed his fingers through a wavy section of hair, lifted it for viewing, then let it fall. "Audrun." He swallowed heavily, expression somewhat peculiar—almost as if he suppressed a laugh, which she found quite odd. His voice sounded rather strangled. "Oh, Audrun, this was a mistake. A significant mistake."

She frowned at him. "Unbraiding your hair? Come now, Rhuan, how can something so innocuous be a mistake? Particularly a *significant* mistake?"

He placed his palm over the upper half of his face, blocking his vision. Yes, he was laughing, if very quietly, which baffled and annoyed her even more. "Audrun . . ." He sighed, then removed his hand. She saw a rueful amusement in his expression, his flickering dimples. "Oh Audrun, I'm so sorry, but by unbraiding my hair, well . . . it means you've married me."

Chapter 18

DAVYN—RIDING a horse with the smoothest gait he'd ever felt, even carrying two—was astonished to discover the karavan grove beside the settlement was mostly upended. And a high percentage of the tents, he saw, were missing entirely, with only a handful standing in the wide, flat, foot-beaten area that had once hosted as many as a hundred families, uncounted diviners, and various makeshift businesses. He saw charcoal raked into piles, a collection of broken tent poles, yards of ruined oilcloth. He smelled dirt, burned paint, damp ash, and death.

Bethid, riding behind him on the gelding's broad rump, said, "Very little is left, thanks to the storm. But the survivors are working together, tent-folk and karavaners both, and we're doing the best we can."

He had been lost in his thoughts and anger on the ride, had not even bothered to ask her if the storm had struck the settlement, and how it had fared. The misfortune of his family, the betrayal by the Shoia guide, superseded realization that others suffered, too. Shame knit a knot in his belly.

"Go on that way." She indicated the direction with her finger. "Mikal's tent is there; see the tankard sign? You can get ale and food if you wish—it's the distribution point—but we can also address your problem."

She made it sound entirely too easy, he thought. And who was "we"? "My family is in *Alisanos*." His tone was acerbic, though he hadn't truly meant it that way. "I doubt anyone here can guide me in without repercussion except the Shoia."

"Then if Rhuan's returned without our knowledge—which is possible for who can say what route he took—you can talk to *him* about recovering your family." She hesitated a moment. "Stop here. Get down. Go on into the tent while I tend Churri." She let herself slide over the horse's rump and tail, dropping to the ground. "Tell Mikal what you've told me."

As he dismounted, Davyn had the impression the female courier was annoyed with him. But then she had spoken in favor of the Shoia, had questioned his conviction that the guide had purposely sent his family into danger. Had Davyn himself not survived the storm, no one would be the wiser. All of his family could be in Alisanos, forgotten by the world.

Distribution point, was it? More than an ale tent? Davyn put the courier out of his mind and went into the tent. The tables, he saw, were filled. Other men clustered in front of the plank bar. Davyn had never been in Mikal's ale tent—in fact, he hadn't been in *any* ale tent for years—so he didn't know if the number was unusual, or if the ale-keep served excellent ale and spirits.

His entrance was marked. One by one men fell silent, set tankards on the tabletops, waited with curious, avid expressions. As conversation died, an aisle to the bar opened before him. Davyn walked it, aware of tensile scrutiny. Every man in the place waited for him to speak. He was a stranger to them; but in view of the storm and the uprooting of Alisanos, he supposed he didn't blame them for the nature of their interest.

The ale-keep—Mikal, the courier had named him—wore a patch over one eye. His bulk was such that he ruled the tent merely by standing in it, especially because his station was behind the bar. Davyn walked the aisle, aware of the smell of redleaf chewed to liquid and spat out, lantern oil, cheese and meat and bread, and an astringency he recognized: men under pressure.

Men like him.

He halted before the plank perched atop two large casks. He shook his head to the offer of ale or spirits. When an inquiry came in the ale-keep's deep voice as to whether he desired food, Davyn surprised himself by saying yes. But then, he was hungry. Thirsty, as well; he had not allowed himself to drink often on the walk from the wagon to where the courier had found him.

"My thanks," Davyn said as the ale-keep set meat and cheese before him on a pewter platter. A tankard of ale, though unasked for, arrived as well. He smiled crookedly, drank down a third before turning to the food, then released a breath of relief. He saw a flicker of understanding in the ale-keep's good eye. "Are you Mikal?"

"I am." The voice was a deep rumble. "You've not been in here before."

Davyn shook his head. "We—my family and I— joined Jorda's karavan on very short notice. I had no time to do anything but prepare for travel."

Mikal examined his clothing, the waterskins arrayed about his person, and the weariness evident in his face. "Eat. Drink." the ale-keep said. "You're in need. If you remain, you'll understand we're rationing, but we'll not deny a man who's lived through a deepwood storm and come out in one piece." Mikal pushed the platter across the bar. "Eat, stranger. You're welcome here."

Ravenous now that food was in his view, Davyn fell upon it. Cheese, bread, meat. All fresh and flavorful. And the ale, when he downed it, made him light-headed. "The guide," he managed, after gulping the whole tankard. "The Shoia. Is he here?"

Mikal shook his head. "Rhuan's been missing since just before the storm."

Davyn wiped a forearm across his brow. His head itched. He needed a bath very badly. "Is the karavan-master here? Jorda?"

"Likely at the grove," the ale-keep replied. "Not the small grove where the wagons used to gather; the old one. Yonder." He gestured. Then, "Do you understand what's happened?"

Davyn grimaced. "Too well. But I'm aware that we might not all see it in the same way." He cast a quick glance around the tent. Men had mostly returned to their drinks, their conversations. This news might regain their attention. "I have reason to believe the Shoia guide intentionally sent my family into Alisanos."

"Do you?" Mikal did not obviously react, which was reaction in itself. "Are you aware that Rhuan came here and bade us all go east, so we might escape the storm? And that many of us did?"

"So the courier said."

Mikal's brows shot up. "Bethid's back?"

"She found me on the Atalanda shortcut." Davyn edited further explanation. "When I told her the guide had disappeared, just as my family did, and I hadn't seen him since, she was willing to turn around."

"You're certain Rhuan's missing?"

The question annoyed Davyn. "He came. He left. He took my children and my wife with him. I've seen none of them since." He met Mikal's single eye. "I've come to speak to him. To ask him to guide me into the deepwood, so I may find my family."

The ale-keep's face was a mask. "You would do best to speak to Jorda. I believe he may be able to answer your questions and concerns—those about Rhuan, that is—better than I may. But let me say this to you: best take care what you say to others about what you *think* happened. Because you don't know that it did."

Davyn felt a sinking in his belly. Why was it so many people trusted the guide? Why could they not see what he saw? The Shoia had sent his family *into* *Alisanos.*

He pushed himself upright, leaving a crust of bread, a few bits of meat, crumbled cheese. The tankard was drained. "Then I'll speak to the karavan-master. I thank you for your courtesy."

Indeed, he felt the ale. It carried him, as if he floated, out of the tent.

RHUAN SAW THE utter amazement and disbelief spring into Audrun's eyes and expression. "I've *what*?" she demanded.

"Married me. According to the traditions of my people, after puberty only one person who is not close kin may unbraid or braid a male *dioscuri*'s hair other than himself. That woman, in doing so, announces her acceptance of his suit."

For a moment she only stared at him, white-faced, eyes huge, mouth partially open. Then she recovered her voice, and with it a crisp tone. "This is ridiculous, Rhuan. I didn't bind myself to you. I didn't announce any acceptance of–of a suit that never existed. I only unbraided your hair to clean your wounds."

The topic was becoming more difficult by the moment. He seriously considered pretending to pass out so he could avoid the discussion altogether, but that would only postpone it, not settle it. In a tone carefully modulated so as to prove his neutrality, he explained, "If the man himself has not indicated his interest in the woman, but allows her to unbraid his hair, he accepts *her* suit. If he stops the ritual, no marriage is made."

Audrun scowled. "You were unconscious."

"But all that matters was that I didn't stop the ritual."

"You were *unconscious*."

Rhuan sighed, and winced in response to a fleeting pain in his midsection. "It's been done before."

"What—a woman unbraiding a man's hair while he was asleep or unconscious?"

"Well, yes."

That diverted her. "Doesn't he have any say about it if he doesn't want the woman?"

"Actually, no. At least not initially. To object, he must bring the matter before the Kiba."

Audrun was momentarily speechless, staring at him fixedly. Then she grabbed a hank of his braid-crimped, coppery hair. "Here, then. I'll braid it up again and no one will know the difference."

He closed his hand on hers, halting her fingers. "You can't do that."

"Certainly I can!"

"No . . ." He was too tired to explain properly, but he tried. "You can't rebraid it here, Audrun. It has to be done before witnesses at the Kiba."

The first edges of panic showed in her voice. "That doesn't matter to me! It makes no difference. Rhuan,

in the Mother's name . . . rebraid it, leave it loose; I
don't care. I'm not married to you. I have a husband
already. What do the traditions of your people say
about that?"

To delay his answer, he scratched at an eyebrow. But
she was waiting, obviously tense, and he continued.
"First, you don't know where your husband actually
is. He might be here in Alisanos, he might be in the
human world, but—"

"That doesn't mean he's not my husband."

"—but—" he continued, "—since you've unbraided
my hair, it indicates that your husband is dead, or you
believe he's dead, or that you're setting him aside. If it's
the latter, you're taking me in his place."

She was seriously annoyed. "I didn't set him aside.
Can't you just explain to–to whomever these things
matter that this wasn't intended? I made a mistake. A
significant mistake, as you said. But it wasn't meant to
be any kind of declaration about you, me, or my husband—who *is* still my husband no matter where he is,
or where I am. It was an accident, nothing more. Surely
they'll understand."

Rhuan sighed. "I'm *dioscuri*, Audrun. There are
forms to be followed."

Annoyance was dissipated by increasing anger. "I
don't care if you are the son of a god. I don't care what
your father the god thinks. This—"

"He's a primary, Audrun."

"—was not intended," she continued firmly. "And I
also don't care if he's a primary—whatever that is—or

anything else. Whatever needs to be done to *un*marry you, I'll do it. What is it? You shave your head? I shave mine?" She grabbed handfuls of her own tangled, tawny locks. It's *hair*, Rhuan. Just hair."

"Audrun, Audrun, Audrun." He offered a rueful, crooked smile. "You're in Alisanos. Our customs and traditions override those you know in the human world."

"I'm already married no matter what world I may be in. I haven't set my husband aside, and I don't believe he's dead. And I *am* human. I don't have to pay attention to the customs of your people."

"Well," he said, "you do. They'll make certain of it."

"Who will?"

"The primaries."

"They're all gods, these primaries?"

"One thousand of them. Yes."

That sidetracked her a moment. "Your people have one thousand gods?"

"We do. But there are many more of us who are not gods, let alone primaries."

Audrun visibly wrenched herself back to the original line of discussion. "Well, since I'm merely human without a speck of divinity, it shouldn't matter in the least what I think."

"But it does."

He watched her struggle to not be rude. She achieved it, just, controlling her tone with extreme effort. "Rhuan—I don't want to be married to you."

"Here, you already are married. Or will be, when you rebraid my hair at the Kiba before witnesses."

She pounced on that. "Then we're not married *yet*."

"Well, technically, no. Halfway, you might say. But the vow has been made, just as in your world you plight your troth. It binds us both."

"The vow I made to my husband overrides that."

"This vow was made later. *It* takes precedence."

He watched the myriad emotions flow across her face. He didn't doubt that she wanted to grab up handfuls of dirt, perhaps even his knife, possibly his heart, and hurl them all across the clearing in a fit of fury. Instead she wound her hands in her homespun skirts, cleared her throat, and began again, speaking with extreme precision so that he could not possibly misinterpret what she said. "When we reach the Kiba, I will discuss this matter with your father. I will explain what happened, that I already have a husband, and that I can't—that I *won't*—marry you."

It triggered a shout of laughter, which hurt. After a moment the worst of the pain faded, and he said, with false cheer, "This will be most interesting to witness."

Chapter 19

ILONA, cradling her splinted arm, followed the riverbank as she approached a forest but recently arrived. The distance was, she believed, approximately half a mile and not taxing, unless one was recovering from a broken arm and fever. But turning back wasn't an option; now piqued, her curiosity coupled with the desire to learn what she could, if possible, of Rhuan, were he in the deepwood drove her onward. In all the moments he had sensed the imminence of Alisanos' movement, in his eerie ability to predict where it might go, she had trusted him. Now she was frightened for him, yet also baffled. How could a man with land-sense strong enough to send folk away from the awakening of Alisanos become trapped in the deepwood himself?

But he had gone to assist the farmsteader family. He had placed himself at risk to save them. It was entirely possible he had been swallowed by Alisanos because he refused to remove himself while others were in danger. Ilona was aware of his feckless, charming ways, his skewed sense of humor, his occasional lapses in judgment. Some might name him irresponsible, but she did not. She knew him better than that. As a guide, he let no one in his charge die or be harmed if he could prevent it. He had killed five Hecari warriors in a matter of moments to protect the farmsteader family. He would do it again, even if he died from it. And he may have, with no resurrections remaining.

A world empty of Rhuan.

Ilona desired no part of that.

She halted abruptly. Something welled up in her body, in her heart and mind. She felt fear, anxiety, and denial tied together into a knot. The back of her neck tingled. Her body rang with the impulse to run, to flee, to escape the imminent threat.

What imminent threat?

The forest lay before her. She was only a few steps away from its verge. But she could not find it in herself to take those steps.

Until she saw a familiar man walk out of the trees and shadows.

"Rhuan!" She stepped forward on a surge of relief. "Are you all right . . .?"

But again, she stopped in her tracks. She was close enough, now, to see that the man was not Rhuan after all; to touch him, if they each stretched out an arm. He wore the braids, the ornamentation, shared coloring and a similar stature, but he was not Rhuan.

Mother of Moons . . . it's the man I dreamed about!

He took two long steps and placed himself immediately in front of her, perhaps a pace separating them. Ilona's initial impulse was to back away at once, to put distance between them, but something in her prevented it. An altogether unexpected stubbornness told her to hold her ground, to not act as prey, to not show submissiveness to this man. Were she to do so, she knew—without knowing *how* she knew—she would place herself in very real danger.

Free of the dream, so close she could smell a faint masculine musk, she saw he was very like Rhuan in many regards, but not in all. As in her dream he wore snug, scaled, thin russet hide, supple upon his body. His smile brought forth no dimples. And it was clear he had an amused awareness of how his physical presence affected others, and a willingness to use it. He was beautiful. Not as a woman was; he was entirely male. But he burned so brightly she could think of no other word. This was a man who could rule others merely by letting them look upon him, by being in his presence. They would answer without understanding the power within him.

Ilona felt that power as he stood so close. She recognized it. She had seen men and women before who exhibited this type of self-confidence, this acute inner awareness of superiority. His was an arrogance that set him apart in ways other than physical. And she felt a tendril of the power questing out of his body, approaching her own.

Still she did not move. But he did, circling her the way one dog circles another on first acquaintance. He *examined* her. She was keenly conscious of what he saw: hastily-donned gray-green tunic and skirt; wide, brass-bossed belt; damp hair hanging to her waist. The top layer had dried just enough that loose ringlets had begun to form.

He circled her twice, as if weighing her against an inner image. Ilona disliked it intensely. She decided to divert his attention—and perhaps blunt that annoying power—by asking a question. "Have you taken Rhuan?"

The sense of examination abated. He halted in front of her, so close she could see the delicacy of overlapping scales in the hide tunic and leggings, gleaming as if wet whenever he moved; whenever he breathed. This close, he was overwhelming.

Coppery brows rose over cider-brown eyes. In faultless Sancorran he said, "Have *I* taken Rhuan?"

She amended her question. "Has Alisanos taken him?"

The stranger smiled. "I haven't been paying attention. Alisanos may indeed have taken him. Perhaps I should see if that's so, since there will be serious consequences if true."

"Can you find him, if he's in the deepwood?"

The smile broadened, displayed good white teeth in genuine amusement. "I can always find my son . . . if I bother to try."

BETHID CONSIDERED LEADING Churri over to where the common tent had stood in case Timmon and Alorn had scavenged enough poles and oilcloth to pitch it again, but a sudden desire for ale diverted her intent. Instead, she untacked the gelding, set blankets and saddle upside down against Mikal's tent, changed out the bridle and bit for a rope halter, then led Churri a short distance away to where grass grew in abundance. There she picketed him, patted him, and returned to the ale tent. But before she could enter, the farmsteader exited. By his expression, by the tautness of his shoulders, it seemed likely Mikal had offered no definitive response to any questions about Rhuan. The man, caught up in his own emotions, barely glanced at her as he walked out of the tent and turned toward the grove hosting karavan wagons.

Perhaps he'll fare better with Jorda . . . Bethid slipped into the ale tent. At once she was assailed by the sights, the sounds, the odors she always associated with an ale tent. In the midst of upheaval within the settlement, this she recognized. It grounded her immediately. And the sight of Mikal, leaning forward on arms braced against the surface of his bar, kindled a rush of relief. As a courier—and as herself, different from her family in so many ways—she had no true home, but this settlement, this tent, with this man present, offered a sense of comfort and familiarity.

He saw her making her way through the tables and

men who stood closely among one another, and set up a pewter tankard of ale. She thanked him with a smile as she arrived and drank a few deep swallows, heedless of the foam.

Mikal waited until she quenched her immediate thirst and wiped her lip. His voice was quiet. "I understand from the farmsteader that Rhuan isn't to be found."

Contentment dissipated. Her smile faded. "Not yet. He seemed certain that he would have seen Rhuan if he were anywhere nearby, but I'm not sure that's so. Things out there are—different. The main road north is now blocked by Alisanos, so I had to cut across a different way to join up with the Atalanda shortcut. Rhuan may have done the same." She shrugged. "Who's to know the route he took? I think many of us will be making new tracks and roads now that the world has changed."

Mikal's expression was grim. "I admit he annoys me from time to time with his unrepentently vile sense of humor, but we need him here. With Alisanos so close, his gifts and experience are vital."

Bethid drank more rich brown ale, wiped residual foam away. "We do need him, yes. But I don't see how we can find him under the circumstances. It's much too dangerous to send out a true search party for Rhuan—or the family. I think he'll have to find *us*." She glanced over her shoulder, marking that no one paid attention to her. But she lowered her voice regardless. "I'm assuming the farmsteader told you his theory that Rhuan sent his family into Alisanos on purpose."

"He did." Mikal shook his head. "That's a dangerous rumor to spread. That Rhuan's Shoia has always either intrigued or concerned folk, probably frightened some of them, and the Mother knows all kinds of tall tales are spread about him, but just now we need no one distrusting him if—*when*—he does return. I did warn the farmsteader about talking to others without knowing what happened for certain, but I doubt it will do much good."

Bethid considered that. "The karavaners knew to trust Rhuan on the journey, even if they did have to turn back. And certainly several of us can speak to his determination to urge everyone *here* to safety. I mean, why would he intentionally send a family into Alisanos? And if all of them, including Rhuan, were taken by the deepwood, can't the farmsteader see that he's a victim, too?"

"I think just now he can't see anything beyond his grief and desperation. And after a Hecari culling and a terrible storm, the loss of goods and lives, it may be that folk here will be all too willing to believe anything."

Bethid frowned. "Brodhi may face the same reception when he returns."

Mikal snorted an abbreviated laugh. "Well, Brodhi's another tale entirely. I don't know anyone here who *ever* trusted him." He sighed then, rubbed a hand through dark hair. "We can only hope Rhuan brings the family here, that he got them to safety and stayed with them until things settled. But if a pregnant woman and four children did end up in Alisanos, and Rhuan did not . . . well, for his own safety he'd better not come back here at all. Having however many additional lives are left won't save him—he'll just be killed again and again until the final death occurs."

Bethid opened her mouth to comment, but broke off as the noise level and intensity in the tent suddenly altered. Its tone was odd. She turned, her back now to the bar, and saw that Naiya had entered. It was immediately obvious that every male in the tent, except perhaps for Mikal, believed she had come in search of a man for the night. Certainly she did not move as if that were so, or invite attention with beckoning smiles, and a light shawl discreetly draped lent her respectability. She did not so much as glance at the men. She came directly to the bar, gaze flicking between Mikal and Bethid.

In a low, husky voice devoid of seduction, she told them Ilona was missing.

IT WAS A delicate line he walked, in the palace of the warlord. Brodhi answered every question as many times and ways as they were asked, and took great care to offer information he'd already reported. A courier's memory for language, inflection, things not said, things not meant, stood him in

good stead whenever he met with the Hecari warlord. He let no impatience show, no weariness, no
boredom, only calm attentiveness. When asked, he
answered. When necessary, he explained at length.
Though seated on a fine, comfortable cushion, he
wished very much to stand. He wished very much to
walk. He'd been riding for five days straight.

But this was the Hecari of Hecari, as the Sancorrans
called him after their own tradition. What his given
name was, Brodhi didn't know, nor did he care. Knowing a ruler's name was not important; knowing his
mind was. And so Brodhi sat upon the cushion and
talked himself dry. At long last, with a glint in his eye,
the warlord gestured for water to be served. One of the
guards responded immediately, setting an engraved
silver goblet into Brodhi's hands and waited while he
drank. When the goblet was empty, the guard re-
claimed it at once and resumed his place beside the
throne.

"We begin again," the warlord said, who also had
drunk nothing since Brodhi was shown into his tapes-
tried chamber. "This place, this *Alisanos-deepwood*,
culled that gathering more heavily than my warriors."

"It did, my lord. I did not take an accounting before
I left, but no whole tents—*gher*—remained, and bodies
were scattered across the grasslands. Men, women,
children."

"And the land itself is changed, in this *tent*-place beside the river."

"It is, my lord."

The warlord's fingernails were painted gold. It did not, on this man, look effeminate. He tapped several of them on the armrests of his chair. Then contemplation ended. "I will send warriors with you, to see this *Alisanos-deepwood*."

Brodhi had expected it. "Of course, my lord. But they must be warned of the deepwood's nature. It may move again at any time. One is not necessarily safe near the forest even if a road runs into it. It is important to stay a safe distance away."

The warlord nodded once. Then he smiled faintly, but it was an edged, cruel smile. "You serve well, but what will you do when I replace all couriers with my own men?"

It came as no surprise that the warlord would, at some point, wish loyal Hecari to bring tidings to him, to carry word of the warlord's edicts. But Brodhi intended, by then, to be back in Alisanos; the warlord's future actions and activities meant less than nothing to him.

He answered carefully nonetheless, because an answer was expected. "Sancorra is not my land, nor are its people mine. Perhaps there will be room for a Shoia in your service."

A flicker of surprise and consideration shone briefly in the warlord's dark eyes. Then he made a gesture. "You may go. To your Guildhall, yes?"

"If I may, my lord."

Another gesture with golden nails. "Go. Go. Warriors will come for you in the morning."

Brodhi supressed a grimace as he rose; he'd been hoping for two or three nights in a comfortable bed with no saddle in sight. But one did not ask that boon of this warlord. Brodhi bowed, showed empty palms again, then followed a guard out of the chamber. Once more he looked at no one, though they made quiet jibes to fluster him; once more he did not step on the golden threshold. And as he went down the steps his mount was waiting, reins in the hands of another warrior.

Many Hecari had come into the square to see the foreign courier. All watched him mount. All watched him ride out.

DAVYN FOUND THE karavan-master in the midst of the grove, counting spare wagon canopies. Jorda was surrounded with an array of kegs, casks, bags of sugar, salt, flour, beans, seed corn, potatoes, medicinal herbs, tea makings, an open trunk heaped with mismatched clothing and bedding, wicker crates of hens and chicks, and such oddments as a man's pipe, a woman's comb, a child's tin whistle. Once the canopies were counted, Jorda took a rough-made sheet of paper pinned to a thin, square plank from a three-legged stool. And he had, Davyn saw, a quill pen stuck behind one ear.

Jorda glanced up from his figuring as Davyn approached. A brief smile crinkled the flesh high on his cheeks; the rest of his face was hidden by ruddy beard. "Rhuan found you in time, then. A fortunate day for you and yours."

It struck Davyn like a hard blow in the gut. He stared blankly at the karavan-master for a long, empty moment, trying to sort through the thoughts crowding into his mind. This man, this man would not be easy to convince of Rhuan's perfidy; this man, in fact, might well be impossible to convince.

His throat was tight. "Please," he said. "If you please . . . tell me where the Shoia is most likely to go when he's not here."

Jorda's brows lifted. "But he must be here—he brought you back."

"No." Davyn shook his head, tried to open his throat so the words were easier. "He didn't. He didn't bring anyone back. All of them are gone."

"All of—O Mother, not your family!" The karavan-master was stunned. "They're not here with you?"

"No. No. Only me." He smoothed broad hands down the nap of his tunic front. "He–he did come for us. He found us in the storm. And he told us to go north."

That mattered to the karavan-master. "North? Not east?"

"North."

"But we were told to go east."

The crux of the matter was upon them. Davyn drew in a deep breath, tried to steady his voice, tried not to be strident. "He drew us a map that night. The night before you took us out onto the road. He drew us a map so we would have an idea where we'd find the shortcut. He told us, too, that he has land-sense, that he can tell where the deepwood intends to move. He knew. He *knew*." Tears brimmed. Davyn dashed them away. "He never said east. Not to us. He sent them north. Into Alisanos."

That told, in the sudden knitting of ruddy brows. "If it was in the midst of that storm, it's understandable that you may have misunderstood what he said—"

"I didn't," Davyn declared. "I will swear . . . I will swear to you by the Mother of Moons that this man— this Shoia—sent my children and my wife into Alisanos."

Jorda was stunned by the statement. "Not intentionally!"

Davyn closed his eyes against the disbelief, then looked at the karavan-master steadily. "I think—I think yes. Intentionally."

"It's just not possible—"

Davyn overrode him. "He took my youngest up on his horse, told my eldest also to go, sent my wife and me after them. That was the last I saw of any of them."

"Lost in the storm, I can see, and yes, if they were in the way of Alisanos as it moved—but because he *took* them there? On purpose?" Jorda shook his head. "Not Rhuan."

An odd calm came into Davyn's spirit, lending him self-control and certainty. "He sent them north, karavan-master. Not east, into safety. Into Alisanos."

He made a forestalling gesture before Jorda could speak again. "I went north, as told. As he told all of us, from youngest to oldest. I found none of them. But Alisanos, oh, yes. *That*, I found."

"Jorda!" A woman's shout, and hoofbeats. Davyn abruptly lost the karavan-master's attention; all of it went to the woman courier on horseback, pale hair cropped short, ear-hoops swinging. Davyn noted that she rode bareback, and the only control she had of the horse's head was a halter and a lead-rope looped and tied as a single rein. She halted beside them, face taut with urgency. "Have you seen Ilona?"

Jorda frowned. "Isn't she sleeping?"

The courier shook her head. Ear-hoops glinted. "The Sister told us she's not in her wagon." She flashed a glance at Davyn, who saw a shade, the barest whisper, of brief but pointed assessment, coupled with something that he thought, in sudden shock, might even be contempt. "Jorda, you know her best of all of us, I think—where might she go?"

For a moment the karavan-master was clearly at a loss. "She's a woman, Beth—*you* might have a better idea. But then, if she's delirious, nothing will make sense. She could be anywhere."

The courier frowned, thinking. After a moment her expression brightened in triumph. "Hah. She'd want a bath! *I* would, after a storm out of Alisanos showered me with grit and dirt and ash. And a broken arm that kept me in bed in the same clothes for days to boot."

"The river," Jorda said instantly. "It must be, with

the bathing tent destroyed. O Mother, Alisanos is now very close to the river, and she doesn't know it!"

The courier nodded, gathering lead-rope rein. "I'll go ahead now. Follow if you can."

"Go on, Beth." Jorda looked again at Davyn. "We shall speak of this more, this tale you tell, but just now this is more pressing."

The words fell out of Davyn's mouth before he could rethink them. "One? One woman against four children and a wife? A *pregnant* wife?"

The karavan-master's brows knit together. "This isn't a competition. Best you remember that."

Davyn closed his eyes, ashamed, wishing he could unsay the words. But it was too late. The karavan-master was already in motion, striding across the grove as he shouted for Janqeril, the horse-master. Later, then. He would apologize later.

Later, yes, an apology. Yet a tiny part of Davyn's heart, regardless of the shame, told him that one woman's welfare was *not* after all equal to the loss of a man's children and his pregnant wife.

Chapter 20

*A*UDRUN, sitting cross-legged beside the cairn of black melons, watched as Rhuan began the slow, painful process of sitting up. She had suggested he not do so; he insisted he should. So she clamped her mouth shut and did not so much as wince in sympathy as he grunted and swore his way through the activity. Upright, holding his torso rigidly still, he saw his leggings for the first time in days.

He was startled. "What did you do?"

"What did I do where?"

He pointed. "My leggings." He peeled back one of the flaps and bared a claw-punctured leg, but seemed far more concerned about his knife-slit clothing. "Both of them?"

"One does prefer to tend wounds in the open," she noted, "as it's a trifle difficult to manage if the patient is wearing vastly ornamented leather trews cut a little on the snug side to begin with." She recalled that on first meeting Rhuan when she accosted Jorda about

letting their family join the karavan, she had assumed
the guide was vain because of all the ornamentation in
braids and on garments. Apparently that assessment
was correct. "They're just leggings, Rhuan. It's not a
fatal thing. Punch a few holes, cut off some of the
fringe, lace the flaps back together." Audrun
shrugged. "I don't know why it should matter. Your
tunic has been used for everything from a sling for a
newborn to a temporary clout." She caught his expression of startled horror. Well, she truly hadn't meant to
tell him the last part. Probably no one wanted to put
on a tunic that reeked of urine, even be it from a newborn. She swiftly changed the subject. "I did the best I
could, but it would be wise to clean those wounds
with something other than water and muslin. Is there
a plant you can point out that I can use for a proper
cleansing?"

He was still examining his leggings, looking for all
the world as if he were in mourning. After a moment
he scowled at her. "You've unbraided my hair, sliced
my leggings to bits, and turned my tunic into a latrine.
Is there any other damage you would care to do?"

"Oh, best you not ask that," she replied promptly,
"else I will do worse. Which my family well knows."
But she would not dwell on family, not until she had
privacy. Instead, she arched her back, stretched her
arms, and rolled her head on its neck. The movements
dropped his knife from her lap to the ground.

The sound he made seemed to be one of disbelief

coupled with outrage. *"What have you done to my knife?"*

"Oh." She glanced sidelong at the rock she had employed as a hammer. "I used it to open the melons."

"Used it *how*?" He reached, stopped short, thought better of it as the movement rekindled pain. Gritting his teeth, he put out his hand, palm up. "Please."

"As a chisel." Audrun picked up the weapon and handed it to him. "Will you hold mourning rites for this, too?"

He looked over the knife, then glared at her. "Why didn't you just smash the *melon* with the rock? You wouldn't have needed my knife for that!"

"Oh," she said again. Yes, she could have done that very thing. Had it occured to her. Chagrined, she offered, "I can lace up your leggings, if you like."

He ignored the offer, very intently examining the damaged end of his horn-handled knife with deep consternation. He glanced up at her as if he wished to say something less than polite, but he didn't. He stared at her a moment, then began to laugh. He winced and clutched at his abdomen, but the laughter continued, if somewhat more muted.

"What?" Audrun demanded.

Laughter died to a grin. Dimples appeared along with a flash of teeth. "We are both of us unfit for polite company. You've hacked apart your underskirt, torn open your bodice, have welts and cuts all over your legs and a few on your face, seasoned with sap. And then, well . . . there's your hair." He shook his head. "I'm not sure it won't all have to come off."

Her hands flew to her head. "My *hair*?"

"Ah," he said, nodding solemnly. "Now she understands." He slid his damaged knife back in its sheath. Audrun was quite certain she would never be trusted with it again. "So. Melons." He eyed her black-skinned cairn. "Perhaps tomorrow I can find something else."

"Tomorrow?" She was surprised. "You aren't well enough for that."

"I heal very quickly. That is, if women don't poke their fingers into my gut." He surveyed the bandage wrapped around his torso. No new bloodstains. "Tomorrow, though. Not today." He shook back a curtain of braid-crimped coppery hair, looking past her to the charred dreya ring. The humor left his eyes. He said something quietly in a tongue she didn't recognize, then looked at her. "Rites," he said. "That first, tomorrow."

She nodded acknowledgment, then gathered the two halves of the melon she'd been using as bowls and rose. "I'll go for water."

He raised his voice as she walked away. "About now, I'm wishing we had spirits!"

"The better to clean your wounds with, yes," she threw over her shoulder.

Much affronted by that blasphemy, he shouted after her as she stepped into the shadows, "I meant the better to *drink* with!"

Which did not in the least surprise her.

BETHID DISCOVERED THE red cloth hanging on a bush down by the river's edge, near the pool used when folk wished not to pay coin to use the public bath tent. Of more concern, however, was that Ilona's soiled clothing was there as well. That she should change into fresh garments after finishing a bath was not in the least unexpected, but finding the others abandoned made no sense. Bethid slid off Churri's bare back and squatted to get a closer look at the stained skirt and tunic. She found nothing untoward. And the rope? She had no idea what that was for. Possibly someone else had left it.

A thought occured, one so obvious that Bethid rolled her eyes in self-derision. She should have known the hand-reader might seek brush other than where people generally left their clothing as they bathed behind which she could relieve herself. "Ilona? Are you here?"

No response of any kind.

She heard approaching hoofbeats and, as expected, Jorda arrived on one of the draft horses. Once he reined in, she gestured at the soiled clothing. "I found these. But no sign of Ilona. I called for her, but received no answer."

Jorda, frowning, contemplated the red cloth and clothing a moment. Then he said, "I don't like this, Beth. Fever can do odd things to people, and Ilona hasn't been herself since she was injured."

"I know she's very concerned about not being able to read hands." Bethid glanced at the grass on which she stood. "Jorda, I can try tracking her. The grass is tall here; it should be easy enough to find where her steps have pressed it down. Will you hold Churri for me and follow along while I track on foot?"

Jorda, nodding, accepted the lead-rope once the end was untied and took two wraps around his saddle horn, snubbing the gelding up fairly short. Bethid searched the verge until she found grass pressed flat, noted that indeed a faint series of indentations progressed along the riverbank, and began to follow it. Jorda fell in behind, keeping the horses well back.

The river swung right in a lazy curve, but the footprints did not follow it. They led Bethid directly to the west, into the open grasslands. Within a matter of moments, not far from the edge of the deepwood's new incursion, Bethid saw Ilona. The hand-reader was walking back the way she had come.

"Ilona!" Bethid broke into a jog. "Ilona—are you all right?"

Ilona looked up and stopped. She waited until Bethid reached her before speaking. Puzzled, she said, "I'm not sure how I got here."

"Here? You walked. I tracked you."

Ilona's frown deepened. "I have no memory of it. I recall bathing in the pool, no more." She glanced back toward the forest's edge, none too distant. "Why in the world would I go *toward* Alisanos?" A brief shiver traveled through her body as she turned back to Bethid. "Have I been gone so long a search party was necessary?"

"It's just me," Bethid told her, "and Jorda. And no, you haven't been gone all that long, but when the Sister couldn't find you at your wagon, she was concerned. So were we." Before Ilona could protest, Bethid placed a hand against her brow. "But you don't feel fevered."

"I feel fine . . . well, as fine as one can be with a broken—O Mother, what did I do?"

Bethid understood the question and concern at once. Ilona's left arm was naked of splint and wrappings. "Well, we can resplint it when we get you back to your wagon."

Frowning, Ilona raised her left arm. She made a fist and rotated her hand, then looked at Bethid in astonishment. "There's no pain at all. It feels like it always did, before I broke it."

"Bones don't heal that quickly," Bethid said. "It will be weeks before you're out of the splint—or *should* be out of the splint, that is." She stepped closer. "May I look?"

Ilona offered her arm. Bethid very gently took it into her hands and began to press carefully in different places along the forearm. She expected Ilona to discover that the arm did in fact hurt, but no such comment was forthcoming. They looked at one another with identical expressions of confusion.

"It doesn't hurt," Ilona repeated. Then she looked beyond Bethid and her mount. "Here's Jorda."

Jorda reined in as he came up on them. His eyes were only for Ilona. "What happened?"

She shook her head. "I have no recollection of anything. Just the river. Jorda . . ." She lifted her left arm once more. "Somehow, I've healed."

He scowled as he saw the arm absent of splint. "It's too soon for you to be healed. Why did you take the splint off?"

She shook her head again. "I have no memory of doing so. But it's *healed*, Jorda." She rotated a fist again. "Ask Bethid."

Bethid nodded as Jorda looked to her for confirmation. "It certainly appears so. When I examined it, she said there was no pain." She took Churri's lead-rope from Jorda and knotted the end into the gelding's halter.

"It's whole," Ilona insisted. "There is no reason for me to claim it's healed if it's not. By the Mother, I swear it feels fine."

Still frowning, Jorda looked beyond his diviner to the edge of the forest. "How far did you go, 'Lona?"

She glanced back a moment, then met Jorda's eyes. "I don't know. All I remember is bathing in the river." Her tone went dry as she glanced down at herself and smoothed the fresh tunic with her right hand. "But apparently at some point I changed clothes, for which I'm most glad." She encircled her forearm with her right hand as Bethid had, moving her hand up and down the forearm, squeezing as she did so. "Truly, it feels whole. There is no pain. But I have no explanation for it."

Jorda glanced at Bethid. "Fever?"

"None that I could tell."

The karavan-master sighed deeply, then looked back at Ilona. "Healed or no, it would put me at ease if you returned to your wagon to rest. Ride behind me, if you would. I'll deliver you." He glanced at Bethid as he dismounted. "I am remiss—I should have collected her other clothing at the river. Would you bring them?"

With the lead-rope rein in place again, Bethid grabbed mane and swung up onto Churri's slick back. "Of course. But first, well, I believe I'll undertake a little exploration."

He knew at once what she meant.

"Beth, that's dangerous. It's too close. You put yourself at risk."

"I have every intention of being remarkably careful." Bethid smiled crookedly. "But if you like, I can make another vow to the Mother concerning this reconnaissance. And I did return from the other one."

Jorda gestured at Ilona to step into his linked hands for a boost up behind his saddle; he clearly didn't trust her left arm to stand for pulling her up. "This is very much different, and you know it."

She sighed, nodding. "I know. But it must be done, Jorda. *Something* happened to Ilona. We need to learn where she went."

Jorda thrust Ilona upward and gave her time to settle her legs and skirts into place, then mounted by placing left foot in the stirrup and swinging his bent right leg forward and across the horse's neck and saddle, since Ilona's presence behind him prevented a normal mounting. "I don't like it."

Bethid expelled a short laugh. "Oh, I don't *like* it. But I think it needs to be done." She made a shooing gesture. "Go on, Jorda. Get her back to her wagon. I'll return shortly. I'm not expecting to find anything, but that in itself may be an answer."

Jorda said nothing more, but his eyes were unhappy. He nodded and turned his horse. Bethid watched them go, then reined Churri in the other direction and rode straight toward the deepwood.

Chapter 21

*T*HE COURIERS' GUILD in Cardatha opened onto Market Square, as did all of the major guildhalls. It was a hollow square of hewn masonry, with three sides consisting of stable blocks, stalls, and paddocks for the horses; in the very center stood a large round pen for breaking and training mounts. The fourth side of the Guildhall contained the barracks: refectory, meeting chamber, private chambers belonging to the Guildmaster and his assistants, and one large communal chamber hosting sleeping pallets. At any given time, the sleeping chamber was inhabited by weary couriers. Those awake, if not seeking amusement in taverns, generally spent their time in the refectory near food and drink, seated around a huge rectangular slab of table, trading stories and jests.

Brodhi rode in through the main gate just off the Market Square, the clatter of shod hooves on stone becoming a quieter thump on the packed dirt. As usual, one of the junior couriers was there to meet him and take his horse; Brodhi dismounted, collected his scroll case, saddle pouches, and personal belongings, then handed the reins over. His first task, now, was to report to the Guildmaster. Later would come food, drink, and rest. Too much later, likely, for the balance of the day and night promised to be short; Brodhi had no doubts that the Hecari warriors would arrive at the Guildhall just after dawn, and he had much to do before he fell into bed.

He made his way through the heavy front door of the main hall, strode down a corridor, and came to a halt before a chamber door. The door stood open. Brodhi placed himself in it, but did not enter. The Guildmaster, going over a logbook at a table, looked up, registered his identity, beckoned him in. Brodhi walked in and waited before the table.

This chamber, too, was of hewn stone, with candle racks in each corner, three chairs set against walls bedecked with tapestries, wooden shelving stacked with unrolled scrolls pressed flat by the weight of others. Pinned to the tapestry directly behind the Guildmaster's table was a large map of Sancorra province made of fine, scraped vellum, carefully inked in rich colors to show roads, passes, rivers, lakes, waterholes, hamlets, villages, cities, forests, and other various landmarks couriers might encounter on the roads. An ornate compass rose in the lower right corner showed the cardinal points, and the entire map was bordered by rich colors touched with gilt. It was art, and it was utility, and it was very nearly priceless.

The Guildmaster, dressed in black, cropped dark hair beginning to silver, set aside his logbook and quill pen and sat back in his chair. Gray eyes were shrewd but unwelcoming; Brodhi knew full well that his attitude irked the Guildmaster. He dropped scroll case, saddle pouches, and other belongings into a chair, then skipped the preliminary courtesies. "Alisanos has moved."

The Guildmaster blinked; Brodhi knew he hadn't been anticipating any news of that sort. "Good Mother," the man said, "tell me this is a very poor jest."

Brodhi shook his head. "I was present."

The Guildmaster closed his eyes briefly, then sat forward and rested his arms on the table. "Where, exactly? Such as you can tell me, of course. What about the roads?"

"There is a settlement where folk gather to join karavans headed out of Sancorra. Near a shortcut to Atalanda, which has been used only rarely in the past forty years because of its proximity to Alisanos. It's not precisely a hamlet or village, just a gathering place. It has no name. But I went there too, when I found it, to announce that Sancorra of Sancorra was executed, as bade by the warlord. Several days later the deepwood moved, swallowing much land. No one knows, now, how its boundaries lie upon the earth. But I can tell you that a portion of the road to Cardatha from this gathering place is now blocked by the deepwood. I had to find another way."

The Guildmaster rose, handed Brodhi a thin, glyph-carved map-stick—skin oils and grime would stain the vellum—and indicated the map on the wall behind him. "Show me."

Accordingly, Brodhi rounded the table, found Cardatha on the map, and began to move the stick westward from the city along the established road. Then he halted the movement and tapped lightly. "Here is where Alisanos encroaches. I went this way . . ." He traced the route he had made, pointed out the crossroads for the northbound and southbound roads, then drew an invisible circle in the midst of emptiness on the map, save for a blue-inked river. "Here, approximately, is where the settlement lies. Because of the northern road, because of the river and two immense groves, karavans began using this area as a gathering place. But some people remained. Now, there may be one hundred people here at any given time, even when there are no karavans." He caught himself. "Fewer now, because of Alisanos going active. But here is where a portion of the deepwood lies now. Very close, as you'll see."

The Guildmaster's eyes seemed distant, as if he were looking elsewhere. Then his gaze sharpened. "I lived through the last movement of Alisanos. I prayed there would be no more."

"There will always be more. Those who believe otherwise are shortsighted, and place themselves in harm's way."

The Guildmaster studied him a moment, evaluat-

ing, Brodhi knew, whether the comment was intended
for him personally, or was about people in general.

"Alisanos cannot be predicted," Brodhi continued.
"I have land-sense enough to know when it's on the
verge of going active, and in what direction part of it
might go, but no one alive may predict what may
come. All we can do is try to avoid it."

After a moment the Guildmaster nodded. "We need
new maps."

"I've begun." Brodhi gestured toward his pile of
belongings. "But it will take time to reconnoiter the
new footprint of the deepwood. Until then, I can
only offer a limited amount of information." He
paused. "The warlord is sending men tomorrow to
ride back with me. He wishes to be certain I'm telling
him the truth. There was a decimation there not long
ago; he wants to know how many folk Alisanos
killed or swallowed, and how many remain."

"Was he aware of Alisanos, and what it is?"

"Until I told him, no."

"Were any other couriers present at this settlement
when Alisanos moved? Were any killed?"

"None killed. Timmon and Alorn are there, and
Bethid."

"Bethid." The Guildmaster grimaced; he had been
one of those most adamantly opposed to Bethid join-
ing the guild. "Well, we are fortunate that none were
killed. They remain there?"

"Many folk were killed. Those who survived have
no alternative for the time being and are determined to

rebuild. Timmon, Alorn, and Bethid stayed to help. I came here."

"Very well." The Guildmaster's mouth was set in a thin, flat line. "By the Good Mother, it is difficult enough having to deal with the warlord, may the Mother one day lift that presence from us. And now Alisanos?" He shook his head. "By morning I need a map of this area, Brodhi, as clear as you can make it under the circumstances; it will be incomplete, of course, until we can send members of the Mapmakers' Guild to survey the area, but any knowledge is vital. For now, with four of you in this place, I need send no more couriers there. Finish the rough map before morning, if you will, and I'll have it sent to the mapmakers for fair copies. When we know more, it will be added to this master." He turned back to his table and chair. "Eat and drink first. Then begin." His casual gesture was dismissal.

Brodhi inclined his head briefly, gathered up his gear, and departed the chamber.

WITH AUDRUN GONE for water, Rhuan felt more motivated to climb to his feet, if at all possible, because then he would have no audience if it proved more difficult than he hoped. What he had told her was true: despite being capable of dying in Alisanos, he healed more quickly even here than a human, as he did in the human world. Her ministrations had indeed kept the wounds clean, so the healing process was not delayed. The abdominal wounds remained the worst, but they too, despite the remaining pain, had begun to heal.

Kneeling, he placed one hand against the earth and pushed himself up. The effort required two tries to gain his feet and he felt a little light-headed, but he managed to stand. Triumph indeed. No doubt after he had a normal meal instead of mashed melon he would begin regaining strength. In the meantime, he wished to reenter the dreya ring, if only briefly. Fortunately it was only a few paces away.

The trees themselves were charred skeletons, many with broken limbs. Living wood had burned through, so that little force was needed to break other limbs. It was possible that if Rhuan leaned on one of the burned trunks, he could knock the tree down entirely. He walked through ash, crunched across charcoal. The heaps at the bottom of each trunk were not recognizable as women, or even as formerly living beings.

Rhuan stopped in the center of the ring and turned in a circle, looking up into the hole left in the forest canopy. The light from two suns, unhindered by leaves and limbs, shone blindingly bright. He dropped the membrane over both eyes, now viewing the world through a red scrim.

He felt plenty of guilt. Had he and Audrun never set foot in the ring, the dreya and their trees would still be alive. He had asked them for help, explaining things to the queen, and they had offered it. Now all were dead

because of providing that help. At the time it had felt
more than worth the risk, to protect an infant. But now,
with Sarith stolen, the dreya had died in vain.

He saw a drift of ash, and something protruding
from it. It appeared to be leather. Rhuan bent and
caught the thing and pulled it free. His tunic. It was
charred in spots, scuffed, with spark holes here and
there, but it was mostly whole. He shook it out, a cloud
of ash wafting into the air, and saw that it was still
wearable. It had been, as enumerated to Audrun, a
sling for a newborn, employed to hold blackfruit and
seedpods, then served as clout for the infant. Some of
the ornamented fringe that ran down the outer seam of
the sleeves was burned, but the tunic still resembled
clothing. Rhuan shook it out again, wiped it down
with his hand, slipped off the baldric with its weight of
throwing knives, then finally worked his head and
arms into the leather tunic despite the pain it caused.
Whatever odor Sarith may have imparted to it was
gone; all he smelled now was smoke and burned
leather. That, he could bear. It wanted cleaning, but
then, so did he.

"Rhuan?" Audrun's voice, calling. "Rhuan!"

"I'm here." He walked out of the circle, settling the
baldric across his leather-clad chest. "What is it?"

She was somewhat out of breath. Tangled tawny
hair looked worse than ever, and her clothing was
filthy. "The creek," she gasped, trying to catch her
breath. "The creek is gone!"

"Did you take a wrong turn?"

Audrun shook her head. "I followed the route markers. When I reached the last one, no stream was there. It's just brush and trees!"

He nodded, loosing a long breath. "Well, either the creek changed locations, or the path you marked did. We'll have to look elsewhere for water."

She pushed hair out of her face and stared at him. "You take it very calmly."

"Audrun, I told you Alisanos changes itself, often overnight. Even with route markers, you can end up lost. We were fortunate the creek remained in that place as long as it did."

"Then what do we do? We need water, Rhuan."

"Tomorrow," he said. "You've brought blackfruit; the meat is moist and will get us through the night. Come morning, we need to start for the Kiba anyway. We should find a stream somewhere along the way."

She looked at the pile of melon, then nodded absent acknowledgment. When she met his eyes again, he saw a weary sorrow. "Can your people at the Kiba recover my baby?"

"We shall ask," he said quietly. "We shall ask if they can give us leave to find all of your children."

Audrun nodded again. She walked shakily to the melon cairn and sat down, taking up the rock she'd employed as a hammer.

He said, as she seemed to be searching for something, "Break the melon open with the rock. You don't need my knife as a chisel, trust me."

She smiled slightly, though it was more of a grimace, then commenced smashing stone into rind.

ILONA, DELIVERED ON horseback to her wagon, ignored Jorda's suggestion that she sleep and instead sat in her open doorway, slippered feet set two steps down. Repeatedly she made a fist of her left hand and rotated it back and forth, up and down, testing her forearm. There was no pain. There was no stiffness. She could have sworn no injury had ever occured.

So, if it were true, as Bethid had suggested, that the broken arm had prevented her from reading hands, her gift should have returned. But she wouldn't know until someone allowed her to try. Jorda was too busy. The Sister had returned to her wagon. Bethid was exploring the land near the deepwood. And Ilona didn't feel strong enough to walk over to Mikal's tent.

She took up the mug of tea Naiya had left her. Breathing in the spiced, herbal scent, she tried to recall exactly what had happened when she left the river to walk to the fringes of Alisanos. She had *known* what it was; how not, when prior to the storm no such forest had existed? Why would she purposely go so close? She had no death wish. She wanted nothing to do with Alisanos. And yet she had walked away from the river, walked across the grasslands, and had stood upon the very verge of the deepwood.

Something had happened, there at the transition between the human world and Alisanos. But she could not say what. When she attempted to search her memories, she found nothing. Everything that had occured between putting on fresh clothing at the river and Bethid coming upon her was a blank.

She sipped her tea, framed by the doorjamb. Jorda had promised a replacement for her wagon canopy come morning. Beneath her feet, wooden steps provided entry to her wagon. Two of the plank steps were clearly new, as yet not worn and weathered by time and weather. They had been replaced by Rhuan—no, not by Rhuan. By Darmuth. That, she remembered.

Ilona frowned. Something teased at her mind, feathering across memories.

She had left the river. Walked away and across the grasslands. Approached the deepwood. And there, something, *something* had occured. Her arm was healed.

Eyes closed, with elbows braced against her thighs and her brow resting against the mug she held in two hands, Ilona tried to remember what had taken place. She could not have gone into Alisanos; she would not be here, and whole, had that been the case. She thought it through, considering what she might have done there at the border. Alisanos was completely unpredictable, as if sentient. It was not impossible to believe that someone might have come to her, that someone had healed her arm, was it?

If so, she would have asked about Rhuan.

Memory flickered like a candle in a draft, then burned more brightly.

She *had* asked about Rhuan. She had asked where he was, if he might be in Alisanos.

But who *did I ask*? No memory of an answer rose at her question. Her mind remained a blank. Whether Rhuan was in the deepwood or elsewhere, she did not know.

Ilona drew in a deep breath, admitted to herself that she was very tired, and rose. Her cot called her. Slightly dizzy, she set the tea mug aside, got into bed, pulled the bright coverlet over her body. Sleep came up like a friendly dog licking at her hand. She began to drift into it, until something kindled in her mind and jerked her to wakefulness. Something she had thought about, but not fully accepted. The knowledge hit unexpectedly hard.

Rhuan was gone. Possibly forever.

Sleep was banished.

Tears were not.

Chapter 22

COME SUNSET, BETHID tracked down Jorda at Mikal's ale tent. She had tended Churri for the night and he was picketed over by the somewhat fragile common tent Alorn and Timmon had raised. Dinner had consisted of fresh fish taken from the river and water. Now she wanted something with a bit more life to it, and to tell Jorda what she'd found.

She sat down at the table the karavan-master had appropriated. Already a jug of ale sat at his elbow; Mikal tossed a tankard from the bar. Jorda caught it, poured, then slid the tankard across to Bethid, who gulped down two hasty swallows, then set the tankard down as she cleaned her upper lip.

"Ilona's footprints led to a swath of charred ground approximately ten feet wide," she said. "It appears to run alongside the deepwood in both directions for quite some distance, rather like a skirt hem. I did not ride into it, just alongside, but I did find footprints. Ilona walked out into that charred area; her footprints, coming out of the grass, were easy to see. She went no farther than perhaps six feet, then stopped. At some point she turned around again; footprints matching hers go back in the other direction, sometimes beside her original track, sometimes overlapping it."

Jorda was frowning. "Then as far as you can tell she just stopped and turned around?"

Bethid shook her head. "I think not. There was another set of footprints. They came out of the deepwood, walked straight to Ilona, and circled her."

"*Circled* her!"

"As if she stood still, and whoever this was walked around her two or three times. The prints are scuffed and some overlay others, but I could make out that much. Both sets of prints were fresh. They appear to have been made at the same time."

"In other words, she met someone."

"Or some*thing*," Bethid said, "since it came out of Alisanos."

Jorda stirred on his stool. "You're certain of that? That it came out of Alisanos?"

"I see no other place it might have come from. The prints were from boots the size of a man's, and with the charred ground it's a simple matter to see footprints. But, Jorda—whoever he was turned around at some point and walked back into the forest. I saw no prints other than in that specific area. Whether Ilona went on her own for some reason and by coincidence met someone coming out of the deepwood, or someone from Alisanos walked out and found her there, I can't say. I can only tell you that she went there, went into that charred border, and eventually turned around and headed back, which is when I found her. Certainly when I rode on toward the forest, I saw no one. Just the bootprints."

Jorda's forehead wrinkled with deep thought. "Do you think it might be possible that it was Rhuan she met?"

"Rhuan?" Bethid found that startling. "Why might it have been Rhuan?"

"Because there's every chance he was swallowed when Alisanos moved. That farmsteader you brought back said he hadn't seen Rhuan anywhere since the storm."

"But why would Rhuan *remain* in the deepwood?" Bethid asked. "I mean, if he could walk free of Alisanos and meet Ilona, why would he return? It makes no sense. And why would she not remember? First of all, we don't know that Rhuan *can* make anyone lose their memory, but if so, why would he want to?"

"Her arm was healed," Jorda said evenly.

"But has Rhuan ever shown any ability to do such a thing?" Bethid shrugged as Jorda shook his head. "I think the only answer we can hope for is from Ilona, if she ever remembers."

Jorda growled, then sat forward and leaned heavy elbows on the table. "I am without both my guides when I most need them. We may never know if Rhuan and Darmuth were taken by Alisanos, just that they disappeared during the storm. What else is one to believe?" He tapped thick fingertips on the wooden table. "Well, if nothing else, we now know that from the river to that burned buffer area there is no obvious threat. That land can be used for planting. It's more than we knew this morning."

"Even if someone can walk out of Alisanos, right there?"

"We must begin," Jorda said heavily, and then broke off any additional comment. He half rose from his stool, arms braced against the table, eyes fixed on the entrance. "No," he said. "She shouldn't be here."

Bethid turned to look. Coming through the entrance flap, wrapped in a green shawl, was Ilona. She had wound her hair against the back of her skull and, as was her habit, anchored it there with ornamented hair sticks. As earlier, her arm bore no splint, and in no wise appeared to be weak or painful.

That the hand-reader was tired was obvious. It affected her movements, set shadows beneath her eyes, lent her face a drawn look. She glanced over the tent, and her eyes lighted on Jorda. Immediately she quickened her pace. Jorda was shaking his head repeatedly as she arrived. "No, Ilona. You should be in bed."

"I was." She found another stool and sat down upon it, even as Jorda lowered his body. "But there is something we must discuss." She looked at Bethid, then sighed. "As I said, I have no memory of what happened when I nearly walked straight into Alisanos. But I have a memory of *a memory*, if that makes sense."

Her smile was slight and fleeting. "I do wish Lerin were alive to read my dreams, but it's left to me to try to sort out the images in my mind. I will tell you what I dreamed while fevered, and I ask you to give it full weight, to not dismiss it as utterly irrelevant. Because odd as it will sound, I feel very strongly that it is related to my experience earlier today."

Bethid raised her hands and displayed palms in a gesture of deference. "Anything a diviner has to say should not be dismissed."

Jorda nodded. "Go on."

Ilona resettled her shawl, drew a breath, then told them. "Some while back, I dreamed of a man I at first believed was Rhuan. He's very like Rhuan. But he's someone else entirely . . . and I don't know who. I might say he was simply a dream construct, but now when I recall the dream, I feel there is more to the story. That I should know more about him. That in some way, he's real. And that, to some extent, I know him." Ilona shook her head. "I feel as though the memory of this dream is what led me away from the river and to the deepwood, almost as if I were somehow *summoned*. Trust me, I have no wish to explore Alisanos! I have no curiosity that goads me to go so close. But I did go. And at some point, as we know, my arm was healed. Is that not a convincing argument that I met someone there?"

"Oh, the tracks are convincing enough," Bethid murmured, then explained when she saw Ilona's blank look. "Someone did meet you. There are two sets of tracks in the burned area that skirts the deepwood.

Yours, and bootprints that look as though they could belong to a man."

Ilona frowned, shaking her head. "I just can't remember."

Bethid exchanged a glance with Jorda. "Ilona, is it possible you met Rhuan there?"

Ilona's head snapped up. "Rhuan? No. No. In fact, I *asked* about Rhuan! That, I remember." Again she shook her head. "But I don't know what the answer was. I don't even know of whom I asked the question." She made a growling sound of frustration and clamped splayed hands to her head. "Why can't I remember?"

"Perhaps," Jorda said very quietly, "because this man doesn't wish you to remember."

DAVYN PAUSED OUTSIDE the ale tent. He could hear laughter and snatches of conversation from within. The sun had set; interior lantern glow illuminated the walls of the tent, so that he could see the silhouettes of men. He felt alone, the one who didn't fit in. But how could he? Those inside were enjoying their evening. He had lost a family; he believed it likely he would never enjoy anything again.

But he had not come here to bury himself in sorrow. He had other business.

Davyn drew in a deep breath and pulled the tent flap aside. As expected, he saw men seated at tables downing ale and spirits. Some were deep in conversation, some played dice, others spoke quietly. And near the bar, he saw the table hosting the karavan-master and two women. One was the courier who had, he believed, given him a hard glance of contempt earlier, as he spoke to Jorda about Rhuan's role in his family's disappearance. The other, O Mother, the other was the hand-reader. Forgetting for the moment what had brought him to the ale tent, Davyn strode down the aisle.

The conversation broke off as he arrived at the table. He was aware of the karavan-master's frown and the expression of surprise on the courier's face. The hand-reader, however, merely looked up, met his eyes, and waited for his words. Of course—she must be well accustomed to being sought for her gift in any place, at any time. She looked infinitely weary, but he dared not allow that to deter him.

Davyn knelt beside the table. On his left was the courier, who blurted a sound of surprise that he would be so forward. On his right, the diviner. "Please," he said, "accept my apologies for this intrusion." He glanced briefly at the courier and Jorda. "I came for one purpose, but now I discover I have another." He looked down at the packed earth floor a moment, then back up to meet the hand-reader's eyes. "Your companions will tell you I have spoken with them only today. Neither conversation went well; you see, I have reason to believe what I do, but what *they* believe is very different." He gestured acceptance. "That is their right. But I come to you now because I believe you might be able to clarify the truth, to *find* the truth, and then all of us may go on knowing what needs to be done."

The karavan-master leaned forward, his tone proprietary. "Ilona has been ill. Reading hands at this time will tax her unduly. She needs—"

"No." The diviner raised her hand. "No, let him speak, if you please. This may be how I am meant to discover for myself if my gift is absent or returned."

That baffled Davyn momentarily, but he went on before he lost his nerve. "My family is missing. We were upon the shortcut that leads to Atalanda; you may recall you and fourteen other diviners felt it was imperative that our fifth child be born in that province." He saw a spark of memory in the hand-reader's eyes and hastened on. "We were caught up in the storm. The guide came to us—to help, he said—and sent all of us north. *North,* while everyone here was told to go east. And so we went north, as instructed, and Alisanos swallowed all but me. My wife, my children—all gone. Because we went north. Because we went where he told us." He tried to keep his tone neutral, but wasn't sure he succeeded. The faces of the courier and karavan-master had closed themselves to him. He chose his words with great care. "Forgive me, but I am in doubt. Were we sent north for a purpose other than finding safety?"

Shadows lay beneath the diviner's hazel eyes. "You believe my reading your hand will answer this?"

"No, no—perhaps not that. But you and the guide were—are—in Jorda's employment; you will know him better, and what he might intend." He drew a deep breath. "I need most to know if I will ever find my family, but I need, too, to know if what happened was done on purpose."

She shook her head. "Reading your hand will tell me nothing about what Rhuan intended but *I* can tell you—I will *assure* you—that he acted only in the best interests of your family. North, east—does it matter? He sent as many as he could to safety."

Despair rose. "But they were taken! All of them!"

Her gaze was unwavering. "As were others. Husbands, wives, children. You have not been present *here*, to see how many bodies were buried. Will you say then that Rhuan's purpose was for these folk to be taken?" Color stained her pale face. "He would not. He would not. What he told you was meant to keep you safe, if at all possible. But no man may guarantee that. Nor can I." He saw, to his surprise, the sheen of tears in her eyes. "I ask you to recall what he did for you and yours when the Hecari patrol came upon the karavan. He *died* for you; were he not Shoia, he would have remained dead, and all for your family's sake. How can you believe that a man who dies for your family would have a purpose other than to preserve it?"

He opened his mouth to answer, but no words came. Only despair, denial, and desperation. Tears welled in his eyes. He said at last, in a broken voice, "What am I to do? What am I to do? They are my life."

It was the karavan-master, after a heavy silence, who answered. "Tomorrow," he said, "tomorrow we will go to your wagon and bring back what is salvage-able. Even the wagon, if we can."

Davyn, puzzled, looked at him. "That isn't impor-tant. I don't care about those things. All that matters is my family."

"It is important," Jorda said, "and you will care about those things, as you should. Perhaps not now, perhaps not even tomorrow, but everything in that wagon speaks of those you loved."

Oh, but it hurt. He could barely speak. "My oxen are dead."

"Then we will take a team. All will be brought back."

- "Before . . ." the diviner said, and he saw she was white and trembling with exhaustion. "Before you go, come to my wagon. I will read your hand."

From the tail of his eye he saw the courier and karavan-master exchange a concerned glance. But he knew, looking at the diviner, that she was not fit to try his hand tonight.

He rose. He inclined his head. He marshaled his voice so it did not waver. "I thank you. I thank you all." He began to turn, to walk back up the aisle to the tent flap. But the karavan-master asked him to wait a moment. Davyn turned.

Jorda said, "There is bedding at my wagon. Take what you need."

Davyn had not considered that. Where and how he would sleep had not been part of his thoughts. Only his family, only the guide. He nodded his thanks and walked out of the tent.

Chapter 23

WHEN BRODHI SETTLED into the refectory with a sheet of clean parchment and fine lead, no one was present. He preferred it that way. But by the time he began transferring the rough sketch he had made to the fresh parchment, couriers began trickling in. At any given time many were on the roads throughout the province, while others returned to Cardatha with messages for city-folk or for the warlord himself. So long as there were no messages waiting to go out, riders were at their leisure. Prior to the war, few enough couriers had time to spend at the Guildhall, but since the Hecari had overrun Sancorra, the business of the Guildhall was under the warlord's control. Couriers did not depart without the warlord's permission, and those returning with messages were required to first go to the huge *gher* palace to report the news to the warlord in person. It was a complete abrogation of a courier's traditional duties, but no one dared protest except in the confines of the Guildhall.

The long slab of a table could host more than twenty couriers. Brodhi, at one end, had pulled a candle rack close to provide clear light as he drew in minute details. He was not a mapmaker, and those of the Mapmakers' Guild would denigrate his work, but it was enough; he knew to provide his own Guild with the information necessary for the proper execution of duties and also enough for the mapmakers to begin what would come to dominate Sancorra: knowledge of where Alisanos now lay.

The Guildhall kitchen with its huge hearth and spit abutted the refectory and nearly every courier stopped there to beg a bite or two from the cook or to gather up a new pitcher of ale and some mugs. In this instance, three couriers came back into the refectory with bread, ale, and four mugs. One, he supposed was for him; it was courtesy extended to every man present, though likely no one truly expected him to partake.

He knew them: Corrid, Gathlyn, and Hallack. Corrid, eighteen, was the youngest of the three, sandy-haired, blue-eyed, with a spattering of freckles across his nose, and a body not yet at ease with its height and length of limbs. Gathlyn was dark of eye, of hair, swarthy-featured, of medium height, past forty. Hallack was brown-haired, with hazel eyes, in his mid-thirties, the tallest. All were garbed in undyed woven tunics and trews, with leather riding gaiters cross-gartered over their boots and lower legs. None wore scroll cases looped over their shoulders, which meant they had completed their current duties, and they had clearly left cases, badges, and cloaks in the sleeping chamber.

Ale was poured. As Brodhi carefully made note on his map of how Alisanos cut across the old road, Corrid, foaming mug in hand, wandered up from the other end of the table. He stood at Brodhi's left shoulder, studying the in-progress map. Without asking permission, he placed a grimy fingertip on the parchment. "What's this? I don't recognize this route. Where is it?"

Brodhi picked up the importunate finger and pushed the hand aside. "East of where the Cardatha road joins up with the northwestern route."

"No!" Corrid's voice contained a note of startled disbelief. "It doesn't look anything like that, Brodhi. What are you trying to do, confuse us all?"

Gathlyn and Hallack also came down to look. They agreed with Corrid: Brodhi had misdrawn the routes.

Brodhi, continuing to work steadily with a careful hand, didn't bother to respond.

Hallack pointed. "What's this? Where is this, Brodhi?"

"You've chosen to disbelieve me; why should I answer?"

Gathlyn made a rude sound. "Don't ask Brodhi anything, friends, he'll give you naught for it."

"Look here." Corrid indicated the tiny trees Brodhi had sketched. "This isn't right. Not if it's supposed to represent the southern route to Ixtapa."

"It does represent the southern route to Ixtapa,"

Brodi said. "What it also represents is that the topography of the entire southwest region has changed. No map is accurate now." He glanced up at Gathlyn and Hallack. "What in this world might prove so powerful as to change the lay of the land?"

"Nothing!" Corrid declared before the older men could speak. "Brodhi, is this a jest?"

But Gathlyn didn't laugh. Gathlyn was old enough to remember. He understood at once. He released a long, low whistle of startled comprehension. "This much, Brodhi?"

"This is but a small section," Brodhi replied. "We've had no time to scout all the changes. But here, you'll see, the deepwood encroaches. I rode north a fair piece, then northeast, to join up with the Cardatha road."

Corrid asked, "What are you talking about?"

Hallack shot the youngest a hard glance. "No schooling, is it? You know naught of Alisanos?"

Gathlyn shook his head, still studying the map. He indicated a notation. "Where is this, Brodhi?"

"That is a settlement. Or was. The Hecari paid a visit. Far fewer are there now, unless you count the bodies."

"Blessed Mother," Hallack murmured. "Decimation."

Gathlyn swore, crying down multiple curses upon the Hecari. He walked three paces away in tight-coiled tension, then swung back. "What else?"

Brodhi went on. "It's near the crossroads of the

northern route to Korith, the southern to Ixtapa, and the Cardatha road. This is a river, as you see; it's a natural gathering place. Unfortunately, this—" Brodhi indicated an area with his lead, "—is Alisanos, now but a half-mile away."

"What's Alisanos?" Corrid asked, young face baffled.

Hallack and Gathlyn, annoyed, each grabbed a shoulder and shoved him down onto the bench. "Did your parents teach you naught about the deepwood?" Gathlyn asked.

And Hallack, in contempt, "It's a young fool, isn't it?"

Corrid looked from one to the other. Then he looked at Brodhi. "What *is* it?"

"Let him up," Brodhi said, and waited until the older men allowed Corrid to stand. He crooked a finger, beckoning the boy closer. "Time you learned," he said, "what all of us under the warlord's fist should know."

FOR MORE DAYS than he could count, Gillan knew pain intimately. He was ashamed of his weakness, ashamed of tears, of begging for something to stop the pain, of begging for his parents to find him. Lost to fever much of the time, he was distantly aware of Darmuth tending his ruined leg, but that only brought renewed pain and Gillan told him time and time again to stop. But Darmuth, possibly because he was a demon and took joy in this, refused. The pain continued. Each day the demon peeled burned skin away; it crossed Gillan's fevered mind to wonder if Darmuth *ate* the ruined flesh. Each day the demon applied to his leg an oil that stank, then slathered on pulp taken from a plant Gillan didn't know, and each day Darmuth wrapped the leg in several huge, flat leaves, binding them on by winding from knee to ankle a thin length of fabric taken from the hem of his tunic. Gillan spent more time unconscious than awake, for which he was grateful, but with that came confusion as to how much time had elapsed since the storm that brought him into the heart of Alisanos.

He asked Darmuth if he would be trapped in Alisanos forever. He asked that question again and again. No answer was ever given. The demon only smiled. And so eventually Gillan stopped asking. He accepted that Alisanos was his future as well as his present. That comprehension brought grief, anger, a terrible despair. He was lame, he was alone. To all things, he was lost.

But somehow, somehow, he would find a way to survive.

AUDRUN AWAKENED VERY stiff. She had spent much of the night jerking awake, waiting to return to sleep, only to be again disturbed by dreams she could not recall come morning. With Rhuan clearly recovering, she didn't seek to share body heat with him—to do so would have made her too uncomfortable. So she slept cold as well, arms and legs knotted upon themselves in a search for warmth of any kind. By the time the double suns rose, she felt more tired than when she had gone to sleep the night before.

Rhuan said little this morning. Waking was a slow process because of his wounds, and he arose carefully, grunting with exertion. But there was no question that he had improved since the day before. He had indeed taken her suggestion with regard to his leggings, and used fringe cut from the seams to close the flaps of leather from knee to ankle. His hair, free of braids, hung to his waist, still slightly crimped. He did use a length of fringe to tie it back into a single tail, but otherwise made no attempt to deal with it. Looking at it brought home to Audrun the memory of Rhuan's words regarding their "marriage." It prompted the same kind of desperate denial she'd employed the day before, as much in her mind as on her tongue.

With no water for washing, she knew herself to be the mess Rhuan had mentioned, her face marred by welts, scratches, and sap, debris in her hair. Audrun collected several of the cloth strips used as route markers for a trail that no longer existed to tie back her hair, but as Rhuan made no comment about leaving immediately, she began to separate snarls of hair, to free them of tangles. She gritted her teeth as some strands tore, combing and recombing her hair with spread fingers, trying to free small sections from larger tangles.

As she worked, Rhuan tended to personal matters, then walked into the burned dreya ring. Audrun recalled he had mentioned wishing to give them some sort of farewell rite. She wasn't certain if she should also go into the ring, or stay without. She was all at sea in Alisanos, now that Rhuan was recovered enough to make decisions. For days she had clung to the drive to care for Sarith, to find water, to bandage Rhuan's wounds, to forage for food. The immediacy of those tasks was lifted from her now; there was time for her to question her actions, to wonder what would become of her.

To wonder what would become—what *had* become—of her children and her husband.

Rhuan walked from tree to tree. At each charred trunk he paused, pressed both palms and forehead against the blackened wood. Whether he spoke, she could not determine. But the posture she understood: grief, sorrow, guilt. The latter stilled her fingers. It filled her up abruptly with identical emotion.

The dreya died for my child.

Tears welled, stinging. She looked at the ring of twelve charred trees, black amid the green; at the hole in the canopy where leaves and branches once thrived.

Audrun rose, ignoring the protests of her stiff body. She crossed to the ring. This had nothing to do with Rhuan, with what he said in the privacy of his mind, in the movement of his lips with no voice evident.

Audrun, too, walked to each trunk, one by one by one, but on the exterior of the ring. At each, she pressed one palm against burned trunks. Inside her mind she thanked the dreya for their kindness, for their protection, and wished them, in Sarith's name, peace in the arms of the Mother, and peace in the presence of whatever deity they claimed.

When she finished, she looked up and found Rhuan standing near. He nodded slightly. "That was well done."

For reasons she could not comprehend, those few words, spoken in his quiet voice, made the tears run faster.

"Audrun." Self-conscious, she dashed the tears away. "Audrun, you have given them honor. There is no cause for tears."

She looked up into his face, her throat nearly closed by grief. "I have lost much," she said unevenly, "more than any wife and mother should, but they—they lost their *lives*. For a human child, they died."

"I know this is difficult to understand," he said, "but Sarith was theirs, too. She is of two worlds, Audrun— the human one and this one."

"And lost to both." She swallowed painfully. "I think it would be easier to bear had she been stillborn than to lose her . . . to lose her that way."

Brown eyes were warm. "But there is still hope. A human child has great value in Alisanos. I doubt very much she will be killed, Audrun. So long as she lives, there is a chance she'll be found."

"And at this gathering place, this Kiba, what exactly will happen?"

"I can't tell you *exactly* what will happen there. But you and I will ask to address the primaries—"

She couldn't help the irony in her tone as she interrupted him. "All thousand of them?"

"As many as care to come. Most will, I think; perhaps all." His smile was crooked. "This is a unique situation."

"And what is the likelihood of these one thousand gods deciding to help me?"

He shrugged. "That, I can't say. I wish I could, to ease your pain. But nothing like this has ever been brought before them."

Audrun frowned. "But you've said hundreds of other humans have been taken by the deepwood, including your mother. Hasn't anyone else ever gone to the Kiba and asked for help?"

He sighed, then stepped close. He closed his hands around her upper arms and steered her to a downed tree. "Audrun, sit. Be comfortable." He guided her down onto the huge log, then sat on the ground next to her with his back against the log. "It's far more complex than you think. First, those who are taken by Alisanos often don't survive the first night, let alone long enough to reach the Kiba. Should they survive, they would then have to know the Kiba exists."

"And lacking that knowledge of the Kiba's existence, no human would think to search for it." She nodded. "And humans also have no knowledge of the existence of your thousand gods, so they'd never think to ask them for aid."

"No, humans ask their *own* gods for aid. But this is not the dominion of those gods."

She thought back to all the prayers she had made to the Mother of Moons since arriving in Alisanos. Words. Nothing more. Nothing that might be answered. It set an ache in her heart. It stole hope from her. She turned her head away, not wishing him to see the conflict in her face.

"I mean no offense by this, Audrun, but humans are innocent, and ignorant. In the confines of Alisanos, humans are children. Infants, as Sarith is. And those who survive any length of time become something other than human . . . there's little likelihood such people ever remember what they were, what they have lost, or know what they have become, which is a mercy. Even if they knew the Kiba existed, they might not survive to reach it. Or along the way they may forget why they wanted to reach it in the first place."

She turned her head back and looked into his face, into his eyes, and saw a measure of sympathy she did not expect. She realized she had not asked the one question that most needed an answer. "If Alisanos has been taking humans for so long, then surely your people, your gods, have seen them in the deepwood, lost and alone."

"Yes."

"And they do not help these folk? They do not take

them to the Kiba for aid? Why is this, here and now, a 'unique situation'?"

He drew a breath, then released it. "One thousand of my people are gods, as I've said. Primaries. But Alisanos is—Alisanos. It is the wellspring. It is wild magic in its purest, most concentrated form—powerful, overwhelming, utterly unchecked. To humans, it is poison. This is why humans are changed when they come here. Their bodies and souls can't withstand the poison; either they die, or they are slowly transformed to something that can survive, but they are no longer human." He held out a hand, turning it palm up, palm down, as if making an example of his flesh. "But my people are vastly different. We are *of* the wild magic, born into its substance just as demons and dreya are. It wraps our bones, leaps in our blood, provides certain abilities. Those of my people who are particularly gifted, the primaries, can manipulate the magic, but *Alisanos itself* cannot be controlled. No more than humans can control their world. Humans live in their world, they are born to it, and some aspects of it they can *affect*, but they truly control nothing." His lips quirked a moment. "You may build a shelter against the rain, but you can't control the storm."

"But we're not *gods*, Rhuan! You say your people are. How can they be gods if they have no control over Alisanos?"

He opened his mouth to answer, but an entirely different voice broke into the conversation. "We're gods, little human, because we say we are."

Chapter 24

*T*ORVIC KNEW FROM helping his mam garden that something wasn't right. Each day, more plants in Lirra's vegetable garden drooped. He and Meggie weeded and watered with great care, making sure the plants had room to grow as needed. But it seemed that no matter what they did, the garden continued to fail. Initially Lirra dismissed it with a smile, explaining what they knew as farmsteader children, that some crops inevitably failed. Weak seed, she said; it was just as well such were not grown to adulthood. But the corn and wheat were healthy, tubers grew well, and melons and squash thrived. It was true they would miss carrots and onions and a few other ingredients in their stew, but they would do well enough.

Without the cow, there was no milk and thus no cheese or butter. But Lirra's snares delivered small game now and again, enough to keep them in meat. They had eggs aplenty from the hens, and the beans grew nicely. There were no true seasons in Alisanos, Lirra explained, because the weather might change from hour to hour, so she had adopted the habit of planting year round, knowing some crops would be lost while others thrived.

But then the vegetable garden in its entirety began to die, and three of the hens stopped laying, and the tubers rotted in the ground. Melons grew no larger than a man's thumb, then split open. Lirra said they would do well enough with only four laying hens, and killed the three not laying. Torvic and Meggie plucked them, and for a ten-day they ate well of roasted chicken. But then the rooster died, and Lirra stopped smiling.

That night, beneath blankets laid before the hearth, Meggie whispered a question to Torvic: what they would do if the other hens stopped laying? And without a rooster, where would chicks come from? Mam and Da had made it quite clear that a prosperous farm required a rooster, even though Meggie didn't quite understand the rooster's role in things. Torvic said he didn't know, but that Lirra would think of something. Lirra had lived alone for several years in Alisanos, and if she didn't know what to do, she wouldn't still be alive.

"We'll plant more seed come morning," he told her beneath the blanket.

"What if *it* doesn't grow? What if *it* dies?"

"We've meat," he answered, "from the snares. And Lirra says that now and again when she forages she comes across a wagon swallowed with its people, with supplies still there. Maybe with us to help, we can find more wagons."

"We'll get lost," Meggie declared.

"No, we won't. Lirra will lay the stinkwood fire. We can follow our noses."

"If the other hens stop laying and we eat *them*, there'll be no more eggs."

He couldn't argue with that. But, "We've the snares, Meggie. We won't go hungry."

Lirra's voice came to them from the bedstead. "Sleep, children. No sense borrowing trouble. Now and again we'll go hungry, but it won't last. It's just a matter of planting and raising what's strong, and culling the weak seed."

"See?" Torvic said to Meggie.

Meggie did not answer. She burrowed more deeply yet beneath the blanket. Meggie had stopped crying so often, but he did see her now and again wiping tears away. Sometimes he felt like crying, too, but he had to be strong for Meggie.

"We'll raise what's strong," he whispered, "and cull the weak seed."

ILONA SLEPT BADLY. The night was filled not with dreams, but with vague memories of the man who so resembled Rhuan, and of the grief and heartbreak living in every line of the farmsteader's face. No longer fevered, no longer with an arm that ached, there were no excuses for her. But she found no comfort in sleep, no cessation of the burdens of life. When she awoke, she felt dull and weary.

She had told both Bethid and Naiya that she wanted no company in the night, asserting that she was well enough to tend herself. Fortunately, they accepted her argument. She slept and woke by herself in the wagon, a film of dew coating her coverlet. This morning Jorda meant to put on a new canopy, but then she recalled that he was to ride with the farmsteader to his wagon, to bring it back, and perhaps her canopy would have to wait.

She pushed back the coverlet and realized she had once again slept in her clothing, though at least these were garments she'd donned only the day before, following her bath in the river. As she crawled out of her bed, reflecting that she'd best go find a bush since there would be no privacy with the nightcrock in the uncovered wagon, she recalled that she'd bidden the farmsteader to visit her before he left with Jorda.

Perching on the edge of her cot, Ilona went very still. O Mother of Moons, she had promised to read his hand! But what if she couldn't? What if her gift was still absent? What then would he think of her, and of her defense of Rhuan? A diviner with no gift carried no weight at all in the world. She might as well be a charlatan, might as well support the man's concern that Rhuan had, somehow, *desired* his family to be taken.

Ridiculous. Ludicrous. Completely unwarranted. But Ilona knew well enough that in times of trouble, such things as logic were often buried under grief and anger. And there was that aplenty in this settlement.

FOR WHAT SHE assumed were days, Ellica lay upon the rude pallet of leaves and branches. The dreya tended her with infinite care and gentleness, often stroking her hair, now untangled; stroking also her arms and legs. At first she had recoiled from such intimate touch, but it became clear to her that the dreya were simply fascinated by her skin, by her coloring. They were silver all over, from hair and eyes to a softly glowing silver flesh showing slightly darker patterning. Ellica was so blond her hair was almost white, and her skin, though fair, had a milky tint to it absent from theirs, with undertones of rose. Veins ran bluish within her flesh, and where her pigmentation was pink, such as her lips, theirs was darker gray.

She could not speak as yet, and they wished her not to try. That she healed, she knew; frequent applications of the sticky substance to the wound in her neck had closed the skin. But fingers told her a scar remained, a ring of puckered tissue encircling her neck. The dreya brought her water, fed her with nuts and something astonishingly sweet with the barest hint of spice. It was a limited offering, but she took pleasure

in the sweet substance. And eventually she recovered
enough that they allowed her to rise without help and
to tend her needs alone; initially her brief trips to a
bush to relieve herself required two dreya to assist her.

The dreya, she discovered, did not communicate
with one another as humans did. That they had
voices, she knew; she heard their soft, chiming laughter. But they were mostly silent, linking hands often
as if touch conveyed speech. They combed one another's hair with bundles of stripped twigs from their
own trees, each twig ivory beneath the silvery bark.
At any given time several might go into their trees,
passing through tall clefts, but Ellica was never left
alone. The ring was her refuge, and she blessed them
for offering it.

When she was strong enough to rise on her own, to
walk without assistance, all twelve dreya escorted her
to the tiny sapling in the center of the ring. With gestures and soft trilling, they made it clear that the
sapling was hers to tend. Ellica smiled and nodded,
kneeling down beside the sapling. It was small recom-
pense, she felt, for how they had served her. And she
understood why the work was necessary; the sapling
attracted all manner of insects determined to feast on
its wood, and birds often flew down in attempts to
break off tiny twigs or to bore holes in its trunk. Ellica
groomed the sapling several times a day, if time be
measured in days within Alisanos, nurturing pale,
fragile leaves as they uncoiled from tiny buds, removing suckers at the ground to make certain a single

trunk grew straight and strong, not weakened by lesser sproutings.

Ellica found a tremendous peace in tending the newborn tree, surrounded by silver women within a ring of silver trees. Her strength slowly returned. She took nourishment from the nuts and sweet substance, aware of no desire for meat, bread, or vegetables. When the double suns rose, so did she, a sense of renewed vitality filling her spirit.

Then one day, as she woke with the sun, she heard the voices of the dreya and saw their tears. Each woman clung to her tree, weeping, reaching out again and again to touch the hands of others. That they grieved was obvious. One by one they began to slip into their trees, until only one dreya was left. She took Ellica by the hand, led her to the sapling, and mimed that she was to devote herself to its care. There was an urgency involved in the dreya's gestures, and a grief in her eyes that did not fade. Ellica nodded, knelt beside the sapling, and stroked its narrow trunk, trying to assure the dreya she would tend the tree. The woman cradled Ellica's head, bowed hers briefly in gratitude, then turned to her own silver-trunked tree. With a final glance at Ellica, she slipped into the cleft. Overhead, in the shining canopy, leaves rustled. Stems and branches wound themselves together. There was no branch of any tree that was not touching another.

Save for the sapling, alone in the ring's center.

As Ellica was alone.

WHEN BRODHI FINISHED explaining matters to Corrid, his freckles stood out more prominently because the skin beneath them was pale. Corrid stared at the map a moment, then looked at Gathlyn as if to ask, in silence, if any of what Brodhi had told him true. Gathlyn nodded before the question could be voiced. Hallack, perching atop the table slab, was markedly grim.

"But no one ever told me," Corrid said faintly. "Why wouldn't they tell me about such a place as Alisanos?"

Hallack drank down ale while Gathlyn asked, "Where in the province are you from?"

"Far northeast." Corrid waved a hand at Brodhi's rough map, though the markings didn't extend that far.

"Aye, well, that's likely why," Hallack said, nodding. "Alisanos has been sitting along the Atalanda-Sancorra border for forty years. It moved there a few years before I was born, but my folk have always lived in the southwestern portion of the province. We're closer, so I heard all the tales as I grew up."

"While I," Gathlyn said, "was alive when it moved. I was but a child, but everyone in the northwest heard about it. My folk, too, have told tales of it ever since."

Corrid stared again at the map. "But it could move anywhere?"

"Anywhere," Brodhi said, "at any time. And when it moves again, which is a certainty, who knows but that it *will* go northeast and swallow your people."

That did not set well with Corrid. He looked at all three men, satisfied himself that it wasn't a jest, then began to murmur a petition to the Mother of Moons.

"Meanwhile," Brodhi said, "we've got the warlord sending warriors with me so they may see for themselves, when I return to the settlement. Tomorrow."

Gathlyn swore. "An active Alisanos and the Hecari. One is enough of a burden, but both?" He shook his head. "Poor Sancorra."

Hallack agreed. "A man could wish the deepwood would swallow all the Hecari for us."

Brodhi said quietly, "A man could wish . . . or a man might do something to further that."

Gathlyn and Hallack made derisive sounds simultaneously, as Corrid gazed at Brodhi. "But he couldn't, could he?" the young courier asked. "I mean, there's really nothing we could do, is there?"

"Die," Hallack said. "That's what we'd do."

"Very likely," Brodhi agreed, and left it at that. For an initial foray into learning what other couriers felt, it was less than effective but it was better than no knowledge at all.

RHUAN FELT THE rage rise up in his soul. The voice he knew at once, and its arrogant tone; it was not required that he see the man to recognize him. But the man did step out out of the shadows, clear for all to see, and Rhuan looked for the first time in several human years upon the man who was his sire.

Audrun was on her feet, clearly startled. Rhuan remained seated with his back against the downed tree, trying with great difficulty to ignore the impulse to rise. Alario would expect it, would expect some form of acknowledgment and deference, and Rhuan refused to give it.

"Audrun, sit down." He tried to keep the anger from his voice. Anger would please Alario.

She looked down at him, face still blank with surprise, then slowly seated herself on the log once again. "Are we in danger, Rhuan?"

"Oh, indeed, always," Alario said. His smile was edged. "Surely Rhuan has explained to you what I am."

"In fact, I have not," Rhuan said before Audrun could answer. "You mean so little to me that it never crossed my mind."

"Ah, but I mean enough to you that you choose to turn your back on all that I could give you, on all that you could be, as Alario's get."

Rhuan laughed. "Because I want none of it. None of you."

"Stop," Audrun said. She looked from one to the other. No fear was evident in her expression or posture, no concern of any kind, except for annoyance. "Very well. I take it you are kin. I take it as well that you are neither of you particularly friendly with one another. I may be only a 'little human,' but this I have

seen before. Therefore I say to you both: explain matters. Plainly. You will not use me to cut at one another."

Rhuan, taken aback, blinked and closed the mouth
he'd opened to respond.

Alario's laughter was startled, but also long and
loud.

Chapter 25

*A*UDRUN LOOKED FROM Rhuan to the man who appeared to be his father. Certainly there was a strong resemblence in coloring, in the arrangement of their features, and of course in the elaborate braid patterns and beading, had she not undone Rhuan's. But the father was, she realized—and not unexpectedly—taller, broader, heavier, and clearly more mature. He strode out of the shadows and into the light of double suns with a powerful elegance that eclipsed what she remembered of Rhuan's uninjured movements. That this man was in his prime was beyond obvious; he carried with him supreme self-confidence, such a strong sense of condescension and casual superiority that she disliked him at once. She blamed Rhuan not at all for the bitterness she'd heard in his tone.

"So," she said to the man, taking the offensive before he could, "since Rhuan has not made the introductions, as you seemed to expect—though I don't know why you should—perhaps you will tell me who you are, and why I should care?"

The bigger man raised an eyebrow, and made the motion seem more eloquent than ten words assembled into a sentence. "I am Alario. Primary of Alisanos. A *god*, little human; and yes, there is indeed power I manipulate to suit my needs, as my get has pointed out, even to suit my whims, which is something he abhors."

"Your get?" Audrun echoed, incredulous. "You make him sound like a puppy!"

"And so he is." Alario, clad in rich, russet hide tunic and leggings, with wide, gold-bossed and -buckled belt and glints of beads in his braids, seemed almost to glow with vitality. Casually, he leaned his spine against a tree and folded his arms across his chest. "He hasn't yet proved himself to be anything else. And I doubt he will."

"Why are you here?" Rhuan asked, as yet still seated on the ground with every appearance of insousiance.

When Alario smiled, no dimples appeared. Rhuan's, Audrun realized, must have come from his mother. "I am here," Alario said, "because it was brought to my attention that *you* were here, where you should not be. Failed already, have you? Given up on the journey—"

Now Rhuan stood, thrusting himself upward with a hand on the downed trunk. "I have not. Neither of those. I am here because Alisanos saw fit to go active—"

"He came to help us," Audrun put in. "He tried to direct us away, and was trapped himself."

"Were you? Trapped?" Alario grinned. "Have you explained to her that you could walk out of Alisanos at any time?"

Audrun looked at Rhuan sharply. "Can you?"

"I can," he affirmed, "but not with you, nor with any of your family. And I choose not to do so just now, journey or no journey, until all of your kin are safe."

"What journey?" she asked.

But before he could answer, Alario spoke over him. "I see, too, that you have gotten yourself married in the meantime." He looked curiously at Audrun. "Was taking down his braids his idea, or yours?"

"I'm already married," Audrun declared coolly. "I have not married Rhuan."

"Where is your husband?"

It pinched. She lifted her chin, allowing no weakness to show even briefly, because she knew it would amuse him even as it gave him a weapon. "I don't know. He may be here in Alisanos, or in what you call the human world."

"Then he is unable to keep this match from going forward." Alario locked eyes with Rhuan. "In Alisanos, what exists in the human world means less than nothing. In Alisanos, you took down his braids. In Alisanos, you have in essence married him already. But we do like ceremony at the Kiba. Thus, you'll marry him again before the primaries. You have no choice."

"I have every choice," Audrun replied evenly, refusing to let him bait her. "I will speak at your Kiba and explain to all of your fellow gods that I took down his braids with no notion of what it means in Alisanos. It was done in ignorance as I tended his scalp wounds. There was no intent on my part to make any kind of arrangement between us."

"But the arrangement is made. It cannot be unmade."

"Why not?"

"Because we the primaries have no wish to have it unmade."

"How do you know what the other primaries want?" Audrun countered. "One thousand altogether, I understand. Can you swear that the other nine hundred and ninety-nine will agree with you? I think not. I think when I explain matters, few will stand by you. Not all nine hundred and ninety-nine can be as arrogant as you."

"Actually," Rhuan murmured, "they can."

She ignored him, speaking only to Alario. "I think you personally will only maintain that the 'arrangement' must remain in place because you know it will prove an annoyance to Rhuan. I think if he were anyone else, you wouldn't care in the least. And if the other nine hundred and ninety-nine *are* as arrogant as you, then I shall deal with all of you."

"You?" One eyebrow rose again. "*You* shall deal with us? And how will you do so?"

"As children," she declared. "How else? I've seen

such behavior before . . . in spoiled children. I think it will prove no more difficult than dealing with arrogant bullies, gods or no."

Rhuan laughed softly. "I'll place a wager on that!"

Alario was far less amused. Audrun saw a flicker of red in his eyes, a faint deepening of the pale coppery hue of his skin. Power purled off him like fog. "Little human—"

She cut him off. "Actually, I'm not. I'm somewhere in the middle, when it comes to the height of human women. *My* name is Audrun, and while I am not a primary, I am a wife and mother. I am a child of the Mother of Moons, and a woman of Sancorra. I have been brought to the deepwood very much against my will, and I shall not accept that I am helpless, inferior, and at your mercy."

Alario deserted his pose against the tree and stood upright. His posture was alert, prepared, and quietly intimidating. "You will not?" He tilted his head a little, as if evaluating her from a different angle. "But you should. You very much are helpless, inferior, and at my mercy. And as my get will tell you, I am entirely ruthless."

"He doesn't need to tell me; I can see that for myself. Ruthless or not, the fact remains that you cannot force me to marry simply because you wish to."

"I don't have to," he said, amused. "You've done it yourself."

Audrun was unfazed. "And now, shall we return to the question of whether you are a god?"

"I *am* a god."

"Because you say so?" Audrun scoffed. "Any number of people may call themselves gods. It doesn't mean they are."

Rhuan sounded uneasy. "Audrun—"

She thrust a silencing hand into the air, never taking her eyes from Alario's. "I will settle this, here and now. I wish to see proof. Have you proof to offer me, primary?"

He walked directly to her, stationing himself to throw her into the shadow of his person and power. "And what would you consider proof, little human?"

Audrun stood her ground, meeting him eye to eye despite the disparity in their heights. "You will, this moment, find my husband, my children. You will retrieve my youngest—just an infant in clouts—from a winged demon who stole her from us even as he set fire to the dreya ring that sheltered us. Then you will transport all of us to the Kiba, where I will explain how I came to take Rhuan's braids down, and *then* you will send all of us safely home to our own world, unchanged in any way."

Both brows lifted. "All of that?"

"Every bit of it."

Alario grinned. She marked again the absence of dimples; the absence, also, of honest amusement. His was ice and edges. "No."

"Because you can't."

"Oh, I can."

"If you could, you would."

Alario burst out laughing. "So predictable, Human Audrun. That argument might be effective in your world, but here it carries no weight. I have nothing to prove. Ask my get. He will tell you." The grin remained as his eyes flicked to Rhuan. "Do tell her, won't you?"

"Show me," Audrun demanded. "You. Here and now."

But she had lost Alario's attention. He focused now on his son and changed the subject. "Your journey is ended. All that's left now is for the primaries to make it official, and discuss the timing of your disposition."

Rhuan shook his head. "You may see it that way. But you are one vote. As Audrun has mentioned, there are nine hundred and ninety-nine others to be cast—and you have your share of enemies."

Alario stepped away from Audrun and closer to Rhuan. He stood before him, staring at him, and Audrun felt the trickle of pure, unalloyed power in his wake. His voice, however, was very soft. "You are not fit. Not fit to be *dioscuri*, not fit to be my heir."

"Perhaps that's best," Rhuan replied, "as I have no desire whatsoever to *be* your heir."

"I should have had you exposed at birth."

"And what then would you have done—abducted another human woman to bear your dying seed?" Rhuan shook his head. "The others would never have allowed it. Only one *dioscuri* has been born to you in hundreds of years. That speaks poorly of your potency, as I have no doubt your enemies realize. Surely word is being passed from one to another that Alario has a fatal weakness. I am very probably the last *dioscuri* you'll sire. You need me to retain your place among the other primaries." Rhuan's smile was thin and edged. "After all, Karadath has Brodhi. Without me in the stewpot, the seasoning you provide is weak. Your brother's will be stronger, and he may ascend to your place because of it. That, you could not bear."

Alario began to circle Rhuan, holding his eyes as he did so, until Rhuan had to break off because he could twist his neck only so far. Alario halted in front of him again. He leaned in, sniffed briefly, then withdrew, smiling. "You are weak. The weak are culled by the strong." Without warning, he caught hold of the hair tied at the back of Rhuan's neck and the neck itself, forcing Rhuan's head into a taut, uncomfortable position. Alario bared teeth in a threat display no less effective because he lacked fangs. His voice was pitched low, very nearly a whisper. "Other primaries may well indeed be my enemies, *but you they will never support.*"

ILONA ORIGINALLY PLANNED to set up her low, lacquered table outside along with the seating cushions for the farmsteader's visit, as she usually did for hand-readings. But as she rose to do so, she realized that would require more strength than she had. Instead, she spread a blanket on the ground at the foot of the wagon steps, sat down on the bottom step, and, when the farmsteader arrived, asked him to sit on the blanket. He evinced mild surprise, but only because when she'd read his hand before, the arrangements had been different. He sat down without hesitation and offered his hand, palm-up.

Before she touched it, she looked into his face. He was weary, tense, grimy, and needed a shave, but what lived in his eyes was desperation and despair, not anger, not hatred. He truly believed Rhuan had sent his family into Alisanos, but the root of that belief was fear, and misplaced logic.

Ilona addressed that. "I must tell you: I read true."

The blond man blinked, puzzled. "I know that, else I wouldn't be here."

"And if what I see disproves your conviction that Rhuan acted with the intention of sending your folk into the deepwood?"

A muscle leaped briefly in his jaw. "You're a diviner," he said. "You've been touched by the Mother, to have such a gift. I put my faith in you. Tell me what you see, good or ill."

"Very well." Ilona placed her right hand beneath his, cradling it. Her left she rested lightly atop his palm. There were several methods for reading hands, but actual contact was the most effective. It also relayed high emotions, occasionally too high, so that it was difficult for the hand-reader to disengage. But Ilona felt this particular reading called for contact because the farmsteader's emotions and thoughts were in upheaval, and she herself was anxious because self-doubt had seeded itself in her soul.

There was blockage, familiar and frightening block-age, as she sank her awareness into his. At first she re-coiled in dismay, but then the blockage abruptly bled away. It opened many doors before her, allowing her entrance. She went through, then down and down, deeper and deeper.

Images began to form. None of them were clear enough to read, merely sparks here and there, flash-ing like fireflies. She felt the grief, the worry, the fear, the determination that he must and would find his family, as well as the acknowledgment that it was possible he could not. That was the terrifying conflict in his soul, the besetting fear that his life was forever altered, forever to be blighted.

The jittery images steadied, slowed. She found them one by one, began to sew them together in her mind, assembling the squares of a quilt, the fabric of his fu-ture. She evaluated, then stitched, or discarded. Took up another square of cloth, examined it, set it beneath the silver needle in her hand. And when all the squares were found, discarded, or sewn, the quilt at last was whole.

Ilona opened her eyes. She saw that the farmsteader, too, had closed his. She pressed his hand briefly, then withdrew hers. It jarred him back into the world. He closed the hand and held it against his chest as if what it contained was the rarest jewel.

What she had seen made no sense to her. Part of her

wished to doubt. But the images had been infinitely clear. She could not mistake what she had seen, surprising as it was. "Brodhi," she said. "Somehow, Brodhi is the key."

His brows knit. "What?"

It still, to her, seemed unbelieveable. "Brodhi is the key. Not Rhuan."

"Did the guide act with intent?"

"He did not. He, too, is trapped." Her mind said, *And Rhuan is gone.* It took effort not to let her own pain show itself, but it was required. This was his reading, not her own. "Your wife and children are in the deepwood. All are scattered, save for the two youngest. With them, the youngest, is Brodhi." Ilona drew a breath, knowing the next would be difficult. "She had the child, your wife. The baby is born."

It stunned him utterly. "*Our* baby? Audrun's and mine? But it isn't due yet! It's too early!"

"The child was born at full term."

"It can't be . . . Audrun isn't due for four more months!"

Ilona saw no way of softening the blow. "She's a child of Alisanos, not wholly human."

"The—my baby? Not human?" Color washed out of his face. "But she's mine! She's Audrun's! How can she—*she?*—not be wholly human?"

"She was born in Alisanos." Ilona tried to gather words that were least hurtful. "This is why . . . this is why fifteen diviners said she must be born in Atalanda. None of us knew why, but that much was understood. Now, the image is clear. Your newest is born, but born in Alisanos. The deepwood has laid claim."

"Blessed Mother . . ." the farmsteader whispered. "O Mother of Moons . . ." His face was oddly devoid of all expression, as if so many emotions clamored for release that none could find the way to the muscles of his face. "What—what am I to do?"

"Gather them up," Ilona told him. "Find the way. Find your family. It's vital they be found soon, if they are to remain human. As each day passes, they all become less so."

"But how am I . . . " He let that go, moving to another concern. "Who is this Brodhi?"

"Shoia," she answered. "Like Rhuan; his cousin, I believe. Brodhi's a courier. I see him there, in Alisanos. He is the key." She turned up her own hands, displaying empty palms in a gesture of helplessness. "I can't tell you why this is so, only that he is."

His gaze unfocused as he stared into distance, the farmsteader rubbed a broad hand through his hair, sleeking it back against his scalp again and again. "But who would agree to go into Alisanos on purpose? *I* would, of course—I plan to—but I thought to make the guide, Rhuan, take me there—"

Certainty shaped her words. "If you go, you are lost."

"But—"

"Brodhi is the key."

Now he rubbed his face with his hand. "How does one convince a stranger to enter Alisanos? I have no coin to speak of. He knows nothing of me or my family. *Why* would he go?"

Ilona said again, "Find the way." Then a wave of exhaustion swamped her, one so powerful she nearly lost her perch upon the step and tumbled to the ground. She clamped both hands on the edges of the steps. "I'm sorry. I'm sorry, but you'll have to leave now . . . I must rest." Dizziness assailed her. ". . . sorry . . ." She tried to rise and nearly pitched forward into the farmsteader's arms.

"Here, here, let me help." He closed hands on her upper arms and steadied her, helped her rise and turn. "Is your bed inside?"

"It is . . ." As he helped her to climb, Ilona grabbed either side of the doorjamb and clung. Without his aid, she knew she would collapse into a puddle of abject exhaustion. "Just inside . . ." Oh, Mother, she was weak! The world appeared to be slipping sideways.

"Here. Lie down." He guided her to the cot atop the chest of drawers, ducking roof-ribs. "I'll send someone to you."

Ilona sat down, leaned, then collapsed into bed. She clamped both hands over her face. "Blessed Mother . . ."

"This is my fault," the farmsteader said. "I shouldn't have asked this of you."

"You didn't." Ilona parted her hands just enough so that her mouth was clear. "I offered." The dizziness was worse. It unsettled her stomach. She began to think the nightcrock was in order, and she wanted no witness for that. She opened her hands, noting that the farmsteader looked more worried than ever. "Yes," she said, "do send someone to me." Just so he would leave, and she'd have some privacy for a few moments. Inspiration occured; she knew it would require more of his time than calling for Naiya. "Go to Mikal's ale tent. Bethid might be there. The woman courier."

"I will. Yes." The farmsteader exited hastily.

Ilona covered her face again as sweat broke out on the surface of her skin. Her mouth dried. She made a very long petition to the Mother to settle her belly, if only to distract it, then turned on her side and pulled up her knees. In one of the drawers below was a small bag of tea that would quiet the nausea, but she felt too ill to make the effort.

"This is not fair," she murmured. "Not fair at all."

And yet there was ironic humor in it: Her gift had returned, and she couldn't celebrate.

ALARIO'S HAND, LOCKED into his hair and the base of his neck, infuriated Rhuan. He wanted no physical contact with his sire at all. But before he could speak, before he could react other than grit his teeth in surprise, Alario released him, pushed him aside. "She's broken through," the primary said.

Rhuan, putting distance between himself and his sire with pronounced alacrity, frowned. He exchanged a quick glance with Audrun, who was equally puzzled.

Alario's awareness was patently not of either of them, but of somewhere very much different. His eyes were full of distances. "She's stronger than I thought." Abruptly, with no further speech, he turned and strode into the shadows, disappearing amid trees and brush.

Rhuan stared after him, aware that Audrun did the same. After a long moment of considering silence, they broke that pose and looked at one another, brows raised. Rhuan sighed, managed a wry smile, and tried to make light of it. "Not the kind of father human sons desire."

Audrun was clearly appalled. "Is that behavior *typical*?"

"With primaries? Unfortunately yes." He sat down upon the fallen tree, feeling at the back of his neck where Alario's fingers had dug in. "And yes, all of them are every bit as arrogant as my sire. Imagine, if you can, nine hundred and ninety-nine exactly like him."

"That's impossible, Rhuan."

He worked the muscles at the back of his neck. "Impossible to imagine, impossible to accept, or impossible to be true?"

"All three, I think! He truly is very like a spoiled child."

"But a remarkably dangerous child."

Audrun, too, sat down, placing herself beside him. "Could he have done as I asked? Found my family, transported us to the Kiba?"

"I think it's quite probable. But I'm ignorant of all he

can do . . . we're reared that way, to not know the extent of the primaries' ability to manipulate the wild magic."

"Why? Aren't you his heir?"

Alario's grasp had loosened the leather thong tying back his hair. Rhuan removed it, allowed the coppery curtain to fall forward of his shoulders. He glanced at her a moment, registering her genuine curiosity, then looked back at the dreya ring. The odor of charred wood wreathed the air. "It's different here."

"That, I understand." Her tone was ironically acerbic. "But if you are his only surviving *dioscuri*, and he is unlikely, from what you said, to sire any others, why does he hold you in such contempt?"

He winced; that truth was painful. "Primaries are extremely long-lived. It's a facet of the wild magic. They manipulate it to suit them, and longevity is a part of that. But the only one who knows how much he or she can manipulate, and exactly what can be done, is the individual primary. It's an advantage, obviously, but it's also a weapon." He blew out a breath and looked at her full-on. "For me to inherit my sire's place, I am required to kill him."

Audrun's lips parted. He saw the shock flow into her face, the widening of her pupils. She was not slow of wit; she grasped the consequences immediately. "And you can't."

He shrugged. "That, I don't know. It's possible. When the time comes upon a *dioscuri*, he often has no choice. He challenges because he must. It's a physical and emotional drive, more powerful than any other. Even the need to procreate, though that's interrelated."

"To pull down the strongest so he can make a place for himself . . . and to sire his future replacement."

"It's the central defining conflict of our people. Primaries are driven to sire offspring so *dioscuri* are born—though not many are—and yet from the moment of that birth the sire and the son are locked in competition. The *dioscuri* is a threat, a promise of the primary's ending."

"Do *dioscuri* always win?"

"Oh, no. Not in the least." He gathered his hair into a tail and tied it off. "Quite often the primary kills his own son." Then, as Audrun stared at him in shock, he rose, caught her hands, and pulled her to her feet. "And now, it's time we went looking for the Kiba. We can do nothing here except further discuss my sire's shortcomings, and while that would undoubtedly fill weeks and months, as humans reckon it, it's not particularly productive."

Chapter 26

*B*RODHI AWOKE IN the middle of the night to the awareness, sharp and intense, that someone knelt by his pallet in the sleeping chamber. There was no light whatsoever and there wouldn't be until dawn broke, but he needed none. He moved swiftly and grasped a wrist. When he heard quiet laughter, he gripped more tightly.

"Why?" he breathed.

Ignoring his grasp on her wrist, Ferize slid down, stretched out full length, and settled her body very close to his. Her scent was subtle, but effective; he felt himself respond. He released her wrist, shifted, placed a hand at the back of her neck, buried beneath her hair. She was, he realized, nude.

"Why?"

Deep in her throat, she purred. He slept only in leggings; her hand found the laced flap.

He stopped her. Most pallets were empty, but several hosted sleeping couriers. He knew very well that Ferize would find this a fillip, but he wasn't in the mood to let her dictate terms such as when, and where, and had no desire to entertain fellow couriers. Undoubtedly young Corrid would be astonished.

He rose to his feet, bringing her up with him. Her breasts against his naked chest were intensely warm. The scale-pattern, he knew, was upon her. He walked her backward, spreading his legs so that hers fell in between. At the door he released her, set hands against the wood on either side of her shoulders. Ferize lifted the latch. He pressed the door open, caught her head in his hands, and turned her, guiding her, bringing his lips to hers. Mercifully, she had not yet undone the lacing of his leggings. He walked again, taking her backward, until they reached another door. Once more she lifted the latch; once more, he pressed the door open. It gave. Brodhi closed it quietly behind them, gently setting the latch so no sound was made.

"Ferize—"

She laughed. "Pleasure before business . . ." She silenced him with her mouth. He bore her down to the floor, down upon the rug. He did not stay her hand as she undid the lacing and peeled the leather back. He had time only to consider that they had best finish before dawn, or the Guildmaster, coming to view his map, would be most annoyed.

BETHID, ALARMED BY the farmsteader's message, hastened to Ilona's wagon. There she found the hand-reader lying on her side in her cot, knees drawn up, one hand pressed against her forehead. Her color was ashen. "Ilona!" She moved in close, shifting Ilona's hand to press her own against the brow. It was cool and clammy.

"Tea," Ilona croaked. "A muslin bag tied with blue string, third drawer down on the left."

Bethid knelt and opened the drawer. "I have it."

The voice was weak, but the tone was faintly, barely, ironic. "As soon as possible, if you would, or my belly is going to be quit of every meal I've had for the last several days."

Bethid grinned and pushed herself to her feet. "I'll see to it immediately. Oh, and just in case, here's the nightcrock."

Outside, the cookfire was banked. Bethid uncovered the coals and prepared the tea as quickly as possible, filled the mug, and carried it back into Ilona's wagon. The hand-reader murmured something in relief and raised herself up high enough to accept the mug and drink half the contents down. She paused, made a face of distaste, then drank the remains.

"More?" Bethid asked.

"No, not just now." Ilona sank back against her cushions. "Bless you."

Bethid set the mug aside and perched herself atop the trunk across the narrow aisle. "Possibly I shouldn't ask, but do you want anything to eat?"

"No eating!" Ilona said forcefully. Then, more quietly, "Later." She pressed the back of her hand against her forehead. "Is there word of any sickness in the settlement?"

Bethid shook her head. "Not that I've heard of."

Ilona sighed. "Then I suspect this is linked to the resurgence of my gift. One can't be ungrateful, but one might wish for things to be less . . . violent."

"You can read hands again?"

"Yes. Or at least, I read *a* hand." She blew out a breath. "The farmsteader's." She pushed herself up higher against the cushions, turning on a hip to face Bethid. "Thank the Mother—and you!—the tea is beginning to work."

"Your color's improving," Bethid noted. "Was there good news in his hand, or am I not to ask?" When Ilona closed her eyes, tension tautening her face, Bethid hastened to make amends. "I'm sorry! I shouldn't have asked. It just came right out of my mouth—"

"No, no, it's all right." Ilona rolled her head away and stared at the ceiling. "It's difficult," she said finally, and her tone was a mixture of so many emotions Bethid couldn't name them all, "and painful, to arrive at the realization that someone means a great deal more to you than you thought—and that he's lost to you. Lost to all." She swallowed heavily. "When someone is *so much* a part of your life, even without intimacy, you expect him always to be in it. And when he isn't . . . well, it leaves a very large hole."

Bethid knew whom she meant immediately, and felt

a pang of sympathy. Quietly, she said, "You're certain he's gone?"

"Oh, yes. No one comes out of Alisanos."

"And he's definitely in the deepwood?"

"I saw him there, in the farmsteader's hand. Not long, only a glimpse—but he's there."

"Mother," Bethid murmured. "I'm so sorry, Ilona . . . but . . . " She recalled Jorda saying the two were not lovers. "No intimacy, you said?"

"No. We seemed never to fit in that way. I lost a lover to the Hecari just before Rhuan hired on, and for all his laughter and fecklessness, he can be very pointedly private. I never asked why not. But then, I never asked it of myself, either . . . until recently." She released a long sigh and closed her eyes again. "Too late. Or not meant."

Bethid sought for something appropriate to say, something comforting, but reflected that at this moment nothing *would* be comforting, except privacy. She rose. "I'll let you rest now. I'll come back later."

Ilona made no reply, and Bethid quietly went down the steps.

DAVYN WAITED UNTIL he and the karavan-master were mounted, each man leading one of the draft horses, before he broached the question. It would take several days for them to reach the wagon, time to replace the broken axle and reload the possessions taken out just prior to the storm, and then several days to return, though Jorda agreed that, in the interests of the needs of the karavaners and tent-folk, he would return more quickly with the two borrowed riding horses while Davyn drove the wagon back. It was as they rode across the river and back onto the northern road that Davyn brought it up.

"This other Shoia, Brodhi. Do you know him?"

Jorda, mounted on a stout gray horse and leading a heavy bay, glanced at him sidelong, mouth twisted. "Mostly I know *of* him. Brodhi isn't one for friends or companionship, though he will visit Mikal's from time to time. Why?"

"I know he's gone to Cardatha to tell the warlord about what's happened with Alisanos . . ."

"Yes, and if the Mother is kind, he'll convince the warlord to leave the settlement alone."

Davyn wished he could press a hand against the string of charms around his neck, but one hand held the reins and the other tended the halter-rope attached to the other draft horse, also a bay. "When do you expect him back?"

Jorda reined his gray gelding around a vermin hole and clucked at his draft horse to catch up. "We're not certain. We don't know if Alisanos has cut off the Cardatha road, nor how long the warlord may keep him. Why?"

Davyn ignored the question. "What might buy his services?"

"As a courier? Coin-rings, of course. But his fee depends on distance, and what the Guildhall sets for their share."

"No—as something other than a courier."

That got Jorda's attention. "What do you mean?"

"I wish him to do me a very great service. A very dangerous service. I need him . . ." Davyn inhaled, then exhaled audibly. "I need him to go into Alisanos."

"Sweet Mother!" Jorda was shocked. "Whatever for?"

Davyn said quietly, "My family."

Jorda's reaction was to rephrase the statement as a question. "Why would you even consider asking him to go into Alisanos for your family? It's more than dangerous, man—it's deadly!"

"Because he can *find* my family. I've been told so."

The karavan-master barked a brief, disbelieving laugh. "Whoever told you that is a fool!" He paused a moment, as if aware he might have committed offense, and mellowed his tone. "I can't imagine Brodhi would ever do such a thing. Who told you he would?"

Davyn chose his words with care. "I wasn't told he would go. I was told he *was* there, with my youngest children."

"In Alisanos?"

"The hand-reader told me so, that she saw it when she read my hand earlier this morning."

"Ilona said that . . ." It trailed off before Jorda's tone made it a question. He frowned thoughtfully for a long moment, weighing the information, then met Davyn's eyes. "Ilona reads true."

"Yes. She said that." Davyn grimaced. "And it seems I have done your guide an injustice. He did not purposely send my family into the deepwood . . . in fact, he himself was caught in it even as they were."

Jorda swore loudly and lengthily, reining in his horse so abruptly the one he led bumped into the gray's rump. His expression, mostly hidden by the beard, was a mixture of shock, dismay, disappointment, and concern.

Davyn, halting his mount as well and sorting out reins and lead-rope, sought a way to amend the baldness of his statement. "Perhaps Brodhi could find Rhuan as well as my family."

Jorda stared at him, brows knitted. His tone was hopeful. "Ilona saw *Brodhi* there—she didn't mistake Rhuan for him? That happens often enough."

"She seemed certain. She said Brodhi, more than once." *That he is the key.*

The karavan-master shook his head. "I just can't imagine Brodhi volunteering to enter Alisanos."

"Neither can I," Davyn admitted. "But she saw it in my hand, that Brodhi is in the company of my two youngest." And that, too, he amended in his head: *In the company of two of my youngest* . . . Now that the new child was born, Megritte and Torvic were no longer the babies of the family. "She swore it."

Jorda chewed absently at the tuft of beard jutting out just below the center of his bottom lip. "That may be the only way that Brodhi's willing to do such a thing; that he has no choice, since Ilona's seen it in your hand. Though I believe he will refuse, at least initially. Maybe what happens is that he is also taken." He grimaced. "I suppose it's possible Brodhi's in the deepwood even as we speak, which means both Shoia are trapped."

That awoke a surge of hope in Davyn's body. Perhaps he wouldn't have to hire Brodhi's service at all; perhaps what the hand-reader saw was the natural result of the Shoia being swallowed as well. He was ashamed to admit he hoped that was so, but he did.

Jorda read his face. "It would save you trouble."

"Oh, indeed!" Davyn, hands full of reins and lead-rope, rubbed an ear against a lifted shoulder to rid himself of an insect buzzing near it. "And it may also mean that he has *already* found Torvic and Megritte." He sent a quick, hopeful prayer skyward, toward the pale Mother Moon that waited in the heavens for night to fall. Hope tranformed itself to excitement. "O Mother, let them be brought safely out of the deepwood and back to me!"

Jorda joined him in that. "May it be so. But you do realize we will have no way of knowing what may have happened, or what *will* happen, until Brodhi either returns—"

"—or doesn't." Davyn nodded. "We can only wait. But I believe it will be an easier task for me now, the waiting." Hope bubbled up again, strong as a tankard of raw spirits. "And if I am very fortunate, he will find more than just Torvic and Megritte." He smiled at Jorda. "The hand-reader only saw a few images. Perhaps if I visit her again, she'll see others."

Jorda frowned. Reluctantly, he said, "We can hope so, but I have not seen it happen that way with Ilona."

Davyn crowed a laugh. "But you're not a diviner, karavan-master . . . *should* you see it that way?"

Jorda opened his mouth to answer, thought visibly, then murmured, "We'll know in time."

"Less time," Davyn averred. "Let it be *less* time!"

But in that, the karavan-master didn't join him. He held doubts, Davyn knew. But now it no longer mattered. *The Shoia courier will bring my family out . . .*

AUDRUN LOST TRACK of time. She had not counted the nights they spent beside the dreya ring, or upon the journey. But she could roughly count the number of times she thought of her children, saw the faces of her children, of her husband, in her mind. Hundreds. Hundreds of times. She never once forgot them. Always, always they claimed her mind, and her prayers.

Few rests were allowed, and none of them was of sufficient length. But Rhuan insisted, and each time he urged her to her feet she answered the request. She grew accustomed to seeing the back of him: broad shoulders, narrow hips, tied-back rippled hair hanging to his waist. It was longer than her own.

When he turned to mark where she was, Audrun saw his face in place of his back, and the strain in flesh and features. Each time, with nothing said, she pushed herself the harder to catch up, to keep up, to follow his track.

So many days uncounted. So many days lost.

So many children taken.

SITTING ON THE guildmaster's rug, Brodhi laced up his leggings. "Now that the pleasure appears to be finished, tell me your business."

Ferize, still naked, still sheathed in her opalescent scale pattern, stretched languorously, arching her back as she lay on the rug. "Some choices are more difficult than others."

"I do know that. What's the business about?"

"That."

"What, that?"

"That some choices are more difficult than others." She sat up, wriggled close to him, perched herself in his lap, and wrapped her arms around his neck. This time, her hair was silvery-white, eyes quite black. "That *is* the business, Brodhi."

He detested it when she was coy and cryptic. He set her aside and rose. "I haven't time for word games, Ferize. I'm expecting Hecari warriors to come for me at dawn. It's nearly that now. I have a long ride ahead of me."

She shook back her wealth of hair and rose as well, somehow in the transition gaining a white silk robe that would have been perfectly modest had the neckline not plunged to her navel. "And it will be longer yet, depending on your choice."

He faced her with hands on hips. "Ferize—"

"Your road may fork," she said, "or it may not. Is that so difficult to understand? The words are plain, yes?"

"The words are plain, yes, but—"

"Then what more should I say? What occurs when you arrive at a crossroads?"

He bit back a retort. She was not, after all, being cryptic or coy. "You choose which way to go."

Ferize smiled. "So you do."

The door latch rattled. Brodhi swore. Ferize just grinned at him, and when a moment later the Guildmaster opened the door to his map chamber, he stopped short in startlement. "Where did that cat come from?"

Brodhi said smoothly, "She must have gotten in yesterday and hidden herself. I heard her calling, and found her here." He bent, scooped up the silvery-gray cat, tucked it under one arm. "I'll send her on her way out of doors."

"Do that." The Guildmaster made a gesture of dismissal and rounded his table. "Hecari are in the courtyard waiting for you. They are not, as a rule, patient."

"Then I'll collect my belongings and take my leave." Brodhi walked out of the chamber, but paused as the Guildmaster said something more.

"Be careful, Brodhi. You've two enemies, now, on this ride: Hecari, and Alisanos."

Brodhi smiled thinly. "Pleasure before business."

Chapter 27

THE TEA, THANK the Mother, was effective. Ilona breathed a sigh of extreme relief, gently patting a hand against her formerly upset belly, and sat up in bed, legs dangling over the side. Jorda had come not long after Bethid's departure and fitted a replacement canopy over the roof-ribs, lacing the oilcloth through holes and tying rope around various davits. Once again she had privacy, with heavy wooden walls providing shelter at either end, and the oilcloth pulled down low on the sides, weighted with lengths of wood to keep the wind from lifting it. Well, normal wind, she reflected; the storm had found easy purchase. Ilona felt at ease again now that she had a choice of raw daylight or privacy and shelter beneath the oilcloth. The Mother Rib still lacked the string of protective charms normally attached to it, but they would be replaced in time. In the meantime, she could send prayers to the Mother of Moons as well as to Sibetha, god of hand-readers, for her survival.

The closed door rattled. Ilona looked up, feeling the wagon shift beneath someone's weight on the steps. She expected to hear a knock, or a voice calling her name, but neither occured. Just as she was rising to go to the door, it was pulled open. A man upon the bottom step filled the doorway.

Her knees faltered. She sat down very hard upon the edge of her cot.

He was as she remembered. Tall, broad, mature, incandescent with something inside that overwhelmed all. Coppery hair, arranged in complex braid patterns, glinted with glass and gold. His clothing, as she remembered all too well, was supple, scaled, russet hide, with a wide, gold-bossed belt riding his hips. His eyes were Rhuan's; his face was not, despite similarities. And as he smiled, she saw there were no dimples.

What shot through her mind were any number of opening comments, none of them particularly effective at underscoring her intelligence. Ilona shut her mouth and stared at him. Just that. It was not wise, she realized instinctively, to let him know she was confused and concerned. Best to show strength, or nothing at all. He was a man who would use any hesitation or momentary lapse as a weapon. She was neither a fool nor a coward, but there was no question she felt the power at his call. As a diviner, she was open to such things, more sensitive to power. He made her senses tingle, but it wasn't desire. It was the simple awareness of threat, and of danger.

His smile grew into a grin. Indeed, no dimples.

"Alive and in the flesh. Though I doubt you recall our last meeting."

She arched both brows, trying not to let him know she was guessing based on information from Bethid. "You must mean the one we shared at the verge of Alisanos, not far from the river."

He had not expected that. She saw a brief, slight downward twitch in his eyebrows, but he recovered easily. "Good. This speaks well of you. Few humans— possibly no humans—might remember that."

He was male. Not human, but male. She knew males. "Well, I suspect you are often remembered— and you may take that in whatever vein you wish."

"A compliment, certainly." He climbed the next two steps and ducked down to get through the low door.

Ilona looked again at the braids, the ornamentation of the complex arrangement hanging down his spine. Rhuan had told her it was a Shoia tradition. But the question begged to be asked. "You're not Shoia, are you?"

He paused, and grinned at her. "Indeed not."

She kept her expression and voice casual. "Then Rhuan also is not Shoia? Or Brodhi?"

"Occasionally," he answered. "It serves very well as explanation for resurrection. The name is a euphemism—there are no Shoia anymore. We assume the name of an extinct race as means to make ourselves comprehensible to humans when we're in the human world."

She recalled Rhuan apparently forgetting the number of "deaths" he had experienced. "Then you don't die at all?"

"We can be *killed* in your world, yes, any number of times—but it's never permanent. We learned it was simpler to give ourselves six deaths in any one place before moving on."

She took the gamble. "And in your world?"

He lowered himself to sit on the trunk opposite her cot. Their knees touched. Ilona moved hers aside to escape the contact. "My world is somewhat more perilous."

It was obvious to her now. "Alisanos."

"Alisanos. Yes."

"Are you a demon?"

Teeth flashed in a grin. "I suppose it depends on your perspective. But no. We are not demons."

He looked so much like Rhuan that she had to ask it. "You're kin, are you not? To Rhuan?"

"To Rhuan, yes, and to Brodhi. Brodhi is to me what humans would call a nephew. Rhuan is my get." He paused, seeing the flicker in her eyes, and amended it: "Son."

He had said "is." Not "was." Hope surged. "Then he's still alive?"

"For now."

"In Alisanos."

He smiled. "For now."

The rush of relief was immediate and tremendous, but seasoned still with fear. Not for herself; for this man's son. His *get*. "What is it you want of me?"

"You have no other memory of our meeting?"

She saw no reason to prevaricate; this man, this—*whatever*—knew the truth. "Only that we met."

"I healed your arm." Before she could stop him, he closed a broad hand around her wrist. "Don't you feel the bone within renewed? Does your blood not sing?"

"I was ill." She removed her wrist from his grasp. "Nothing was singing."

"And now?"

Now—yes. Weariness was banished, the last dregs of dullness. She felt entirely well and strong. Indeed, her blood sang. "You did this. Just now."

"Then, and now. Do you see how your body answers mine?"

"Why did you do it? Why heal me?"

"Because you will be most useful to me." He leaned forward, elbows set on thighs. "I wish to make you my *diascara*. In your tongue: wife."

Of all the answers she might have expected, that was not one of them. Ilona stared at him blankly. "Your what?"

"Wife."

"Blessed Mother of Moons! *Why?*"

"Because I'm in need of one."

She gave up trying to recapture a casual demeanor; things now had gone well beyond dissimulation. "And you come to *me*?"

"You," he said, smiling, "may be the answer to my prayers." His grin flashed. "Should I pray to myself, that is."

Ilona made a tremendous mental effort to snag her wits away from various odd wanderings, each incited by this man to follow a different line of thought. "Setting aside the undoubtedly great honor you do me," she wondered fleetingly if he understood irony, "—why in the Mother's world would I become your wife?"

Surprising her with his swiftness, he caught one of her hands, raised it, and kissed her palm. Softly, he said, "Because I wish it."

She snatched her hand back. It made him laugh. "You have little experience of humans, don't you?"

"My most recent *diascara* was a human."

Ilona cocked a suspicious eyebrow. "Where is she now?"

"Quite dead."

It seemed not to touch him in the least. There was neither sadness nor even acknowledgment that a death might be undesireable. But then, he was not human. "If you are not Shoia, nor demon, what are you?"

"I am what is worshipped."

Ilona laughed out loud. "Women fall at your feet, do they?"

He didn't smile. "I am quite serious."

"*Why* would you be worshipped?"

Somehow both hands were in his. She did not recall how they got there. "Because I am a god."

Ilona stood upright, nearly cracking her skull on a curved roof-rib as she yanked her hands free. "*Oh,* no. No. No such thing. I am not so stupid—nor am I remotely swayed by what I admit, in all honesty, is your undeniable attraction—as to accept that as truth."

He was tall enough, even seated, that his head was not particularly lower than hers. "I can, of course, prove it to you. What would you like me to do?"

"*Leave.*"

He laughed at her. "No."

"Then bring Rhuan here."

The laughter died. For all the heat in his eyes, in his body, his stare now was glacial. "I think not."

"That is what I ask."

"Alas, you will simply have to wonder if it can be done." Brown eyes remained cold despite the upward curving of his lips. "You humans value explanations, even if proof is presented. Very well. I am in need of an heir."

She could remain standing, or sit down and take support from the steadiness of her cot. Since he made no attempt to touch her again, Ilona sat down. "If Rhuan is your son, you're in no need of an heir."

"That get is . . . inferior."

Her brows arched up. "*Rhuan* is inferior?"

He took her measure carefully, evaluating expression, posture, tone of voice. Something flickered in his eyes, something briefly red and wholly hostile. But it passed, and she couldn't be certain she had seen any such thing. Until he spoke. "My recent—wife—was initially uncertain. Let me assure you that she came to understand the needs of my people, and embraced them wholeheartedly. She gave me a son who might have grown to be everything I wished in an heir, except for one abiding flaw."

Ilona kept her mouth shut precisely because he expected her to speak.

His lips twitched briefly. "He lacks dedication, my ge—my son. He would rather spend himself in cheap human whores, spilling his seed with no regard for his kin-in-kind. Do you believe he is above that? Be not misled. You are a hand-reader, and you have a true gift. But has he ever allowed you to read *his* hand? Or has he always found a way to refuse?"

She could not hide the flicker of her own eyes as he touched on what had always troubled her.

"My son," he said, "is beautiful, as are all our people, and I understand at times he can be quite charming. He has the flame inside, but it is banked. He might one day have grasped my power, become the greatest of all the Thousand Gods, even as I am—but he has no sense of responsibility. He turns his back on his people and—"

"—and wastes his time on humans?" Ilona didn't smile. "You have yet to provide a single argument for why I should believe that Rhuan is unfit."

"Ah, he has blinded you." The tone was sorrowful. "Ai, he is a rogue who attracts women the way honey draws flies. I am sorry—I believed you too wise to be trapped as others are."

She might have smiled triumphantly, but did not.

"Then apparently I am not well-suited to be your wife after all."

The humor in his eyes died. "Allow me to speak plainly."

A startled blurt of laughter escaped her mouth. "Oh, *please* do!"

"I have a brother. Karadath. In our world, kin who are primaries compete for position within the pantheon. Attaining the highest level is dependent upon many things, not the least of which is the number of *dioscuri* we sire, and of course grooming the one we feel best suited to inherit after us. The *dioscuri* compete as well, and kill one another until eventually only one remains. All of my *dioscuri* are dead, save one. He should have been killed by one of his half brothers. He wasn't. Karadath, too, has only one surviving *dioscuri*—"

"Brodhi . . ." She felt numb—numb and battered.

"And Brodhi is far more fit to inherit Karadath's place than Rhuan is mine, which provides Karadath with an edge. It is a stain on me that Rhuan is so inferior—"

"Wait." She stopped the flow of words with a raised hand. Something inside her had turned cold, painfully cold. "Are you saying that Rhuan and Brodhi are supposed to try to kill one another?"

He frowned. "No. Of course not. The heir is supposed to kill the *sire,* to assume his place. But the challenge can only be approved when the heir has completed various tests, when he is believed to be mentally and physically fit, and when the true need comes upon him. All are required elements." He lifted one eloquent shoulder. "If the *dioscuri* is killed by his sire, then the sire is expected to bring another candidate forward if any are living. If not, he is expected to sire another. This competition among siblings, among sires and *dioscuri,* makes certain only the strongest ascend."

"Your people . . ." She drew in a breath, trying to parse out a clear, precise response from all of the things she wished to say. "Your people have a frighteningly brutal way of living."

"At the next ascension, Karadath will hold a higher place than I because Brodhi is more fitting. Rhuan is weak. He is inferior—"

"And thus you are vulnerable to challenges by others."

"None of them is capable of killing me," he said matter-of-factly, "but yes, having an inferior heir does weaken my standing among the pantheon. Karadath is gaining support. I must prevent that. Therefore I wish to sire another *dioscuri,* one who will raise my standing. I believe it is possible you may provide me with that son, a true *dioscuri,* strong enough to one day kill me, fit to inherit my place. I believe you *will* do so." His clear, cold gaze locked on hers. "And I believe that to arrive at that result, one must do as one sees fit."

She knew enough of him now to take that as a threat. Precisely as he meant it.

Ilona rose. She moved past him, bumping his knees,

and opened the wagon door. She stood there in the sunlight, meeting him eye to eye across a distance of eight feet. "Leave."

Once again, he evaluated her. His thoughts she could not decipher. He rose, ducked, moved to the door. They stood so closely her breasts nearly brushed his chest. She was not unaware of the power of his presence, the incredible *maleness* that reached out to her.

She clamped her teeth closed. Lifted her chin. Held his eyes, and did not waver beneath them.

Surprisingly, he smiled. "Precisely what I want."

She stared after him as he dropped from floorboards to ground, disdaining her folding steps. He walked away from her wagon, away from the grove, striding easily toward the trees a half-mile away.

Toward Alisanos.

Ilona sat down in the doorway, one leg bent beneath her. She felt quite strong, stronger than one might expect after her experiences, but her mind felt bruised by so much startling information. Information she could not believe, but felt she must. If she were to survive.

Rhuan is expected to kill his father.

As Rhuan had, apparently, killed all of his brothers.

GILLAN PRESSED HIS spine and the back of his skull into the tree he leaned against, grabbing up fistfuls of tough groundcover as Darmuth changed the dressing on his leg. The pain was immense as air touched the burns. A few days prior, when he shamefacedly begged for a way to stop his screaming, the demon handed him a modest length of tree branch, cleaned of bark, and told him to bite on it. Gillan did. The stick did not halt the cries or suppress them completely, but they were muted. His teeth left impressions in the wood.

This time as Darmuth unwrapped the bandaging, Gillan looked. He had avoided doing so for several days, afraid of what he would see. But when Darmuth muttered absently that it was "much better," and "it's taking," Gillan forced himself to view the demon's handiwork.

What he saw shocked him into nausea.

"What did you do? What have you done?"

Darmuth said matter-of factly, "Given you flesh."

Gillan trembled so hard he thought his teeth might chatter. "But—but . . . it's not . . . it's not—"

"Human? No." Darmuth began to wrap more shielding around the wasted lower limb.

"Wait—" Gillan lurched forward off the tree and grabbed Darmuth's hands. "Let me *see*—"

Accordingly, the demon removed his hands. He waited.

Still, Gillan shook. He stared in shock at his calf. It lacked muscle to define the shape from knee to ankle, but it was a leg. It was *his* leg. Except for the flesh covering the bone. That was scaled.

"O Mother . . . O Mother . . ."

"You will walk," Darmuth said. "Be not so ungrateful."

"It's—it's—"

"Demon flesh. Yes. So?" Darmuth lifted an eyebrow. "Would you rather have lost the leg?"

Part of him wished to scream *Yes!* Part of him remained so horrified that all he could do was stare. Gray, gleaming flesh, tissue quite fine, overlaid with black-edged scales. He could not bring himself to touch it.

Gillan fell back against the tree, aware of tears in his eyes. But shock was fading and now the pain returned. He winced, closed his eyes, fumbled for the stick.

Darmuth put it into his hand. "Recall, if you please, that a demon has kept you alive."

He knew that. He knew that. But it was one thing to be tended by a demon, and another to have demon flesh become a part of his body.

"I took it from my thigh," Darmuth said casually. "It had to be living flesh, not from a corpse; and I know of no demon who would, while alive, give up his flesh to a human."

Gillan's eyes popped open. He took the stick from his mouth. "*You* did it."

"You may thank Rhuan for that." Darmuth's hands, skilled and efficient, began wrapping the limb. "He cares about your family more than any other. And I suspect you *will* be able to thank him in person. In the flesh, as it were." He displayed perfectly human teeth in a sardonic grin.

As the leg was covered, some of the pain diminished. Gillan still trembled, but speech was easier. "Rhuan's here, too?"

"He was with your mother when the storm came down." Darmuth applied a length of cloth stripped from Gillan's tunic. "He will be making his way to the Kiba to address the primaries. We should be there."

Now he was confused. "Be where?"

"At the Kiba."

"But—"

"He has displayed an increasing tendency to protect and defend humans," Darmuth continued, "which no doubt will infuriate Alario, but it will also please Karadath and those who oppose Alario. I suspect he will ask the primaries to let you and your mother, provided she still lives, be returned to the human world."

Hope leaped painfully within his chest. "We can go back?"

"Pin no hopes on it," Darmuth suggested. "It's highly unlikely—and will you wish to go back, wearing demon skin?"

Gillan stared at the bandaging. His thoughts tumbled in his mind like creek water over stones. "I wear trews," he said finally. "Who will know?"

Darmuth's eyes were pale, pale gray. The pupils elongated. "Living skin grows."

Gillan blinked. "What?"

"Eventually, no amount of clothing will hide your scales."

His reaction was instantaneous. Gillan cried out,

pushed himself sideways off the tree, scrabbled away. The limb would not support him. Pain renewed itself. Eventually he fell backward, landing upon his elbows. He stared at Darmuth in almost paralyzing shock. "Take it off! Take it off!"

"The skin is living. Your blood runs in its tissues."

"Take it off! *Cut* it off!"

Darmuth raised an eyebrow. "The leg?"

"Cut it *off!*"

"How will you survive Alisanos with only one leg?" Gillan screamed.

Sighing, Darmuth picked up the forgotten stick. He rose, went to Gillan, and squatted down beside him. With no ceremony at all, he shoved the stick into his open mouth and held it there. "Your choice, boy. Be a man, or be a child."

Sweating from pain, trembling in shock, Gillan stopped screaming. Tears coursed down his face.

"Better." Darmuth removed the stick. "Weeping is quieter."

ILONA SAT FOR a long time in the open door of her wagon. She watched the sun set. She watched twilight come. She watched the first stars appear in the sky, and Mother Moon brightening among them. She heard snatches of conversation from others carrying within the grove, karavaners sorting out cookfires and the evening meal. She won-

dered why she wasn't hungry. She wondered why
she remained on the floor of her wagon when there
were things to do.

Rhuan's father wanted to sire a child on her.

It was a small sound at first, a brief, choppy exhala-
tion coupled with something that was precursor to
laughter. Ilona closed her eyes, leaned her head
against the doorjamb behind her, and gave way to
honest if quiet laughter shaped by a plethora of emotions, most of which she could not name. They passed
through her mind too quickly. It was ridiculous. It was
ludicrous. It was entirely, absolutely, incontrovertibly
unbelieveable.

When the laughter stopped, leaving behind a grin,
she brushed her hair back from her face and opened
her eyes. And found a woman waiting at the bottom of
her steps.

Ilona was instantly aware of the tableau she presented, slumped in the open doorway with one leg
doubled under her, the other trailing down the steps,
skirts tumbled awry. She saw doubt in the woman's
blue eyes as well as reticence.

Immediately her professionalism asserted itself.
"May I help you?"

The woman had light brown hair, though much of it
was hidden beneath an enveloping shawl. She was
young, her face a lovely oval, but strain printed her
face with an unattractive tautness. "You're the hand-
reader?"

"I am." Ilona smiled crookedly. "Though at this par-

ticular moment, that may strike you as unlikely." And
it bloomed again in her mind, in her heart: she was
able to read hands again, when for a while she could
not. "I'm afraid I haven't had time to arrange my table
and cushions outside; would you like to come in?"

The woman glanced past her, looking inside the
wagon, though with the sun gone the interior was
murky. She nodded.

Ilona got up, realized one leg was nearly asleep,
and set about finding flint and steel, a lantern containing wick and oil, the means to illuminate her tall
wagon with its new canopy. She jerked the rumpled
cot coverlet into order, then turned and gestured for
the woman to enter. And as Ilona waited for her to
seat herself on the cot, she reflected that the time
spent with this young woman would do more to restore her sense of self than anything else. Smiling,
happy, she sat down beside the woman and took the
work-roughened hand into her own.

Chapter 28

THE HECARI WARLORD sent four of his warriors to accompany Brodhi back to the settlement. They were as all Hecari males: dark-skinned, black-eyed, skulls shorn save for a black scalplock, faces painted indigo from mid-face down. Heavy ear-spools stretched their lobes. They carried warclubs and blow-pipes and poisoned darts.

He discovered within a matter of moments prior to departing the Guildhall that either they spoke almost no Sancorran, or spoke it well and hid it. Brodhi's grasp of Hecari was quite good but he saw no reason to indicate that. He said only what was necessary; otherwise, he rode in silence.

In the evenings, over dinner, the warriors spoke quietly among themselves but without excessive conversation. At night, two were always on guard duty while the other two slept. Brodhi let them tend that duty; it gave him opportunity to sleep the nights through.

As at last they left the Cardatha road, cutting northward across open grasslands, the warriors' alertness level increased tenfold. They exchanged a few terse words concerning the new route, but did not question Brodhi. They watched him, fixing black, fathomless stares on him. Days had passed since Brodhi journeyed this way headed to Cardatha, but his horse's hoofprints were still visible. No rain, no wind, no one else upon his tracks. The world felt immense, untenanted.

When the smudge upon the horizon formed itself into forest, Brodhi noted the warriors exchanging glances. In his company they were neither voluble nor expressive men, but he was well aware that the appearance of the forest where none had been before, and their awareness of it, suggested the warriors had at one time ridden this way. Possibly they had been part of the culling party that decimated the settlement. They knew very well that they followed no familiar track, that the forest now stood where none had stood before. All maps, all knowledge of routes, were suddenly obsolete. To a nomadic people whose overriding goal was to conquer provinces, such things as disappearing roads and unexpected forests was of great concern. Alteration of the land was potential alteration of their warlord's plans.

Brodhi smiled. The four men made deft, quick gestures to one another that conveyed precisely how concerned they were. He saw it in their eyes, in their faces, in their postures. Now and again their black eyes flicked in his direction, searching his face for telltale signs of fear or superstition. Brodhi maintained a bland quietude that little by little added to their concern.

He took them up to the narrow opening, to the gateway through the curving arms of Alisanos. There he reined in. He waited as they did, watching their eyes shift from his face to the opening, to the close-grown forest on either side. It was the beast's maw, and they knew it. The warlord had obviously told them what Brodhi had told *him*, and these men knew enough to take Alisanos very seriously.

They were not, Brodhi knew, men who would willingly ride into the deepwood simply because he suggested it, ignorant of consequences. They reined their horses into a single line, pointedly placing him at the front. Each right hand now held a blowpipe.

Brodhi said, in Sancorran lacking intonation or emphasis, "Don't go into the forest. Devils abide there, and they will behead, dismember, and eat you."

There was no reaction from the men save continuing suspicious stares.

In fluent Hecari, he repeated the warning. As they exchanged startled, frowning glances, hands tightening on blowpipes, Brodhi calmly lifted the reins from his horse's neck and led the warriors single-file through the opening.

 A DAY OUT from the settlement, Davyn halted the team for the evening, pulling off to the side of the nearly impassable shortcut. Chores took up the twilight, actions so familiar he need not think about what he was doing: placing wheel chocks; unhitching the borrowed team and hobbling them, freeing them of the harness, brushing them down; laying a modest fire so he might have tea. As night spread around him, cloaking the grasslands, he ate dried meat and fruit, smoked his pipe, drank tea. It was the first time he had undertaken ordinary tasks since his family had been taken; all of his mind had been utterly focused on his loss, on the absence of those he loved, on ideas for their recovery. Desperation now was banished because of the hand-reader's description of what she saw in his hand. Worry remained, as did anxiousness and a sense of urgency, but there was room now to breathe, space within his mind to find a small release from the crazed fear and lack of self-control that had driven him to the settlement, to accuse the Shoia guide of intentionally sending his family to the deepwood.

Ashamed, Davyn looked up at Mother Moon, gravid in the heavens. He asked her forgiveness for behaving so poorly, for making assumptions about a man's character. He vowed to her that he would apologize to the guide, once his family was safe from Alisanos.

Nightsingers filled the evening with continuous sound. A breeze ruffled the grass. He heard the horses snorting as they grazed, blowing dirt out of nostrils. Fireflies flickered near the ground. With his spine against a wagon wheel, the hub softened by a folded blanket, Davyn felt a measure of relief trickle into his soul. The world smelled of grass, of woodsmoke, of horses and tea and seasoned meat. The blanket behind him carried the scent of his children. Time, only time, and patience, were needed. Brodhi would find Torvic and Megritte, and then they would search for the others. And Rhuan, Rhuan was with Audrun. He would see her safe.

On the journey to the settlement, Davyn had slept out of doors with Audrun, leaving the wagon to the children. But this night he craved company as best he could get it. Instead of a sleeping mat spread upon the ground and absent of Audrun, he climbed into the wagon, found the family bedding, and settled down for the night upon the floorboards. In his mind, he could hear his children, recalling snatches of conversation, glimpses of their faces. For the first time since the storm, he went to sleep smiling.

MIKAL, WITH JORDA back from accompanying the farmsteader to his wagon, quietly called a meeting of certain men in the karavan and from the settlement as the sun went down. Bethid learned of the meeting from Timmon and Alorn, and accompanied them to the ale tent. As she entered she saw Mikal note her presence and smile crookedly, with an expression that suggested he should have expected her. Jorda took note of her and merely indicated a table near the bar with a tilt of his head. Within moments all benches and stools were filled.

Jorda and Mikal stood before the bar. Quietly, with economy and clarity, each man spoke. They outlined their thoughts, described details, offered suggestions, answered every question without hesitation. Bethid realized the topic had likely been on their minds for some time, discussed at length, and they had finally felt the occasion was right to bring it to the survivors. But they knew better than to address everyone; they had chosen certain men in order to keep control of the discussion, knowing these men would carry clear word to the others without the freight of excess emotion. It would prevent dissention, curtail panic. Wise, Bethid thought.

She disagreed with none of it. She wondered, however, if any of the survivors would be able to do what Jorda and Mikal recommended. She wasn't certain *she* could.

Then Bethid remembered watching Kendic die in a sea of Hecari, recalled the panicked screaming, the shrieking of the children, the sound of skulls being pulped by warclubs, the odor of burning oilcloth and human bodies, and knew that yes, she could do it.

The only question, she realized, was *when*.

AUDRUN DISCOVERED THAT Rhuan's stamina was far superior to hers. It did not come as a surprise; it was confirmation of something she hadn't thought about, but admitted to readily as he led her through the deepwood. This was home to him. She understood now that the membrane in his eyes, akin to a third eyelid, was necessary in a land with two suns, as was the coppery tint to his skin. The interwoven tree canopy, Rhuan explained, provided shelter against the suns, but not all of Alisanos lay under canopy. The suns were small, he said, not like the single one she was accustomed to in the human world; she simply would have to adjust to having two hanging overhead. Long sleeves, he advised, and a broad-brimmed hat, when they left the forest. Also there were plant oils she could use to protect her skin.

Progress was difficult. Without paths, tracks, or trails, their way was obscured by any number of trees, vines, thorny underbrush, ropelike groundcover that caught at the ankles, twisted roots hidden beneath leaf mold. Her legs felt battered and sore, her hands were victim to numerous cuts from swinging branches and fronds, and from time to time she simply fell down. Each time, Rhuan walked back to help her up, then calmly suggested they go on without delay. *He* managed not to fall down, but then he was taller than she, his legs were very much longer, and he was simply stronger. He had been born to this deepwood, reared in it. To her, it was nightmare come alive.

She fell into the habit of asking him, each time they stopped at a stream for water, to catch a breath, or to relieve themselves, how much farther they had to go.

By the sixth stop and her sixth version of the question, Rhuan simply looked at her.

Audrun shoved loose hair out of her face and stared back. "Well?"

"What was your answer each time your children asked how much farther it was to the settlement?"

"It depended on whether it was the same day, or another."

"The same day."

She opened her mouth, then shut it.

"Exactly," Rhuan said. He gestured. "Shall we?"

She watched his back retreat. Several different responses warred in her mind, but none made it as far as her mouth. She needed her breath for walking. For crashing through the obstacles Alisanos saw fit to put in her way. Once again she batted branches aside, ducked sharp-edged fronds, tore a foot away from vines wrapping around her ankles, slapped at the insects that flew toward her face. Rhuan was approximately three paces ahead of her, and she was unable to close the gap no matter how hard she tried.

"*You*," she gasped, "never had a baby. *You* never carried a child for nine full months. You never had four months of pregnancy escalate into a matter of hours . . . you have no idea what it is to deal with sore, leaking, overfull breasts . . . or to completely lose your sense of balance because your belly is huge and your back is tired . . . nor have you had to tend other children while pregnant with the next. You haven't the *faintest* idea of what it is to be a woman who's recently given birth. You—"

"I," he said from very close by, and she glanced up in time to stop herself from crashing into him.

She muttered an apology, caught her balance, pushed hair out of her face again, and looked up at him, panting.

"I have done none of those things, it's true."

"Well—" She yanked a booted foot free of an encroaching vine, spat out the foul taste of tree sap. "It isn't easy! Any of those things! It's cursed difficult!"

"Audrun—"

She stomped on grass attempting to insinuate itself beneath the remains of her skirt, picked out a twig hanging from her hair in front of her eyes, peeled away from her neck a delicate but tensile clinging vine. "I," she said, "have done all of these things. Several times—well, no, I haven't had more than one escalated pregnancy, but the point is—"

"Audrun—"

"—that I'm tired!" She wiped a forearm across her face, still breathing hard. "I'm tired." Her voice and emotions ran down into exhausted blankness. "I'm . . . just . . . tired." When he said nothing at all, merely waited as if he expected her to add more commentary, Audrun gestured. "All right. We can go on now."

"Are you sure?"

"Yes." She picked a soggy strand of hair out of her mouth. "Yes."

"Are you very sure?"

She glared at him. "Just *go!*"

Rhuan went.

THE VEGETABLE GARDEN died. The chickens died, depriving them of eggs. Blight struck the wheat. When ears of corn were stripped, kernels were discovered shriveled on the cob. Snares remained empty. Melons rotted in infancy. They ate up every scrap of food remaining in Lirra's cabin, rationing it so carefully they all were hungry night and day. Lirra's expression was frozen into a taut, stricken mask. Meggie, again, cried every night.

"We could fish," Torvic offered as they all sat on Lirra's bed, contemplating their straits. Meggie was on his left, Lirra to his right.

Lirra was distracted. "We're nowhere near a stream or river."

"We could *find* one," Torvic said. "We could leave here for a few days and go looking."

She glanced at him sidelong. "You and Meggie?"

"You could stay here and check the snares, tend the stinkwood fire . . . we'd look for fish. And fruit!"

Lirra sighed. Her eyes were distant again. "It's a brave offer, Torvic, and I thank you, but I fear it's much too dangerous for you and Meggie to go alone."

"A river might come *here*," Torvic said, who had at last grasped the unpredictability that was Alisanos.

"Rivers don't do that," declared Meggie, who hadn't.

"They do here," Torvic muttered.

"They do," Lirra agreed. "And it's true that a stream may be closer to us now." She chewed absently at her lower lip. "If we built a large enough stinkwood fire, I could accompany you. We couldn't go very far, I don't think, but if we sorted out our directions very carefully and went out each way a certain distance before returning to build up the fire again, we might have some luck." She leaned forward to see Megritte beyond Torvic. "Would that suit you, Meggie?"

In a very small voice, Meggie said, "I'm hungry."

Lirra smiled. "Then that settles it. We'll gather up the biggest pile of stinkwood ever seen in the deepwood, and go hunting for fish! Shall we begin now? Meggie? Torvic?"

Torvic scooched himself to the edge of the bed and let himself down. "Come on, Meggie."

Meggie crawled across the bed. "Stinkwood stinks."

Lirra laughed. "Indeed it does! Which is a very good thing for us all, don't you think?"

Torvic did not miss the worry that remained in Lirra's eyes. "We'll find fish," he declared, to lessen that worry. *"We will."*

Chapter 29

RHUAN KNEW AUDRUN was exhausted and badly in need of rest, but the very kind of rest she needed was not what he dared allow any time soon. It was too dangerous. The longer they remained in one place, even to sleep, the more likely it was they might be attacked by beast, demon, or devil; the more likely it was that Audrun, with momentum halted, would not be able to continue; and, of course, the longer it would take for them to reach the Kiba. It was vital they reach the Kiba as soon as possible, either to mitigate the damage Alario might have already done them, were he there; or to, in fact, prepare their own offense before he could arrive. And so Rhuan insisted Audrun keep moving; insisted they could stop only rarely, and only if absolutely necessary; woke her at dawn and urged her on yet again. She was flagging, but he saw also a core of resilience within her she very likely was unaware of. Were she weaker, were she less deter- mined, were she the kind to give in, pushing her so hard would have been unnecessary because there would be no hope of winning over the primaries at the Kiba. It was precisely *because* he felt Audrun capable of confronting the primaries on their own ground, entirely unintimidated by them or by her surroundings, that Rhuan was willing to make himself resented and hated.

Unhappily, he recognized that by behaving in such a manner, whatever the reason, he risked being viewed more like his sire than he ever anticipated.

The forest canopy overhead began to thin. Trees grew farther apart, copses and groves grew sparse. Two suns blazed overhead, dazzling their eyes. Audrun took to holding a wide, flat plant frond atop her head to shade her face and shield her eyes. The forest floor, dense with leaf mold, deadfall, and underbrush, became firmer underfoot, giving way to terraces of stone. The terrain altered from mostly flat to uneven, rocks forming shoulders, crude steps, upthrust spines upon the earth. To avoid slipping on inclines, they grasped vines to lower themselves down the steeper areas, soil and leaf mold sliding away beneath their boots. Audrun lost her frond when two hands were required. Her nose and cheeks slowly reddened.

Down and down they climbed, slipping, sliding, losing footing frequently. Audrun no longer asked how much farther they had to go, when they might rest, what they could eat. Either she had no breath for it, or she conserved and banked her anger for a time she viewed as ideal to confront him.

As the suns stood sentinel overhead, Rhuan sought and found the rock formation he had guided them toward all along. On the downslope of a steep hillside, huge, tall outcroppings of grainy, gray-purple stone presented a narrow chute, a slotted opening that appeared to end in a wall of rock. But Rhuan knew the slot bent left behind a gleaming bulge of faceted, ruddy stone that was visible only during brief periods of the day, at dawn and dusk. As he paused on the cusp, followed by Audrun, who was breathing hard and sweating, he lifted his arms in a wholly spontaneous gesture of success and relief. He swung around, smiling, took a long step to her, and grasped her shoulders.

"Almost," he said, *"almost."* She stared at him blankly. He tightened his grip on her shoulders. "Audrun, we rest here the night. We may take time tomorrow as well. The Kiba is very close."

"Don't touch me," she said with exquisite clarity.

He released her as if she burned his hands. "Audrun, I'm sorry. I'm sorry—"

"Be quiet." Her voice was ragged. "Silence from you, in fact, would be best of all."

He opened his mouth to apologize again, to say he understood, but nothing in her eyes suggested that was wise. After a moment he inclined his head in brief acknowledgment, then indicated the slot in the twin walls of stone. "The path is clear."

She slanted him a sharp look. "Prey goes first?"

Rhuan shook his head. "Guests go first."

The brief expulsion of breath was a scornful laugh lacking in humor, devoid of forgiveness. Audrun walked past him and entered the slot.

For a moment he remained where he was, staring after her vanished body. A vow wholly alien to one born of Alisanos, but somehow oddly fitting, rose in his mind: *Mother of Moons, let her come to understand.*

IT WAS NEARING sundown as Brodhi led his complement of Hecari into the settlement. In his absence a large bonfire area had been raked and tended, rocks set to ring it, a pyramid of wood leaning against one another in its center. Small cookfires dotted the surviving grove; the bonfire, obviously, was for communal gatherings. Mikal's tent stood where it always had, appearing somewhat sturdier than when he had left; other tents, some with multicolored patches in place of uniformly-colored oilcloth, had been pitched as well. This time it was not a helter-skelter jumble of tents raised by whim and inclination, leading to tangled skeins of footpaths, but a clearly delineated circle around the bonfire area. Karavan wagons still inhabited the grove of elder trees, but even the immediate environs of each wagon appeared to be neatly tended. This was not a haphazard transient stopover thrown up by those in a hurry to depart, but a true settlement.

Riding ahead of the warriors, Brodhi was nonetheless aware of their low-voiced commentary, the tension infiltrating their tones. Blowpipes remained in their hands, and warclubs hanging by their knees were tested for ease of unhooking. They broke out of their single file to spread themselves behind him, horse by horse by horse by horse, with room between each mount. He heard the word for *culling*. He heard the word for *decimation*. He heard them say to one another the warlord would not be pleased, that a place so recently culled would come out of the experience with a greater sense of permanence.

Brodhi halted his horse six paces or more from the bonfire ring. The Hecari behind him halted as well. By the moment, twilight deepened. Mother Moon, in the sky, had begun the aging process to become the Grandmother. Using courier training, Brodhi pitched his voice to carry. In Hecari he called, "Who is warlord here?" He followed it in Sancorran, "Who is in charge?"

The entry flap of Mikal's ale tent stirred. Then came a slight figure with short-cropped fair hair and glinting brass ear-hoops. She stopped equidistant between ale-tent and bonfire ring.

"I am in charge!" she called.

Brodhi turned in the saddle to the Hecari, translating, and saw the horrified disbelief in the faces of the warriors.

For their sakes, Brodhi laced his tone with scorn as he turned back. "You are? *You?* You are a woman!" He repeated it precisely, in like tones, in Hecari.

"I am in charge!" she repeated.

By her tone and posture, it required no translation. Brodhi reined his horse in a tight circle to face the four warriors. He spread his hands in a gesture akin to annoyance and helplessness, in effect asking for advice. The men shot brief, hard glances at one another, muttering angrily among themselves. The woman would never be accepted. That she dared to claim herself a warlord was insult of the highest order. Women in Hecari culture were completely subservient, refusing even to meet a warrior's eyes.

In Hecari, Brodhi said, "The warlord would order a culling."

They agreed emphatically.

"Shall I kill her now?"

That pleased them. Black eyes glittered as they looked briefly at the woman who dared to call herself in charge, then fastened avid but questioning gazes upon Brodhi.

He shrugged with exquisite nonchalance. "*I* am not Sancorran. *I* work for the coin-rings. Your warlord pays me well."

One of the warriors raised his chin, lifted his war-club from his saddle, and let loose a ululating cry of approval and encouragement. Brodhi wheeled his horse, set the gelding on a leaping course over the pyramid of wood in the center of the ring, and roared in Sancorran: *"Kill them now!"*

As the warriors gazed in fervid anticipation, as Brodhi neared Bethid on a galloping horse, karavaners and settlement men, bearing such weapons as they had contrived, rose up in the dusk from behind the tents and fell upon the Hecari, hamstringing horses to bring them down, dragging warriors out of their saddles. Even as Brodhi veered around Bethid, who wisely stood her ground, and spun his horse back again, the killing was over.

He glanced at Bethid. "Whose thought was it that you claim yourself the leader?"

"Mine." She smiled grimly. "I suggested it would distract the warriors more than anything else, being as how they view women as worthless."

He nodded. "That was well done, Beth."

Her expression was odd as she looked across the bonfire ring to where some men surrounded the dead warriors while others killed the hamstrung horses. "No, I think it was *ill* done, but it was decidedly necessary."

Brodhi left her then, riding around the ring to the other side. Jorda and Mikal were directing matters. Both were blood-stained. Jorda glanced up as Brodhi reined in. "You placed your sentries well," Brodhi told him. "All went smoothly."

The karavan-master nodded, saying nothing. The crease between his brows had deepened.

"If I may make another suggestion . . . have the bodies taken as close to the forest as is possible. Beasts will come out to fetch them. And then, should the question ever arise, all can say in perfect honesty that Alisanos took the warriors."

"Clever," Jorda murmured. Then his eyes focused more sharply on Brodhi's. "Rhuan is in Alisanos."

"I'm aware of that."

"I still need the boundaries surveyed and mapped. Will you do it?"

Brodhi uncapped his scroll case and pulled a rolled parchment from it. "I have already begun. Have this copied as best you can; it shows the new route to the Cardatha road, and the way into the settlement." He handed it down. "I will begin with the other areas tomorrow."

Jorda accepted the scroll with a word of thanks, then glanced up in open curiosity. "You are being very generous, Brodhi. If I may be blunt, more so than I was led to expect from you."

Brodhi considered saying something such as, *I have to deal with you because it's a test I must complete on a personal journey you could never possibly comprehend,* but he had meant what he said to Bethid about dealing with the Hecari. The karavaners and tent-folk, directed by Mikal and Jorda, had acquitted themselves far better than he had ever anticipated. "It's quite true I have no patience with the extreme emotions your people exhibit so frequently, and other habits I find inexplicable or deplorable. Many humans I consider worthless. But

a few of you, in the face of terrible odds, have occasionally proven yourselves somewhat competent."

Jorda's brows twitched upward, then leveled again.
His tone was expressionless. "Ah. I see. High praise,
that."

Brodhi nodded, then turned his mount away from
the bodies of Hecari and horses and rode through the
settlement to the common tent he shared with the
other couriers. His gelding was due untacking, grooming, and a meal; once those tasks were completed, he
thought he would make his way to Mikal's tent for ale.
The journey with four Hecari had made him quite
thirsty.

AUDRUN MADE HER way along the chute
winding through the massive rock formation.
She was aware of Rhuan following, though he moved
very quietly. She supposed she had been quite rude
to him, but was too tired to spend much thought on
it. She knew if she stopped moving, she would not
begin again. All of her reserves were spent. Her body
trembled with exhaustion. Knees threatened to
buckle. Much of the time she placed one or both
hands on the chute walls just to remind herself she
was upright, gaining momentary support, a slight encouragement for continued momentum. When she
rounded a slight curve and a vista spread out before
her, she stopped short because it was so unexpected.

The chute widened itself into a roundish, rectagular cave opening out of a cliff face. Audrun stood nearly at its edge on a broad shelf of stone, astonished by the world presenting itself to her. Across the way her eyes met a cliff similar to the one housing the cave. But below it, and below the cave she stood in, spread wide, shallow terraces of red rocks, each containing a pool of brilliant blue-green water. To her right, at the edge of the uppermost pool, the two cliffs merged into one, forming a slot for a narrow fall of water to the pool below. Surrounding the pools, in hummocks within the cliffs and along the crowns, spearlike trees stood as sentinels. At their bases yellow flowers bloomed.

Rhuan stepped up beside her. Though still angry with him, she could not prevent the question. "This is the Kiba?"

"No. This is merely the vestibule." He pointed. "The deepest of those pools below are no higher than your shoulders. The current is slight—you'll see that each spills into the pool immediately below it, all the way down to the stream that cuts through the canyon. There you may bathe, or just float in the water."

She was stunned. "This doesn't even seem like part of Alisanos. It's beautiful!"

"The deepwood has many faces." He glanced at her briefly in profile. "Are you ready to go down? We'll spend the night here, and rest tomorrow."

"There's a way down there?"

He smiled and extended a hand to the right side of the cave. "There. That shelf extending beyond the cliff leads down to the upper pool, and additional pathways skirt the edges of the others below it."

The way down he indicated was a steep, narrow shelf of stone jutting sideways from the cliff face, girded on the right side by vertical stone. In descent, the left side of her body would be next to open air.

"It's all of stone," he said. "It's a part of the cliff itself. There's no danger of any portion breaking away."

"*You* say," she muttered.

"I have climbed up and down this path more times than I can count. If you like, I will descend in front of you, and if at any time you feel unsafe, say so. I will be happy to provide a steadying hand. Or you may place your right hand on the wall if it serves your sense of balance."

She looked at him, prepared to answer sharply, until she saw that he, too, was weary. At some point he had been transformed from the dimpled, laughing guide she trusted to a man with tension and tiredness etched in his face. He had nearly died in defense of her baby. For all she knew, his wounds still troubled him.

But still, she had to say it. "You pushed too hard."

"It brought us here."

"You asked too much."

"No," he said, "Oh, no, that I did not do. The spirit dwelling inside you can survive much more. And once we reach the Kiba, you will need every bit of it." His lips twitched briefly in a tired smile. "Tonight, and tomorrow, we can give our souls and bodies the rest they deserve, but only if we first descend this trail."

After a moment, Audrun nodded. But before he could move to take his place before her, she took the first step, and another, and another, upon the path of stone.

Chapter 30

*D*AVYN MADE HIS way into the ale tent and found Mikal there as well as Jorda. No one else was present. They shared a table companionably, with jugs and tankards at their elbows and a wheel of cheese set on a platter. Heads were bowed over a sheet of parchment weighted down in the center of the table. They glanced up as he entered.

Smiling, he went directly to the karavan-master. "I've left my wagon in the grove and returned your team to your horse-master with my thanks for his aid. Now I tender you the same, and an offer of any help you may need, at any time." He thrust out an arm and Jorda gripped it. "I see much has been done since the storm—tents repaired and raised, and an orderly arrangement! Much improvement. And the bonfire ring will do well as a place all may gather." He nodded. "Well done."

Jorda and Mikal exchanged wry glances. "We decided," Mikal said, "after hearing from a few wives and mothers, that if we wished families to be part of the recovery, we needed to offer a place more appropriate than an ale tent."

"Join us, if you like," Jorda said. He gestured at the parchment. "There have been developments over the last two days."

Davyn looked and saw the beginnings of a crude map. The circle of tents had been inked in, as well as the karavaner grove, the river, and the road leading southeast out of the settlement. He frowned, studying it. Parts of the map looked familiar, but other portions did not. "It's changed," he noted, "the way we came." He indicated markings denoting a forest. "Is all of this Alisanos?"

Jorda touched a finger to the parchment, tracing a route. "This is the old road, this beginning—here. But Alisanos encroaches now, as you can see. We must swing northeast two full days through a narrowing cut before we reach open grasslands again. But there is a way. Brodhi came through it. This map is his."

Davyn glanced up sharply. "Brodhi's back?"

"He is scouting for us," Mikal said. "With his land-sense, he can tell where the edges of Alisanos lie. Within a ten-day or so, we should have a better idea of where we may go safely, without fear of stumbling into the deepwood."

Dismay was abrupt. "Then he's not here now? I need to see him." He met Jorda's eyes. "I told you what I must ask of him."

The karavan-master looked beyond Davyn. "Then I would say you can do so in short order."

Davyn swung around abruptly, feeling his heart lift as he saw the Shoia entering the ale tent. He didn't believe he had seen Brodhi before, but found him very like Rhuan in appearance. They shared coloring, build, complex braids, and yet there was an austerity, a coldness in Brodhi's face Davyn had never seen in the guide's. He wondered, idly, if this man ever smiled.

Brodhi strode to the table with a scroll in his hand. "Somewhat more," he said, "and more yet to do."

"Brodhi." Davyn cleared his throat. "May I speak with you? I have work for you."

The Shoia glanced at him as he handed over the scroll to Jorda. "You wish a message carried?"

Davyn shook his head, looked briefly around the tent, then pointed to a table tucked into a corner. "May we speak privately?" He paused, shot a questioning glance at Mikal. "May I offer you ale or spirits?"

Brodhi contemplated him a moment, then hitched one shoulder in a casual shrug. "Ale will do. I'll hear what you have to say." He turned and headed toward the table, the heavy cluster of braids filling the space between his shoulder blades.

"It's midday," Mikal said, rising from the table. "I'll set you out food as well."

Davyn thanked him and followed Brodhi, seating himself across from the courier. He began without preliminaries. "My family was taken into Alisanos when the storm came down, on the Atalanda shortcut." He paused, but Brodhi said nothing, nor did his expression alter from one of something akin to boredom. "I haven't many coin-rings, but I will give you all of them if you will do me this service." He drew in a deep breath, then said it all at once. "I wish you to go into the deepwood and find my family."

Brodhi ignored Mikal's arrival with two tankards of foaming ale clutched in one big fist, and the platter of bread, butter, and cheese in his other hand. The ale-keep set all down on the table and departed. Davyn waited, trying not to squirm, twitch, or babble with impatience beneath the Shoia's steady, emotionless gaze. He knew he was being weighed, and likely came up short in the other's estimation.

"No," Brodhi said.

Schooling his face into a similar austerity, Davyn picked up his tankard, drank several swallows, then set it down again, brushing foam from his lip. He was not surprised by the response, but felt he himself was in control of the situation—yet how did one *tell* a man he had to do so, because a diviner had seen it? "I am offering to hire you."

"No."

Davyn met the cold brown eyes with his own and held them, unflinching. Quietly he said, "I think you must."

Brodhi's eyebrows arched up. "Must? I *must*?"

Davyn nodded. "The hand-reader says so."

"The hand-reader."

"She saw you there, in the deepwood. In my hand. She saw you with two of my children."

"I have no intention whatsoever of entering Alisanos."

"The hand-reader said—"

"I care nothing at all for what this hand-reader said. I will not do it. She will have to admit her reading is wrong."

"I believe her." Davyn hung on to self-control with great effort. "I have to. All of them are in Alisanos. Can you understand what that means to me? My wife, four of my children—" He stopped short. "No. *Five* of my children; the diviner says the baby is born. Yes, I know it is dangerous; I know that very well, if you please. But this is my *family*. I would go—I told the diviner so—but she read my hand and says that *you* go. She saw you with two of my children."

The Shoia's expression was no longer bored. "You believe that on the word of a hand-reader, who may well be a charlatan, I will enter a place known to all as deadly. A place all avoid. A place that even now I am mapping precisely so that no one ends up there by mistake." Brodhi leaned forward, hands resting palm down on the table top. "Are you mad? Or are you simply stupid?"

"She said—"

"I don't care what she said, human! Go yourself. This is your family—*you* take the risk."

Davyn spoke quietly, deliberately, relying on fact,

avoiding emotion. "My oldest boy is sixteen. His name is Gillan. The next oldest is Ellica, fifteen, his sister. The younger ones—"

Brodhi stood up so quickly his stool fell over. He was clearly furious. For a moment Davyn believed he saw something red flicker in his eyes. "This is Ilona, your hand-reader?"

Davyn nodded. "She reads true. Everyone says so."

"*Do* they?" Brodhi picked up his brimming tankard and upended it, spilling ale onto the floor. "I will not drink your ale. I will not take your coin-rings. I will not enter Alisanos to search for your family. But what I *will* do is have a word with your diviner."

"My younger ones are five and six. Megritte and Torvic. The baby—her name is Sarith."

Brodhi turned on his heel and strode out of the tent, slapping the entry flap aside. Davyn slowly drew in a breath, then released it. When he lifted his tankard, he saw his hands were trembling.

But Ilona had seen it. Ilona read true.

 "IT'S TIME," DARMUTH said. "We must leave now."

Gillan, awakening slowly and stiffly, peered up from the rude pile of leaves he used as a bed. The demon stood over him. "Time for what?"

"Time to go."

Brilliant sunlight cut through openings in the tree

canopy. Gillan shielded his eyes with a flattened hand, squinting from under it. He had not slept well until near dawn, and was slow to grasp such thoughts as arising for the day. "Go where?"

Darmuth leaned down, closed a firm grip around Gillan's left arm, and pulled him up from the bedding. "To the Kiba."

Gillan scrambled up in ungainly fashion, keeping weight off the burned leg. When Darmuth released his arm, he grabbed the tree beside his bedding, taking all his weight onto his sound right leg. "Now? It's barely morning."

"Time to go," Darmuth repeated.

Rising from the confusion of an abrupt wakening, Gillan scowled at the demon. "Is this a jest? If so, it's a poor one. I can't walk anywhere yet."

"You'll be riding, not walking." Darmuth closed a hand around Gillan's upper arm and took him from the tree. "There is a log just there, see?"

Gillan, completely taken up with attempting to stay upright, hopped to catch his balance. "I see it. What about it?" The guiding hand was inexorable; he had no choice but to follow its lead. "Darmuth—"

"Sit a moment," Darmuth directed, placing Gillan immediately in front of the log. "When I'm ready, use it to help."

Gillan sat down hard on the log, hissing as it jarred his ruined leg. "Use it to help what?"

But Darmuth didn't answer. Darmuth was, in fact, losing substance. Gillan gaped as the demon's form thinned nearly to transparency. A moment later substance returned, but was completely reshaped. What stood before Gillan now was a four-legged creature in place of a man who usually appeared perfectly human.

"You're a *horse*—?"

A gray horse, in fact. And it bent its neck around to place its mouth atop Gillan's shoulder, which it proceeded to bite.

"Ow!" Gillan jerked away, rubbing his shoulder. The message was clear enough, as was the means to mount. Gillan sighed. "Yes, I see. Be patient, if you please; this will be difficult."

The horse sidled a step closer, dropping its head down as if to graze. Nodding, Gillan grasped mane. He pulled himself upright; then, using the horse to steady himself, he hopped one-legged up onto the surface of the log. Balance was nearly lost, but the horse stepped closer yet. Gillan clung to him a moment, found his balance on the one leg, then spread his hands along the horse's back. His left rested at the gray withers. His right was at the beginning of the horse's rump.

Gillan had ridden since early childhood. He had mounted this way many times when there was no saddle, once he was tall enough. But never, never using only one leg. Never when the other leg hurt unremittingly.

Gritting his teeth, Gillan dropped his body as if to crouch, bent elbows outward, bounced three times, then thrust himself upward. Pain shot through his bad leg, but he was in motion. Momentum carried his body up and over. He landed belly-down across the horse's back. Trusting to instincts, Gillan immediately swung his good leg across the broad rump and scooted into place behind the horse's withers. He reeled there a moment, contemplating vomiting from pain and dizziness, but clamped both hands tightly into the mane before him. The horse moved one way, then the other, barely shifting its weight, until Gillan's sense of balance reasserted itself.

He was weak and in pain, and sweating. But he had grown up on horseback; this, he could do.

"How far?" Gillan asked, before he recalled that a horse could not speak. Grimacing, he recalled Darmuth's dry tones. "As far as it is, yes?"

The horse snorted, shook its head, and began to walk.

RHUAN STOOD WATCH as Audrun waded out into one of the shallow blue-green pools. The ill-used hem of her skirts, at its longest point, touched barely below her knees. She caught the skirts up by habit, then waded carefully out a little farther. And finally, as if surrendering every portion of her awareness, Audrun sat down. Water reached to the top of her hips. She put her hands below the water and scooted out farther, seeking depth. Finding it, she leaned back and back, floating, upper body held in place by the tension in her arms as she clung to the shallower stone at the edge of the dropoff. She arched her spine, tipped her head back, let the water take her hair, then lowered her upper body. All of her was afloat within the pool, though she anchored herself with both hands.

Long overdue, he knew. He had pushed her hard, had asked a great deal, but had not pushed *too* hard, nor had he asked too much. What she didn't realize was that going into the Kiba to confront the primaries would demand even more. This was merely the prelude.

He had stripped off his boots, tunic, and baldric. Now he stood on stone beneath the water, wet above his ankles. It didn't matter that the bottom of his leggings were soaked. His tunic had served a newborn infant in all of her needs. He looked away from Audrun to where the cliffs met, lifting his eyes. Water poured down as if from a bottomless pitcher, sun-dazzled mist rising. He lost himself in it. So many human years since he'd been in Alisanos . . .

"What are you thinking?"

He glanced back, breaking from his reverie. Audrun sat again in shallow water, legs crossed. She was working at wet hair, trying again to split out the snarls and tangles. She was cleaner, tension washed away, hair slicked back from her face. He saw for the first time that without constant family cares, without the worries of travel, she was attractive. He had always viewed her as a *mother*, not as a woman. Now he revised his estimation.

But her question was due an answer. "That all I ever wanted to be was *not* like my father."

"From what I saw of him, I can attest that you aren't." Head tilted as she tended her hair, Audrun smiled. "What was your mother like?"

He shook his head. "She died not long after I was born. I never knew her."

"I'm sorry. But you must be very like her."

"I don't know how. We are raised in the creche, not by our parents." He walked back toward the pathway beside the pool, sloshing through shallow water. "We are *expected* to be like our sires."

"What does it mean if you're not?"

He turned. "It means—*Audrun*." He kept his tone even, free of alarm, but nonetheless quietly urgent. "Audrun, come out of the water. Try not to splash. Make haste, but carefully." He fixed his eyes above the cliff opposite the pools, watching the winged creature rising on the air. It was some distance away, but the eyesight of the creatures was legendary. "Audrun."

She rose up dripping from the water, face gone pale. As instructed, she moved carefully toward the pool's edge, gliding feet along the stone beneath the water to save splashing. "What is it?"

"Draka."

"What is a draka?"

"Something you don't want to meet." He extended

a hand for her to grasp, bringing her out of the water onto the pathway. "There is an overhang back by the cliff face, this side. Walk steadily to it. Don't run. Make no sudden moves."

She twisted her head briefly to follow his own line of sight. *"Mother of Moons!"* Before he could urge her to move again, she began to walk away toward the cliff face.

Rhuan held his ground, watching the draka. Its body was a sinuous, gleaming, coppery mass beneath the double suns. Enormous wings lifted it high, higher yet. He willed it to turn away, to take another direction. But in a moment he knew its path lay toward the pools.

Swearing beneath his breath, Rhuan began to back slowly away from the pool's edge. He hoped Audrun had reached the cliff face, was pressed against its stone beneath the overhang. He continued moving slowly, trying not to react when his bare feet met sharp stones and thorn bushes. Steadily he made his way through the brush, arms spread for balance, hands open, eyes fixed upon the creature in the sky.

Finally he risked a quick glance over his shoulder to mark the cliff wall. Audrun was there, white-faced, squatting, making herself small. Her eyes tracked the draka. Red dirt clung to the ragged bottom of her skirts. Rhuan covered the last one hundred paces as quickly as he could without crashing through the brush. Relief filled his chest as he reached the overhang, and then he turned and squatted as Audrun did, placing his back against stone.

"Blessed Mother." Audrun's tone was a mixture of disbelief, fear, and awe.

The huge draka soared up to the cliff opposite their own. Now its wings were clearly seen, huge membranous structures of pale copper-gold, shining wetly in the sunlight. Those wings steadied the body as it settled slowly, uncurling legs to extend scaled feet, to grip soil and stone with dark talons. Wings folded. The tail unfurled over the cliff's edge. The long, sinuous neck counterbalanced the weight of the body, lifting the head high in the air.

"Can it see us?" Audrun whispered.

"Not if we don't move. The brush shields us, and the shadow beneath the overhang."

"What is it doing?"

Rhuan sighed. "Sunning itself."

Audrun bit back the quiet, startled laughter, but he didn't blame her. One did not think in terms of a creature such as a draka, with its deadly talons and fierce eyes, undertaking an activity so benign. "How long will it stay here?"

"Unfortunately . . ." Rhuan very slowly, very carefully, lowered his body out of its squat to sit upon the earth, ". . . as long as takes its fancy."

Chapter 31

*B*RODHI FOUND THE hand-reader outside of her wagon, kneeling by her cookfire. She'd hung a kettle from a small shepherd's crook planted inside the rock ring. A mug was in one hand as she cloaked the other in layers of shielding rags and reached for the kettle handle.

He walked right up to the other side of the modest cookfire and stopped, glaring down at her. She glanced up, registered his expression, and said, ironically, "I suspect you aren't interested in my tea."

He freighted his words with scorn. "No indeed. I came here so you could instruct me in my actions."

A faint frown passed briefly across her face. Then comprehension came into her eyes. She looked at her kettle, mug, and folded rag, sighed, then set everything aside. She rose, shook out her skirts, and met him eye to eye across the cookfire. "Whatever you came to say can be said while I'm seated."

He watched her walk to the back of her wagon,

climb three steps, then seat herself in the door frame, booted feet planted two steps down. After a moment he followed, halting at the foot of the bottom step. Her wagon was tall; he did not have to look down far to meet her eyes.

"I read true," she said as he opened his mouth to speak, cutting him off. "I am sorry if that inconveniences you, but I won't apologize for it. Yes, Brodhi, I did read the farmsteader's hand; and *yes*, Brodhi, I saw you in Alisanos. With two of his children. My obligation wasn't to you, it was to the farmsteader who engaged my services. I saw what I saw."

He had lost his temper with that farmsteader. He would not do so again. "You are a charlatan."

She laughed at him. "Of all the things in my life of which I am, and which I am not, charlatan falls most decidedly into the latter category. I realize that for a *dioscuri* that is hard to understand, but it's quite true. I saw what I saw, Brodhi. It matters to me not at all that you choose to disbelieve me; many have, over the years. And they have regretted it."

He had never told her he was *dioscuri*. He had never mentioned the word to any human, here or elsewhere. Rhuan knew, of course, as did Ferize and Darmuth. But humans did not. A chill coursed through his belly. "Ilona—"

"I understand you are the last of Karadath's children who are *dioscuri*. Did you kill all the others?"

Brodhi stared at her, stunned.

Ilona smiled without humor. "Oh, yes. I know. I understand what faces you when you return to Alisanos. In fact, I know rather a great deal about you. Alario was most forthcoming." Hazel eyes were clear and cold. "Yes, Brodhi—*Alario*. Rhuan's sire has visited me."

She had completely undermined his planned attack. Now he was aware of thoughts tumbling one over another, portions of them rising to the surface, settling onto his tongue, and yet he spoke none of them. "Alario was here."

"Twice."

"Why? Rhuan is in Alisanos."

"He didn't come to see Rhuan. He came to see me."

It was preposterous. "You? *Why?*"

"He feels Rhuan is inferior get."

"He is."

"He feels you are more suited to be an heir than Rhuan."

"I am."

"But you happen to be *Karadath's* heir, not his own, and it troubles him. He feels he's losing his standing among the primaries."

Brodhi wished he could dismiss everything she said, but it was clear to him she spoke from actual knowledge. She knew too much. "He *is* losing his standing among the primaries."

"And so he has decided he should get a new son, make a new *dioscuri*. One more fitting, he says, than the one he has now." Ilona shrugged. "I personally feel Rhuan is worth far more than you *or* Alario, but that seems to make no difference."

Now Brodhi smiled. "No, it doesn't. You're a human. You aren't expected to understand, and what you feel doesn't matter in the least."

She tilted her head slightly, studying his expression. "Human or no, it matters enough that Alario has decided to get this new son on me."

He went cold to the bone. He couldn't disbelieve her; what she said Alario intended was exactly the action that a primary in Alario's position should do. Particularly since it *would* harm Karadath's position.

"I'm curious, Brodhi—how many of your brothers have you killed?"

He found a cool smile, trying to regain lost ground. "I've lost count."

"And Rhuan?"

"Rhuan? Rhuan's weak; he hasn't killed anyone. And you wonder why Alario feels he needs a new heir?" For the first time he paid very close attention to the hand-reader, examined her as a possible piece upon the primaries' gameboard instead of discounting her because she was a human. His own mother had been human. "I am aware this is not how humans conduct their lives. But if Rhuan wishes to survive beyond childhood, he should accept what must be done."

"*Child*hood!"

At last, he could tell her something Alario hadn't. "We are, in the human tongue, adolescents. In your years, we are young. We are on the cusp of adulthood, he and I . . . that we are *here* is because of that. I have heard a human term, a human phrase, rite of passage.

This is ours, Ilona. If we wish to become adults, accepted as adults, we must become more than *dioscuri*. We must prove to the primaries that we belong among them."

She sat stiffly upright within the frame of her doorjamb, staring at him fixedly. "How do you do that?"

"Many methods, among them various tests. A journey. The latter requires five human years in the human world."

"And then?"

"Then we return to Alisanos. We face the primaries. We explain our actions, defend some of them. *They* decide if we are fit to become adults."

"And if not?"

"If we are not fit to become adults, we are not fit to procreate. And so the primaries make certain we cannot."

Ilona frowned. "How in the world can they do that? If your seed is alive, it's alive. You can sire—"

"Castration."

The color flowed out of her face. Horror shone in hazel eyes as her lips parted.

"Our world," Brodhi said, "is somewhat more rigorous than yours."

"Mother of Moons . . ."

"Yes, we kill our brothers. It is necessary so that one day we may challenge our sires. Only one of us may do that; it is how our sires are replaced. If we fail our journeys, fail our tests, provide the wrong answers, we remain children. And the opportunity to challenge our sires, to become as they are, never arrives." He stared at her. "And I think even a woman may understand that castration is not an acceptable outcome."

"Brodhi—"

"You do read true," he said, "though in this case perhaps not for the reasons you believe. Yes, I will enter Alisanos. You have made it necessary." He shook his head. "Karadath should know what Alario intends."

TORVIC AND MEGRITTE straggled into the cabin not far behind Lirra. On the trip back, Meggie had from time to time said she was hungry, even after they'd eaten the berries found along the way, but for the most part none of them spoke. Lirra had, for the first time, seemed despondent over their inability to find rivers, creeks, or ponds containing fish. It had been their last real hope. But now they passed the stinkwood fire, the rotted melon patch, the deceased vegetable garden, the small field where wheat and corn ordinarily grew. With all the chickens dead, there was no comforting noise of their clucking and squawking around the cabin. The well still gave water, but they all of them wanted something solid.

No bread. No tubers. A handful of herbs. Nothing more.

As Torvic followed Meggie into the cabin, he saw Lirra standing in front of the shelving, digging through the contents once again. Nothing was to be

found, he knew; she had done the same thing repeatedly before their last trip looking for fish. Meggie
crawled up onto Lirra's bed and sat against the wall,
knees drawn up and arms hugging her belly. Exhaustion was obvious in her features, with circles beneath
her eyes and bones prominent. Pale hair straggled
loose of its braids.

Lirra stopped rummaging. She looked at them both,
lines etched into her forehead and at the corners of her
eyes. Brown hair, ordinarily tucked into a neat knot at
the back of her neck, was coming undone. She pressed
fingertips against her forehead and rubbed. He saw
fear in her eyes, and a terrible hunger. After a moment
she crossed to the table and sat down in one of the
chairs. Her hands, folded atop one another on the
table's surface, trembled.

She looked at him. Looked at Meggie. Closed her
eyes, as if she prayed.

Torvic took the deadfall fruit he had found along the
way from the hem of his tunic. He went to the table
and set it beside her hands. "I'm not hungry, Lirra. You
eat it."

She looked at the fruit, then to him. "Ah, Torvic, no.
It's for you."

He shrugged. "I ate along the way." So they had,
each of them, finding berries, nuts, a few deadfall
fruits from a tall tree. Those they had indeed eaten. But
they had found nothing more. None of them had truly
eaten for two days.

She looked past him to Meggie. "She's so tired, poor little thing. See her? She can't even stay awake."

Torvic looked. His sister was slumped against the wall, head fallen forward in something akin to sleep.

"What can we do?" Lirra asked. "She's the youngest, the smallest, the weakest. I fear we'll lose her first."

For a moment he wasn't sure what she meant. Then he knew. "No! Meggie won't die! None of us will!"

"Hush, hush." Lirra lifted a hand to halt the flow of words. Then she leaned forward, resting her face in her hands as she braced elbows against the table. "O dear Mother, have you abandoned us?" She looked upward, tears running down her face. "What are we to do?"

"I'll go." The words jumped out of his mouth. "I'll check the snares. Maybe they've caught things while we looked for fish."

Lirra nodded, attention only partially on him. She looked terribly worried, exhausted, and desperately hungry.

"I'll find something," Torvic promised.

Lirra's gaze sharpened. She stared at him, almost as if memorizing his features. Her expression was stark, then altered into decisiveness. Her tone now was crisp. "Be thorough, Torvic. Take your time. Be very *thorough*."

He stared back at her, then broke from his reverie and promised once more that he would find something to eat. He turned and hastened out of the cabin.

AFTER BRODHI'S DEPARTURE, Ilona returned to her tea. She took an extra fold with
the rag intended to protect her hand since the kettle
had ended up over the fire longer than intended. She
had filled the mug and was blowing on the surface of
the tea when Bethid came around the end of the
wagon.

"Ilona? Have you seen Brodhi? Someone said they
saw him coming this way."

Ilona nodded, still blowing. "Yes, he was here." Hot
steam rose up from the mug into her face. Loose hair
around her face began to curl. "Would you like tea? We
may not be able to drink it until sundown, but there
can be no complaints it's too weak."

Bethid shook her head. "I need to catch up to him.
Do you know where he went?"

Ilona looked through steam at the courier. "I don't
think you want to catch up to him, Beth. He's going
into Alisanos."

Shock flowed over Bethid's face. "*Why?*"

"It would be to his credit," Ilona began dryly, "if he
were going to help the farmsteader's family, but he's
not. Well, he *will* help the family whether he intends it
or no, but that isn't why he's going." She considered
attempting to sip, then decided against it. She had a
feeling she might burn her lips off. "Bethid, there are
things about Brodhi you don't know."

"There are things about everyone I don't know,"

Bethid replied, impatient. "But why is he going into Alisanos? Is he mad?"

"Angry," Ilona said, "but not mad." She blew on the tea again, ruffling its surface. "Don't fear for him, Beth."

"He's going into Alisanos! How can I *not* fear for him?"

Ilona weighed Brodhi's undoubted preferences for keeping the truth secret against Bethid's very real concern for his safety. "He isn't Shoia, Beth. He's *from* Alisanos." She lifted a hand before the courier could blurt out a response. "I know. I do know. But it's true."

Color had bled out of Bethid's face. "Did you read his hand, to know this?"

"No. He told me." And then she reflected that Brodhi had done no such thing; Brodhi's *uncle* had told her. But she feared that would prove too much for Bethid to assimilate just now.

In fact, Bethid glanced around absently as if looking for something, then simply sat down upon the ground beneath the spreading tree. She crossed her legs as if perfectly at ease, but the expression in her eyes, the tone of her voice, belied that. "Then what is he?"

"That, I can't tell you." Ilona risked a small sip. The tea was quite hot, but not undrinkably so. "I don't know what they call themselves, his folk."

"Then Rhuan is also . . . not Shoia."

Ilona sighed. She moved to the nearest of the high wooden wheels and squatted down, balancing herself against the spokes as she sipped again at tea. "Not

Shoia. No. Neither of them." She smiled crookedly at
Bethid. "We have either been particularly gullible, all
of us, or they are extremely experienced at hiding the
truth. But Rhuan always refused to let me read his
hand. I did catch a glimpse once, just one brief
glimpse, when he was dead. The night we met."

"What did you see?"

"I saw . . . chaos."

They stared at one another for a long moment.
"Mother of Moons," Bethid murmured. "Alisanos?
You're sure?"

Ilona nodded.

"Is he coming back? Brodhi? *Can* he?"

"I don't know."

Bethid nodded, her eyes full of thoughts. Finally she
met Ilona's again. "What do we do? Do we tell Jorda
and Mikal? Do I tell Timmon and Alorn? Do we say
nothing at all?" She rubbed a hand through her
cropped hair. "What do we *do*, Ilona?"

"I think—I think we must let this be what it will be."
Ilona grimaced. "I know that sounds trite or intentionally obscure, as if I'm a charlatan trying to make you
believe. But the Mother must surely have a plan. Certainly I see sense in telling Jorda and Mikal, but anyone else?" She shook her head. "I think it's best we
keep this to ourselves, for now. If we tell everyone that
Rhuan and Brodhi are actually from the deepwood,
we would very likely seed panic. And those maps
Brodhi has drawn to keep *us* from Alisanos would become suspect."

Bethid nodded after a moment. "Yes. Yes, I think you're right." She tipped her head back against the tree, making a strangled sound of frustration. "It just becomes more difficult, doesn't it? Day by day!"

"Moment by moment." Ilona raised her mug. "Tea? I promise it won't burn a hole in your throat."

"No." Bethid rose. "No, I think I want something stronger than tea." She cast Ilona a weak smile. "Probably a great deal of it."

Ilona watched the courier slap at trews to free them of dirt. "Jorda will likely have questions. Tell him that when he has time, he should come to me."

"I will."

Bethid strode off. Ilona leaned her head against the wheel behind her and gazed up through the storm-stripped tree limbs to the sky overhead. It hurt, she realized, to acknowledge that Rhuan was not Shoia. That he was in truth a child of Alisanos.

The get of a god.

Or merely the unwanted child of someone who *claimed* himself a god.

Chapter 32

*T*ORVIC CHECKED EACH snare with hope filling his chest, and each time it was dashed. Of eight snares, seven were empty. *He* felt empty, and hungry, and sick. He approached the final snare slowly, almost afraid to look, thinking how and what he would tell Lirra and Meggie if he returned to the cabin with nothing. He was so hungry he trembled, and his belly ached, but he refused to give in to it. He peeled back the leaves hiding the last snare, and saw that it also was empty. The final failure. All growing things had died, all living things had died, and they found no rivers with fish in them. Torvic fell to the ground, trying very hard not to cry, but he was so tired, so weak, and so very hungry he had no strength to halt the tears. They ran down his face until, at last, he wiped them away with the back of his hand, trying to repress the terrified sobs that wanted badly to be released.

Da wouldn't cry. *Gillan* wouldn't cry. He, Torvic, was the man of the cabin. He shouldn't cry, either.

But he was very hungry.

He swiped again at his face, gulping down a sob, and then he heard, cutting through the forest, a thin, high shrieking.

Meggie. *Meggie.*

He ran. He ran and ran. He ignored vines and brush and trees that slapped at his body, leaped over roots, tore his arms free of thorns. Meggie was screaming.

He ran past the stinkwood fire, still smoldering. He ran past wheat and corn, all dead; ran past the melon patch, all rotted; ran by the shriveled vegetable garden. He ran into the open door and stopped on the threshhold.

Meggie was screaming.

At first his mind refused to believe what it registered. But then he knew. He saw and he *knew.*

In Lirra's left hand was Meggie's wrist. In Lirra's right was a knife.

The rope belt around her waist had unwrapped itself and rose upright in the air. No: tail, not belt.

Lirra had *a tail.*

She saw Torvic. As she tried to yank Meggie close to her body, she bared her teeth at him. "Weak!" she cried. "Weak! We raise what's strong and cull the weak seed!"

Meggie still was screaming, pulling and jerking, feet scraping against the floor, trying to wrench herself free of Lirra's hand.

"She's weak!" Lirra cried. "My husband was weak! I had no choice! He was weak! I had to live! *I was hungry!* I had no choice!"

Torvic whispered, "Let her go . . ."

"Cull the weak seed!"

"Let her *go*!"

Lirra's knife glinted. She yanked Meggie closer. Her hair, free now of its pinned coil, hung loose on either side of her face. Her eyes suddenly reminded him of a mad dog his da had once killed in the cornfield. "Do you want to live, Torvic? Do you want to *live*?"

Screaming. Screaming.

Again Torvic ran. He ran out of the cabin, past the vegetable garden, past the melon patch, beyond the wheat and corn. He ran to the still-smoldering fire and grabbed a length of stinkwood from it. It was burning at one end.

From the cabin he heard Meggie screaming. Lirra was still shouting that she *had to eat*.

Back and back he ran, and into the cabin. He saw Meggie, saw her scrabbling on the ground with one arm strung up in the air, screaming and screaming as Lirra pulled her closer. Meggie was small. Meggie was weak. Meggie hadn't eaten in two days. How could she withstand a grown woman?

Torvic ran at Lirra. He ran at Lirra with burning stinkwood in his hands, and thrust it directly toward her face. Flame leaped to her hair.

Now Lirra, not Meggie, screamed.

"Meggie!" Lirra had let go, was beating at her hair. Torvic grabbed Meggie's hand. "Meggie, come on!" He pulled, he tugged, dragging his sister across the cabin floor. "Meggie! Come on!"

Lirra screamed and screamed.

He dragged Meggie to the cabin door, released her hand to reach down and grab whatever he could grab, and pulled her partially upright. "Meggie—run! Run! Run!"

Still Lirra screamed.

"Meggie, we have to run!" He pulled, he pushed, he dragged. He got her across the threshhold. "Run, Meggie, run!"

And then hands came down, man-sized hands, and caught them both. Meggie screamed. So did Torvic.

"Hush," the man said irritably.

Torvic sucked in a breath. *"She wants to eat my sister!"*

The man set them aside, set them out of the cabin and away from the door. "I have no particular use for human children, but neither do I eat them."

Meggie was on the ground beside the bench. As the man went through the door, Torvic pulled her close, wrapping his arms around her the way Mam and Da did it. Meggie wasn't screaming. Meggie wasn't screaming.

Inside Lirra's cabin, Lirra stopped screaming, too.

AUDRUN, SEATED WITH her back against the cliff beneath the overhang, gazed up at the creature Rhuan named draka. Still it perched atop the cliff opposite them. The coppery tail spilled over the edge, dangling loosely, and massive wings were partially opened to rest against the clifftop. Sunning itself, Rhuan had said. It certainly seemed so. The creature had tucked its head back against itself just beneath its right wing, and to all appearances appeared to be napping.

"Could we just go on to the Kiba?" she asked. "You said it isn't far."

"The way is too exposed."

"Is there a possibility we could . . . I don't know, shoo it away? The draka?"

Rhuan looked at her a moment, then deep dimples blossomed as he grinned widely. " 'Shoo it away?' It's not a cat, Audrun. Draka don't 'shoo.' "

But she wasn't amused. "I need to reach the Kiba as soon as possible, Rhuan. The lives of my family are at stake."

His grin faded. "I know. I do know, Audrun." He looked up at the sky. "The suns will soon begin to set. The draka should leave then."

"And then we go on at night?" Audrun tried to rein in the tension in her voice. "Or will we have to remain here until the morning?"

"I think—*wait*." His hand came down on her forearm. "It's moving."

She looked up, and relief shot through her body. The draka indeed was moving. It folded its wings, shook its head on its long, sinewy neck, then rose up onto extended legs. The tail slid up the cliff face and disappeared.

"Is it leaving?"

"Just wait."

With a snap the draka spread its wings. Audrun saw again how huge they were, gleaming russet-gold in the sunlight. Abruptly it launched, leaping off of the cliff, and glided down, down until Audrun feared it would crash into the ground. But it skimmed the terraced pools, made a lazy turn, then with one beat of its wings lifted itself up into the air. Downdraft stirred wavelets across the pools, set the brush to rustling. The draka flew high and higher, climbing into the sky, and Audrun's last view was of the scaled, gleaming body carried on wide wings into the distance.

"Shoo," she murmured.

Rhuan, laughing, pulled her to her feet. "Now," he said, "we will start for the Kiba. We won't reach it by nightfall—we'll have to sleep along the way—but if we leave not long after dawn tomorrow, we'll be there by midmorning."

Apprehension abruptly filled her belly. They were close, so very close, but there were no certainties that Rhuan's primaries, gods or no, would accede to her demands.

ELLICA GROOMED THE earth around the sapling. She groomed the sapling itself. She waited for the dreya to step back out of their trees, but they did not. She waited and she waited.

Twelve trees surrounded her. Twelve trees made a

ring. The were tall, mature trees, patterned branches reaching high and higher yet, gleaming in the sunlight, silver-gray in the shadows as the suns went down. She knelt beside the thirteenth tree, the smallest of all, grooming its trunk, grooming its soil. She kept no count of the days. There was no such thing as time in Alisanos, not the kind of time she knew, the day by day accounting of her life. Days, weeks, months. Here, time did not matter. Only the trees. Only *her* tree.

The dreya had left her. They had slipped through clefts, leaving her behind. She was not one of them. She was only human.

But I have a tree.

"Ellica! Ellica!"

She looked up, reacting to the sound. The name was unfamiliar.

"Ellica!" A boy. It was a boy. He fell down beside her, pale face smeared with dirt. "Ellica!"

She looked beyond him. A man stood there, holding a young girl. A many-braided man, glass and gold glinting in the strands of his hair.

"You're human," he said, "or so this boy tells me. Have they taken you for their own?"

She moved closer to the sapling, providing it with shelter.

The boy cried out again. "Ellica!"

The girl in the man's arms stared. Her face was frozen. Her eyes were made of ice.

"I have no time," the braided man said. "Stay, or come; it matters not to me."

"Ellica!"

The boy put hands upon her. Human hands, hands made of flesh. So much could harm flesh. So much could bruise it.

"Boy," the man said, "she's lost to the dreya. Leave her to them."

"She's my sister!"

"So is this one, boy. You may save one, it appears, but not the other. She won't leave her tree."

"EllicaEllicaEllica!"

She stared at the boy. Stared at the man. Saw the young girl with eyes that didn't blink. A word formed in her mind. "Meggie?"

The boy flung himself at her. She caught him, to save the tree. So he wouldn't land upon it.

The man said, "Bring your tree. It's young enough to travel." He shifted the girl in his arms. "Or stay. I don't care. But the boy does. This one . . . well, this one may never know if you come or stay. Your tree may in fact be better company."

"Meggie," she said again.

"Boy," the man said, "I have no time. These are your kin, not mine."

"Ellica!"

She sank her hands deep into the earth, avoiding fragile roots. The soil was soft. It compacted easily, and then she brought the rootball out of the ground. She set the soil and tree into her skirts, wrapped the rootball carefully, then stood up. The man cradled the girl. She cradled her sapling.

"Three children and a tree," the man muttered in disgust. "The hand-reader didn't bother to tell me about all of *this*."

BENEATH THE SHELTER of trees with the sound of running water in his ears, Rhuan did what he could to feed them both. Fruit, a tuber, seeds and nuts. Water they had aplenty but steps away. Audrun said she despaired of ever tasting meat again, but her heart wasn't in the complaint, nor, he knew, was her mind on food.

The suns sank below the top of the cliffs. Now twilight reigned. As Audrun ate slowly, making the simple fare last, he began to tell her of the Kiba and of his people's dwellings. They lived in stone, he explained, within natural cliff caves, behind walls of ruddy, rough stone chunks hacked out of rock. Piled and mortared as needed, the hewn rock offered shelter and defense.

Audrun's tone was ironic. "And what would *gods* need defenses for? Why don't you just summon this wild magic and make yourselves invulnerable?"

"We have enemies," he said simply; then, as she began to repeat the second question, he raised his voice. "I've told you before: wild magic is unpredictable. We are at risk, too."

"So while they are gods—or so they claim—your people don't rule Alisanos."

"Alisanos rules itself."

Audrun efficiently sucked her fingers clean of fruit pulp. "Tell me more about this Kiba. Tell me what I may expect."

He looked straight into her eyes. "Cruelty. In plenty."

TWILIGHT FELL AMID the forest. Ellica, seated at the foot of a tree with a smaller version held tightly to her chest, watched the Shoia courier. He had said very little as they walked toward a place he called the Kiba. Now it was time to settle for the evening. He'd found a pocket of trees he said would do for shelter, such as it was, then set Torvic to searching for rocks with which they might build a fire ring.

Ellica objected. "Don't send him away from us! This is Alisanos!"

The Shoia, gathering deadfall wood from their immediate environs, fixed his gaze upon her. She saw something in his eyes akin to contempt and frustration. "I would set you to the task, but I see you won't release the tree you treat as a child."

She opened her mouth to retort, but shut it again when no words came to defend her actions. It was in her, it was *in* her, that she tend the sapling.

"The boy needs a task."

Busywork. She understood that.

"But you might put down that tree and tend your sister."

Ellica looked at Meggie. The youngest of them had not spoken at all, and, when she lagged, the Shoia eventually lifted her into his arms and carried her. Now Meggie sat at a foot of a tree as well, collapsed into a huddle of knees and elbows. Her face was not visible.

"Meggie," Ellica got up onto her knees and, still cradling the sapling, moved awkwardly the several paces to the tree. She settled again, sitting close enough that their bodies touched. Ellica felt the stiffness in the girl's body, the trembling of her limbs. "Oh, Meggie."

As she made shift to tend both tree and child, she was aware of the courier's watchful gaze.

Chapter 33

"COME," BRODHI SAID, "time to go. Now. Not tomorrow."

He doubted they had gotten much, if any, sleep. Torvic and Ellica had settled Meggie between them throughout the night, half buried beneath a light layer of leafy boughs Brodhi had cut and arranged over them.

When there was no response save a slight shifting of the boughs, Brodhi began tossing them aside. "Time to go. We'll make the Kiba today."

Ellica's head came up. She blinked at him blearily through bloodshot eyes, then began to push away the boughs. When free of them, she knelt beside the sapling kept close throughout the night. "What will happen at this Kiba?"

"Someone else will have your tending." He bent and pulled more boughs off of Torvic and Meggie, baring their bodies. "I'll be quit of you." He jostled Torvic's shoulder with a booted foot. "Up, boy. Time to go."

Torvic sat up, frowning. "Let Meggie sleep. She cried all night."

"Oh, I am *most* aware of that." He made an imperative gesture. "Now, boy. Or I'll leave your sister here."

"You wouldn't do that!" Ellica cried.

He told her the absolute truth. "Oh, but I would. When survival is risky at best, the weakest often must be left behind."

"Or culled?" Torvic lunged to his feet and stood stiffly, trembling. "You would *cull* my sister?"

"Mother of Moons," Ellica breathed. "You're a monster."

He had once called Rhuan that very same thing. Brodhi sighed. "Then get her up, and readied, and we'll all go together. But *waste no time.*"

THE PRIMARIES, AUDRUN discovered, were all very alike. Whatever they were, gods or no, they decidedly stamped their get. Were she breeding foals or calves, she'd say that someone, somewhere, was prepotent: sire or dam. All were tall, even the females, all of robust stature, brown-eyed, all with the faint copper tint in their skin she had marked in Rhuan, and they, too, wore reddish hair in multiple, complex braids. Males and females were clad in rich, glossy hide; wide, ornamented belts; and snug tunics and leggings colored copper, russet, and bronze.

She stood beneath the double suns in the Kiba, in

the gathering place of Rhuan's folk, in its very center.
It was a deep, steep bowl in the ground carved out of
red rock, with round, vertical walls and two wide
ramps of steep stairs set across from one another. The
bowl was quite large and open to the sky, with blocks
of carved stone set upon the floor against the walls.
Audrun had counted one thousand blocks of stone.
Above the bowl, looking down upon it and its surrounding area, rose tall, ruddy cliffs. Dwelling places,
as Rhuan had said, were hewn out of those cliffs and
caves, linked together by steep, interconnected stair-
ways, shielded by walls.

Nine hundred and ninety-nine primaries were
ranged around her, seated casually on the stone
blocks. There was no single individual to keep order in
the proceedings. They said what they said, asked what
they asked, as it struck their fancy. She believed her
head might crack open if she listened to much more.

Rhuan stood behind her left shoulder. He was not
allowed to speak. He waited, legs slightly spread,
knees slightly flexed, hands linked behind his back.
Before descending one of the stair ramps into the Kiba,
he had pulled the leather thong from his hair, which
hung to his hips, loose and shining. *Her* hair was far
less tidy than his; she had braided it while wet, taming
the worst of the tangles, but was acutely aware that in
her tattered clothing she presented an entirely unpre-
possessing appearance. The primaries were beautiful,
each and every one, powerfully scintillating in the way
of a deadly, elegant weapon.

Nine hundred and ninety-nine. Alario was missing.

"Again," a female said, one knee drawn up with her booted foot atop the block, a forearm propped casually across that knee.

"Again?" Audrun was entirely exasperated. Courtesy had achieved nothing. "How many times, *again*? Are you deaf? Are you stupid? Are you children, to forget a thing as soon as it is said?" She drew in a breath. "I am married already. He's human, as I am. We have five children. I want them returned to me, husband and children, each of them. You're gods. You have that power."

"We also have laws," the female said. "You may have your human husband, if he survives the challenge. If there is to be only one man for you, the other must die. But if Rhuan survives, then *he* is your husband."

"No," Audrun said, making a chopping gesture of emphatic refusal. "No, no, and no. No challenges. No deaths. I have only one husband, and Rhuan isn't he. Whether my husband is here in Alisanos or free in the human world, I can't say. But you can. Tell me where he is."

No answer was forthcoming.

"Refusal to tell me suggests you don't know," Audrun pointed out. "And if you don't know, then you aren't gods, are you?"

Rhuan murmured, "I'm not sure this is the best tack to take."

She turned and glared at him. "I have to take some

tack, do I not? This is ridiculous, Rhuan! There's no reason for them to refuse to tell me this, unless they have no answer."

"Or unless they don't *wish* to."

His expression was odd. After a moment Audrun turned in a slow, complete circle, looking at various primaries as she moved. "Is this the truth? That you don't *wish* to tell me? Does it amuse you to withhold the information? Does it provide some preverse form of pleasure?" She halted where she had begun, looking at the female who'd spoken. "Is it that you view humans as toys? Are we dolls to you? Puppets? Do you play with us until we break, and then throw us on the rubbish heap?"

And then an idea kindled in her mind. She recalled Alario and his arrogance. She recalled how he had infuriated her.

Audrun left the center of the Kiba. She walked, as if wandering idly, toward the ring of blocks used as seats. "Alario told me something not so long ago. I was questioning if you truly were gods. And he said something I find very interesting, now that I am here. Alario said: 'We're gods, little human, because we say we are.' " She paused, then walked on. "What if that is true? What if Alario told me the *precise* truth? What if you aren't gods at all, but simply say you are?" She turned her hands palm up and spread her arms. "It could be done, of course. One may claim oneself whatever one chooses to. I could claim myself a male, if I wished, though I think none of you would believe it. It

SN

would be a simple thing to prove I lack certain physical characteristics that define males. But it's a much more difficult thing to prove you *are* something when it isn't obvious. Alario, though claiming himself a god, refused to bring my family to me. I ask you if my husband is even in Alisanos, and you refuse to answer." She turned and faced the other direction, looking at other primaries. "Could it be," she said, "that you *aren't* who, or what, you say you are?" She walked on, glancing at dozens of brown eyes staring back at her. "Could it be that you are not gods at all, any of you, but something entirely different? Something less significant? Something *in*significant. Perhaps in fact you are merely the descendants of a people who were taken by the deepwood just as my family was, and you have been poisoned by the wild magic. Could it be that you have become less than what you were because of that poison, and thus must hide the weakness? What if, in truth, you are *just like humans*?"

BETWEEN MIDDAY AND sundown, Ilona received six people who wished to have their hands read. Part of her wondered if accepting so many clients so close to when she could read no hands at all was wise, but how could she turn them away? There were no other surviving diviners in the grove or the settlement. And though she could always tell when a person was accustomed to seeing a different kind of

diviner, she made no comment about it. All were desperate. There was no one else to see.

Ungainly with exhaustion, she planted shepherd's
crooks around her wagon, lighted pierced-tin
lanterns, tidied the low, lacquered table with its silken
cloth, and prepared a light supper. She needed rest,
yes, and perhaps a better meal, but she was weary.
This would do.

She climbed up into her wagon to light the lantern
that hung over the folding steps. Once the wick had
caught, she blew out the spill she'd taken from her
cookfire and stepped down carefully, making certain
the lantern remained lit. Satisfied that it would, she
turned to descend the balance of the steps and stopped
short at the bottom.

Alario smiled.

The step gave her somewhat of a higher vantage
point than usual, with him. She stayed upon it, not
stepping down to the earth.

"Will you come?" he asked.

She didn't even trouble herself to ask where. "I will
not."

His smile remained in place. "I can show you places
you've never seen before."

Ilona lifted a brow. "So can my employer."

"I need you, woman."

"Woman." And that was to impress. Ilona shook her
head. "You don't need me."

"I do."

"No. You merely need a womb."

"Have you not asked yourself *why* I chose you? If it's as you say, that I only need a womb, why do I come to you?"

"If I were younger," Ilona said, "and more impressionable, I might surrender to your argument. I might feel most flattered. Were I were stupid and foolish. But I am neither that young, nor that impressionable, nor that easily flattered, and lately not at all stupid. Are you?"

He blinked. "Stupid?"

"Yes. Why else would you come to me again when you know I'm not interested?"

Though the sun was not yet gone, the lantern over the steps nonetheless painted him in highlights, russet, gold, and copper. Light ran like liquid over the warmth of his clothing, the sleek, supple scales of a long-dead beast. "What do you want, hand-reader?"

Ilona smiled. "Merely to be left alone. Truthfully, I can see how women give way to you. I dismiss none of your appeal, Alario. You have it in abundance . . . and much else to offer, I suspect, to a woman who answers to you. Just not to me."

His smile had faded. Fire leaped in his eyes. "Are you cold to men?"

Ilona laughed. "No man I have been with would say so."

He examined her the way other men had, men who claimed no courtesy. She was accustomed to that, as she drank ale in tents where other women did not, unless they be Sisters of the Road.

"There are women," she said, "far more beautiful than I. Lusher of flesh than I. More accomodating than I. Seek one of them, Alario."

But he had not surrendered. "I will take you to my son."

She hoped very much she kept her reaction from showing on her face. "What, you think to win me with him? Why would I wish to go to him when you are right here?"

But neither was he a fool, Rhuan's sire. "You desire the lesser being. You long for the *dioscuri*—while *I* am a god!"

Ilona smiled. "But I am only human. I would never look so high as to seek a god."

The first flicker of red showed in his eyes. "He has married the woman."

That reaction she feared very much he saw. "Then I wish him joy."

"She is fecund."

Still she held to her smile. "Then I wish him joy of children."

Alario arched his brows. "Do you so? Another woman's get?"

He was ruthless, and she knew it. He would tell her anything. Possibly even the truth. "Say what you like, Alario. I will not go with you."

"You will."

She stepped down to the ground. "I will not—"

He closed his hand around her throat. "No? You say me no? You defy *me*?"

Ilona shut her hands over the one embracing her throat.

Red flooded his eyes. "Then *say* no, woman. Say no to everyone!"

He flung her backward, hard, smashing her full force against the wagon steps.

Chapter 34

"AUDRUN—"

She raised her voice over Rhuan's, infusing it with more confidence, giving them arrogance for arrogance. "How sad that would be. How tragic. Not gods at all, but ordinary people—just like humans. Taken by the deepwood, just like humans. People who are helpless, just like humans, but who choose to name themselves gods because to be and to act otherwise is to admit the truth: that *Alisanos* is the god, and you are merely its toys." She met the fierce eyes of the female who had questioned her and refused to give way. "Prove it," she challenged directly. "Such a small thing for gods: bring children and the man who sired them to their mother."

The female rose. She was quite tall, Audrun noted, certainly taller than she. And though she lacked the hard bulk of the males, she was clearly a very strong woman. The contours and angles of her face resembled those evident in the males, but there was a decidedly female cast to her features. No one would mistake her for a man.

She strode forward, moving with a powerful grace. Braided sidelocks dangled from her temples, weighted with beading. The rest of her hair was gathered back from her face, comprised of long, ornate braids that were themselves braided into one another. Audrun recalled how much time was required to take down all of Rhuan's braids.

The female circled Audrun and Rhuan. Audrun watched her, though Rhuan kept his eyes fixed on the rank of primaries immediately within his line of sight. He made no attempt to follow the female's movements. Audrun was again put in mind of an animal examining another, assessing scent, posture, and other visual signals.

Then the female halted immediately in front of Rhuan. "I see you are no more reconciled to us than you were before you departed."

"No, Ylarra," Rhuan said.

"Your dam's blood runs strong."

"It does."

"Alario is ashamed of you."

"And I of him."

"Do you want this woman?"

"Forgive me, Audrun," he murmured quietly, then raised his voice. "I do not want this woman."

"She's human. Isn't that what *you'd* prefer?"

"When the time comes to choose a woman, I will choose her for myself, not because she unknowingly takes down my braids when I am unconscious. Ylarra, this woman has a husband. Let her keep him."

The woman prowled, hands clasped behind her back. "Darmuth tells me you bed many human women."

Audrun glanced at him sidelong. His mouth quirked. "Darmuth says too much."

"But that is Darmuth's duty, Rhuan. To observe you, and to report to us. How you conduct yourself is very much a part of this journey." The female—Ylarra—glanced at Audrun. "Your human husband is not, nor ever has been, in Alisanos. Whether he is alive or dead in your world is not known to us."

Relief nearly took her legs out from under her. "Thank the Mother," Audrun whispered as tears welled.

"Audrun." Rhuan's voice sounded odd. "Audrun, turn around. Look at the top of the steps."

She did so, and cried out. At the top of the steps four of her children waited. Gillan stood with weight on one leg, Darmuth next to him. Ellica held what appeared to be a sapling wrapped in her skirts, cradled close to her breasts. Torvic stood beside Brodhi, who held Megritte in his arms. None of them spoke. All merely stared. But in Gillan's eyes, in Torvic's and Ellica's, she saw a stark, desperate hunger for her presence.

"Wait." Rhuan caught her arm as she began to move. "Audrun, wait."

She tried to wrench free and couldn't. "Let me go to them!"

His face was tense. "The primaries are not done with us, Audrun. This isn't your world. We are not free to act as we will. Your children are safe for the moment. Let them be."

"Wise words," Ylarra said dryly. "And to think Alario believes you empty of them." She walked around to stand in front of Audrun, blocking her view of the steps. "No doubt you wish to return to your husband and take your children with you."

"*Yes.*"

Ylarra turned to the other primaries. "What say you?" She looked at one particular male. "Karadath?"

He rose. His eyes were those of a predator. "Alisanos took her. Alisanos keeps her."

"My children," Audrun appealed.

He met Audrun's eyes, and she saw nothing of humanity in his. Only cruelty, as Rhuan had warned. "Alisanos took them. Alisanos keeps them."

RHUAN SAW THE FURY rise up in Audrun. She was nearly incandescent with it, and in that moment every bit as commanding as a primary. He watched her let all of the anger, all of the frustration, all of the fear for her children build within her, and watched too as she let it flow into her voice. The scorn was so thick it was palpable.

She didn't shout; she did not need to. "And so I am

proven right. You are *not* gods. Alisanos rules, and you and all of your people are its sycophants."

Every primary rose. An angry, deep-throated roar filled the Kiba.

She had given him the opening. Rhuan raised his voice before Ylarra or Karadath could say anything. "This woman has challenged you within your own Kiba, questioning whether you are gods or no. In your own house, she challenges you. And I add my voice to hers: *prove yourselves.*"

He had surprised all of them: Audrun, Ylarra, Karadath.

"There is war in the human world," Rhuan said. "One man has made himself a conqueror, claiming land that belongs to others. Thousands have died. Thousands have lost their homes, their livelihoods. More yet will die as this man enforces his rule. Because of him, folk like Audrun, alone and with their families, are fleeing their homeland to begin again in another. And it is because of this war that this family put itself in harm's way. They had no wish to tempt Alisanos! But in their journey to escape the depredations of this conqueror, they ventured too close. The deepwood took them. And while I understand that what Alisanos takes, it keeps—there is a way to give this family back much of what it has lost."

He saw the alarm in Audrun. "What are you saying?"

"In the human world, I am a guide," Rhuan continued. "And Brodhi is a courier. We were reared here in Alisanos, knowing that there are no fixed, reliable routes through the deepwood. But we have lived, too, in the human world, and now understand the value of such things. What I propose, then, is that you prove to this woman that you are indeed gods, not sycophants. Give her a road."

Ylarra's tone was startled. "A road?"

"If she and her children can't return to the human world, let the human world come to them."

Ylarra's response was immediate. "Impossible!"

"Because you can't do this thing, or because you refuse to?" He turned sharply as Karadath took two long strides into the center of the Kiba. "Will you say the same, uncle? Ah, forgive me, that is a human word. But will you admit before this human woman, in direct response to her challenge, that this is impossible?" He flung out an arm toward the steps, pointing. "Your own son, your last *dioscuri*, has returned before his time. Would you have said that *Brodhi* was capable of such a thing? Impossible, is it not, that he would do so. Yet here he stands." He lowered his arm and looked again upon the primaries who stood within the Kiba. "Safe passage through Alisanos, to Atalanda province. That is the challenge." He met Audrun's eyes, lowering his voice. "Anyone who wishes it can be brought through. Undoubtedly Davyn will be first."

"Through Alisanos?" Her voice trembled. "To what would you bring him and the others? To death? To physical transformation?"

"To safe passage, Audrun. Alive. Whole. *Human*, as long as they're on the road." He flicked a glance at Karadath, whose face was stone.

She was white to the lips. "You could do this thing? Make a road, and bring Davyn to us?"

"Not I." Rhuan's smile was wry. "I'm merely a *dioscuri*, and an inferior one at that. But yes, *they* can do this." He glanced briefly at Ylarra, at Karadath. "Brodhi and I have private business, and you need to meet with your children. If given leave, I will come to you after."

She heard something in his voice. She flicked considering glances at the two primaries standing closest, then looked back at him. "Are you in danger?"

"Among the primaries?" He smiled. "Always. But then, I have always refused to play the game."

"Rhuan—"

He lifted a hand. "Let it be, Audrun. For now, let it be." He turned, then, to Ylarra. He took the leather thong he had used to tie back his hair from his belt, and offered it to her. When she took it, he held out his arms and crossed his wrists.

But it was Karadath who stepped forward, who ripped the thong from Ylarra's grasp. Rhuan gritted his teeth as his wrists were too tightly bound, the thong too tightly knotted.

"You should know," Audrun cried as Karadath turned him toward the steps, "that this 'inferior *dioscuri*' has more honor in him than any of you! Than *any* of you!"

THE SUN HAD set. Bethid, in Mikal's tent sharing a table with Timmon and Alorn, was working her way through a second tankard when the Sister of the Road, the woman named Naiya, tore open the tent flap and stepped inside. Her face was drained of color.

"Bethid," she said breathlessly, as if she had been running. "Mikal. Jorda says to come. Come at once." Her eyes, too, were stunned. "The hand-reader's dead."

Bethid was aware that she moved, that she thrust herself to her feet and kicked aside the stool. She ran through the aisles, ran past the Sister, ran out of the ale tent. She heard footsteps behind her, male: Timmon. Alorn. Mikal.

Not Ilona. Not Ilona. Not Ilona—dead.

The settlement was now in an orderly circle. Easier to navigate. Bethid ran through it to the karavan grove, to Ilona's wagon.

People were gathered there. Karavaners. They had left their wagons to go to hers. Bethid pushed through even as they gave way.

Jorda sat on the steps. Ilona was in his arms. She was a doll cradled there, a child cradled there, while Jorda wept.

"O Mother . . ." Bethid's knees faltered, gave. She knelt in the dirt beneath the huge old tree. "No, no, no. Mother, not *Ilona*."

"Sweet Mother," Mikal whispered. "No, not Ilona."

The lantern over the steps shone down on Jorda's head, burnishing ruddy hair. His beard was soaked with tears. "She's gone."

"Are you . . . is there . . ." Bethid tried again. "Could you be—"

"Mistaken?" Jorda shook his head. "Her neck is broken."

One couldn't tell by looking at her. Jorda held her too closely. Her head rested against his shoulder.

Bethid sat down. Her own eyes filled. She had no words, no words to speak, now that Jorda had said those that destroyed all hope.

Mikal's voice was thick. "How? What happened?"

Naiya had come up. "I heard nothing," she said. "No outcry, no scream. My wagon's closest. I heard nothing."

"Murder," Jorda said. "There is a handprint on her throat. But I found her on the steps. She's all broken."

One of Ilona's hair sticks lay in the dirt at the foot of her wagon. The other remained in place, but much of her hair had fallen loose. The wild ringlets cascaded over her shoulders and into her lap. Her face was hidden.

"Who would *do* this?" Bethid asked. "*Who* would do this?"

A tear rolled down the right side of Mikal's face. Below the eyepatch, the flesh was dry. "Jorda." He stopped, cleared his throat. "Jorda, perhaps it's best to put her in her bed. Let the women prepare her. She'd be wanting dawn rites."

"Who's to officiate?" Jorda asked. "All the diviners are dead."

Bethid closed her eyes.

All the diviners are dead.

WHEN RHUAN CAME to Audrun and her children, the crying was ended. Audrun sat on a stone bench beneath a massive, spreading tree with Megritte in her arms, poor mute Meggie, who had, Torvic explained, said not a word since Brodhi pulled them out of Lirra's cabin. He sat next to her on the bench, a warmth against her side. Ellica crouched upon the ground, tending her sapling. And Gillan, aided there by Darmuth—who was, Audrun learned, far more than merely a karavan guide—sat perched upon a large shelf of stone. She saw the shadows beneath his eyes, the tautness of his features, the pain in his posture whenever he shifted position. Damaged, Darmuth had said before he left them, *but recovering*.

Rhuan's wrists were freed of their binding. She saw a pensiveness in his features as he approached, and an odd consideration as he looked at the cliff wall just behind them with its multitude of staircases hewn out of the stone, the stacked and mortared walls. But when he joined them, she saw again his smile, and the dimples.

"Is your business concluded?" she asked.

"It is."

She recognized the look of a chastened young man who wished to hide it. "You're to be punished, aren't you? I don't know what it is you've done aside from saving my life, but that is, apparently, worthy of punishment among your primaries."

He gazed at Meggie, whose face was turned away, then looked briefly at the others. A muscle leaped in his jaw. "My punishment is nothing compared to what Alisanos has done to your children." He looked again at Audrun. "Have they explained?"

"Oh, thoroughly." A part of Audrun wished to cry again; another portion wished to be angry. But she would show neither to this man, who had done so much for them. "We can never leave Alisanos. My children have been made flesh of its flesh." Bitterness rose against her wishes. "We are to be *guests* of your people."

"That, only temporarily," he replied. "Only until trees are cut, and materials are brought, and men who can build are found, and a karavansary is constructed at a place of your choosing along the road. A proper karavansary, where travelers may stop on the way to Atalanda. Then you will have a home again, and a husband." He gestured briefly, indicating the children. "When you found yourself in Alisanos, you said nothing about your own welfare. You wished only to find your family. And so you have. You have your chicks back. You have accomplished, against all odds, what you wished to do."

Audrun nodded, acknowledging that. "And this

road will be safe? Davyn may travel it without fear of being changed?"

"All will be safe, and infinitely human, so long as they stay on the road."

"Will *you* bring him to me?"

Rhuan smiled. "It would be my honor."

He had done much for them, but she had to ask it. "Could you not bring him here? Now?"

The smile faded. "I may not. I'm sorry, Audrun. Not until the road is underway. If I brought him, he would be at the mercy of Alisanos. I think you would not wish that on him."

It hurt not to cry. "No," she agreed. "I would not."

She knew she should rejoice that Davyn would be able to come at all. Yet when would that be? How long must she wait?

But still, she had more now than when she had first awakened in the deepwood. Her children, safe; herself, safe.

Except one child remained missing. A child she had had no opportunity to know.

To distract herself from that, she asked a question. "Why are you being punished?"

"I came home too soon. Or perhaps I should say I came *back* too soon; this is not my home."

"I don't understand."

He shook his head. "It doesn't matter. It means that my final disposition, as the primaries call it, must be put off. Some argued against it, saying that the decision should be made now, but others said there were extenuating circumstances. And so I am to begin all over again."

"Begin *what* all over again?"

"That journey Alario mentioned. Brodhi is quite furious . . . I think he would happily kill Ylarra for suggesting it, but Karadath agreed. So he and I are to return to the human world for another five years. Five human years."

Audrun blinked. "Is that all? *That* is considered punishment?"

"Brodhi considers it so." Rhuan grinned, and dimples appeared. "It means we're still children, as the primaries view it."

Audrun rather thought there was more to it than that, considerably more to it, but as Meggie moved in her arms she let the subject drop so she could resettle her daughter. "What will you do now?"

"I have a job as a karavan guide. I intend to return to it." His eyes softened. "And there is someone I need to see. Someone whom I have had to treat as a friend when I desired otherwise . . . very much otherwise." He grimaced, lips twisting. "It's more than a little taxing, keeping secrets from one you esteem—"

Audrun's brows rose. "*Esteem?* Is that what you call it?"

It showed in the lowering of his lids. "No."

"Keep no secrets from a woman you love."

His head came up, and she saw the desperate appeal for her understanding. "I had to, Audrun! It's part of the journey."

"But how can you start over again without *continuing* to keep those secrets?"

"From her? No. Not again. Not this time. Because I know, I *know* that I can trust her to keep them as well." His mouth jerked briefly in a self-deprecating hook. "As you say: 'keep no secrets from a woman you love.' I won't do it again. I will offer my hand, so that she may read it and know all that I am. But others? Well, still I shall tell them nothing beyond what is always said: I am Shoia. I can survive six deaths, but the seventh is the true death." He chewed briefly at his bottom lip, considering something. "One day . . . perhaps one day such secrets will not be necessary. Perhaps one day all humans may be told who and what we are."

Audrun studied him a moment in speculation, seeing within her mind the olive-skinned woman with dark, wild ringlets, hazel eyes, a slim, tall body, and secrets of her own. "Will you ask her to braid your hair?"

He shook it back from his face. "I think possibly so—if she'll allow me to braid hers."

She could hold him to her no longer. It wasn't fair.

"Then go," Audrun told him. "Waste no more time here. You have done much for me and mine. I bless you for it, and I thank the Mother of Moons. But it's time now for *you* to accomplish a goal—one, I suspect, you've set aside for too long." She managed a smile. "Go to her, Rhuan."

He nodded. Then he stepped forward and bent down over her, placing a gentle kiss atop Meggie's tangled hair. "May the Mother of Moons bless you, little one. May you find your way home."

As he turned and walked away, Audrun fought back tears.

It was Torvic who asked what she wished to ask, and did not. "What about the baby? Who's going to find her if Rhuan isn't here?"

Audrun drew in a deep breath, filling her lungs. Then expelled it sharply and declared, "We will." She steadied her voice, and felt her spirit respond. "We will, Torvic. We're her kin."

Epilogue

BETHID HEARD HER name echoing through the grove. She could not imagine who would shout so, when all knew what had happened, when all knew she was sitting with Ilona through the night. It was customary. That anyone would disturb the vigil was astounding.

She rose from the trunk across the narrow aisle from the cot. Earlier she and Naiya had washed Ilona's body and replaced her clothing with the traditional linen burial shift. Night had fallen; illumination was dim. The only lighted lantern was the one at the door hanging over the steps.

"Bethid!"

Furious, Bethid stepped to the door, preparing to tell the man in no uncertain terms that he had no business interrupting the vigil.

But it was Rhuan.

Rhuan.

She registered the pallor of his face, the horrified

shock in his eyes. *O Mother, he* does *love her*! His hair was unbraided, swinging behind him as he ran. He wore a soiled tunic and leggings missing much of their ornamentation.

Jorda, she thought. Jorda had told him.

He stopped at the foot of the steps and stared up at her almost blindly, as if waiting for her to give him different news.

Bethid couldn't. She couldn't say anything at all because of the pain in her throat and chest. She just walked down the steps and away from the wagon, so he might have privacy.

But he had, she knew, seen confirmation in her eyes.

HE FELT HIS knees falter as Bethid walked away. He took a step forward to steady himself and caught hold of the doorjamb, one hand braced on each side. It set the lantern above him to swinging. Beneath his foot the bottom step was still new, the wood raw. Darmuth had replaced it, because he hadn't.

Rhuan closed his eyes. He believed for a moment he couldn't mount the steps. But he did. One foot, one step, three times in all, until he ducked beneath the lantern and entered the wagon.

She was very still beneath her colorful coverlet. No mark marred her face. The dark ringlets, usually wound in a coil and anchored against her head with rune-scribed sticks, had been loosely plaited in a single braid. It lay atop the coverlet.

No words. No words at all. Only a great and terrible pain in his heart and throat.

He lingered there, looking. And then he bent down over her, slid his left arm beneath her shoulders and raised her up, cradling her head. He slid in behind her very carefully, holding her in place until he sat against high-piled cushions with one leg tucked beneath him, one foot on the floor. He settled her against his body, wrapped arms around her torso and held her there, her head against his shoulder. He pressed his cheek into her hair and believed it was possible he could not give her up, when they came to take her.

"I'm not Shoia," he told her, finally hiding nothing. "I'm Alisani. *Dioscuri.* Born of the deepwood. It was why, when you asked, I dared not let you read my hand. You read true, and always have. You would have seen it. You would have known the truth." He drew in a breath, let it go. Her weight was no burden. "That first night we met in Mikal's tent, the night I died . . . I knew it when I saw you. My heart leaped. It knew. There was no question in my mind. But the journey requires that we tell no human who, and what, we are. *Then,* I cared." He drew in a breath, let it go. Her weight was no burden. "And so I locked away my feelings. I accepted the rules."

"You've *never* accepted rules."

He began to smile. Then he went still. Warmth was in his arms. A breathing woman was in his arms.

Ilona said, "Your heart just skipped a beat. No, two."

He let her go and slid out of her bed far faster than he had gotten into it. He stared at her, lips parted, struck completely speechless.

She hitched herself up on an elbow and demanded, "What in the Mother's world were you doing in my bed? *With me in it*, no less?"

Eventually he rediscovered the human language. But in his shock, he said the only words he could find. "You were dead."

"I was no such thing." She held her arm out, considering the linen sleeve over it. She looked down at her breasts and touched the fabric. "Blessed Mother—am I in a burial shift?"

"You were *dead*, 'Lona."

"I'm not dead, Rhuan!"

He was very precise with his intonation. "You *were* dead."

She stared up at him. "How could I have been dead? How could I have been dead if I'm alive now?"

His heart was beating far faster than normal. He worked it out even as he spoke. "Unless, unless Jorda was wrong and you never were dead . . . which I very much doubt based on what he told me—you can't truly mistake a badly broken neck—there is only one explanation." He thought about that another moment. "But—but I suppose, when you consider it, it's not entirely out of the question that the primaries may have made a completely wrong assumption. As gods, they leave much to be desired." He sat down upon her trunk heavily. "Apparently . . . apparently the Shoia aren't an extinct race after all."

That left her perplexed. "Are they supposed to be?"

She had, of course, as had all the humans, been told by him that he was Shoia. It was the common fiction that all *dioscuri* maintained among the humans while on their journey. "Well, the primaries said—" He made a chopping gesture, abruptly silencing himself. "Never mind. They were wrong. Or they lied. It doesn't matter; it's not important." He paused. "Well, there is *one* thing that's important. Always keep count, Ilona. It's very, very important."

"Of my deaths? If I'm Shoia?" She pressed a hand against her forehead. "What am I saying? I can't be Shoia—"

He overrode her. "Just remember, the seventh is the true death. You have five left."

She remained perplexed, peering up at him from beneath her hand. "But how can this be? My parents never said anything about being Shoia! Not before they turned me out for . . ." It was her turn to break off and make a chopping motion. "Never mind. Maybe they lied. It doesn't matter; it's not important." She looked at him. "I would prefer to limit dying to just the one death."

The last of his shock dissipated. He recalled Audrun telling him it was time he accomplished his goal, even as she had accomplished nearly all of her own.

And so. His goal. Very nearly accomplished.

Rhuan slid off the trunk and knelt down beside her

cot. He raised his hand so that she could see the palm. "Read it," he said. "No more secrets."

Ilona never took her eyes from his, to look at his hand. She placed her palm against his. "I don't have to, Rhuan. I know what I need to know."

He smiled briefly, but then it faded. The joy of a wholly unexpected reunion on the heels of seeing her dead was set aside. There would be time for endless discussions later. For now, one overriding question begged to be asked. He tried to keep it as light as possible; she always argued with him if she believed he wanted to commit violence.

"Jorda said it was murder, not an accident." He moved her braid aside. "The marks on your throat are eloquent." It took all he had not to shout his question, to retain self-control. "Who did this, Ilona? Who killed you?"

Her smile, too, faded. A darkness came into her eyes. She interlaced her fingers with his very tightly, as if she might defend him against pain. He thought she meant not to answer. But then she did, saying quietly, "Your father."

It was nothing, *nothing* he had expected.

Alario? Alario?

"*My* father? Here?"

"Alario. Yes."

The shock was so overwhelming all the flesh rose up on his bones. He felt sick to his stomach. His mouth worked stiffly. "Alario. *Alario* killed you . . ."

"I'm sorry," she said. "Rhuan, I'm so sorry."

Sorry for *his* pain, not her own.

"Ah," he said. "Well." From the coldness of his bones, from deep within his soul, a hot ember of hatred, of utter conviction, kindled in his belly. But he kept it from her, crafting a casual smile. "Well, we shall have words, he and I."

And the reluctant *dioscuri* would, after all, at the time of his own choosing, challenge his sire.

But in the meantime, he was here, and she was here, and both of them were alive. With fingers locked into hers, he said, "My hair, as you see, is loose. Will you braid it for me?"

Jennifer Roberson

The **Karavans** series

"The first volume in a new fantasy saga from
Roberson establishes a universe teeming with
fascinating humans, demons and demigods.
Promises to be a story of epic proportions."
—*Publishers Weekly*

"High-quality action fantasy." —*Booklist*

"Roberson's prose is compelling, the book's
premise is well-presented, and the pages almost
seem to turn themselves."—*Romantic Times*

"Set in one of the most vividly described and
downright intriguing fantasy realms to come
along in years, *Karavans* is arguably Roberson's
best work to date..This is a "must-read" fantasy
if there ever was one.
—*The Barnes & Noble Review*

KARAVANS   978-07564-0409-6

DEEPWOOD   978-07564-0482-6

To Order Call: 1-800-788-6262
www.dawbooks.com

DAW 120

JENNIFER ROBERSON

THE NOVELS OF TIGER AND DEL

Volume One 0-7564-0319-7
Sword-Dancer & Sword-Singer
Volume Two 0-7564-0323-5
Sword-Maker & Sword-Breaker
Volume Three 0-7564-0344-8
Sword Born & Sword-Sworn

CHRONICLES OF THE CHEYSULI
Omnibus Editions

SHAPECHANGER'S SONG 0-88677-976-6
LEGACY OF THE WOLF 0-88677-997-9
CHILDREN OF THE LION 0-7564-0003-1
THE LION THRONE 0-7564-0010-4

To Order Call: 1-800-788-6262
www.dawbooks.com